SEEKING ASYLUM IN UTOPIA

B. G. Cox

Copyright © 2025 Barry Cox

All rights reserved. No part of this publication may be reproduced or transmitted in any form or by any means, electronic or mechanical including photocopying, recording or any information storage or retrieval system, without prior permission in writing from the publishers.

The right of Barry Cox to be identified as the author of this work has been asserted by him in accordance with the Copyright, Designs and Patents act 1988

First published in the United Kingdom in 2025 by
The Choir Press

Paperback ISBN 978-1-78963-493-8
Ebook ISBN 978-1-78963-490-7

Acknowledgements

This book is dedicated to my wife, Fiona Hillary, and to my four children – Buster, Hella, Ben and Cleo. Their patience and encouragement have been so much more than I deserved.

My thanks go to The Literary Consultancy and their mentors for their assistance; to Ralph Jones, for his wisdom at key points in the process of production; to the late Pat Coyne; and to Sir David Scott, for his periodic enthusiasm and continuous support.

To my good friend John Lloyd, for his willingness to chat about my progress.

And a special thanks to Rachel Woodman and her team at The Choir Press, for actually getting this book published.

Prologue

The passengers in the Airbus were in the brace position; they could feel the aircraft going down, but it was not yet too scary. The captain had warned them of a failure in one of the engines, and that this was an emergency; they were above the Atlantic, and he was hoping to bring the plane down on the only island within the time and distance that seemed currently available to him.

"This is an island called Libance," he announced over the audio system. "I've just called Heathrow and asked them to tell your relatives where we are, and about the emergency landing. In addition, they need to pass on what's happening to your offices, particularly if you are travelling to New York on business.

"A word about the airfield we are approaching. I gather it can take an Airbus like this one, though I have no idea if there are any actual flights to it these days, or what condition it is in. So we will evacuate via our air chutes in an emergency operation; make sure you know where the nearest exit is."

The pilot signed off in the same calm, cheery tone. There was an instant anxious buzz among the passengers, while the cabin crew took a final chance to walk through the plane, checking and reassuring those people who needed it, before taking up their own emergency landing positions.

One passenger was rapidly making an assessment of possible alternative solutions which might suit him better than going back to London. He began to think that the best bet might be to apply for asylum – from the limited knowledge he had of it (some kind of free market free for all that had cut itself off from the rest of the world) he reckoned that even a place as weird as this one must have a way of dealing with refugee applications. His professional position as a journalist, if presented as a flight from bad guys in London, would surely give him some credibility.

Yes, Bob Rowgarth thought, taking temporary refuge in the apparently libertarian society of Libance ought to give him the material for some rather good features, for print, TV, or the internet, when he got to New York. There must be some way of getting off this isolated place in due course. They may be cut off but these days surely there was nowhere on Planet Earth that couldn't be reached – or left.

He suddenly realised there was total silence in the plane. It was touching down, shakily, in Libance.

Chapter One

My first encounter with Libancer folk was somewhat disconcerting; the two officials whom I spoke to on the tarmac looked very confused by my attempt to explain that I was seeking asylum in their country, and they tried to usher me into one of the three buses that had drawn up on the tarmac, and into which the rest of the Airbus passengers were being shepherded. Luckily, the captain of our aircraft spotted the argument, which was becoming increasingly heated, and adopted a sufficiently authoritarian manner to get me taken instead into a rather scruffy office in the terminal building, clearly not one much used.

"Well, here you are, old boy, I wish you well in your adventure. It will be a little awkward to explain to Heathrow why we are returning with one passenger missing, but we've got your signed note saying that this is all your own idea, so let's hope that will do the trick." He left me sitting rather forlornly with my suitcases and a smaller case containing my laptop. After ten minutes or so, a uniformed woman came in.

She sat down at the desk, plugged her communicator into the electronic terminal, tapped a few keys, and then inserted my passport card into her machine.

"Good morning, Mr Rowgarth. My name is Friya Alling, and I am under contract with the Western Guardian Security Company. We handle all security matters at this airport. I understand you have asked for asylum."

I nodded.

"That is very unusual. According to our records, no-one has asked for asylum in Libance for more than forty years. My company is prepared to offer you a one-month contract to deal with your case. I therefore have to ask you if you will accept my services. My fee is 500

US dollars a day, 50% refundable once you have found work and we can then have a straightforward commission relationship. Should you want it, of course. May I have your credit card?"

"Hey, wait a minute. I thought you were an immigration official. I don't need any security services, thank you."

"You do not understand, Mr Rowgarth. We do not have immigration officials. I normally deal with breach of contract cases. My job is to find you the best possible way of financing your needs while our Security Association works out how to handle your situation. You cannot of course simply pay for your food and lodgings as if you were on holiday, as we don't have an old-fashioned currency, but since you say you want asylum, I assume you would like to start earning a living as soon as possible. I cannot act for you without a contract between us. You can of course refuse, but then you won't be covered by any insurance. This is definitely not advisable in our country."

I knew Libance was a weird place, but I hadn't expected my first encounter with an official to turn into a session on career advice, and advice I was going to have to pay for. I had no choice at the moment but to let her carry-on accumulating information about me.

"So," she said eventually, "to sum up. You are a 37-year-old freelance journalist, living in London, divorced, with two children. You specialise in investigative features, mostly these days for the American papers and TV networks, because the European media owners won't employ you. You were en route to New York when your plane ran into difficulties and was forced to land here. You claim that you have received death threats from criminals associated with businessmen and politicians in Britain that you have written about, that neither the UK or European police will protect you, and that you were going to America (because you already have a Green Card) to try to settle there. This is why you are refusing to go back with the other passengers to Heathrow, and why you want asylum here, at least until you can arrange to go to the United States. Which will of course be difficult, given the effective non-existence of travel arrangements between Libance and the USA. If you don't go on your plane once whatever is wrong with it has been sorted out, you could well be here for a long time."

I thought that was a pretty accurate summary. During this time, I had formed a pleasant impression of Friya Alling. She was polite and seemed efficient; she certainly asked some pretty sharp questions. There was nothing particularly attractive about her, at least at first glance: a medium height, medium build, brown-haired woman with glasses, in her late 20s or early 30s at a guess. But there was a warmth and vitality that made itself felt over the two hours, so much so that I nearly forgot that her usual customers were people who couldn't pay their debts.

Asking for asylum had been pretty much a spur of the moment decision. I didn't want to risk going back to London and then make a second attempt to fly to New York. Various people would by now know that I had been on the diverted plane and would make very strenuous efforts to stop me leaving Europe if I went back and tried it again.

In that sense staying in Libance, at least for a few months, made better sense. People rarely came here, because it was such an odd place, and difficult to get to. I mean, it didn't seem to have any kind of government, which was a pretty good start. If I stayed a couple of months, I should get enough material for several lucrative articles and TV shows. But I had a more immediate problem; getting some cash now.

"Miss Alling," I said, assuming from her ring-free finger that she was a Miss, "how can I pay you if there is no exchange system for foreign currencies?"

"An interesting question. But the insurance clause in our contract will take care of that until we can open a bank account for you here," she said. She looked at my debit card with some fascination but handed it back to me and sighed.

"I see, Mr Rowgarth, I am going to incur an immediate deficit on your account. Give me a moment." She then turned to her computer and tapped for a couple of minutes. "There, I have booked a grade 3 room in the prison hostel, with breakfast only. That will be the equivalent of 80 US dollars a day. They won't bill you until the end of the month, and I think we will have found you proper work by then. Please authorise this arrangement. Then we can get down to business."

I looked at her. "You are putting me in prison, and making me pay for the privilege?"

"You need only stay there at night, and only until I can get you registered. Of course, you will pay. What happens in prisons in your country?"

"Lots of things, many of them unpleasant, and some I wouldn't want to describe to a lady. But at least you don't pay the governor for the favour of locking you up."

She grinned broadly. "How fascinating. I knew I was right to take this contract. You and I can have wonderful talks about your country and how it works. I have read such strange things, and once saw an amazing TV documentary about the USA. We so rarely have outsiders visit us, and I've never had the chance to talk to any of them. Mind you," she said on reflection, "that could well be because there haven't been any for a long time."

Friya Alling said she would conduct me to the prison she'd fixed up for me on her way home. She waved up a horse and cart. I looked at her and began to ask why she had such an out-of-date mode of transport, when she laughed. "Of course, you don't realise we have been living with, or in anticipation of, climate change. Our oilfield will run out in twenty-five years, so we are adjusting now to a pre-petrol age. Only a few security vehicles run on petrol. The rest of us use our feet, cycle, ride on horses, or ride in pony carts."

She certainly handled our cart well enough, weaving expertly round slower ones, and avoiding both pedestrians and the big horse-drawn buses. She started to tell me about the couple of job interviews she hoped to arrange over the following days with some financial services companies with an interest in foreign events, who might be willing to take me on as a short-term consultant. I was half-listening, but more interested in the passing scenery.

It looked superficially like most rides between an airport and a big city, except for all the non-petrol carts and wagons and bicycles. I'd remembered from somewhere that Libance had a climate like Belgium's (not that I was sure how Belgium's weather differed from England's). This, even though Libance was an island and a thousand miles from anywhere else. Anyway, this afternoon it was grey, overcast and mild – which sounded like Belgium to me.

Then we got stuck in a traffic jam. It was soon clear why – large crowds were streaming towards a big arena. This was emblazoned with banners and slogans, and catchy music was blaring out from the sound systems. As we slowly made our way past the stadium, I saw a number of stalls selling the usual promotional merchandise: disks, picture books, T-shirts, posters, speciality food and souvenirs. It all looked very lively and jolly.

"What's going on?" I asked Alling. "Is it a big match? Or a rock concert?"

She laughed. "No, no. It's an election meeting. We have to vote for a new Senate in four weeks. This is one of the first big events in the campaign of Kris Myer – he's leader of the National Democratic Party. He is a wonderful performer. He can always attract big crowds. And he's got a pretty good supporting line-up tonight. I had intended to go myself, but then you came along. But I can catch the highlights later on my video box."

I was impressed. I'd never seen cheerful, enthusiastic crowds like this at a political event back home. The Cup Final, yes; but not an election. I was about to ask if this Myer was government or opposition when I remembered Libance didn't have a government. "What does your Senate do if it doesn't provide you with a president or prime minister?" I asked.

"Why, it debates a variety of things of course. And it has to approve all judicial appointments and public franchises."

"Well, who proposes the debates if it's not the government?"

Alling looked puzzled. "Anyone can if they can get the necessary minimum number of supporters. I thought we were famous as the most democratic country in the world. In a real democracy any citizen should be able to propose a new debate, surely."

I couldn't begin to summon up the energy to argue with this, and anyway, given my distrust of politicians, I didn't want to suddenly find myself trying to defend them. I decided to leave my basic lesson in the Libancois constitution for another day. Then I remembered that I was supposed to be finding out how to get hold of some local currency.

"Say, could we stop at a bank or an ATM so I could get some cash? I have only got dollars and Euros on me, and I don't suppose they take those in your shops."

She laughed. "Mr Rowgarth, don't they teach you anything about us in your schools and colleges? I thought we were famous not just for our democracy but because we have abolished coins and notes. We have no cash. Every transaction is done electronically."

"Well, of course we are getting there too," I said rather huffily. "But we still do many things with cash. We do sometimes use contactless credit cards for a few euros' worth of sweets or newspapers, but cash still rules for a lot of people."

She shrugged. "We have got used to our way. Anyway, it's the only way to make sure everyone is insured. And it has the great advantage that it makes most theft and robberies pointless."

There she went again: two more casual statements that left me totally puzzled. What had insurance to do with the price of sweets? And how did a cashless economy eliminate robberies? I added these to my tuition list of local customs to be explained at some future date.

We pulled into the drive of what looked like a large but ordinary hotel. A large and ordinary-looking porter picked up my bags. Friya Alling smirked and nudged me. "It's one of the little tricks the Guardian chain of prisons go in for," she whispered. "They get the inmates to act as porters and receptionists. Makes everyone feel better."

Actually, it made me feel rather nervous. If this was a prison, and these people hanging around the lobby were prisoners, where were the guards? Who the hell was in charge?

Friya took me over to the reception desk, where she seemed to be well-known.

"Hi there Friya," said the man behind the desk. "You've got an interesting one for us this time." He turned to me. "Welcome to Guardian Central, Mr Rowgarth. Everything is ready for you. Just sign the book here, please. It's a shame I can't take an imprint of your card, but Friya says you will be able to pay soon, so who's to argue?"

Friya held out her hand. "Good night, Mr Rowgarth. I will come for you at ten o'clock tomorrow. Get a good night's sleep."

I followed what, in any other country, would have been a porter down what looked just like hotel corridors to what definitely looked like a hotel room door. The porter gave me a key card. "Please hand this in at the desk whenever you leave," he said. I went to give him a tip and realised I couldn't. "You're not locking me in then," I said feebly.

"Ho ho, very good," he said. "If you feel anxious you can lock your door yourself from the inside. But there is no need. We have a very good record at Guardian Central."

Good record for what, *exactly*? I thought as I lugged my cases into my room.

Chapter Two

My room was tiny, but decently furnished – very decently furnished for a prison cell. There was an ingenious shower and toilet arrangement which meant you couldn't use both at the same time, but then I don't imagine anyone ever tried to. A tiny flat screen was attached to one wall just below the ceiling; the keyboard remote looked reasonably sophisticated; I thought of logging into my London server and collecting any messages, but I realised there wasn't any way I could get in touch: indeed, it might be better if people in England didn't know precisely where I was. There were curtains on the window, and a view over a rather pleasant garden where several men and women were taking the air, which calmed me down a bit.

I was just finishing unpacking when the screen bleeped with a message – "Rowgarth interview with Chief Executive Delene 19.00 hours."

I had just enough time to use the neatly packaged bathroom and smarten up. At 18:53 a cheerful young man, whose name failed to register but who appeared to be a PA, arrived and walked me to the chief executive's office. Delene herself was a slightly overweight but handsome woman in a smart jacket and dress. She looked as if she'd had a hard day, but perked up when we were introduced.

"Our European visitor. How wonderful. Please sit down. Have a drink – I am."

For an hour she grilled me. Like Alling, she seemed constantly surprised at my account of the way we did things in Europe. Finally, she offered me the chance to ask her questions, but only if I agreed to have dinner with her in her office, since she was starving. Since I was as well, and since I had no idea how I was supposed to get a meal in this place, I readily agreed. She leaned towards a communicator box and ordered some food.

"Okay, let's start with this place. This is like no prison I've ever seen. What kind of criminals do you get in here?"

She smiled. "We don't have criminals in Libance, at least not in your sense of the word. There is no criminal law, so we don't have crimes. The people who come here do so because they have broken a contract in some way and cannot pay the fine, or cannot pay compensation, or their insurance doesn't cover them, or they have lost their jobs or homes. They stay here until we have got them back into a state where they can function normally in the outside world."

I pulled a face. "No criminal laws? What kind of laws do you have then?"

"You seem to forget – Libance is not a state in the way you understand it. We do not have a government which brings in legislation, raises taxes, and runs an administration. Everything here is run by individuals and organisations which enter into contracts with each other. Therefore, our paramount law is the law of contract, and most litigation concerns breaches of contract, or arbitration of disputes. We do have specialist courts which deal with competition law, and with the supervision of referendums and franchises. But there is no criminal law for them to deal with."

"Yeah, I know about not having any government, but I didn't realise that meant you don't have crimes. Suppose I steal someone's wallet, or beat someone up – do I just get away with it? What if I murder someone? Don't the police come after me?"

"There would be little point in stealing a wallet. We do not have money, or rather we don't have cash – everything is electronic. And your personal data card, which you would use for any transaction, cannot be used by anyone else, so there would be no point in stealing that either. It is true that sometimes people steal objects, like paintings or antiques, but it happens rarely since a thief could not sell such objects to anyone else – the electronic record of any attempted transaction would catch them out – and therefore they would only steal something to keep for their personal use."

"As for beating someone up, yes, we do have fights and other acts of violence. But it wouldn't be the police that investigated such actions; we do not have a police force. It would be the security company with which the victim of the assault was registered. They would deal with the matter. You, for example, are registered with our sister company, Western Guardian, so you do not have to worry." She smiled, sweetly, on the mistaken assumption that I would find this information reassuring.

"How would they do that, if there is no criminal court in which to bring an attacker to trial?"

"In various ways. If you knew who the person was who attacked you, they could approach his insurance company for compensation. That company might or might not be willing to accept the claim, depending on what their client said about the matter. If there was a dispute, it could go to arbitration. Or your security company might decide – with your agreement – simply to send some of their guards to beat the other man up, as revenge. They would of course only do that if they were sure that that person's security company wouldn't in turn take action against you."

"Good grief, that's very primitive. Does that sort of thing happen often?"

"More often than you might think, particularly if you yourself do not have a record for getting into fights and the other person does. The security companies concerned would recognise that this was the simplest way of dealing with the matter."

"What if I didn't know who attacked me?"

"More difficult, but ultimately the same process. Depending on your insurance terms, the security company would be obliged to spend some time trying to find out the identity of the person who attacked you. If they ran out of their contracted time, you could pay them to continue – or let the matter drop."

"As to murder, there are very few cases – but I can tell from your reaction just now that you will not approve of our approach. It is very similar to what I have just described, except that the investigation will be either on behalf of the murdered person's relatives - or even by their security company for its own sake – they will want to be seen to be doing the proper professional job. If they find the murderer, they will try to negotiate compensation for the victim's relatives. However, the relatives are entitled under certain circumstances to ask for the murderer to be killed in turn. Naturally this can only be done with the agreement of the murderer's own security company – so they have to be satisfied with the evidence against him."

I tried to imagine how this would work in England. Your brother has been murdered; Securicor come and say, "We have found the killer and it's okay, Group 4 have said, 'yup, he's the guy, you can have him.' So if you want we will go and take him out." It sounded terrible, put like that, but I had a sneaking suspicion that if we had the same system in England the great majority of my fellow citizens would cheerfully say, "Sure thing, go ahead and get the bastard."

"So these security companies take the place of the police – and do everything as a matter of individual contracts? Don't they end up fighting each other?"

"Oh no, that would be hopeless. No, they have a very carefully drawn up professional agreement which prevents that, and which determines how they handle individual cases. Anyway, most matters are dealt with by negotiation, or failing that, by arbitration by the court."

I remembered what Friya Alling had said about it being advisable to be insured in this country. "So good insurance is a must," I said.

"Absolutely. Your insurance agreements are the most important things in your life. And the insurance companies are the most important organisations in our country. The Guardian company, I am proud to say, is one of the best."

"Guardian company? You mean the people who own this prison?"

"That's right. We are a subsidiary of the main group. Our security company is one of the best too." And she gave me that sweet reassuring smile again.

"So, if everybody has insurance, how come some people end up here in prison?"

"As I said earlier, sometimes people do things which aren't covered by insurance, or they can't afford to take out the right insurance, or their insurance company refuses to accept their claim. Usually, it is because they have let their insurance premiums lapse – and that is generally because they are out of work. Because it is very dangerous to be uninsured, people in that situation will either themselves seek to be interned here or their relatives will ask the insurance company to get them committed here, if that is a condition in their original contract."

I thought about that for a moment. If you were unemployed or uninsured you went to prison – sometimes of your own free will. This was barbaric. It must mean there were plenty of prisons, and they must be pretty full. On the other hand, if this place was anything to go by, they weren't much like the prisons back home.

"So how do people get out again?" I asked. "And don't they have to pay to stay here anyway? How can they afford that if they couldn't keep up their insurance payments in the first place?"

"People leave once they have found new jobs, or new homes – whatever it was that they lost, and which forced them to come here. One of our tasks is to help them achieve this. While they are here, they have to work for us – sometimes in the prison itself – you have already met people doing that – but more usually on one of our outside contracts. Of course, we are able to offer workers to other employers at a good price, but still one that covers our own costs."

"That sounds like slave labour."

The chief executive frowned, and then shrugged. "Not at all. Anyone can leave here any time they wish to. Of course, we deduct our costs from what people here earn. Indeed, we take a commission for up to two years on what they earn after they leave here. We are not a charity. We must make a profit."

"But why can't the state pay for this out of taxes?"

Delene smiled. "At last, we have come to the main point. We do not have a government and therefore we do not have any taxes. It is a fundamental principle of our Basic Law. We regard government and taxation as profoundly oppressive. Every citizen must be free to do what he or she wishes with whatever income they have."

I tried to take this in. No taxes. No taxes meant no state schools, no public health service. Okay, I could just about see how that might work – though it must be very tough on people with low incomes – and she had already explained how they managed without a police force. But surely some things had to be paid for by the state.

"Look, what happens to people who are seriously disabled? Do they come here? If they do, how on earth do you make money out of them?"

"That is complicated. I shall first explain what happens when people have sex together."

I pretend to look shocked. "Don't tell me the Libancois have sex with each other in a totally different way to the rest of us?"

She smiled faintly. "I doubt it. No, what is very different is that whenever a man and a woman first make love to each other, they have de facto entered into a contract with the other person, and they are obliged to register this formally as soon as possible after the event."

Now I wasn't pretending. I was seriously shocked. "You are telling me that after every new sexual encounter the man and the woman must trot along to some office and record the fact that they have screwed each other? That is the most appalling thing I have yet heard."

Delene looked at me almost wearily. "They do of course record the fact electronically. And, needless to say, it is confidential to the Institute of Human Relations, which holds the data. The record is only relevant if the woman gets pregnant from that encounter. At that point the two of them must strike a contract with each other, and with the as yet unborn child."

"Hang on, that's all very interesting, but I can't believe everyone sticks to these rules. Surely lots of people must disregard them."

"Actually, no, very few people do – and they are usually caught out later. If you think about it, you will see why. The whole point is to make sure people take responsibility for their own actions. If a woman becomes pregnant, she and the man responsible must make adequate arrangements for bringing up the child, unless, of course, they mutually agree to abort it. So they make a contract. There are some half-dozen basic types, ranging from financial support for the single parent from the other parent – that's if they don't want to live together – to a full-blooded marriage contract with detailed provisions for the upbringing of the child. And of course, minimum insurance arrangements for all three persons involved."

"Of course," I said sarcastically, "the insurance companies were bound to have a slice of the action."

"And that is why," she went on, ignoring my intervention, "people basically must play by the rules. A pregnant woman has to inform both her employers and her insurers. They will want to see the 'couple contract', as it is popularly known. If she hasn't got one, they will try to persuade her to get one, using the universal DNA database to discover the father. If necessary, they will assist her via his insurers, in making sure the father signs up. It is very rare for a pregnant woman to refuse at this point. Doing so would put her in breach of all her contracts – a desperately vulnerable position for a mother-to-be to be in. Everyone knows this, even the men, and everyone knows there is no escape. So pretty well everyone does what they are supposed to do straight away."

"But what if you are using contraception, so there is no risk of pregnancy? Surely people don't rush to their computers in those circumstances?"

"Well, it's true that quite a few people leave it for a while, but in the end nearly everyone does enter the appropriate records. After all, it isn't just pregnancy: there are various infectious diseases to worry about. And your insurance company isn't very happy if you turn up a couple of months after a sexual fling trying to claim for treatment when you should have logged it immediately."

"What about prostitutes? Surely, they don't go in for this rigmarole. I would have thought it would put most punters off if they thought that after a visit to the local brothel they were going into the database at the Institute of Human Interference, or whatever it was."

"Of course, prostitutes electronically record their transactions. Apart from anything else, that's the only way they get paid. We are not a cash economy, remember?"

My God, I thought, *these people don't seem to have any privacy whatsoever.* I was by now prepared to learn that every sneeze and cough was itemised on a database somewhere in this country. How on earth could they conduct adulterous affairs if they had to make them a matter of public record?

"Look," I said, "if you and I were married to each other, and I started an affair, what's to stop you checking with the Institute of Human Busybodies to see if I've got into their records recently?"

"I would find it extremely difficult," she said. "No-one, not even the insurance companies, can interrogate the records without the consent of the person concerned. Of course, I could, if I were suspicious of you, challenge you to allow me to check the records. And in fact, that is one of the most basic ingredients of marriage contracts: whether or not the couple include a clause binding the two of them to agree to such searches if requested. Actually, the majority of people specifically exclude such clauses, precisely because they do not want to get married on that basis."

It was very annoying – she always seemed to come up with a rational answer which I found difficult to dislodge, however absurd the situation seemed at first glance. But I ploughed on, nonetheless.

"Okay, so you can agree from the start whether or not you are going to allow the sex police into your marriage. But what about hackers? All the evidence over many years is that no database, however well secured, can't be broken into by really determined hackers. They must have a great deal of fun checking on who's having it off, and with whom."

"Actually, the records are pretty secure. All names are encrypted, so simply getting illegal access to the data isn't enough – you would have to break the encryptions. And even if you managed that, you couldn't do much with the information. Any publication of such data would automatically lead to you losing your contract with your server company, and no other company would be willing or able to take their place, which would severely handicap you in today's digital world. Yes, you could pass on such gossip by word of mouth, but it wouldn't be much reward for a great deal of effort and a high risk of serious penalties.

"In short, Mr Rowgarth, hacking into the Institute scarcely ever happens."

"Well, I am amazed that you people seem so relaxed about this extraordinary lack of privacy. But then pretty well everything I've learned so far about the way Libance goes about things is extraordinary. Look, if you don't mind, I'll take myself off to my bed. It has been rather a tiring day."

"Of course. But I didn't answer your question about what happens to disabled people, which was how we got onto sex in the first place."

I had totally forgotten that. I asked her to finish her account, as briefly as she could.

"When a couple who are going to have a child draw up both their own contract and the contracts with their insurance companies, they have to have a genetic scan. This, along with the other normal tests that go with pregnancies, reveals any existence of disability in the foetus, or the likelihood of such disabilities after birth. The results determine the attitude of the insurers: what to charge, indeed whether to offer insurance at all. This in turn usually determines whether the couple are prepared to have the child. The net result is very, very few disabled children are born. Of course, people do develop disabilities in later life but again this is covered in most health insurance policies."

"So the insurance companies have the power of life and death, do they?"

"Not entirely. Some people choose to proceed despite negative results from scans. However, as you might guess, they tend to be wealthy people who can commit to bringing up a disabled child, and indeed securing its future for its life after they themselves are dead."

I shook my head. It was very difficult to get inside the Libancois mindset, or to empathise with the calm way they appeared to accept this approach to life. But I was grateful to the prison governor for spelling things out so clearly. She said she would be happy to talk again, since there were doubtless many more aspects of our different societies that we could fruitfully discuss.

When I got back to my cell, or rather my room, I saw a message on the wall screen. It was from the Guardian General Insurance Company, telling me that my application for tier one emergency insurance had been accepted, and that I could now safely go about my business. I am ashamed to say that I really did feel relieved.

Chapter Three

I didn't sleep that well; far too many thoughts and questions were buzzing in my brain. I got up soon after dawn and saw that my screen was helpfully showing a plan of the prison and how I could get to the dining room, as they called it. I let myself out of my room and went down as soon as it opened.

The dining room looked rather more like a factory canteen. It was remarkably busy for such an early hour. I collected a tray and served myself some juice, bread, coffee and eggs, and with difficulty found an empty space next to a kid of 14 or 15 on a small side table. I asked if he minded if I joined him.

"That's OK," he said, scarcely glancing at me. Then he looked more closely. "Hey, you're the guy on the news last night. The visitor from Europe. What a freaky number."

I nodded, smiled, and inevitably had to provide a succinct summary of what I was doing in Libance. My breakfast companion was called Axal, and, it turned out, had been living in the prison with his parents and family for some four months or so. He was supposed to earn money helping to clean the prison before he went to the prison school, but decided he'd skip that so he could talk to me. I think I was supposed to feel flattered.

Axal and family had voluntarily come to Guardian Central at the insistence of his mother after his father had failed to give up gambling. His father owed a lot to the betting company – more than someone who worked as a bus driver could afford to owe – and his mother, who was a part-time cleaner, had invoked the clause in the wedding contract which allowed her to insist on prison as a protection against the claims of the gambling houses. So now his father drove trucks on a prison sub-contract, and his mother could clean full-time as the four children were all taken care of at the prison school and nursery. At the same time the Guardian group was negotiating a deal with the betting company, which was owned by one of their rivals, the United group.

"We hope to be out of here in six months or so," said Axal. "Pop's debts should be paid off, and they'll find us a place to rent. The main thing will be that the Guardian people will have got deals with all the betting companies to refuse to take Pop on as a client. He'll hate that but there's not a lot he can do about it."

I asked if there were many families in this kind of situation in the prison.

"Oh yeah. Loads of them. Most of them, I would guess. It's quite common for people to spend time in prison. You said that in Europe it was a disgrace to be sent to prison. Well, it isn't here."

"What's it like going to school here?"

Axal grimaced. "Bloody hard work. That's why I was trying to finish my maths homework when you arrived. I did two hours last night, but it wasn't enough."

"Why can't you go to your old school now you are in prison? Won't they take you now?"

He laughed. "Yeah, 'course they would. But one of the reasons Mum wanted us to come here was so that we could go to Guardian Central School. It's one of the best in the country."

I shook my head. "Wait a minute. The prison school is one of the best in the country. How is that?"

"All the prison schools are good. Everyone knows that. In fact, quite a lot of rich people pay good money for their kids to come here. I've got several in my class."

This I found hard to believe. "Oh, come on. Why would rich parents want to send their children to a school inside a prison?"

"The discipline is very tough, and we all have to work hard. They put guards outside any class that might give trouble – any hint of a disturbance and they are in straight away sorting it out. It's a grim sight I can tell you. You don't want to be there when it happens. So, it doesn't happen very much.

"And if you don't do the homework or any extra study the teachers give you, you are put in solitary after school and stay there until you have done it. I was in for a week once – never again. Of course," he added, "the rich kids don't like staying in overnight." And he laughed at the thought.

I thought of our English schools. Many teachers I knew (and parents too, I reckoned) would like the idea of instant solitary confinement for trouble-making students. I asked Axal what normal schools in Libance were like. What happened to pupils who cheeked teachers there?

"That depends on the school. The good ones and the expensive ones can get rid of you pretty easily if you don't behave yourself. But there are loads of places that need the money they get from parents, even from parents like mine who don't earn much and can only afford cheap schools; the people that run them don't like the idea of expelling you. So, it's a lot easier to mess about in places like that. In fact, I know some parents who get so fed up with either their kids or the school they are at that they pay to send them to the prison schools. There are a dozen of those in my class right now."

His class of 15-year-olds had over 40 students in it. "Of course, no-one can pay much so they pack them in," but no-one messed about.

"Surely, Axal, you can't enjoy being at this kind of school. Your old one must have been better."

"Sort of; maybe. It is hard here. But I will get much better grades than I would have done outside. And the teachers are usually better. They can make you interested in the subject."

I reckoned with that kind of discipline to back you up you probably did have a better chance of making a subject interesting. I switched to what their rooms were like.

"Our cells, you mean?"

I flinched. I had deliberately not called them that. I imagined Guardian Central would have got way beyond the prison cell by now.

"They are grim. Mum and Dad share a small one, and the three of us kids share another one just as small. There's no room for anything, and there is a toilet and shower we share with another family."

He looked at his watch. "Tell you what, you can come and have a look if you like. The others will have gone by now. I've got a free period. If we're quick I can show where we live and still get my maths finished."

As we walked through a maze of courtyards and small squares, with increasingly dour buildings on every side – Guardian Central was much bigger than I'd realised when I arrived – I asked Axal where they put the really tough prisoners: the hard cases.

He was puzzled. "Hard cases? I don't think there are any. You come here if you are unlucky, like us and my dad."

"But there must be some people who have done something bad. Stolen stuff; done heavy drugs; or killed someone."

I had forgotten what the Governor had told me the night before. I still assumed that even in Libance a prison must contain some conventional criminals.

"No, no-one like that. You would only come here for stealing if you couldn't pay the compensation when you were caught, and most stealing that I know of is for small stuff. Drugs? You can get what you like where you like. If you overdo it you can end up in hospital, and if your insurance runs out you can ultimately end up here, but that doesn't make you a tough nut, as you suggest. As for killing someone, well you'd usually be killed yourself by the victim's security people if you did that. So, you could hardly end up here for that either.

"The only hard cases I can think of," he went on after a brief pause, "would be the kind of people who go to the Island. But they wouldn't want to come here anyway."

"The Island? What's that? I don't know about that."

"You haven't heard of the Island?" He frowned. "It's up north. It's where the outlaws are. Most of them are hard cases all right."

Outlaws? How could there be outlaws in a country with no criminal law and courts that only dealt with contracts and competition cases? Who decided you were an outlaw?

"I don't understand. I thought Libance didn't have the kind of laws that might make someone an outlaw. How do you become one – and who runs the Island?"

Axal looked bemused. "I've no idea who runs the Island, or if anyone does. I mean, it's not part of Libance, as far as I know.

Outlaws is just a name for the people on the Island – they are also called Outsiders, or Refusers, or Rejecters. Basically, you become one of them by your own choice – you decide to go to the Island. No-one sends you there – at least I've never heard of that. It's for people who refuse to work, or to take out insurance, or refuse to go to prison. I suppose that's why some people call them Refusers – 'cos they refuse everything."

This was a revelation indeed, but I couldn't get more out of him, partly because I could see he didn't want to talk about it, and partly because I don't think he knew much more anyway. Besides, we had reached the block where he and his family lived.

It was a tall brick building, similar to others we had passed. The windows were small and showed few signs of life – no curtains or window boxes, everything a uniform dull brown. No-one was putting much love or care into the place.

We climbed two flights of stairs – Axal said it wasn't worth waiting for the lift even if it was working – and trudged down a long corridor. The smells were unpleasant – there were obviously too many people in too small a space with too few facilities. At the far end of the corridor Axal used a key card to open the door into a room about 16 metres square. There was a window opposite the door, and two double bunks along each of the side walls. I noticed a small chest of drawers beneath the window – and that was it, apart from a jumble of clothes and possessions piled in any available space.

"Me, my brother and sister share this. You can see why I do my homework in the canteen. My parents have the same next door. And I don't think you want to see the shower room."

This was indeed fit for prisons as I knew them back home. "You have to pay good money for this? Do you know how much? And what's happened to the rest of your stuff?"

"We had to sell or get rid of a lot of it. There are a few special things in store, but it's expensive to rent space so we can't keep much there. Of course, the prison people don't want us to stay too long so they are not going to make the place nice and comfortable, are they? I'd leave tomorrow if we could. I don't know what it costs – you'd have to ask my mum."

I looked at this tiny messy place where three large and hyperactive young people were supposed to live. "How do you amuse yourselves? There's no kind of screen or terminal here that I can see. No TV or internet or games."

"Oh, you have to go to the Prison Comms centre for that. You have to hang around for your turn, and anyway it costs. All three of us spend a lot of time in school using their facilities, since these are free. Or training, of course. We are all in junior prison sports teams."

From his description these sounded like a version of the scouts or the cadets, only run by the prison security people. It wasn't compulsory – that wasn't the Libance style – but I got the impression that families like Axal's, with active children and teenagers, were encouraged to sign them up. Not that parents in confined spaces would need much encouragement. I wondered if there were equivalents for adults.

Axal said he should go and finish his maths. He felt sure his mum – though not perhaps his dad – would be keen to meet me. Fine by me, I said, and gave him my room number. I didn't imagine his mother would want to invite me round to their place.

Chapter Four

Friya Alling's schedule of interviews for me with various financial companies proved disappointing, at least to her. Two of them plainly said they had nothing to offer, and while the others had been less overtly dismissive, I agreed with her view that they were unlikely to come up with anything either.

I assumed she was concerned because she had failed to win her commission in the shortest possible time, but this may well have been unfair to her. "What can we do with you?" she asked, as we had a drink in a bar at the end of the afternoon. "I have nothing fixed for you for tomorrow – and anyway I have other clients and appointments. What kind of work should I be looking for for you?"

"Well, why not try the media? It is my trade, after all."

She looked dubious. "You know nothing about our country. How can you be of use to a media company?"

"That's just it – maybe they would like something from a stranger. 'The European perspective on Libance'; it doesn't have to be a full-time job, just a feature of some kind. Maybe even a TV documentary: something to keep me going."

This cheered her up. "A very good idea. Tomorrow I will make some calls. With luck we can meet some editors the day after tomorrow."

Relaxed, she agreed to another drink. There were various things I'd noticed during the day that I wanted to ask about. Also, I wanted to see if she would agree to go out with me one evening soon, as I wasn't looking forward to spending all my spare time in my prison room.

Being driven around the town that day in a small, horse-drawn carriage had been rather odd. The different districts had varied greatly, not so much in the variety of houses, offices and factories, all of which were not that different to what we had in Europe, but in the quality of the roads. And we seemed to be constantly monitored by cameras and other electronic surveillance. Sometimes we even had to go through what I took to be tollgates on a regular basis, not that we stopped, just slowed down to be recorded. But this could be on quite minor roads; perhaps obviously, they didn't seem to have motorways or anything like that. I asked Friya to explain.

"Of course, the roads vary. It depends on how much traffic there is, what you must pay, how well off the local community is. We have hundreds of local societies and associations. Most of them try to raise money from charging people to use their roads. And they spend wildly different amounts on maintaining them."

"OK, here we go again. I don't suppose you have local councils who raise local taxes – that would be an act of oppression, as Governor Delene would say. So, what are these local societies, how do they work, and who is in charge of roads?"

She smiled. "An act of oppression. Yes, I suppose that is right. I hadn't thought of it like that. Of course, before the Revolution we had local councils, but not for many years now. What happens is that every household belongs to a local society or association and has a contract with it to provide, or arrange to get provided, various services that the household needs. In the country this can be very little, while in the towns it usually includes water and sewage services, rubbish collection, things like that. Sometimes electricity and gas, though often people make their own arrangements. But always roads – even the most self-sufficient country dweller has to have a road contract."

"Has to have? I thought no-one in Libance was compelled to do anything. How is it different for roads?"

"In theory you don't have to have a road contract. There isn't any law about it. But in practice every house or apartment block has one. It has become over the years a requirement of selling a house or flat that the contract includes an obligation on the person buying the property to join the local society and meet the society's minimum conditions, and that includes agreeing with the way they provide and pay for the roads. If you are lucky, you will buy or rent a house in an area where they make money from the traffic that uses the society's roads, so you don't pay anything."

"Suppose I didn't want to join this local society, let alone pay for the roads. Who can make me?"

"The person selling the property couldn't sell it to you if you didn't agree to those terms. It would be in the contract that they made when they purchased it themselves. So, if you took the attitude you describe, you would never be able to buy a house or flat. If you rent a place, then of course your landlord would hold the contract with the local society."

"I see. So, the system is self-perpetuating – once it has started. How did it start, by the way? What happened when you abolished the local councils? It must have been anarchy."

"According to the history books, it was. It took about ten years for the new system to become universal. There was an awful lot of confusion and chaos, with people – probably people like you – refusing to join societies, and other people getting very angry with what were called free-riders. But I think what happened was that the Constitutional Court and the Contract Court eventually agreed that every local society could require house purchase contracts to include this obligation, and the insurance companies refused to insure houses that didn't belong to a local society – so rapidly everyone did join up. And that was that."

The insurance companies again. They really did seem to run the place. But I wasn't finished with the road question.

"As a matter of interest, what did it cost us to do our little journey today?"

She checked a dashboard I hadn't noticed before and said, "Thirty-two euros. Which will of course be put on your bill."

"That's outrageous – not for charging me for it, but for the whole idea that people have to pay that much to use ordinary roads. It must be horrendous for people on low incomes."

"Everything is more difficult for people on low incomes. Why should roads be any different? It costs money to maintain them. Why shouldn't the people who drive on them and cause the wear and tear pay for that maintenance?"

"Because … because it's a basic right to be able to travel around freely. This is going back to the Middle Ages and keeping people in their places."

"A basic right? Of course, everyone is free to travel. That isn't the same as travelling for free. Someone must pay the costs of travel – why not the traveller? Our system means that you only take out your cart or carriage when it makes economic sense to do so. Not when you walk, of course. But that is why our traffic is manageable."

It was true that there hadn't been much cart or horse traffic around, much less than I'd expected in a big city. But I thought of another objection.

"OK, I can see that these local societies can sort out the roads they inherited after your Revolution, but what about new roads? And what about main roads between the towns? These would run through lots of local society areas, wouldn't they?"

"New roads within the area of a local society would have to be agreed by a vote of all the society members – the exact rules would vary from society to society. We don't have new motorways and the old ones from years ago and other big roads are owned by the road companies. If they are new, they have to be negotiated with the people who own the land on which the road companies want to build. The roads that existed at the time of the Revolution were all auctioned off to road companies – the money raised went to set up the new legal system, as I remember from my school days."

"That sounds horribly complicated. How can a road company negotiate a new 200-kilometre motorway with all the people who own the land along the route?"

"Well, it would take a long time and I can't remember when it last happened. I think if some people are being difficult the road company can run a national vote asking for permission to approach the local societies concerned. In theory since the rest of us usually want the new road they normally win such a vote easily. Then the local society holds a vote of its members. If they agree, and they often don't, then the society can go to the Contract Court to get the various individual contracts changed to make the landowners reach a deal with the road company. But it is all very cumbersome and expensive, which is one reason why most of our roads date from before the Revolution."

"This is ridiculous. How can a modern country operate with such a negative system? There are always people who object to changes that affect them directly, but you seem to have given them a veto."

"I am sorry you find it ridiculous. And yes, it does mean we don't get many new roads. But like paying for every road you use, this is environmentally friendly. It means we only travel by road when we really need to."

"But this must constrain economic growth. If you can't build roads to meet increasing demand, then surely many businesses must stagnate." As someone who had frequently voted for the Greens, I was rather surprised to find myself saying this, but the logic did seem impeccable.

"I am not an economist, but from what I have learned from the media on this it hasn't affected us that much, we have just become very ingenious about dealing with this fact of life. Goods are produced much nearer the markets in which they will be sold, for a start. Do we look as though we are stagnating?"

Actually, from what little I had seen Libance did look poorer and shabbier, generally more old-fashioned, than most of the places I knew in Europe and North America. Whether or not that mattered much was less certain. I didn't feel up to getting into a debate on this, so I let it pass.

"OK, OK, you can make your unfair and stultifying system work, at least to your satisfaction. But there is something else that I have discovered today that I want you to explain. What is The Island, and who lives there?"

Friya had looked confident in defending her country's road-funding policies but now, suddenly, she was uncomfortable.

"The Island? Who told you about that? Never mind, it doesn't matter. The Island lies about a kilometre off our northern coast. It is quite big – I think 20 kilometres long and 15 wide at its widest point. It is connected to the mainland by a causeway which is covered at high tide. Before the Revolution it was part of Libance and was owned by one of the richest families in the country. They treated it as their private estate – only people who worked on the estate lived there.

"After the Revolution the family fled to the United States. Their home on the Island, and the other buildings around it, were abandoned. I think for a while some people squatted there, but they must have found it hard to keep themselves alive, because it became deserted. No-one who could afford to buy and maintain the place seemed to want to – either that or the legal situation was too difficult – legally the old family must still have been the owners.

"Anyway, after a while, something odd happened. There were three families living in the country up North who had persistently refused to accept the way the country was working after the Revolution. They wanted cash for their farm products, they wouldn't get insured, they wouldn't go on the internet. For a while they were left alone to survive as best they could. But eventually they became involved in a big compensation case, but neither the insurers nor the security company involved could get them to pay it. They wouldn't go to prison either. Prison is of course largely voluntary in Libance, as I am sure you know by now, Mr Rowgarth. So, the insurance company said it would evict all of them from their farms, and they would have to find somewhere else to live. This would of course have been impossible; I guess they would have starved to death if they had been evicted. However, one of the families suggested that they all move to the Island, thus removing themselves from Libance and the way it now operated. The insurers agreed to take over the farms, so they were happy, and the families moved to the Island and must have found some way of making themselves self-sufficient. No-one knows for sure, because they were very aggressive to anyone – journalists mostly – who tried to visit them.

"That was nearly twenty years ago. Obviously, it became widely known that there was this odd place where presumably a few people were managing to live without any contact with the rest of us. A couple of men who were real trouble and who even the prisons couldn't cope with decided to try to join the people on the Island. Apparently, they walked across the causeway and must have persuaded the families to let them join them – they certainly never came back. Something similar happened a few months later. And again a few months after that. It began to be a custom – if you really didn't want to, or couldn't, live in our system, you took yourself off to the Island.

"As far as I know, no-one ever came back. A few times bodies of people who had gone there washed up on our shores. The security people who dealt with them said they had been tortured. But that was in the early years – no corpses from the Island have been found on our shores for a long time. Security boats would occasionally circle the Island and establish that it was still inhabited, but none of them tried to land there; there wasn't any point, and of course it had become convenient to the insurance and security companies that the Island existed as a way out for difficult people.

"Then some years ago there was a new development. A small group of Islanders came down to the causeway and approached the security barrier at our end of it. I should explain that each of the big security companies takes it in turn to staff the barriers that were put up years ago to prevent any attempts by Islanders to raid the mainland. Not that they ever tried, incidentally. I have myself served a three-month tour of duty there, which is why I know so much of the story – most people here don't know anything like as much. Anyway, this group came with a proposal. They were in desperate need of medical supplies and equipment and would also like to get decent fabrics for clothing. They wanted to barter fruit and vegetables that they grew in exchange for these items.

"The company on duty consulted with the other security organisations, and it was agreed to try it out. It worked – now twice a week there is what's called the Island Market held on our side of the causeway. But it is carefully controlled; only a few accredited people are permitted to trade with the Islanders, who themselves are very careful not to reveal what is going on on their side of the water.

"The security companies keep a record of who goes to the Island as a Refuser, which is what we normally call the people stupid enough to do this. I think something like 500 people – mostly men, naturally – have crossed the causeway in the past 25 years. Obviously, a number must have died in that time. And it seems likely, given there were a few women of child-bearing age in the original group, and a few that have gone there since, that there must be some people who have been born there. But we really don't know how many there are, how they live and how they organise themselves. Personally, I think there must be some kind of dictator."

She stopped and didn't seem to want to answer any questions. I was anyway so surprised by her story that I hadn't the wherewithal to ask any immediately. So, we sat in silence for a moment.

"Maybe outlaws are the right word," I said eventually. "There can hardly be any law in such a place."

"Oh, I don't know. They must have some way of enabling themselves to live together. We might not regard it as law, but it must achieve something of the same results."

"The law of the strong and the nasty? Not anything I would want to designate with the term law." I went on, "Your point about it being convenient for the insurers and security people here in Libance – that's interesting. What exactly did you mean?"

Friya looked a little cross. "What I said: very occasionally there are very troublesome and difficult people that we don't know how to deal with. It's not usually that they are violent – violence we can treat in kind – but that they just won't play by the rules. If someone refuses to get insurance it becomes almost impossible for them to live; they can't get a job, let alone buy food, find shelter, anything. The prisons don't want them because they can't or won't do anything to pay their way while they are there, and that's if they are even willing to submit to prison, which most of them aren't. Sometimes they can beg for food for a while, but eventually someone complains, and they are moved on – and on, and on. In the end they either make their way to the Island themselves, or some security team picks them up and drops them at the causeway, and then refuses to let them back into Libance."

"Hm. I guess it's your alternative to a system of welfare benefits. Nice one too – doesn't cost you anything."

"It is their choice," she said with waspish emphasis. "Our system is perfectly capable of helping people in trouble, but only if they want to be helped."

"You are right. I hadn't quite appreciated how much your tax-free, Government-free way of life depends on everyone being very responsible. No backsliding, opting-out, dropping-out, sodding-off mavericks allowed. Off to the Island with them."

"Well, you asked, and I have told you. I apologise that it is yet another thing about us that seems to offend you. Thank you for the drink. I will call for you again the day after tomorrow, unless I fail to arrange any meetings, in which case I will leave a message at Guardian Central. Goodbye."

She rose to go, and I suddenly realised I hadn't asked her out. "Hang on," I said. "Look, I am sorry. I don't mean to give the impression I disapprove of everything. I don't at all. It's just that it's all so surprising and different. Please, let me buy us one more drink." I looked around. "I really like this place. It's fun, and you are very interesting. It's certainly better than my room at Guardian Central."

The appeal to her pity worked. She sat down again. We had another drink. And another. She agreed to have dinner with me in two days' time. Result, as we used to say when I was young.

Chapter Five

Friya had offered to give me a lift back to Guardian Central, but after checking a street map she had given me I said it looked a relatively easy walk, that I liked the idea of seeing the town for myself, and that anyway I doubted I could afford the road charges. The joke nearly, but thankfully not quite, undid all the good the last couple of drinks and my attentive behaviour had done. She was about to storm off at the insult to her generosity but fortunately she had got to know me well enough to realise that, at least in my own view, I was trying to be funny.

It was a pleasantly mild, dry evening. There were a fair number of people on the streets, of all ages. They seemed to be enjoying themselves. Many of the shops were still open, even though it was nearly 9pm. There were only a few cafés and restaurants, presumably doing a reasonable business. At first it didn't seem much different from strolling through a comfortable London suburb – Richmond, say, or Islington. The same mix of food and clothes stores, with a sprinkling of estate agents, and music and electronics specialist shops, though all of them looked old-fashioned, rather like the shops I remembered from my childhood, more than thirty years ago. But gradually I noticed there were no banks; there were on the other hand several insurance companies. After twenty minutes or so, I decided that in addition to the Guardian Group the main companies appeared to be the United Assurance, the National Insurance, and the Health and Prosperity Group. All very reassuring names, while offering distinctly more comprehensive services than insurance companies in the UK.

I had imagined that, with there being no local councils to invent and impose regulations, there would be a chaos of cables and wires flung across the streets and round the buildings, and all kinds of visual display and advertising rampant everywhere. (To say nothing of an anarchy of roadworks all over the place.) In fact, it was at least as orderly as London or Paris, and rather more so than New York. If this was the result of decisions by the local societies that Friya had described earlier, then their members in this area were demonstrating an impressive degree of good taste and responsibility.

The upcoming Senate elections, which Friya had mentioned on our ride in from the airport yesterday, were being well promoted with a mix of posters, banners and video boards. Friya's man – Kris Myer of the National Democrats – had film star good looks, and an attractive manner on the video displays. His main opponent seemed to be a woman from the Progressive Party called Lisja Tuller. She was a handsome older woman, with distinguished grey hair and a kind but firm face. The party slogans were of depressing vacuity: Lift Your Spirits, Vote for Kris, as against Vote for Tuller and a Secure Progressive Future. I decided Myer was going for the youth vote and Tuller for the old folks.

There seemed to be a Referendum on at the same time. I couldn't work out from the dominant slogan – Yes To Proposition 72, For Cheaper Insurance – what the issue was, though it was no surprise that it involved insurance.

However, the big difference with what I was used to at home were the drug shops and what were called 'Sex Apartments'. The drug shops were as frequent as London off-licences, and seemed as well fortified with metal cage protection for doors and windows as the London booze shops. The window displays were simultaneously exotic and banal. Variants and derivatives of marijuana, tobacco, coca and opium were on show next to a range of pills in boxes and bottles, an unfamiliar mix of presumably alcoholic drinks, and a generous diversity of what I took to be Chinese medicines and herbal supplements. It was all very soberly done. Each shop had prominently displayed the same two notices. One was a list of 'safe' quantities of consumption provided by what must have been the Insurers Trade Association. The other was a list of those products which would only be sold to people with a doctor's prescription.

After passing three of these cornucopiae I couldn't resist going into the fourth. It was as placid as any British chemist, and the point-of-sale advertising would not have offended anyone from Tunbridge Wells. However, only the alcohol was stacked on open shelving. The staff – two serious-seeming young men – were protected by more security grilles. It was obvious that the drugs (including the cigarettes and other tobacco products) were kept out of sight elsewhere. Libance may not have had much conventional crime, but clearly this was one organisation that felt it necessary to take precautions against robbery. After a brief discussion I bought three nicely packaged and lush-looking ready-rolled joints, which they produced from the back room, for six euros. The experience was as nearly as low key as buying sweets back home.

The sex apartments were however a different deal altogether. They were blocks of flats, some large and free-standing, others, much smaller, above ground-floor shops. Externally, there was no attempt to promote their wares; some appeared to be branches of nation-wide chains, others independent, but all confined their displays to text-only offers alongside the entrances, which summarised the services available inside in an almost decorous manner. Indeed, there seemed to be a system of categorisation by star-rating – five was the highest I saw – based on the range of options available. This rating system assumed the prospective customer could decode it without further help, since it was certainly not made clear what the stars signified.

I couldn't resist trying one. My drinks and conversation with Friya had left me feeling randy anyway, so, when I was passing a nicely painted three-storey block called the Elysian Sex Apartments – three stars – I went in.

The foyer was small, discreetly lit with side lamps, and Vivaldi playing quietly from somewhere. You had two doors to choose from, according to gender. I took the one for men and found myself in a small reception area – four seats and a middle-aged woman behind a desk with a workstation.

"Your card, please."

I assumed she meant the charge-card Guardian Central had given me and which I had been using in the bar. She looked at it, frowned slightly, and put it in a slot in her computer.

"How interesting – a foreigner. Since you are not registered with the Institute of Human Relations we will have to charge you an additional 20% insurance premium, and you will have to choose from a restricted menu. Is that acceptable?" I nodded. "You haven't been here before, have you? Do you know what to do?" This time I shook my head.

"If you take that door over there, you will find yourself in a room with six booths. These are video booths. You can use anyone of them, they are all free at the moment. In each booth is a wall with 12 small screens, each with a picture of a different member of our staff. Three of them are busy at the moment, but you can choose any of the others. Superimposed on the pictures is a basic price and services guide. You can use the keyboard either to find out more information about any member of staff – the instructions are simple – and then select one of them to talk to by video-link. If you prefer, you can go straight to the video-link.

"Once you have agreed an arrangement, you insert your card in the machine in front of you and confirm the price and details. Your chosen partner will then direct you to the room in which they will be waiting for you.

"When you leave you will find by the exit another couple of booths. We would very much appreciate it if you could go in and take two minutes to complete a very simple feedback questionnaire you will find there.

"Have a nice evening. And thank you for choosing Elysian."

I did as she had directed and found myself in another small booth with the screens, keyboard and card-slot as she had described. There were pictures, with names, of seven women, three men and two transvestites, though one each of the women, men and transvestites had a 'Not available' notice superimposed over their picture.

It was fascinating. I started to punch up the data on each person by turn. It was all in the first person: age, where they were from, what they were offering, what they charged. There were interesting variations in approach and price, the men and the transvestites being on average more expensive. The differences between the women did not seem to be based on age or looks, indeed the most expensive person of all twelve was a 37-year-old woman. I was so involved with reading all this, and was taking so long about it, that the woman and transvestite who had been busy became available, while two of the other women found customers who must have come in after me but been quicker off the mark.

I selected a 29-year-old dark-haired woman called Eirene whose description of herself had suggested a sparky personality, which was soon confirmed when she appeared on the video-link. She was intrigued to find she had a European client and regretted the need to charge the 20% premium. Eirene provided exciting accounts of her various services, but I decided to settle for a straightforward arrangement this time around. My charge-card confirmed half an hour at 80 euros, and Eirene told me how to find her on the next floor up.

Our encounter was perfectly satisfactory – I gave straight fours ("very good") on the exit questionnaire – and I found the chance to ask Eirene a few questions about a business which, to me at least, was highly unusual in the way it was organised. (I admit I have never used the facilities available in Holland, Germany, or Nevada.)

Apparently most 'sex apartments' provided equally for men and women, though there were a few specialist gay houses. About a quarter of the Elysian's male and female workers were willing to transact with both sexes. No-one was worried about their details being automatically recorded at the Institute – the sex workers certainly regarded it as a useful protection, according to Eirene. She said there were some illicit operations that were unregistered and uninsured. These were used by people who wanted risk with their sex or who really didn't want their details recorded, but these outfits were hard to find since they frequently moved to avoid the sporadic interests of security companies dealing with complaints from clients (usually the partners of people who had gone to one of these bootleg brothels.)

The star-ratings weren't really to do with quality. One-star meant there were no more than four people available at any one time; two-star, ten or fewer; three-star, over ten. At a four-star establishment you could contract with two or more partners without prior booking; five-stars (though there weren't many of these) would accept customers in groups of up to six who wanted multiple partners – orgies, basically – but by appointment only. No star-rated establishment would offer under-age sex; they wouldn't get insurance if they did. Only the bootleggers did that, and it was very high-risk.

I concluded from my short foray into the sex and drugs sectors of Libancois commerce that these were very well organised and consumer-friendly businesses, offering good value for money at minimum risk to the customer. I intended to congratulate Friya Alling on her country's good sense when we next met. (Well, maybe I would. I might need to suss her views on sex and drugs first.)

When I finally arrived back at Guardian Central and saw the uniformed security personnel in the entrance hall, I realised that not only had I not seen any policemen on my walk through the city – not a surprise since there was no police force – but almost no sign of any personnel from the security companies, with their different uniforms, either. If the Elysian had had any security, they had kept themselves out of sight. All in all, the city did seem a remarkably self-controlled place.

Back in my room there were two text messages on screen. The first was from Axal's mother – her name was Janica Leonz – asking if I was available for a coffee next morning before she went to work at 12 noon. The other was an invitation to Sunday lunch at the home of Governor Delene and her husband. I said yes to both and went straight to bed. I was beginning to warm to Libance.

Chapter Six

Axal had given me the impression that his mother was the driving force in their family, and having coffee with Janica Leonz the following morning reinforced that picture. She was a short, intense woman about ten years older than me, but looking more than that; the result, I imagined, of the stress and hard work involved in holding her family together in difficult circumstances.

It wasn't clear why she wanted to meet me, other than out of simple curiosity. She couldn't have expected that I could do anything to help them get out of prison. Possibly she had heard from her son about the "European" view of prison, and wanted to show me that decent people could through bad luck end up in prison in Libance but that there was nothing shameful about it and they could and would work their way back to a normal life.

What interested me was how a family on a relatively low income could manage in a country which offered nothing in the way of welfare safety nets and expected everyone to take total responsibility for their own lives. That middle-class professionals like Friya Alling and Governor Delene could cope wasn't a surprise; how a carpenter and a call-centre operative with three teenage children got by was more intriguing.

Janica didn't seem to mind me asking about these matters. Though they didn't of course pay any taxes, they spent over half their income on insurance and on purchasing services like health, education and security. She regarded that amount as broadly what her friends and neighbours would pay. "Of course," she said, "there are those who never go to the doctor even if they are ill, who buy the cheapest education for their kids, and who don't have any security. They're a rough lot, who believe in sorting out any problems by themselves – though of course that can get 'em into trouble with other people's security teams. I tell my kids to keep out of the way of people like that."

She thought they would have been able to put their children through what she called 'contract schooling' – the minimum years laid down in her partnership contract with her husband Mika – had it not been for his gambling addiction. "One of the reasons I insisted on us coming to Guardian Central was 'cos they provide counselling services as part of the package. Sure as hell when we get out of this place Mika isn't going back to all that betting, not if I have anything to do with it."

When I explained that in Europe people like her wouldn't have to pay for their children's education or for most health services, and that there were policemen paid by the state to provide security, she was amazed, and asked who did pay for all this in that case. I described as simply as I could the various ways in which taxes were levied. "Oh," she said, "so people like me do pay for it then. It's just that you don't do it direct. You give it to your governments, and they decide how to spend it, do they? You don't get to choose none of it yourself? Don't think I like the sound of that. I want to know where my money is going, and if I'm getting good value."

I then tried to suggest that the European system was fairer, in that the better-off generally paid more in taxes than the less well-off. But she wasn't having that either. "What's fair about that? Suppose I got richer than I am now – I would want to get the benefit of that, not give more money to the Government just so people who didn't work as hard as me could pay less. You call that fair? Sounds like robbery to me."

She then wanted to know who decided what teachers and doctors got paid if they weren't selling their services directly to customers. That forced me to describe trade unions and professional associations and national collective agreements. This flummoxed her even more.

"You are saying that teachers basically get paid the same all over the country? That it doesn't matter if some of them are better than average, and others are worse? Why should anybody try to do their best in that case? And if you are a parent and don't think your kid is getting taught very well, what can you do about it? Doesn't sound as if moving schools would be of much help."

I decided not to tell her that a parent of a child at a state school might actually find it very difficult to move schools without moving to another town or district. This would so affront her sense of liberty and the individual's right to choose that I feared that Europe would lose any surviving credibility as a sensibly organised modern society.

I switched subjects. Did she mind telling me how exactly she could choose to take her husband and family to prison? We certainly couldn't do anything like that in England.

"It's in our marriage partnership contract. We agreed to take out prison insurance, that is, under certain circumstances either of us could insist on putting ourselves under the protection of Guardian Insurance, which could mean going to prison if they recommended it. One of the circumstances was either of us getting into serious debt. Believe me, Mika's gambling debts were seriously serious. The insurance people came round and discussed the situation and worked out the best way of helping us get out of the mess Mika had got us into. Mika didn't like it, and he huffed and puffed a lot, but he knew if he didn't agree I could get an automatic divorce for breach of contract. In which case the insurance people would have taken care of me and the kids, and he'd have been left totally high and dry. So, he gave in. He's OK about it now. Says he sees it was for the best. I think he means it. What would have happened to people like us in your country?"

I said I wasn't sure, but that I thought they would have had to sell their home, and the council would have found them somewhere to live, though it probably wouldn't have been a very nice place. In an extreme case their children might have been taken into care. Janica was horrified. Sell her home when it wasn't her fault? End up in a dump? Lose her kids? What kind of a society was that? How was anyone supposed to get themselves out of the gutter in those circumstances?

I'd lost again. It was clear by the end of our conversation that, to my shame, I had completely failed to convince her that the European – or indeed North American – model had anything to offer Libance.

Indeed, she gave the impression that, however difficult her current situation was, she firmly believed she was much better off than if she had been living in England. She left for her job at the Guardian Central call centre in a positively jaunty mood.

Since I had nothing else on that day, I decided to read up on what had happened in Libance since the Revolution that both Friya and the Governor had referred to. This would certainly do no harm if I was going to meet media editors to sell them feature ideas the next day. I went to the prison's Communications Centre to do some research. It took a good few hours, but it was worth it. I had a much better idea of the place as a result.

*

The Libance Revolution, which had ultimately abolished government, taxation, and the criminal law, had taken well over 20 years to complete, and had had two distinct phases.

The first had begun at the start of the 1980s. The National Democratic Party had embraced the neo-liberal ideas that had inspired the Reagan presidency in the United States and the Thatcher government in Britain, but had taken these to their logical conclusions, unlike the Americans or the British. However, while there had been a very substantial reduction in both the scope of government and the level of taxation in this phase, the early ND governments had felt it necessary to keep control of the police and the armed forces, and had paid for these out of a sales tax, since they had abolished all income, inheritance and property taxes.

During this period the Libance constitution had been radically revised. A Basic Law had laid down very narrow limits for public authority; all criminal law was abolished, since the State now scarcely existed, and certainly didn't have the job of stopping people from doing anything they wished to do, however bad, nasty or downright evil that might be. Everything was left to civil and administrative courts, like the Contract and Competition Courts that Governor Delene had described to me a couple of nights previously. A Constitutional Commission was created to oversee the regular referenda that now began to take place, and also the award of public franchises and appointments – all done by the votes of the general public. (This included the election of the members of the Commission itself.)

I have to say this constant use of the referendum did seem extremely democratic. If a new regulation was proposed, say, to allow retailers to refuse to deal with customers who did not have credit protection insurance, the draft regulation would have to be first approved by the Commission, which had to satisfy itself that the proposal accorded with the Basic Law. (Though the Basic Law didn't like regulations which constrained individual freedom, it did recognise that property owners could with justification act on occasion to protect their freedoms.)

Once it had passed this test, an electronic referendum would be held. Everyone over 18 was entitled to vote. A proposition needed both a simple majority of all those entitled to vote and a two-thirds majority of those who voted; a tough test if any sizeable number of people didn't bother to take part, which I assumed often happened. Finally the Senate had to endorse the result, though this seemed to have become a formality in recent years. I couldn't find any instance of a positive referendum result being vetoed by the Senate, though there were plenty of examples of the Constitutional Court prohibiting proposals and even more of negative referendum results.

Franchise awards, for example, to operate the Libance Diplomatic Service for five years, went through a similar process. The groups or companies bidding for the franchise had to get prior approval from the Commission that they were 'fit and proper persons', and capable of doing the job. Those who got over this threshold, and quite a lot didn't, then faced an electronic vote of all the citizenry. The winner emerged by a process of elimination (by a simple majority of those voting). The Senate had to ratify the result; again, this seemed a formality these days. Public appointments, like getting on the Contract Court legal panel, went through a similar process.

I reckoned the people of Libance had the opportunity to vote on something or other at least once a week. The numbers voting varied greatly, of course: some of the appointments attracted the interest of fewer than 5% of those entitled to vote, while some controversial new regulatory proposal could inspire a 90% participation. Every vote had to be preceded by a minimum two-week campaign (Senate elections required two months, even though Senators didn't seem to do much serious work in my view). Many campaigns were no more than website and chat room battles; others attracted conventional media coverage; and in what were obviously the most significant contests the candidates spent their own money on advertising.

It scarcely seemed possible that ordinary people could be particularly well-informed about the respective merits of, say, financial service companies bidding for the Central Bank franchise, or be able to evaluate the qualities of lawyer X as opposed to lawyer Y competing for a vacancy on the Competition Court panel. Nonetheless that seemed to be how the system worked.

Arriving at this constitutional settlement had taken years and seemed to have been both bloody and chaotic at times. It was during this first phase of the Revolution that the big insurance companies had gradually assumed their dominant roles in Libance society, as they extended the range of their products and services to fill the holes left by the abolition of taxes and the privatisation of pension, health, education and welfare services.

The second phase saw the abdication of the residual Government, the abolition of the sales tax, and the transformation of the police and armed forces into a number of private security companies (now nearly all owned by or associated with different insurance groups). The police and military seemed to have been instrumental in forcing this change. Their leaders had become disillusioned with their deteriorating relationship with the rest of society, as they were resented as the sole beneficiaries of tax money, boxed in by the lack of a criminal justice system, and increasingly unable to justify their existence, they had sought the freedom of an existence based on commercial contracts with individual customers.

Reading all this lot (which took most of the rest of the day) made me realise why the outside world thought Libance was on another planet, and why over the years fewer and fewer people visited it. While my own experience since I arrived showed that you could get along without cash and that you could get temporary insurance and security cover, it wasn't the sort of thing that either tourists or even businessmen would readily take to. In effect the world had decided it didn't need Libance: and Libance seemed to get by without needing the rest of the world. This certainly explained the absence of any trading with the outside world; Libance was steady, self-sufficient and this also probably explained why everything seemed so old-fashioned; they weren't exposed to the new ideas from all over the globe that swamped the rest of us on a regular basis. Libance seemed like 1940s Ireland – without the dominant Catholic church.

*

That evening, I ate in the prison canteen – no-one wanted to chat to me this time – and watched some TV back in my cell. It was very odd having to rely on old-style channels, and there weren't many of them to choose from. I couldn't tell whether, as a prisoner, I wasn't allowed to access the internet for entertainment or whether I hadn't been able to find the right way to do it, but either way I couldn't do much but flip about between about twenty free channels. I did briefly find one with a rather fierce discussion going on; it must have been to do with the upcoming Senate elections, but I couldn't be sure. It appeared to be about a proposal to allow two of the big insurance companies to merge. One side thought this would make insurance a lot cheaper for everybody, the other that this would be the end of Libancois democracy, which sounded a tad extreme. The thought that the only thing that was exciting the citizens of Libance that evening on telly was an argument about insurance was too depressing, and I went to bed early to see if my dreams could put together something more interesting.

Chapter Seven

"You have done really well. I am just cross you managed all this without me. I am not sure I can really claim my commission."

"Rubbish," I said. "You set the meetings up. It wasn't your fault you got called away on an emergency case. Anyway, the media is my trade. I ought to be able to deal with newspaper editors and TV producers by now."

Friya and I were having dinner in what she said was a typical Libance restaurant. Actually, given my growing sense that Libance was not only old-fashioned but seriously limited for both clothing and food supplies, the unimpressive menu did not surprise me. Still, I did not blurt this out; and thus we were both able to enjoy ourselves. I relished being out on a Saturday night with a young woman whom I was definitely beginning to find attractive. Friya had, as she had promised, fixed me interviews with one of the Libance national papers and with a local TV station, but she had called that morning to say she couldn't go with me, as she had an urgent security issue to deal with. So I had had to go to them on my own.

Both had produced satisfactory outcomes. The newspaper, the *Tribune*, had commissioned four weekly features to appear over the next month, with a promise of more to come if these worked well. I could pretty well pick the subjects myself, but all were to be based on the straightforward idea of a European's view of Libance. The TV station, Metro TV, wanted to team me up with its documentary department to come up with a proposal for a half-hour film, hopefully within the month. It would be on a similar theme to the newspaper articles; neither the paper nor the TV people seemed to mind if they overlapped. If Metro liked the programme idea, they would shoot and edit it (with me as presenter) in the following month.

I would get five thousand dollars for the articles, and six thousand for the TV research, plus another six thousand if the film went ahead; not bad money, and even better when I remembered that none of it would be taxed. Friya's commission, or rather her employer's, Western Guardian Security, would be eleven hundred dollars.

She wanted to know what I had made of the press and TV people I had met. Were they like their European counterparts?

"Well, sort of," I said. "The Metro people were young, bright and buzzy, trying to outdo each other in instant ideas for what the film might include, not very interested in the substance of what I might say but clearly trying to judge how I might come across on camera – and there were as many women as men. So, they were just like the TV folk I knew back home. The *Tribune* guys were both middle-aged men, and seemed quite a lot like broadsheet journalists in London, except they weren't interested in politics at all, at least what I would call politics. When I said I would like to write about the general election campaign they looked extremely puzzled; why would I want to do that? It was a bit of fun, but it wasn't very important. I said that was precisely the point; in Europe big elections still mattered.

"They replied that in Libance what mattered were the specific referendum propositions, like the one arguing for the merger of two of the insurance companies – United and the HPG, I think they said. Not apparently that it would actually be put to the vote: the Constitutional Court was likely to throw it out, according to them. I think it was called Proposition 72: I'd seen posters around the place telling people to vote for it. Anyway, we compromised; I said I would do both."

Friya nodded. "They are right about the merger referendum. United and HPG together would be over half the market and would dominate the other companies. They would be bound to take business from the rest of us. It would be a disaster for the country. That is why the Court won't allow this Proposition 72. No-one can work out why they are even trying to get a referendum on it."

"Forgive me if I can't get as worked up about insurance mergers as you Libancers seem able to do. Anyway, there was something else they said that was much more intriguing. I said I would quite like to write about the absence of crime in Libance. They looked surprised, and said why did I think there was no crime here? So, I did a shortened version of what Governor Delene had told me the first night I was here, and they laughed and said well, she would say that wouldn't she, and then told me about the Special Administration Districts, the 'bad SADs', they called them. Told me I should be very careful about going into any of them without security back-up, and certainly not on my own. They were running out of time by that stage and said their news desk people would fill me in next time I visited the building.

"So, let me ask you: what exactly are the bad SADs? And where are they?"

"Yes, I wondered why Governor Delene didn't mention these to you. Don't worry, I wouldn't have let you go near any of them, at least not on your own. There are three here in the metropolitan region, and seven more in various other parts of the country.

"What happened was that after the abolition of local government and the emergence of all the local societies and associations that we talked about the other day, some areas began to deteriorate badly. People living in them had only minimal insurance, just enough to get basic work. More and more of them stopped paying rent. At first the landlords sent security people in to seize their goods, if they had any, and then to send them to prison: but the prisons began to refuse to take them, since many of them couldn't do much in the way of jobs, and anyway the landlords were finding they couldn't rent their properties in these areas, which were getting a bad name. So gradually they gave up and abandoned them. The utility companies weren't getting paid, so they would cut off water and power to more and more homes. The local associations of residents collapsed: not enough people would join, so there wasn't enough money to maintain the roads or organise any services. Young men, who couldn't get work or didn't want to, formed gangs and fought regularly with the security companies and each other. They would hijack vehicles driving through the areas, or attack and rob people who were visiting them. Soon the security companies refused to take cases involving these areas, and the insurance companies stopped paying out on them."

"Hang on a minute – what did they rob these visitors of? People don't carry cash in this country."

"Oh, personal stuff, watches, jewellery, the clothes they were wearing. Anyway, all this began to have a bad effect on the neighbouring districts. The gangs would invade them and cause trouble. Diseases went untreated and spread infections in all the surrounding areas. So the local societies in one particular area – not that far from here, actually – got together and organised what was in effect an invasion of the trouble spot. They paid the security companies to put together a special joint force, and basically told them to go in and kill all the gang members they could find. It was a terrible fight, apparently. Hundreds of people were killed. The worst flats and houses were demolished. Some two hundred women and children were rounded up and put in a special camp. The only people allowed to stay were those in half-decent homes who either had, or had only recently given up, insurance, and who had jobs or were willing to go to prison until they got jobs.

"Of course, this caused a terrible row. Some people living in unaffected parts of the country said this was against the spirit of the Revolution, that it was unconstitutional, and organised a referendum proposition which would have required this special action to be abandoned, and compensation paid to those who had lost their homes. Fortunately, all the insurance companies were strongly opposed to this idea, as well as the security companies, and it was easily defeated.

"However, the companies recognised that something formal needed to be done, especially if, as looked very likely, other districts suffering from these problems decided to adopt similar tactics. So, they jointly proposed in a referendum that any district where the local society collapsed (or was non-existent) could be taken over by a consortium of neighbouring societies under a Special Administration Order from the Constitutional Court. Later this was extended to allow people living in an area which was collapsing to ask the Court to take the initiative and create an order requiring the neighbouring districts to take it over."

I was smiling to myself listening to all this. Sounded much like a compulsory form of local government to me. "Who pays for these special administrations?" I asked. "Must be expensive for somebody."

"That was a problem initially," said Friya. "On the first occasion the group of local associations that organised the take-over paid for it themselves, but when the debate on the SAD referendum was taking place all the districts which faced similar problems argued that this was a national issue and that everyone should contribute something. Of course there was a lot of opposition from other areas to this, and some people argued that this would be in effect creating a national tax, which would have been illegal. It looked as though there was going to be deadlock. So, the big insurance and security companies got together and agreed that they would create a special joint company to fund and manage SADs when they were approved. And that's what happens."

I thought about this for a moment. It seemed to me it was indeed a stealthy way to create a national tax, collected through the insurance premiums paid by everyone. However, I knew Friya wouldn't accept this, so there was no point in getting into an argument about it. Instead, I asked her why, if there was this system for dealing with failing districts, crime still persisted in them and why they were thought to be unsafe.

"Well, the truth is that creating a special administration district enables the situation to be contained but does nothing to deal with underlying problems of poverty and disorder. People who can't seem to organise their lives in a responsible way (or people who just don't want to live responsibly) still have difficulty in making ends meet and still – some of them, at any rate – cause trouble when they can, especially when they are congregated together in large numbers, as they are in SADs. Gangs still exist, even if they can't create the kind of havoc that they did before. Security teams still have problems in dealing with incidents in these areas: people won't talk to them, so usually they can't get information except through electronic surveillance. If people are attacked, whether they are visitors or people who live there, the assailants do quite often go unpunished in a way which wouldn't happen elsewhere in the country. So now everyone knows that, if they do have to go into a

SAD, they should take the kind of precautions that your newspaper people described."

"Sounds really grim. Do people who have the misfortune to live in such places ever manage to get out, move somewhere better? Indeed, does any SAD ever manage to get itself reclassified, become a normal area once again?"

"Actually, that has happened a couple of times. When there are local people who can be helped to take leadership roles, and enough decent people who can be organised effectively, it does seem possible to reverse the downward slide. It helps too if the area itself has some natural advantages which can be commercially exploited. One SAD here in the capital was close to the centre, and had a long riverside frontage, much of it old industrial buildings which had been abandoned some years ago. Some bold property developers decided to buy the run-down and derelict riverside factories and houses and convert them into attractive homes for wealthy people who wanted to live near to the centre. It was a gamble, but it worked. Within ten years the SAD was wound up.

"And yes, people do manage to get out of them. I have met some of them at work. It just depends on your attitudes; if you want to make the effort you can do it."

I wasn't sure about that; I could imagine people who did have the right attitude and did make an effort but who could still be defeated by the desperate circumstances in which they were living. But talking to Friya was like talking to Axal's mother – it was impossible to dent their Libancer conviction that people could control their lives successfully if they wanted to.

Anyway, Friya was losing interest in discussing this rather negative subject. I had decided she was a basically optimistic person, who, while not blind to the bleak side of life, had no great wish to spend time talking about it. She began to plan how she might help me get organised in my new career; find a flat, buy the right electronic equipment, get the right insurance.

This rapidly turned into a trickier conversation than I had anticipated. My private intention was to stay in Libance for a few months, enjoy myself as best I could in that time, and get to the States as soon as possible thereafter. I wasn't looking to enter into long-term arrangements, or burden myself with kit I didn't really need. However, technically I was seeking asylum, which implied a long-term stay in the country. Friya recognised that I couldn't be expected to go out and buy a home that would last me for years straightaway and would need to settle for temporary accommodation in the short-term: but no such considerations affected my insurance needs. She got quite excited as she sketched out the kind of comprehensive package I could go for.

"You could go for the Guardian's favourite comprehensive deal, that does all the personal stuff you need, like security, health, family (including children's education), pension, property, employment protection, personal indemnities, and is really good value. Trouble is you will also need professional insurance, and of course," here she giggled nervously, "you don't need the family cover just yet. So maybe we will have to design a more customised set of packages for you. I have a friend at the Guardian head office who could help us work this out."

"Er, excuse me a minute. Do I have to take all my insurance from one company? And does it have to be the Guardian?"

"Well, no, you can pick any company you wish. Go to all of them for something if you really wanted to. But it would be absurdly expensive. No-one does that. We nearly all pick one company and stick with it. I suggest the Guardian, not just because it does my insurance, nor because I work for it, but because it is the best. And anyway, since you are an existing client, if only for a few days and on an emergency account, you would be entitled to a 15% discount."

I realised I was in murky water here in all sorts of ways and got us off the subject by agreeing to meet her friend and give the Guardian first shot. I was determined to go for the minimum I could get away with without ending up back in prison. Thankfully Friya was happy to move on to the equally interesting topic of where I was going to live.

We cheerfully batted around what my truly minimum needs might be, we settled on a bedroom, a work room, a kitchen, and a bathroom, and where I might get something in a reasonable location at a price I could afford. Friya nominated a couple of districts where we could start looking – she rather sweetly assumed I would want her to help, which of course I did – and we agreed a couple of evenings early next week. This prompted a question from me about boyfriends and so on; it appeared she had split up with her latest a few months earlier and was currently not doing much socially. So of course, I had to try my luck.

"In London, at this stage of an evening like this, I would invite you to come back to my place for coffee or a nightcap," I said. "I can't really do that here. My cell isn't exactly suitable for entertaining, not that I suppose Guardian Central would allow prisoners to take people in for a drink."

"Oh, I think they would. But I agree, it wouldn't be appropriate for us."

There was a silence while I waited for her to say a bit more than this. She just looked at me with slightly raised eyebrows and the tiniest hint of a smile.

I gave in. "Right. Well, of course, you could invite me to your place."

"Is that what I would do in London?"

"Undoubtedly. And I would of course accept."

"Of course. And after our coffee, or night cap?"

"Well, that would depend on how we felt. Ideally of course I would stay the night."

"Of course."

I felt I was being gently skewered by all these 'of courses'. But this time I was determined for her to speak next. It must have taken more than a minute; in which time we made what I suspect we both hoped were sophisticatedly slight facial movements to each other. At last, she said, "In Libance we too might make such arrangements. But we would agree certain important matters in advance. You know how seriously we treat such things. You told me what Governor Delene had said to you on this subject."

"Oh yes. Notifying the sex police and all that. Taking out new insurance. Making a plan for any children that might result."

She smiled, beautifully. "Perhaps not all of those. Indeed, in some circumstances, none of them would be needed. Are you willing to do exactly as I say, and not try anything I haven't myself suggested?"

"Absolutely." It sounded better than 'of course', and I was excited by the mystery of what it was she had in mind that would not involve any of the Libance-style contracts and precautions.

"Well then, Bob," it was the first time she had used my Christian name, "I would very much like to invite you to my flat where we can have coffee or a night cap, or both, where we can get to know each other better, and where you can stay the night if you wish to, which I can see from your expression you would like to do. Incidentally you should let Reception at Guardian Central know you won't be back. They won't ask where you are going to be, so don't tell them voluntarily."

I made the call – I loved the idea of a prison being so accommodating – we split the bill, and she drove us home in her horse and carriage. I recalled then that there had been a fair number of what looked like stables in the town when I had taken a sedan chair to the restaurant; Friya had parked her horse and carriage in one such establishment, a big place with at least 20 horses and a mess of carriages large and small. Friya pointed out that a big city like Libance needed many such parking spaces to cope with people riding to work every day, and which were then readily available for folk going out in the evening.

We reached Friya's home in twenty minutes or so, dodging great piles of horse shit en route. Her home was an airy flat in a modern block, sensibly furnished and decorated with not too many frills and female clutter; there was the standard mix of living room/kitchen/bathroom, and two bedrooms. I was sincerely appreciative, and we settled down into two comfortable armchairs for drinks.

After a few minutes of cheerful banter, I felt entitled to turn to important matters. "So, Friya, I have made my promise; what exactly are you going to suggest?"

"Well, I am happy to try a bit of sex." This was a funny way of putting it, I thought.

"I want to have an orgasm and I am sure you do too. We will take our clothes off and sit in these two chairs opposite each other. You can stand if you prefer, but I will sit here. We will both bring ourselves to orgasm in whatever way we wish; I have some toys if you want them. I will probably take longer than you, so I trust you will be patient, sitting over there. Then we can go to bed, yours is in the spare bedroom, of course. I hope you find this proposal acceptable. If it makes you embarrassed, I will understand, and we can simply go to our respective bedrooms now."

"Embarrassed – good Lord no. Intrigued – yes, a bit."

Actually, I was more stunned than intrigued. This was not an outcome I had imagined in the slightest. I had pretty well assumed we would stop short of actual penetration, but that there would be plenty of embracing and grappling and close order activity. Solitary self-pleasuring with the added dimension of a potentially disconcerting voyeurism was nowhere in my list of possibles.

In the event it was rather more fun than I expected. I did try to suggest that we might kiss before we started, just to show some sort of affection, I thought, but this was firmly rejected. (I was however offered the prospect of a kiss when we met in the morning.) So, we stripped off, Friya more seductively than I could manage, and sat in our chairs, six feet apart, and brought ourselves off, as they say. She had a great figure, and looked at me in a steadily compelling manner, and it was all rather erotic. Afterwards she smiled gently, thanked me, and said I could use the bathroom first.

Next morning, I got two kisses: one at breakfast, the other when Friya dropped me off at the prison. Both were satisfyingly sensual.

Chapter Eight

I just had time to collect my clean clothes from the laundry (the franchise for this was held inside the prison by some enterprising women inmates); use the tricksy toilet arrangements; and as I was trying on my shoes, the video monitor bleeped with the message that the car had arrived to take me to Governor Delene's home for lunch. The car, I thought; this showed her status. She had earlier left a message telling me who the other guests were going to be. They included a lawyer, a TV chief, a banker (that was Delene's husband), what looked like a very senior executive from the Guardian Insurance group and someone I would have called a political apparatchik for the National Democrat Party, had I thought Libance went in for conventional politics.

The journey took half-an-hour, passing through some featureless districts but ending in a very pleasant suburb with comfortable detached houses and green leafy gardens. Delene herself welcomed me at the door. She looked very glamorous – I would never have guessed her occupation had I not already known it – and wrong-footed me immediately.

"Well, who's a mysterious stop-out then? Didn't report back to base last night, did you? I won't ask what you were up to, but I am amazed you have discovered enough in your few days here to be sufficiently confident to stay out overnight. I must admit I was a bit worried when they first told me; I thought you weren't going to get here in time, which would absolutely have ruined my arrangements, but here you are and it's lovely to see you."

I got a couple of kisses on the cheek, which might just have concealed my blushes, and was introduced to her husband, Tomas Kryk, whom she described as the top man in the Metropolitan Investment Bank. (It turned out that among many other things in the

Libance marriage contracts women had to decide whether to keep their own names or take their husband's. It was no surprise to learn that Delene had kept hers.) "Tomas, this is Bob Rowgarth, our delightful European visitor, currently one of my clients, though not," here a glance at me that managed somehow to be both coy and flashing, "for much longer, I suspect. Bob, you are to call me Rilka, not Governor Delene. We are in my home, not my office. Now come and meet everyone else."

Rilka, as I must now call her, swept me out to her garden terrace, and round half a dozen men and women whose names I scarcely took on board but all of whom welcomed me with a mixture of warmth and curiosity. They had the collective confident air of the successful middle-aged that I had experienced on similar occasions in London. I was briefly introduced to four teenagers, two of whom, I learned later, were the children of Tomas and Rilka, but they disappeared somewhere to entertain themselves separately and I only saw them again to say goodbye hours later.

I found myself talking to the TV executive, a woman called Christine Abbass, and the ND Party worker, a man called Josep Stilo. The woman knew all about my commission from Metro TV, unsurprisingly, since she turned out to be the station's finance director. She was as bemused as the newspaper people had been when, asked what ideas I had for the documentary, I mentioned the upcoming election. "Well now, this is some good luck. Here is Josep, who oversees all communications matters for the National Democrats and is a close friend of Kris Myer himself. Now Josep, are you going to help our English friend here make his documentary for us?"

Josep, of course, was ostensibly deeply sympathetic, though he explained that they already had many television commitments, including a very important Saturday night entertainment show on Metro itself. What kind of thing did I have in mind?

I said I wanted to find out what made people vote in the Libance elections, given that the Senate didn't seem to have the kind of power its equivalents had in Europe. I mean, why bother?

Because people were very engaged with the campaigns, said Josep.

It wasn't a bother at all, as you sat at home and voted electronically. It was all great fun, particularly in the early stages, which were just about to start, where potential candidates were eliminated by TV voting. Each party had its own show, where their applicant candidates were put through their paces, assessed by a panel of experts, and then judged by the viewers. Those who were approved formed the party teams at the next stage, where they competed directly against the other party teams in a series of TV shows. The votes they won from the audiences at this stage determined how many actual senators each party could have. In the next round each party again had its own TV contests to select the actual senators, according to the number they were now permitted. The grand finale was a live TV contest between the party leaders, supported by their elected senators; and the viewers voted who they wanted to be Senate Leader.

I kind of knew, from listening to Josep, that somehow, whatever else formed the content of these various games and contests, it wouldn't be matters of political substance. Nonetheless I ploughed on. "So, what qualities do these various TV shows seek to discover in the candidates?"

"All the qualities one would want in a Senator. Intelligence, charm, the ability to think quickly on your feet, a capacity for working with other people, a willingness to take decisions, a wide general knowledge. And, of course, being able to entertain. Surely in Europe you want all these qualities in your legislators as well?"

"Most of them, yes. But we would also want to assess their competence in running the country, and what policies they would adopt if elected. We would be particularly interested in what they might say about taxes. Here in Libance I suppose you no longer need to worry about any of this."

"Indeed not. But I am not sure how you could make a television programme based on this difference."

Stilo was probably right. Making a documentary about something which was absent from the location in which you were making it is a pretty challenging proposition. So, I agreed with him, and said I would have to think harder about it. Christine Abbass said surely there were many other easier subjects available for me. What about the fact that they had given up using cash completely?

"Well, it is another negative, isn't it? Same problem, we in Europe have something which you have given up. How do I show that visually? Still, it is an interesting difference, and I will think more about that too." At that point Tomas and Rilka clapped their hands and told us to move to the dining room where lunch was ready.

I was seated in the centre, presumably so everyone could grill me and hear my fascinating accounts of how we did things differently where I came from. However, my immediate neighbour on my right was Tomas Kryk, the banker, who insisted on discussing our respective financial environments. In fact, these didn't seem so different, with a very similar range of financial services in both places. What struck me, was once again the dominance of the insurance groups, who either owned, or were the biggest shareholders in, most of the major institutions; and the way the governing council of the central bank, the Bank of Libance, was appointed.

I tackled Kryk on both matters. "Of course, the insurance groups occupy a dominant position," he said. "Everybody has to have insurance; the majority of people have to invest around half their incomes in our policies. In turn we must do something with all that money, so we invest it in as wide a range of profitable opportunities as we can find. Not surprisingly, many people with surplus income who want to save some of it (in addition to the insurance policies they already have) either come through banks owned by their insurers, like the one I run for the Guardian, or invest in companies that they know we favour. They rightly assume that we will be the best-informed people in this respect."

The Central Bank was, it transpired, elected every four years by the votes of every adult in the country. It both set interest rates and regulated all financial services, duties it had inherited from its pre-Revolutionary predecessor. It was a non-profit making corporation financed by the fees from the services it licensed. The Council was composed of people from the various financial sectors, the Big Four insurance companies naturally being guaranteed a place each, while other sectors had to make do with single representatives. What was interesting was that at least two people had to be nominated for each post; even the big guys couldn't just shoehorn who they wanted onto the council. But I still found it difficult to see how most of the electorate could offer an informed view of their respective qualities. I mean I was hard pushed to recall a single member of the European Central Bank in Frankfurt, and I was a professional opinion former.

Not a problem, according to Kryk. Fewer than 40% voted in most central bank elections (I thought that was pretty good, considering), and many of them followed the suggestions made by their own insurers, but in general all the candidates were well-qualified people, and genuinely independent voices did get on. The Bank was well-run, witness the relative stability of the economy for the past decades. (It turned out they had missed the various global recessions because they couldn't trade finance with anyone else, and similarly, with the great covid pandemic, since they had stopped the cargo flights to the USA from the beginning, and there was no other way of infected persons getting to them.)

Not being a financial expert, I was prepared to take him at his word on this. But I was curious about his remark about the amount of income people had to set aside for insurance. It didn't seem to leave much for the rest of their needs and desires.

"Well, when I said roughly half, I was including what they would spend on educating their children and so on, some of which is done through savings policies. I have always understood that it was like what in your country you would have to pay in taxes and insurance and other financial obligations taken together."

Maybe, I said. But let's look at education as an example of what was puzzling me. A family on even average income in the UK couldn't afford to pay for private education; they benefited from the fact that everybody, whether they had school-age children or not, paid the taxes that funded the state schools. How could a family on average income afford to pay for schools here in Libance? (As I asked this I was thinking of Axal's family. Before they went into prison his parents couldn't have been earning more than 40,000 euros a year between them, if that. In the UK, private schooling for three children would have taken most of that.)

Kryk smiled. "Ah, this is a subject you should write about. We are very proud of the way we have transformed the cost of education. Your observation is in one sense quite correct; after the Revolution we quickly found we had a crisis in education for precisely the reasons you have given. But the invention of contract schools solved that."

I remembered the conversations about the partnership or marriage contracts requiring the parents to fund the schooling of their children. Kryk explained that some smart businessmen had realised that, while traditional education wasn't affordable for most people now that they had to pay for it directly, in the digital age children didn't need to be taught in classrooms by expensive teachers, they could sit at computers and do it all on their own. At first the new education programmes and software were designed to be used at home, but this didn't work very well for most families, since they needed to get their kids out of their homes while they (the parents) went to work. So vast learning factories were created, which took thousands of students between the ages of 7 and 18 and put them all in individual cubicles for five hours a day with their computers and education programmes designed for whatever stage they had reached. There were no teachers in these factories, just security teams, administrators and carers or counsellors. The work of each student was monitored electronically by a central staff of educationists; reports were emailed to the parents each week; you were entitled to a minimum face-to-face conversation with your child's education mentor of one hour every three months, but you could buy more time (including specialist education time, pastoral care and counselling) if you wanted to. In this way all children could be educated for less than a thousand euros per child each year, though of course most parents spent more than the minimum, depending on what they could afford.

This was astonishing, and I immediately had a host of questions, like how did they make sure the kids stayed in their cubicles and worked at their programmes, and how did they manage breaks or going to the toilet, and wasn't this all pretty grim and anti-social? (No wonder Axal preferred his prison school, at least they had individual lessons there.) Kryk laughed and said there were answers to all these questions, but I really ought to visit such a school and see it first hand for myself. He offered to introduce me to the chief executive of one of the big education companies, who would, he felt sure, let me go and visit one of their institutions.

This did sound like a very good idea for a story, and I accepted his offer readily. But I pressed Kryk on one point. If kids went to these factories for just four hours a day ("five, with breaks," he said) what did they do for the rest of the day, particularly if their parents both worked, which seemed to be essential in Libance? This was, said Kryk, one of the great beauties of the system; it allowed children over twelve to get jobs for the other half of the day, and many of these, particularly for girls, involved looking after children under twelve at day-care centres, a lot of which were attached to the learning factories. The money teenagers earned in this way was often, at least in part, used to fund extra education for themselves.

"But that's child labour," I protested. "Great reformers devoted themselves in the 19th century to ending this abuse."

"Nonsense," said Kryk. "These are decent jobs, like child-care or working for delivery firms. We don't send our children down the mines or up chimneys. Believe me, most of them prefer it to going to school."

If going to school meant they had to sit in a cubicle for five hours slaving at a computer I wasn't surprised but decided not to say so. Besides Kryk had switched his attention to what had become a general conversation around the table about the proposed merger between United and HPG. It was clear that although they all worked in different professions and occupations everyone here was closely linked to the Guardian Insurance group and was as a result very hostile to the idea of this merger.

The senior executive from the insurance company itself, a woman called Elli Dyvers, was particularly vehement about how it would make life impossible for everyone else, and how we would all end up in the grip of a giant monopoly if it were to happen. The lawyer, a sharp younger man called Timo Jankel, whom I took an immediate dislike to, was pompously explaining to her why it wasn't going to be allowed.

"Look, my dear Elli, I know you are very important at the Guardian, but you mustn't go around spreading alarm and despondency in this way. Let me spell it out for you. There are six judges on the panel of the Constitutional Court. Everyone is sure, based on their track records, their known personal connections, and the accepted interpretation of the Basic Law, that they will divide four-two on this in favour of rejecting the referendum proposal. It won't even be put to the voters.

"Even if, by a remote chance, Justice Akerman, who was once a legal adviser to United many years ago, were to switch sides and make it three-three, the chairman of the panel is old Victor Riccardo, a long-time Guardian man, as you must surely know, and he will have the casting vote. So, no problemo."

Elli Dyvers, who looked as though she didn't like this legal smartarse any more than I did, said she was reassured by his account of the maths involved, but when would the Court make its decision? It was extremely nerve-wracking having to hang around waiting like this.

"In ten days," said Jankel. "It is scheduled for Wednesday week. No-one expects them to take more than two days reaching a decision. So, the weekend after next we can all celebrate and then get on with normal business."

Rilka Delene, who was sitting next to Jankel, looked at me. "Now that would make a good story for you, wouldn't it, Bob. You could interview Timo here to explain it all to your viewers and readers." And she beamed at him in a way that dropped her several points in my estimation of her.

I said that, from all the interest there seemed to be in this business, all the Libance media would have it covered comprehensively and I doubted I would have much to add to it, which visibly annoyed Rilka, who was clearly used to having her advice accepted unquestioningly. To make amends I added that the way Libance used referenda so frequently was indeed a difference with Europe – even Switzerland was more restrained, I said – so that might be a way into the subject. This mollified her somewhat, and she said surely, I agreed that allowing everyone to have a direct say in all the various policy and business decisions that affected them was the best form of democracy.

"I am really not sure I agree with you," I said. "Obviously I must wait and see how your system works in practice, but I believe, as a basic bit of political philosophy, that electing representatives to govern you, and paying taxes to enable important national services to be provided collectively, rather than as a matter of individual choice and personal payments, is in principle likely to make for a better society.

"For a start, running a country is complicated, and requires detailed knowledge from those making the decisions. There is no way in which voters as a whole can hope to have all the relevant information, whereas there is at least a chance that full-time politicians would be reasonably informed. And secondly, as Tomas Kryk and I have just been debating, it is hopelessly unfair on many people if they must bear the whole cost of educating their children. They can't do it, and as a result many children would be badly educated, which couldn't be in the interest of society. And that must apply to other matters, like defence and welfare and health."

There was a widespread murmur of disagreement round the table. Not surprisingly the egregious Jankel intervened more loudly than anyone else. "That is of course the traditional theory, but I cannot see how you can defend the way it works in practice. Politicians are corrupt, lazy and partisan, and don't make much effort to inform themselves in the way you describe, but just vote the way the party machine tells them to. As to the quality of service provided through enforced taxation, well I mean everything I have read about what has been happening in Europe, and particularly in your country, says that those delivering the services run them in their own interests rather than that of those needing those services, that there is great waste and inefficiency, and that those who have to rely on public services because they cannot afford to pay for private ones have to put up with a very poor quality product. Our experience absolutely demonstrates that requiring individuals to make their own choices and pay for these choices directly is a vastly superior system." And he really enjoyed the enthusiastic agreement that came from Rilka.

"I totally disagree with your view of politicians. There are inevitably a few who fit your description, but most of the ones I know, and I have met many in my work, are decent honourable people trying to do the best for the country. Of course, needing to get elected means you have to go around telling part truths a lot of the time, but that is as much the fault of the papers and TV stations, who aren't interested very much – some of them not at all – in serious issues but only gossip and sensationalism and personalities.

"I have more sympathy with your point about public services; we do have real problems in reconciling public funding with the delivery of quality services; nonetheless it remains true that most people are getting services they could not afford if they had to pay for them individually. And I am sure I will find that you have a problem here in Libance in this respect."

"Well, I am glad our European reporter is approaching the subject with an open mind," sneered Jankel. I regretted giving him the opening for such a retort, but he got up my nose so much that my better judgement was suspended.

Tomas Kryk came to my rescue. (I guessed he didn't much like Jankel either, if only because of the way his wife did like him.) "Now, Timo, you make it sound good, individuals paying for everything themselves as they need it or want it, but you are ignoring the whole point of insurance, which is to pool money collectively so that services can be provided to those that need them – inevitably a minority at any one time – more efficiently and cheaply. It is still collective provision: the difference is that this is provided by private companies not the Government. We may have done away with taxation, but we still raise money for important necessities on a co-operative basis."

Jankel looked briefly as though he intended to make a contemptuous reply but obviously thought better of it. He simply said that the important point was that people were able to choose for themselves how much they spent on insurance, not have it decided for them by some government or set of bureaucrats.

I was still thinking about this, how important a distinction this was, or whether it was a real distinction at all, when Rilka, who looked as though she had not enjoyed the rather acerbic turn in the conversation, hustled us all outside again to have our fruit, cheese, and coffees.

The ND Party functionary, Josep Stilo, took me aside. "I have been thinking about what you said before lunch about elections. Can you explain to me what happens in your country?"

So I did. He was especially interested in what his equivalents did. I told him about opinion polling and focus groups, about the stormy relationship with the media and trying to make sure election campaigns worked to your agenda, not those of your opponents; about email data bases of supporters, about raising money, and about old-fashioned door-to-door canvassing (which he found particularly intriguing).

At the end he said, "I found your comments about your politicians very interesting. I am sure Kris Myer has those same qualities of honesty and decency; it's just that we don't really expect to need them to come into play. Would you like to meet him?"

Of course, I said. He promised to fix it up very soon.

The party began to break up. Rilka said my car was due soon and took me back into the house so I could use the toilet. When I emerged, she was waiting for me.

"I am sorry if that got a bit out of hand," she said. "Timo is a sweet man, but he can sometimes let his urge to tell everybody what the true situation is carry him too far. Now I expect you will be leaving Guardian Central soon, won't you?" I confirmed that I would indeed start looking for a place to stay the very next day. "Do you know where to start?" she asked. I felt obliged to tell her that Friya Alling had offered to help. "Ah, it is the delightful Miss Alling, is it," she said, and gave me a look that combined mysterious significance with more than a trace of disappointment. "Well, I am sure she will be very good, but if you need my help, please let me know. And I insist you take me out to dinner before you finally decide to leave us. Or very soon afterwards."

How could I refuse?

Chapter Nine

Well, the Libance approach to education certainly gave me a great first column for the *Tribune*. Tomas Kryk got me an introduction to the chief executive of the Knowledge Corporation, a man called Isaiah Raeburn, who turned out to be extremely keen to tell me all about his learning factories, as he quite cheerfully called them.

His company certainly sweated its assets more effectively than any educational institution I knew back home. Each 'factory' (though formally they were still called schools or colleges) ran three shifts: 8am to 1pm: 1.30pm to 6.30pm; and 7pm to 10pm. The first two each day were for children (the 7 to 18 range Kryk had described); the evening was for adults: and the half hour breaks were to clean the places thoroughly and make any straightforward repairs to equipment or facilities before the next shift arrived. All of his establishments had nurseries and day-care facilities attached, with very flexible hours, so that parents could leave children up to the age of seven for whatever hours they needed (as long as they could afford it; as Raeburn said, it was more expensive to provide nursery care than education, since even in Libance they hadn't worked out how to look after small children without responsible adults in attendance).

He proudly showed me round the corporation's Control Centre. Here around a hundred teachers, – I found myself calling them that even though they didn't do any teaching as Europeans would understand it: Raeburn himself called them 'content specialists' – monitored the various subject programmes, and were available for the more detailed telephone or email discussions with students or parents who were willing to pay for such conversations. The bulk of calls were handled by teams of much less qualified staff, who also did the basic monitoring of student activity.

These teams worked in a vast room, like any large call-centre, I suppose. Raeburn said that one of their most important tasks was to monitor what he called 'negative behaviour' by individual students, particularly where it was persistent, or a pattern was developing. This needed to be reported in clear terms to the students' parents: the basic weekly electronic reports were done automatically, and though they would show negative behaviour as it manifested itself on their systems, Raeburn said it was essential to supplement this with individually written addenda requiring a response, so there was no risk that parents could claim they hadn't noticed what was going on. It was, apparently, very much part of the contracts between parents and the corporation that the parents took active steps to correct such behaviour; failure to do so in serious cases could lead to the exclusion of the student.

The software and programmes used by the students were designed and manufactured at another location; this was the most expensive, and vital, part of the operation and demanded close working relationships between the content specialists and the software designers. The quality of the product, its efficacy as a learning tool, its ability to handle a wide range of aptitude and attitude in those using it, the sophistication of the interactive features, above all its market appeal to the customers and the reputation it won around the country, all this was of crucial importance. "Our programmes have consistently been in the top three of each subject, at all ages," he said. "Our students have the best overall track record for gaining the desired qualifications. We are without doubt the market leader in mass education in Libance." Many of his rivals had given up competing with him directly; they had gone into more specialist, niche markets where they had some of hope of making a mark for themselves.

"Surely," I said, "you must have some failures. I just don't believe you can put thousands of children through such industrialised processes without some casualties, some drop-outs and refuseniks."

"Well of course," he said, but the incidence of such failures was tiny, less than 3 per cent a year. One of the important features of the system was that students proceeded at their own pace; you could have 15-year-olds doing the same programmes as some nine-year-olds, particularly in core subjects like literacy and numeracy. In the end even the most reluctant, most stupid 15-year-old found it preferable to knuckle down and do the work, get the basic qualification.

But what about medical or psychological problems, kids with real learning difficulties that weren't about laziness or stupidity? He had two answers to that. First, if such medical problems were detectable before birth the parents could (and usually did, given the problems they would face if they didn't) abort the foetus; as a result, there were very few such cases. Where a child did develop serious difficulties that couldn't be corrected by the standard professional techniques used by his counselling teams, they would have to go to special institutions – and you had to hope the parents had got the relevant insurance. Or not get educated at all. The parental contracts did have a get-out in such sad circumstances. You did occasionally come across such people; they usually ended up in one of the prisons doing very basic manual work.

"How," I said, "could parental contracts and all that work with adolescents who were out of control? Quite a few families back home couldn't handle their teenage children. A contract with a school wasn't much use in such cases. Why should it be different in Libance?"

Raeburn provided two reasons. In the first place most parents' contracts with their security companies entitled them to call on assistance in these circumstances, like physically making sure their children got to school, even if they didn't want to. The stroppiest adolescent was no match for three tough security guards determined to do their duty. Of course, if they persisted with their negative attitude at school, the school had the right to expel them, which put the problem back in the family's hands, who then had to try another school. Often this worked; but in extreme cases, where a succession of schools had failed, or when the parents ran out of schools willing to take their child, the child (or even the family) would end up in prison.

"But don't kids in Libance ever run away from home?" I asked. "It's sadly quite common where I come from."

"Hell, no," said Raeburn. "How could they live? Until you are eighteen you don't have a legal personality here; all big things have to be done with your parents' consent. Let's say you're a sixteen-year-old with your own bank account, and nearly all children of that age do have them, because that's where the money they earn is usually paid. That can only be set up by the parents, who can close it down if a child runs away. (Indeed, they would be at risk themselves from their insurance company if they didn't do that.) So, this home-leaver couldn't buy food or anything else; no access to their account. Nor could they get a job, they need signed parental consent for that.

"They can't beg on the streets; no-one carries cash here. In the early years after the Revolution there were instances of young people living wild and stealing food and so on, but they were caught quickly. There was one notorious case where a rich man picked up a runaway boy and kept him effectively as a sex slave for several months, but the boy escaped eventually and went home and reported what had happened to him. The kidnapper had to pay out a fortune in compensation to the parents, for both the assaults on their son but also for in effect inducing them to breach their own marriage contracts with each other in respect of their son's upbringing. The paedophile also got terrible publicity, and indeed killed himself a few months later. No one tried that adventure again.

"So, all young people here recognise that they have little choice but to make some accommodation with their parents until they are eighteen. After that of course they are on their own and take the consequences of their own choices and actions."

"OK," I said, "so they don't run away. But don't tell me they don't have sex with each other. If they don't have the legal right to enter into contracts on their own, how do they deal with the little matter of notifying the sex police what they have done? I thought everyone who fucked here had to log the fact with the Interferers' Institute. And what happens to teenage pregnancies? I can't believe that even in hard-nosed Libance these are all ended through abortions."

Raeburn smiled. "Interferers' Institute. I like that. I hadn't thought of it like that, and I do see what you mean. And of course, there is plenty of under-18 sex here. Sensible kids tell their parents, and it is logged, as you put it, with the Institute. If a pregnancy results in such cases, it is usually terminated, but there are instances where, with the agreement of both sets of parents and the consent of the relevant insurance companies, the girl has the baby, and an adult-type contractual arrangement is set up between her and the father which only comes fully into effect when they both reach 18. This really only happens with reasonably well-off families who can cope with the financials for the early years.

"The child can also be put out for adoption, but that must be arranged early on; the adult parents would not be allowed by their insurance companies to let their offspring just wait and see how they felt after they had had the baby.

"Naturally there are a few times where the youngsters involved don't tell their parents, or the parents don't find out, at least not in time for an abortion. It amazes me sometimes how a young girl can be six months pregnant, and nobody notices, but it does happen. If the adult parents are rich enough, they can buy their way out of the problem, either through an emergency adoption (permitted in such circumstances) or by agreeing to fund the upbringing of the child. Those that can't afford such a solution end up in prison as breach of contract cases, and the prison and the insurance company take over responsibility. They can secure late adoptions; if that fails, there are a handful of orphanages, generally run by charities, but there are a couple funded and run by the insurance companies, which bring up the children and take on the contractual responsibilities for them."

I told Raeburn that this was all rather authoritarian and must certainly be in breach of Human Rights legislation, but this didn't faze him. "Look, we quit the United Nations after the Revolution. Since we didn't have a government capable of fulfilling international obligations everyone saw that that was inevitable, so we aren't covered by any international conventions. More important, no adult here has either rights or obligations that they haven't voluntarily signed up to. There are no Human Rights, only contractual rights. I have no right to have sex or not have sex; rights don't come into it. As an adult, I can do what I like, provided I am able to live with the consequences. Those under 18 have to do what their parents tell them. That's not because we are dreadful authoritarians, indeed we pride ourselves on being the most libertarian country on earth, but because a society which has few laws and no taxation can only function if parents have the power to make their children behave responsibly. And what I have described to you is the way we have found to make it work. Anyway, I don't have a problem with the idea that if you have children you have to take responsibility for them rather than leaving that job to the rest of us."

It was back to that eternal Libancer mantra, taking responsibility for your actions. Of course, I couldn't disagree with that as an idea, just challenge the way it worked in practice, since few of us behave responsibly the whole time and some otherwise perfectly decent people find it hard, through no fault of their own, to take on all such responsibility without help from the state, that is, the rest of us. I made the point to Raeburn, who just shrugged and said, well, we would have to disagree about that. If I wanted to see how it worked in practice, he could suggest the right Knowledge Corporation learning centre just a couple of kilometres from where were. And he fixed for me to go down there right there and then.

It was impressive in a rather chilling sort of way. Imagine a battery chicken farm, only with every little cubicle filled with a child or young adult. Unlike a factory farm operation, it was totally quiet; every cubicle was sound-proofed. That was almost the most eerie thing about it. This college had three thousand students under 18, half of them there at any one time. (Even at weekends many of them came in to do extra work.) The college had six floors for students, 250 on each floor, in two-year age groups with the youngest on the ground floor. Yet there was no noise at all.

The deputy director, a pleasant middle-aged woman, showed me around. Apart from the age differences, it was pretty much the same throughout the building; students with headsets earnestly staring at screens and typing keyboards. A few were on telephones, having brief conversations with their mentors at the central control centre. Quite a few were reading books: my guide explained that in many courses, literature and languages being obvious ones, the computer programmes were designed to be used alongside good old-fashioned books, which students could borrow from the college libraries if they (or their parents) didn't own copies already.

On each floor there were two adults and half a dozen teenagers in uniforms. These apparently provided security and crowd control. "The teenagers are salaried prefects, usually taken from the other shift," the deputy director told me. "Right now, all the ones you see were here this morning as students. They stay on at lunchtime and change into these uniforms. They are always older than the students they are supervising, which means of course that on the top floor, with the 16- and 17-year-olds, we use adults.

"During study time each student is allowed one visit to the toilet. Basically we encourage them to go during the two half-hour breaks we have each session, but of course you can't be totally strict about that. A prefect will let them out of the cubicle, which are all locked, and make sure they go and come back swiftly. At break times, staggered so that only two floors are on the move at the same time, the doors are unlocked electronically, and the prefects marshal the movements into and back from the playgrounds. Actually, the students are very disciplined about this, they know too well the consequences of taking too long, or being rowdy. So, despite the numbers we have here it generally works well enough."

"The cubicles are locked?" I asked. "What happens if there is a fire?"

"Any alarm signal automatically unlocks all doors. In the rare cases where this doesn't work, usually in the regular testing of the systems rather than on real occasions, the security teams on each floor can unlock the doors mechanically, or in extreme cases, manually. There has never been a problem in all the years we have been doing this."

"But why lock them in in the first place?"

"We didn't, at first. But we found that too many of the students would wander out into the halls, for whatever reason, and it took a lot of prefect time to get them back and prevent disruption. The choice was either to increase the security team personnel dramatically, with serious cost consequence for the students and their parents, or lock the students in. We did major customer research and consultations on this, and by a large majority, once people saw the system would be safe, they voted for locking in. It went to a national referendum, and we won easily."

I shook my head. It sounded horrendous, even if done by consent. For this allegedly most libertarian of countries had had to invent a great deal of excessively repressive measures to deal with the consequences of their supposed freedoms.

The deputy director arranged for me to talk to a couple of 15-year-old students during the second afternoon break. These seemed to accept this way of getting educated well enough, not that they had experience of any other kind, though they were aware of the few expensive schools which had conventional classroom teaching.

"It's OK," said one of them. "I mean of course it gets boring often enough, and if you don't keep going at a steady pace you can end up in trouble with your parents or your mentor, but in the end that's down to you; no-one can force you to go faster than you want to. It would be good to be able to put more questions directly to the control centre, but that costs money and my family certainly can't afford it."

"Yeah," said her companion, "but they do let us text each other for help as much as we like."

"Sure. And here at least, I'm not sure about other schools, they don't mind if you use text for personal stuff, or just to have fun with your mates, as long as it doesn't get out of hand. They seem to realise you need a bit of space, stuck in that hole for hours on end."

I asked whether there were any all-school assemblies, or any out-of-school activities like sports teams or music or drama.

"Nah," said the girl, "least ways not included as part of the basic deal. I mean we don't meet to say prayers and sing hymns like they do in the church schools, and no-one lectures us on morals," here they both giggled, "like what I hear they do at some of the rich schools. It's all dead business-like, as my dad says."

"There are sports teams and that," said her companion. "They are organised by either the staff or some of the older students, but you must pay to join them. It doesn't cost a lot, and I play football for the under-16 team, but it's entirely voluntary. I reckon about half the school takes part in stuff like that."

This aspect of the Knowledge Corporation's approach to education I approved of. I had always hated the compulsory sport at the

London school I'd gone to, and the way the staff tried to build a 'school ethos' at assemblies and tutor groups. A 'dead business-like' philosophy seemed definitely preferable.

Before I wrote my column, I checked back with Axal at Guardian Central. He hadn't gone to a Knowledge Corporation school, as apparently the savings scheme his parents had joined when they got married was linked to another company, and his school had been what sounded like an awkward mix of conventional classroom teaching ("done badly," he said "because the classes were far too big") and a less comprehensive version of the computer-cubicle approach. He reckoned, and I was inclined to agree with him, that you got a better deal out of either of the two extremes, the prison school or the learning factory, than you got out of any in-between, hybrid system.

As I said, this first *Tribune* column was a great success. I called it The Price of Freedom. I basically argued that Libance was trying to be the country with the greatest individual freedom in the world, but in practice it was in some ways extraordinarily repressive, and I used education as an example. It provoked a storm of response, mostly hostile; but the paper loved it. I thought Isaiah Raeburn at the Knowledge Corporation would be angry, or at least irritated, but he called me to say what an interesting argument it was, and he had already had the article programmed into several courses, from history through law to journalism. I would of course be receiving the standard royalties.

Chapter Ten

While there was no doubt that Friya was a great help in finding a flat for me to live in, the process did create tensions between us. She was all for finding something unfurnished with a minimum of a year's lease, on the grounds that it was much better value, and I would need the furnishings in the long term anyway. I said though that might be true it would be crazy to make that financial commitment until my asylum application had been accepted, and by her own account that could take three months or more. Better therefore to accept the short-term extra costs of a furnished place, or even a cheap hotel, until I had cleared that hurdle.

I instantly regretted mentioning the idea of a hotel. "That makes you sound like a tourist," she said. "Are you really serious about settling down here?" I tried to sound as positive as I could, and rapidly withdrew the hotel proposal. By the end of the week, we had found a small apartment in a block near the river. It was, according to Friya, a reasonable location, with good shops and transport, though the district was not one of the better ones, and the local association did not have a great reputation for efficiency or good value. On top of that the furnishings were rather shabby, though the flat itself had a couple of nice rooms with good light. I promised Friya that I would buy enough stuff, pictures, flower vases and the like, to brighten up the place.

One good thing was that I could move in almost immediately. Friya had a lawyer acquaintance who OK'd the contract, which I had to say was full of clauses that we wouldn't have in Europe, to do with the range and detail of the insurances I would have to take out if I didn't already have them and giving the landlord carte blanche to handle the dealings with the local association. Friya advised that I should allow a week to sort out the insurances and accept that I would have to stay on that much longer at Guardian Central.

A couple of other matters also kept things gritty between us. I let slip that Rilka Delene ("Oh, it's Rilka now, is it?") wanted to have dinner with me before I left the prison, which Friya viewed with suspicion. "She has a poor reputation, you know. Runs rings round her husband, even though he is a very important man. I would take care if I were you." I said I had every intention of doing so, and anyway I imagined it was simply to continue our discussion about the differences between Libance and Europe.

That wasn't the smartest thing to say, because it enabled Friya to revisit the argument we had had about my newspaper column on education and the new repression. "Hm, I suppose Governor Delene will approve of your argument that our ideas about freedom are deeply flawed. Really, I don't know why I bother to talk to you about life here. You are so prejudiced against us."

This was nonsense, I said. There were many things I had seen already that I admired – I was going to mention the sex apartments and the drug shops, but thought I'd better leave out the former – and there was much more to see, most of which I was sure I would like. And she wouldn't want me not to write the truth as I saw it, would she?

It wasn't helped by the fact that she was very busy, or said she was, and that we couldn't find time to go out for a meal or to any of the many leisure events that the capital had on offer. The one thing she did get enthusiastic about was when I told her that I had fixed to see Kris Myer, the National Democrat leader. "I really envy you," she said. "He is truly wonderful. What a shame you cannot take me with you. I want to hear all about it afterwards." Having said this, she then had to follow through and agree an evening when we could meet for a meal. The best time seemed to be on the evening of the day I moved into my new home – we could celebrate properly, I said, and she frowned and said, maybe.

I have to say I saw what Friya meant about Kris Myer. He was an impressive and charming man, in his early 50s; tall, elegant, slightly thinning hair, with a generally lively and animated expression and laughing eyes, a warm smile and a deep, resonant voice which must have made many women feel weak in all kinds of ways. He had that great politician skill of making you feel you were the most important person in his life at that particular moment; I suspected he could calculate within seconds the tone and frame of reference that would work best with whomsoever he was talking. He certainly managed it with me, apologising within minutes for the fact that Libancer politicians were really rather poor examples of one of the world's great professions, and that people like him had lost – or no longer needed – the ability to offer leadership in difficult circumstances.

"In truth, Mr Rowgarth, our Revolution, for all its many blessings, has emasculated real politics, and I am afraid we are the poorer for it. What was it that Californian woman sang all those years ago – you don't know what you got 'till it's gone – well, that is certainly the case with Libance and good government."

"Joni Mitchell, 'Big Yellow Taxi', and she was Canadian, actually. But I am slightly amazed, Mr Myer, to hear you say this. Everyone I have met has told me how wonderful it is not to pay taxes and not have people like you laying down the law. Indeed, given how little there seems for senators to do, I would love to know why you have chosen to be one."

We were sitting in his office at the NDP headquarters, along with Josep Stilo. They were not like any political party offices I had been in; more like the offices of a smart advertising agency or financial consultancy firm. There was a formidable amount of activity, I assumed it was to do with the election campaign and the associated TV shows. Myer's own office was tastefully furnished, largely in black, and uncluttered, with a large flat screen on one wall showing what seemed like a dozen TV channels. We sat round a low table with our coffees and water. I had said straightaway that I wasn't at this stage proposing to write up our conversation, just get some background, though I might ask for a formal interview at another time.

Myer smiled at my slightly blunt question. "Let me describe how I fill my time – that might start to answer your inquiry. I get into the office here just after ten; no point in travelling in the rush hour. Most mornings are dealing with the planning and preparation of our TV shows – we have something on the go throughout the year, not just at election time – or our events on the road. After lunch I go to the Senate House; sessions start at 3 and finish by 7pm. Mind you that is only for half the year: we have two terms a year, between March and June and then between September and November.

"In the evenings there are usually events of some kind to go to: a TV recording, a dinner, or a big public occasion in a stadium or conference hall. The Leader of the Senate is, alas, in great demand for a wide range of occasions. But I enjoy that kind of thing. I am a show-off; I love meeting people; I like the attention. And there is always something new that I have to form an opinion of; it keeps me stimulated. On top of everything I am well paid. Not for being in the Senate, of course: you only get expenses for that. But the National Democrats are a very successful business – you must get Josep to show you our accounts. We are the number two production company, and number three in the music market. Our concerts and festivals are very popular, and we intend to move into the exhibition and fitness markets. We are not allowed by the Basic Law to own media, or I am sure we would be very good at that too."

That a political party could be a successful entertainment corporation was a novel idea, but I would have to pursue that another time. I wanted to find out more about Myer the politician. "That sounds like the life of a TV celebrity to me," I said. "Nothing wrong with that if you like that kind of thing. But what do you do as a senator? Not that you seem to have much time to fill in that role; four hours a day for half the year must make it the least demanding political job in the world."

"Most of the business in the chamber is formally approving senior appointments and the results of the latest referenda – and there are a lot of those. I am sure you have discovered already how much we Libancers love voting; we can usually exercise a vote twice a week if we want to in the busy parts of the year. Then there is the weekly debate on Wednesdays; each party takes it in turn to choose a subject and the party leader introduces it for a full two hours of discussion. It is televised, of course, and is a favourite programme with daytime viewers. Not surprising really, since pretty well every senator has shown they can perform well on TV – they wouldn't have survived the election campaigns otherwise. I assure you all that keeps us busy."

"OK, let me try another tack. What are the political or ideological differences between the parties? What do you get to argue about? Why would I vote for you rather than that lady who seems to be your main opponent?"

"Those are all very different issues, yet you seem to think they connect together. There are no political differences between us: how could there be? I have already admitted that real politics has almost disappeared from Libance life. Oh, historically there were differences. The National Democrats were the party of the Revolution; it was our leaders who had the vision of what needed to be done. The Progressives were the main opponents of the Revolution: they liked the idea of big government and plenty of taxes. But all that was years ago; we have kept the names, but all the ideological content has drained away. I suppose we keep the parties, including smaller ones like the Liberals and the Republicans, because we have to have some mechanism by which we can organise an institution like the Senate. We couldn't all run as independents – we need decent organisations supporting us.

"What do we get to argue about? Anything and everything. The whole point is that we are all supposed to be good at arguing. You really must come and see a Wednesday debate once the Senate has reconvened after the elections. In the last session we had some very good set-pieces, one on who was more admirable, a football star or a nurse, and another on whether we should lower the age of majority from 18 to 17. I was particularly proud of my contribution to that one.

"And why vote for me rather than the delightful Lisja Tuller? Well, that depends on whether you find ageing matinee stars, as they so charmingly used to call us a hundred years ago, more appealing than someone who reminds you of your mother. It will be a hard contest, I know that. It is the first time Lisja has run as leader, and I don't underestimate her at all. Her real problem is that everyone likes her but no-one gets enthusiastic about her. And as far as I can tell, people still seem to get positively worked up about me. God knows why, and I don't suppose it will last much longer. But enthusiasm is what usually makes the difference."

I shook my head. "It is still a puzzle. When I saw your election posters, soon after I got here, I assumed you were going for the youth vote and Ms Tuller for the grey vote. Now I am not so sure."

"Indeed, you shouldn't be. We both need to get votes from all sectors of society; it would be fatal to be associated with one particular group. That is why we make sure our Senate candidates come from all age groups and both sexes. We want a comprehensive demographic profile. Just because we National Democrats are good at doing TV and music for the young audiences doesn't mean we neglect the others. Indeed, we have to try that much harder with them."

"So when people come to vote for Senate Leader in a few weeks it will on the basis of which of you they like most? Nothing to do with what you stand for?"

"I am afraid so. I stand for nothing other than offering you an entertaining time in an acceptable manner."

I was getting a bit desperate. I couldn't believe that elections had been reduced to this. "But what about when you have to approve a referendum decision, or an appointment? On what basis do you reject them? Surely people have got to know something about your approach to those decisions."

Myer shook his head gently and smiled condescendingly. "But we don't reject anything. That would be entirely wrong. Our approval is a foregone formality. If the people have made a decision themselves, who are we to overturn it?"

"Well why on earth ask the Senate to vote at all?"

"A fair question, to which the only answer is tradition. The Senate had these powers both before and after the Revolution. Gradually it became the custom not to exercise them except in a formal, you might say ceremonial, way. There has occasionally been talk of abolishing the custom, but it is there in the Basic Law, and we have been advised that the Constitutional Court could not accept a referendum proposal on these lines, so there we are – the legislative chamber of last resort, in law at least, though not in practice."

Josep Stilo, who had been sitting listening attentively all this time, now intervened. "Kris, I'd like you to hear Bob describe some of the stuff they do in their election campaigns in England. I think there are some tricks we could usefully learn."

So then we got into a discussion of voter databases and how to use them. It emerged that the political parties of Libance didn't have members as such, which was not surprising, since there wouldn't have been much for party members to do, so no database there: the commercial arms kept the usual files on their customers, but that wasn't of much use in elections; and the idea of compiling a database of who voted and how in the course of the TV shows that made up campaigns in Libance did not seem to have occurred to them. Myer and Stilo got very excited and were so deep into their own enthusiastic exploration of this new concept that they almost didn't notice a secretary come in with an urgent message for Stilo. He looked peeved at being interrupted but left Myer and me to carry on on our own.

I was amusing him with accounts of the way we used to do door to door canvassing in London in the old days, when Stilo came back in a state of great agitation. "Dreadful news. Chief Justice Riccardo has just had a heart attack. He is in hospital, but they don't think he will survive. That totally transforms the situation in the Court. It means Proposition 72 could well go to referendum."

Myer looked devastated. "God, that can't be. We have all assumed it stood no chance. You really think Ackerman will go with the Proposition?"

"More than I think he will vote against. Even if he abstains it will give a casting vote to Schneider, who will take over as chairman until a new Justice is elected, so it will still get through. I think you'd better talk to the Chief."

Myer nodded, looked at me and said, "I am very sorry about this, but you will have to excuse us. I am sure you appreciate the dreadful significance of what has happened. I am very glad to have met you and I hope we can continue our conversations in less dramatic circumstances."

I said of course and took my leave of them. Stilo was too frantic to accompany me to the front lobby and left the task to the secretary. She kept saying how awful this was, and I kept agreeing, though I wasn't totally sure why it was. When I got to the street, I realised that this had been the first long conversation I had had in which insurance hadn't come up as an important topic – at least, not until Stilo had come in with his dramatic news and even then it surfaced only obliquely. So why was Myer so concerned? Were the National Democrats in hock to the Guardian Insurance Group? I kicked myself for not asking. I might just have missed the most important point of all about the attenuated world of Libance politics.

CHAPTER ELEVEN

Actually, I hadn't. It turned out that all the big insurers supported all the Senate parties, if not equally then pretty damn close to it. I learned this from Rilka Delene when we had our dinner a couple of days before I moved out of Guardian Central. It was simple good sense, she said: you never knew which parties would provide the Leader of the Senate, nor how many of their candidates would get through the TV steeplechase, nor which ones: so you had to spread your bets, as it were.

It was true that Kris Myer was closely linked to the Guardian Group, and Lisja Tuller to United (or, more accurately, Health and Prosperity, the junior partner in the proposed merger). But that was an accident of their personal histories. It was extremely unlikely that Caldor, the chief executive of United and the driving force behind the merger, had anticipated that Tuller would emerge as the Progressives' leader – no-one had until very recently. So, he wouldn't have timed his referendum proposal to fit with the elections. And anyway, the Senate would have scarcely anything to do with the outcome; they might just get round to a Wednesday debate early in the new session, not that that was going to affect anything, but it was just as likely that the whole thing would be over by then.

She was nonetheless deeply depressed by the turn of events. Riccardo had died within hours of being admitted to hospital; Schneider had taken over as acting chairman of the Court. The decision on Proposition 72 was delayed out of respect for the dead Chief Justice, but it would be decided in the following week. It all depended on Ackerman, and no-one knew what he would do; but from all the excitement and activity in the United/HPG camp they seemed to think they would get what they wanted. A fresh burst of posters and video ads had appeared, and why would they spend that money if they didn't think they had it sewn up?

I was surprised that it all seemed to depend on the decision of the Constitutional Court. Even if they accepted the legality of the proposition, it still had to win the majority of votes in the referendum, and wouldn't the Competition Court have a say as well?

Rilka dismissed these attempted consolations. "United and HPG will get all their customers to vote for the proposal; they all stand to benefit from the 10% bonus discount on their premiums that the two are offering on completion of a merger. There are rumours they will make a similar offer to new customers for the first six months afterwards, and if they do, they will get some of our people voting yes to take advantage of it. Even without that it will be very difficult to persuade many of our lot to vote at all; people find the whole thing complicated, and probably think that if it brings the price of insurance down that must be a good thing. Yes, we can tell them that in a year or so when the new United group has got us and the National on the run the prices will not just go back to where they are now but even higher, but that will just sound like scaremongering and sour grapes. No, if the Proposition is put to the vote, it will be carried.

"In theory you are right about the Competition Court," she went on. "They certainly have the power to stop the merger before it happens. But if it has been approved by a referendum on a decent turnout, they will be very reluctant to do that. They will want to see what happens in practice, which means two or three years from now. And by the time they take action, the damage will be done, we will have lost significant numbers of our people, and there will consequent knock-ons into all the other businesses that the big insurers dominate. Indeed Tomas, my husband, thinks that is Caldor's game plan. He can reckon that even if he is forced to demerge the insurance groups in three or four years' time he can retain his position in most of the other businesses they will have acquired or got effective control of in the meantime. This is precisely the scenario that those who led the Revolution said would never happen. All the safeguards they built in were supposed to stop the emergence of a single powerful group dominating the entire economy. So much for political theory."

I finally began to realise why all the people I had met were so worried by what I had hitherto regarded as a purely business matter that ought to be of limited interest to most people and with little likelihood of having much impact on them. Since the whole country seemed to rely on the big insurance companies so much, and since they dominated so much other economic activity, if the equilibrium between them was upset and one organisation permitted to get much bigger than everyone else then indeed it might be as critical for Libance as Rilka and her friends clearly thought.

"Right," I said. "Well, you can't do much about your constitutional judges; there are only five of them and they will do what they will do, they won't be much influenced by outsiders at this late stage. So, the referendum is crucial. You talked about the significance of a 'decent turnout'. Tricky question – do you work very hard to maximise the no vote, even if you are convinced you will lose, or do you urge people to abstain, so that there is a low turnout and the Competition Court feels more confident about stopping the merger on competition grounds?"

Rilka looked impressed. "No-one has put it like that. I must tell Tomas and the others." She looked at me imploringly and put her hand onto my arm. "Would you help us? This is a completely new situation for us, and I don't think many people know how to deal with it. But I get the sense from you that out there in your world things like this happen more often and you do have some idea of what to do."

I thought about that for a moment. It was pure accident that I had found myself in the Guardian camp, and I wasn't at all sure that it was sensible to get involved. However, my journalistic love of a good story, and desire to be at the heart of something big, overcame any scruples, so I said I would do what I could behind the scenes, though I thought she was overestimating my ability to be of much help.

"That's wonderful," said Rilka, giving my arm a big squeeze. "I will tell Tomas and he will be in touch with you tomorrow, I am sure. I hope you aren't too busy with your newspaper and TV work, and with moving into your new flat."

That got us onto those topics. My second column had been about my experiences at Guardian Central, and was much more positive about the Libance way of doing things than the first one had been. Rilka had naturally been delighted that her prison had featured so prominently and in such a good light. I told her I wanted to do a piece with a security team, ideally in one of the SADs, the special administration districts, which she had so carefully avoided mentioning when we had had our first discussion about crime in Libance.

She pretended to be affronted. "I didn't deliberately conceal the SADs, they just didn't come up. I said there was violence in our country, but not organised and not particularly significant. The fact that we have to make special arrangements in a few unfortunate districts where our normal way of doing things doesn't work doesn't alter the general truth of what I told you."

It wasn't worth arguing the point, especially as I wanted names of contacts and introductions, if Rilka had them. As I expected, she did, and she promised to put me in touch with a good Guardian security team here in the capital. I thought at one point that she was going to say that Friya Alling ought to be able to help but seemed to stop herself halfway and decide to do the job herself. When we got round to talking about the new flat, she was very complimentary about Friya's willingness to help me. "I hardly know her, though she has a good reputation for her work, and she is clearly a very nice woman to put herself out for you, especially when there is nothing in it for her. But then I am not really surprised; you are a very attractive man and I suspect most single women would be keen to help you if they could. And not just single women either."

I am not very good at dealing with compliments, so I nearly missed the implication of the last remark, and my confusion meant I certainly didn't know how to respond to it. Rilka smiled, and said she hoped I would be willing to show her my new home when I was settled into it. Yet again she had made a date for the future that I couldn't refuse. She insisted on taking me back to prison in her chauffeur-driven car, even though she had finished work, and it was out of her way. She sat closer to me in the back seat than was strictly necessary, and when we touched as the car swung round corners didn't move away. By the end of the 15-minute journey, I was very conscious of her powerful sexual presence, and was so stimulated by her farewell kiss on the mouth that instead of going straight to my cell I needed to pay a visit to the Elysian sex apartments to get some relief.

Chapter Twelve

Naturally the day I was due to leave Guardian Central and move into my new flat turned out to be the only day in the near future that Commandant Keely Stavros, head of security in Special Administration District Six, could see me. It was also the day that I got a surprise call from the Tribune news desk asking me to get in touch urgently with the office of Dirk Caldor, the chief executive of the United Insurance Group. And Axal and his mum wanted to see me off properly by taking me out to lunch.

All this took me back to high pressure days in London, trying to juggle too much into a single day. Fortunately, Caldor's office were available early; the great man apparently had read my columns with interest and wanted to see me, and we fixed something for the following week. I had to fob Axal off by saying I would come and see him and his mum (if available) for a coffee after his martial arts class that afternoon, and before I finally left the prison. That gave me the bulk of the day with Commandant Stavros, and I needed it.

SAD Six was a depressing-looking suburb about half an hour's drive from the centre. You could tell when you entered it even you hadn't had to pass a security barrier with a notice advising you of the fact: the roads and pavements were in an unusually poor state, shops and houses were boarded up in significant numbers, graffiti everywhere, streets empty apart from occasional gangs of surly youths lounging around, and a much greater presence of security vehicles and patrols. That and the fact that the taxi driver that took me there not only charged a whacking premium but kept up a running commentary of abuse as soon as we had passed the barrier.

The Administration HQ was a fortress inside a formidably protected compound. Apparently, a few years earlier a gang had got hold of explosives and driven a booby-trapped truck into the original

HQ's lobby, with devastating results. The new version was designed not only to prevent a repeat ram-raid of this kind but to withstand mortar attacks from outside the perimeter. I thought this rather undermined Rilka Delene's claims about the 'insignificant' violence prevalent in Libance, but Stavros told me that it had been an excess of enthusiasm on the part of the architect at the time. No-one had ever tried to mortar the place and he himself doubted anyone ever would.

The Commandant was a tall, greying man in his early 50s, more quietly spoken than I expected from the account of his career which I had found on the Guardian Security Company website. (He had been with them since leaving the former Libance army after the Revolution; he seemed to have a strong intelligence background.) He was smartly turned out: he told me that, given the quality and character of many of those who worked as security guards, firm discipline in every aspect of the work was essential, including uniforms and appearance.

SAD Six had been in special administration for more than ten years and showed little sign of being ready for returning to normal status. Indeed, five years before, following the bomb attack on the administration building, the consortium of associations managing the district had fired the previous security contractors and brought in the Guardian team. Stavros was proud to say they had achieved some results, but it was hard going.

"We don't have any of the advantages of old SAD Three," he told me as we sat in his rather austere office. (SAD Three was the riverside district in the capital which Friya had described to me, and which had been declassified after successful gentrification.) "We are a poor location with dreary housing, no opportunities for interesting conversions for either domestic or industrial use, and a sullen population with few people with ambition or aspirations for a decent life. The education provision is mediocre at best," (apparently Isaiah Raeburn's company had refused to set up one of his learning factories in the district) "and it's the devil's own job to find any kind of work for the young men, though thankfully the women are more employable. Indeed, it's the women that keep the place going."

The real problem was that turning the district round would require serious money, and there was no way of raising that if private investors didn't want to do it themselves. "The Guardian's contract has no budget for this; and the consortium's deal with the insurance companies has only limited funds available for non-security work. When the SAD was approved by referendum, it restricted the money the insurance companies could put in; the rest of the country only agreed enough money to contain the problem, not solve it."

The only real revenue available to the Administration was from road charges. Not only were these steep, well above average for the capital, but as I had seen, little enough of the money raised was spent on the roads themselves. "We have no choice," said Stavros. "We have to spend something on trying to improve the lives of people here, and better that than on the roads."

So how did people stay alive in this area, if there was little work available, and if so much money had to go on insurance?

"Ha, it's amazing how little you need to spend on insurance if you are in a SAD," he said. "Most people don't have either homes or possessions worth insuring. They don't have contracts with the local association – there isn't one. We have to provide basic services like water and power even to those who can't pay for them, though that can be very basic: standpipes in the street and water, like gas and electricity, available only for a few hours a day. Many of them don't have marriage or partner contracts, or rather they do, but the provisions in them are suspended indefinitely, and unless you have a real job you don't have an employment contract. You can't take out any health or welfare insurance, so if you are ill you have to go and join the massive queues at one of the two medical centres, and the treatment you will get will depend on how much of a risk you are to other people: we can't afford to be interested in your health on any other basis.

"As to work, well, one of the best things we did when we arrived was to do a deal with the Guardian North prison, which is just over the district boundary, whereby they take on as many of our workless as they can to add to their own clients needing jobs, and sell them on as a package. The prison doesn't have to assume the responsibility for our people that it does for its own, which can be rather limiting, but it's better than nothing. But joining that scheme is entirely voluntary – we can't force people here to do it, and if their wives or daughters have got proper jobs many of the unemployed men here will only 'do prison', as they call it, when they really need the money, and then only for a few weeks at a time.

"The result is what you saw on your way here, I suspect – lots of men hanging around the streets. You would think that is a certain recipe for trouble, and sometimes it is, but funnily enough it doesn't occur as often as you might think. No doubt because of the excellent security measures I have put in place."

He smiled as he said it. (I didn't find out until later whether it was a joke or a boast.) If it's as bad as that, I said, don't people try to leave and go somewhere better? How can they, said Stavros, when they haven't got the jobs or insurances they would need outside the SAD? Most of them are effectively trapped here for life. Some of the brighter kids will do just about well enough at school to get proper jobs, and if they stick at them for a few years employers and the insurance companies will then give them a chance. That way a few people do get out, enough to offer some kind of model and a small morsel of hope to some parents, enough to encourage some children to take school seriously. But that just wasn't realistic for most people, and understandably they gave up. Truanting from school was endemic, not that the school or anyone else much cared, since those truanting weren't working at school, just causing trouble; and the security teams made no attempt to enforce the parental contracts on education, as they would elsewhere.

I assumed that in this kind of culture and poverty crime must be at a high level. Not really, said Stavros, at least not serious crime. "There isn't the opportunity. You can't run a racket: all those vices, as you call them in your country, are legal here – sex, drugs, alcohol, gambling. When people can indulge themselves in these activities as much as they like there is little scope for criminals to make a living out of providing them. As for protection rackets, effectively we and the other security companies are the legal versions of those. There is theft but it's very low grade: the absence of cash makes stealing a low reward business. There is quite a lot of petty thieving, some of it violent, here in the SAD, but there isn't much we can do about it, and to be honest we don't try, unless the victims are one of those relatively few families trying to make a decent life for themselves – we want to encourage them if we can.

"Likewise with assaults and even murder. In the conditions people live under here the strains can become horrendous. Inevitably violence breaks out frequently. If it's public, we deal with it hard; and if it involves a decent family, then, as with theft, we take it seriously and find and punish those who did it. But if it's in private, or in one of the grim places that call themselves bars here, then unless it's obvious who did it, we don't get involved. Our job is hard enough without taking on unrewarding tasks like that."

"So you tolerate the gangs?"

"I wouldn't quite say tolerate. Rather, reach an accommodation with them. There are unwritten rules about what they can and can't do, lines to which, if they cross, they know we will react. It was my big new policy change when we took over the franchise. I knew we couldn't stamp out the gangs, as they are one of the few things around here to give young people pride and any sense of identity, but I persuaded most of them most of the time to keep their activities within bounds that I, and, as importantly, the rest of the people living here, could accept. In many areas they effectively do a lot of our policing for us. It is one of the reasons we don't chase after all the cases of violence; a good few are gangs dealing with anti-social behaviour in their territories. And if we know about it in advance, we will even allow them occasional fights between themselves to sort out any particular aggravation."

"How do you know what they are up to, to be sure it's within your rules? How do you stop them slipping out into neighbouring districts and causing trouble there?"

"Electronic surveillance and paid informants. We have a visual record of everyone who leaves the SAD, even at night. We tag the most problematic individuals and track their movements inside the district as well as out, though we don't usually let them out unless we know in advance where they are going and why. And I have enough informers spread around to tip me off in advance if there is something being planned that I won't like. It's a combination that works most of the time."

"It seems to me you have pretty much carte blanche to do what you like, provided you keep a lid on trouble here. That's a terrifying amount of power for one man to have."

"You are forgetting, or perhaps you don't know about, the protocols and rules within which I have to work as a member of the Association of Security Officers. If I break any of those, I can lose my job, and in some cases find myself sued for breach of contract as well. I assure you these set seriously effective limits to what I can do."

I asked him for examples.

"I can't deprive any adult of their liberty for longer than a day, unless the Contracts Court has found them in breach of contract and ordered them to be sent to prison. I cannot interrogate anybody for longer than an hour without their recorded and independently witnessed consent. Of course, for most people their insurance contracts require them to co-operate with security officers so that isn't a problem, though it can be here in SAD Six where more than half the population doesn't have that kind of insurance.

"Yes, I can keep people under close surveillance, but I can only use information gathered in this way in a formal case, say, a negotiation with another security company about incidents involving both our clients, or a breach of contract application.

"And yes, I can physically assault someone, or order my men to do so, under various circumstances, carefully defined. It is true the rules in a SAD are more relaxed in this respect, but they still basically apply. I can't decide to kill someone, or even beat them up, on a whim; after all, most of what we security teams do is recorded on camera, in both public and private locations."

That surprised me; I asked him to explain.

"Any team of more than two people has to have a camera operator attached to it, recording continuously with time code burnt in, while on duty. That means almost all units here in SAD Six, as we rarely send out teams of fewer than four officers. In a two-man unit one man must record key incidents when possible; failure to do so could lead to breach of contract actions. It is as much for their protection as anything else. Indeed, I cannot force an officer to undertake an action on his own for precisely this reason, though sometimes people volunteer in a particular case."

I said this must make security work very labour intensive. Stavros agreed. It was a factor in the high cost of security insurance but it did mean that many men with limited skills had proper jobs. "We are far and away the biggest employers of men with only basic educational qualifications. I have often said the Revolution still works only because the security industry has effectively wiped out unemployment among unskilled males."

This prompted me to ask about the relations between the different security companies. Given they were in competition with each other for business, didn't that lead to awkward incidents? Indeed, how did those in charge prevent direct conflict, even physical violence, between their respective employees?

"Well, it's rather similar to our officers' association and its rules. In the first couple of years after the army and police were disbanded and everything handed over to private security firms there was all kinds of trouble of the kind you mention. Everyone realised this was hopeless, and indeed, there was a strong movement in the country demanding the return of the police. So the security companies got together and hammered out a comprehensive agreement binding all members of the industry. All the Courts – Constitution, Competition and Contract – approved the arrangements even though you could argue they breached the Basic Law in certain respects, since the judges realised the country needed something like this to supply essential law and order. These rules have been in place ever since, and the Courts have upheld them in several important cases, so now everyone in the security industry knows what they can and can't do in respect of each other.

"Let me give you a few examples. We have two kinds of contracts; those that we bid for in open competition with each other, which is most of them, like this one that we have here in SAD Six. The other kind is what we call a public interest contract, and we take these in turn on a rotating basis. Examples of these would be the Island causeway contract – you know about the Island? – or the naval patrols or providing security at the Senate. These are fixed-price, based on the revenues available, which sometimes don't quite cover the agreed cost of the service, so we all end up subsidising them a little. The Security Companies Association manages these and determines the economics, with the approval of the Contract Court auditors.

"Then there are what we call case protocols. Let's say you are attacked and robbed of your watch. Yes, it does happen. You have a contract with the Guardian, so their security people investigate the case. They find the perpetrators, a couple of teenagers whose parents have insurance contracts with, say, United and HPG. The Guardian team negotiates compensation with United and HPG within agreed guidelines, and one that is acceptable to you. It could be financial compensation; but maybe the parents' insurance doesn't cover this, in which case you are entitled to get a percentage of their parents' earnings for a fixed term, or – in extreme cases – send them or their parents to prison until they have, through their prison work, earned enough to compensate you. Of course, in a minor case like stealing a watch it is usually easy to sort out, unless you have sustained injuries which merit a heavier punishment, which the other side feel they have to dispute.

"All this is negotiated under the terms of the Agreement protocols, with recourse to the Contract Court if necessary. But suppose you want physical retribution as well as financial compensation, which the guidelines permit in certain circumstances. Again, the Guardian team fix this with their counterparts in United and HPG – the key point being that no counter action can subsequently be brought against the Guardian team for any injuries they have inflicted."

I interrupted him at this point. "This is barbaric. Governor Delene described this to me when I first got here. She said you can even have someone killed in revenge for a murder. I can't believe that."

Stavros looked at me steadily. "Yes, I can see that it would seem barbaric to an outsider. And there were many people here who said, when the Agreement was put to the vote in a referendum, that it was a return to the blood feuds and vendettas which civilised states had long since stamped out. Nonetheless the Agreement got a massive majority in the referendum, because this legalised form of revenge was the only way we could see to prevent widespread private feuding. Since we have no laws affecting private behaviour, we had to put something which dealt with physical violence in their place. This was the best we could do.

"And, which may surprise you, it works very well. Calculated violence is rare, because the person making the calculation has to take on board the likely consequences for themselves. Within a couple of years of introducing the Security Agreement the number of physical assaults, and murder in particular, dropped dramatically. Which was just as well for those of us in the security industry, because managing physical retribution was proving very tricky, and having a detrimental effect on our staff, who divided very quickly into those who liked administering physical violence and those who didn't; and as a manager you had problems with whichever camp you chose in such cases."

"Have you ever had to do this in your career? I mean kill anyone in cold blood as part of an insurance deal?"

Stavros didn't flinch. "Yes, twice. In both cases I chose to do it rather than order someone else to. Not pleasant. And thankfully, nothing like that for a good few years now."

"But what happens if there's a fight and both parties turn to their security companies for revenge on the other person? How does that get sorted out?"

"It depends on the circumstances. If it's a Friday night pub brawl it is usually dealt with like most car accidents, with 'no fault' clauses: in other words no action is taken on either side. If there is sufficient evidence from witnesses to say one person was the instigator, then the two security companies will agree that, and fix the appropriate compensation, and the instigator can only challenge that decision by taking a breach of contract case too. That rarely happens because of the difficulties of proving your case in such circumstances, and anyway most people know if they really are to blame. On the rare occasions where it is both a serious incident and there is no obvious culprit it goes to a special tribunal to decide the outcome, which often ends up back as 'no fault', so the companies try to discourage such action if they can."

I found this absence of a police force, and the reliance on private security firms, one of the hardest things to accept in Libance; but twice now I'd gone over the subject at length and failed to dent the confidence of serious and intelligent Libancers in their system. Stavros and I then talked about the details of his operation in SAD Six, and he showed me round his control centre and operations room; and we fixed for me to go out with a unit in two days' time. He also suggested that I should take a couple of days to go north and see the Island causeway security operation, which the Guardian force was due to take over in the following week, and he promised to put me in touch with the right people for this.

I had arranged for the same taxi to take me back to Guardian Central as brought me in the morning and was subjected to the same diatribes about SAD Six. "These roads are shit. These people are shit, worthless. Why you come here? Nothing good here. Here, you get your throat cut and no-one cares. And who pays for this shit? We do. We pay plenty through extra insurance. Every year your insurance go up plenty. And you know why? Because of this shit." And on and on in the same vein, until we were back in a normal district. It was good to know that at least one group of people in Libance had the same view of life as their peers in the rest of the world.

Chapter Thirteen

I got back to Guardian Central in time to watch the end of Axal's martial arts class; at least, that was what he called it: it looked more like hard physical training to me. There were about 50 youngsters and young men, between the ages of 15 and 25 I would guess, working under the guidance of an instructor who gave the impression he had been expelled from the US Marines for brutality.

I wondered what the point of it was. Axal said it made him feel good, but more important it was a modular course, and you could get a succession of diplomas which were highly regarded by employers, as testimony to your stamina, determination and general good character. The class was also used by the Guardian Security people as a recruitment pool for better quality candidates, not that that had any appeal for Axal. He wanted to be a lawyer.

His mother was still at work, so we went down to the prison canteen where we had first met to have our farewell coffee. Actually, I insisted on tea, and explained about the British mid-afternoon ritual, which Axal warmed to when he learned you could also have sandwiches and cakes if you wanted to. We had a good talk. I was still grateful to him for his valuable introduction to Libance life and promised to keep in touch. He said if I ever wanted to write a column about what young people in Libance really thought he could put me in touch with a good gang, as he called it.

It didn't take long to move into the flat. Apart from the two large bags of clothes I'd had on the plane, I'd bought some bed linen, towels and cutlery from a department store recommended by Friya. Metro TV had loaned me a flat TV screen, and I had opened a rental account with the local cable company. I had my mobile computer and handset, and Tribune had given me a printer. I stocked up with food and drink from the nearest local store. I was settled, and ready for business within two hours.

I had some time before I was due to meet Friya, so I thought I would run through what was available on my screen. I had only taken the most basic package of free channels and connection to the web, with the option to pay for individual films or programmes as I wanted them. There was the usual mix of entertainment repeats, music, shopping, promotion and news channels (though all with an odd Libance flavour), but one service was decidedly different: the referendum update site.

This had a wealth of detail. Top of the list, in flashing red text, were the two referenda with voting deadlines in the next two days. Then, in vote date order, were those that were current; fifteen within the next two months, including the three Senate election rounds. Beside each of these seventeen were the percentages of votes cast so far (I learned later these were updated every four hours). If you clicked on any one referendum you were then offered a series of choices for further information, some of considerable complexity. (The level of complexity depended on how much information or supporting material proponents and opponents, or rival candidates, were willing to pay for or provide.) And, where appropriate, you were offered the chance to vote using your remote handset. Finally, there were the results of the last half dozen voting events, with additional descriptive material.

The people of Libance had a fascinating range of issues to vote on. There were appointments: including the vacancy on the Constitutional Court, which was listed with a deadline of six weeks' time, though as there were as yet no declared candidates there was no other supporting material. There were public franchises: right now, several companies were bidding for utility contracts in four different districts. (Friya later told me that voting in these was confined to householders in those district associations, but the process was in each case visible to everybody in the country.) There were three proposals to build new roads: again, only those in the districts affected could vote. (Interestingly, in all three the No votes were currently well ahead.) And there were a number of elections: apart from the Senate, people were running to be presidents or chairmen of animal welfare, heritage and disability societies or charities.

For a journalist like me it was all very intriguing. I read the various biographies and enjoyed the different approaches to wooing the voters exhibited therein. The utility applicants seemed generous with their financial information, though I couldn't of course tell how accurate it was. (Very, according to Friya later: if anything was found to be wrong or misleading, the Courts could ban you from competing for future business for anything up to three years, as well as cancelling the result of the relevant referendum if appropriate.)

I tried voting on all of them and wasn't surprised to find that usually my attempt to vote was immediately rejected. In fact, I was most surprised when I found that my vote for the chairman of the animal welfare society was accepted; its election rules were clearly more generous than everyone else's.

And of course I soon found that, because Libance had rapidly stopped paying for international telecoms connections after the Revolution, there was only a small, limited use of the internet. A sort of Facebook was there, with a rival chat forum, but no Google, Amazon or Apple. I thought at first that this was a major drawback, but I fairly soon changed my mind on this. Friya turned up on time. We had arranged to go out to a local restaurant that she knew, but she wanted to see me in my new home first. She admired (or pretended to) my choice of bedding and towels, declared that I had already made it a home, and was generally enthusiastic. She even accepted a celebratory drink.

However, the meal itself went less well. Something was clearly upsetting her, though it took a while for me to get what it was. She wasn't as attentive as she had been before to my account of my recent encounters, even the one with her hero, Kris Myer. She remained almost silent during my description of the dinner with Rilka Delene, even though I emphasised the Governor's concerns about the burgeoning merger crisis, which Friya clearly shared. She was more responsive to the story of my trip to SAD Six and the meeting with the Commandant earlier that day, even making suggestions about what to look out for when I went out with the security unit the next day. And she definitely perked up when I reported the Commandant's idea of going up to the Island Causeway for a few days.

"Ah, I can help you there. One of my oldest friends will be in charge of the Guardian Security team when they take over responsibility for the Causeway operation in a couple of days' time. I will call him and then you can arrange to go there as soon as you like."

I was of course very grateful for this and took it as a sign, wrongly as it turned out, that the earlier chill in the conversation was now melting, and I could move on to more intimate topics, like inviting her to spend the night in my new home.

"No, I don't think so, Bob. It is very nice of you to suggest it, but I have to get up reasonably early tomorrow. There is a lot on at the moment."

"Friya, you can get up as early as you like – I will still get you breakfast. You saw how well-stocked the fridge is."

"That is sweet of you, but I need a good night's rest. I will not get it if I stay with you."

"Oh, it's because there is only one bed. Fair enough. Well, why don't I come back with you to your well-appointed two-bedroom home?"

"No, no, that would be silly when we are within walking distance of your flat. No, let us enjoy our evening together here, and look forward to other times when we can be more relaxed."

"I am puzzled. You are being very kind and helpful to me. You seem to like me. I certainly like you, like you a great deal. You were willing for us to be, well, very good friends when we had our first night out together. What has gone wrong? What have I done?"

She looked at me steadily. "Nothing has gone wrong, as you put it. Yes, it was good fun last time. And I am sure we can have good fun again. It is just that I have to sort out quite why I am seeing you. I haven't done that yet."

"How can you sort that out if we are going to behave in this kind of distant way?"

Mistake. Not even logical. It got the riposte it deserved.

"On the contrary it is precisely the best, perhaps the only way, to sort it out. I want to continue to get to know you, to have evenings like this with you. But I have to decide how important it is to me to trust you. I haven't been able to do that yet."

"Trust me? Why don't you trust me?"

"I am sure you know why I don't at the moment. But you are missing the point I was making. It isn't whether I trust you or not, it is whether it matters whether I trust you or not."

I was silent. I saw the difference. Then I said, "Yes, well, there isn't much I can do to help you there. Though what I intend to do is to show you that you can trust me. But I see that that might take a little more time."

She laughed. "Well, it is good of you to try. And now let us pay the bill and go to your new home, collect my car and say good-bye until next week, perhaps, after you have been up to the Island, if we can arrange it quickly. I will call my friend – his name is Jorge Reinhardt, and he is a captain – first thing tomorrow."

And that was that. I took her to her car. She kissed me before she got in. It was even more disturbing than Rilka's kiss after my dinner with her. The sensuality was as great, though very different. But it did more than that. It made me feel something that was almost sad. It was very odd indeed. I couldn't remember when I had felt this strange with a woman.

I sat alone in this new home and had a drink. I realised I hadn't told Friya that I had agreed to help the Guardian people (and Kris Myer) in their campaign against Proposition 72, and I wasn't sure why I hadn't. I would tell her when she rang after her conversation with this Captain Reinhardt fellow. Hm – I bet he was a former lover.

New home. Of course, it wasn't really a home, and I had no intention of making it one. But perhaps that was the problem. It was ridiculous to think I would want to stay in this absurd country. With luck they would turn my asylum application down. And if they didn't, well, tough, it would turn out that I would change my mind. But as I tried to imagine telling Friya that, as and when it was necessary to do so, I couldn't. (If I wasn't a perfectly healthy male in early middle age, I would have said it made me feel sick even to try to imagine it.)

Chapter Fourteen

We were sitting in our armoured truck for half an hour before the two investigators turned up. I have had better waiting experiences. The truck was supposed to take eight people, but that was on the assumption that at least two of them were prisoners in the secure section at the back; the front part, used by the security patrol team, was unpleasantly cramped with six, particularly with all the weapons and equipment they carried.

And normally it would carry just five people: the sergeant, the three patrollers, and the cameraman (who was usually, and was in this particular case, a woman, but was still called cameraman). One of the patrollers, the one doing the driving, was also a woman. So, the members of SAD Six unit seven, called 6/7 for short, were not particularly pleased to have me along with them. They didn't want publicity, and they didn't want the stuffy discomfort that I created either.

I had met them just before 8am in the HQ canteen. I had turned up early, a special effort for someone like me who didn't like getting up before 7.30 at the best of times, in the hope of getting to know the members of the patrol unit that Commandant Stavros had chosen for me before we went on the road, but I hadn't been able to find them. (I became pretty certain they had been in the canteen but had told their colleagues not to point them out to me.) So we had only met as they were about to leave in their truck.

I say 'truck'; it was more like a large people-carrier or SUV, but armoured and with one-way windows. The sergeant in charge of the unit, a well-built man called Charles Rodier in his mid-40s, inevitably called Rodie by his colleagues, was polite enough, but the others did their best to ignore me. The two male patrollers were particularly hostile, and I can't say I liked the look of them either. The older was a thin, dark-skinned and sharp-eyed fellow called Archer, who never seemed to smile. I instantly decided he was the kind of person who would enjoy any task which required hurting people. The other was a balding overweight brute in an ill-fitting uniform with small eyes and a couple of teeth missing who looked as though his favourite leisure activity, if he had been in England, would have been the Friday and Saturday night fights after the pubs closed. He was called Shuts, though whether that was his real name I never discovered.

The woman patroller was almost as off-putting. She was in her early 30s, a little overweight (though nowhere near Shuts in that respect) but neat enough in her uniform, with cropped, rather badly dyed blonde hair. The most disconcerting thing about her – she was called Jeannie by her colleagues – was the dead quality of her pale grey eyes. Rodie and the three patrollers all carried side-arms and clubs the size of baseball bats, and had mobile communicators clipped to their ears. There was other weaponry in the truck: a couple of heavy automatics, grenades of some kind, gas canisters and masks and a marksman's rifle with night sighting. For an ordinary street patrol, the team seemed equipped for an alarming range of possibilities.

The cameraman was a wiry woman in her 40s called Tina. She had lively features and shortish dark hair. She was the only one of them who, during the course of my time with them, revealed enough about herself for me to learn she was married and had children. Like the patrollers and Rodie, she wore an armoured vest, and like them had a helmet available, though they tended to leave these in the truck. Tina at least was reasonably happy to talk. She showed me her two cameras, before fixing one at the rear of the passenger section. This apparently recorded continuously and transmitted everything back to HQ, which I suppose in part justified the general silence of the unit when I vainly tried to engage them in conversation. (There was another slot for the second camera, directed at the rear, prisoner section, of the truck, which Tina had to put there if they were holding anyone in that section. Normally, however, the second camera was the one she used outside the truck.)

Rodie did explain, in a rather brusque way, their schedule for the ten hours they would be working that day. SAD Six was divided into four quarters, each with a dedicated patrol unit: the first task of 6/7, having collected the brief from the overnight team, was a thorough sweep through their quarter. After that there were three specific jobs at different times of the day: to accompany two United insurance investigators on a job in the quarter; to do a similar job for two case negotiators later on; and later still to attend the District Court where they were likely to have to pick up prisoners from the day's breach of contract cases and take them to Guardian North or some other nearby prison, depending on the prisoners' insurance arrangements. In between they would make regular sweeps, available to deal with any incidents or alarms (and go to other quarters if needed). They would have a couple of hours at HQ to get something to eat and do desk work, though again this could be disrupted in emergencies.

There wasn't much happening on the first sweep. A couple of times Rodie muttered something when he saw particular individuals or groups on the streets, and once ordered Tina to tape one group, and transmit it back to the Castle, as they called their headquarters. Presumably the unit knew these people well, and their significance or otherwise, but there was hardly any discussion, so I never learned what it was. At least I got the chance to take a better look at this particular section of SAD Six.

It seemed to be split between three different neighbourhoods: a few streets with functioning shops and a park which was better cared for than I'd expected, with ordinary people seemingly on their way to work or school; another area with old multi-dwelling houses in a poor state of repair, plus scatterings of burned-out factories and warehouses, and empty spaces where buildings had once been; and what looked like a relatively modern estate of what I would have called public housing if I had thought any such thing existed in libertarian Libance. However, this was in even worse state, at least on the surface, than the streets with the older run-down houses. The 6/7 truck nosed its way slowly through the maze of the estate, past wrecked cars and vans, dumped rubbish, broken glass everywhere, open spaces that must once have been, however briefly, pleasant oases of green but were now just dusty shit-heaps of detritus. There were scarcely any people about; a few scurvy cats and dogs fought and scrapped amongst the rubbish. Rodie looked briefly at me and nodded at the empty landscape. "Too early in the morning for the inhabitants of this paradise."

Clearly the rest of the team were inured to what they saw. They looked almost relaxed: I learned later that this early morning tour of their quarter was the time when were least likely to encounter trouble.

After this sweep we drove back to the decent-looking area and parked near a row of shops. This was where we would wait for the United investigators. I saw a café among the shops and offered to go and get coffees for everyone. No-one accepted: Rodie said the coffee there wasn't very good. They all produced flasks of their own, and Tina offered me some of hers. I asked Rodie what the investigators would be doing here: he shrugged and said he didn't know. All he had been told was their names, where they were from, and the address of the house they were going to. Since it was a United case, the team had no interest in it: all they had to do was to ensure the investigators' safety.

It was a tedious wait. A couple of times Rodie's communicator beeped, and he held brief muttered conversations. The second time he said, "As usual," to the rest of the team, who shrugged and said nothing. He told me afterwards that United investigators were notorious for turning up late for appointments with security teams from rival firms; the calls to him had been from today's pair offering excuses for the delay. The general theory was it was an attempt to reduce (however marginally) the cost-effectiveness of the rival operations.

A few times Rodie exchanged greetings with passers-by. Once someone banged heavily on the truck roof, which annoyed Shuts a great deal, and he made as if to get out, but Rodie ordered him to stay put. "Just Rexy on his way to get his late breakfast," he said. Rexy, it turned out, was one of the local gang leaders.

It was so stuffy that I said I would like to get out and stretch my legs, but Rodie wouldn't let me. "Not safe," he said. "You are my responsibility." I was annoyed, as the street looked peaceful enough, but stayed put. Luckily a car drew up a few minutes later and a man and woman got out and came towards us. "At last," said Tina, picking up her second camera. Rodie told Shuts to come with him, and got out of the truck, followed by Tina and me. The sergeant looked for a moment as though he wanted to order me back inside, but then nodded for me to follow them.

The conversation with the investigators was cursory. They declined Rodie's offer to accompany them inside the house they were visiting, leaving us on the pavement outside. "Small stuff," said Rodie. "Someone can't keep their payments up. Not surprised round here. In fact, it's more of a surprise that they have any insurance at all."

"What will happen?" I asked.

Rodie shook his head. "Case must be pretty advanced to send the suits out here. Probably setting up a prison spell." I looked at the house the investigators had entered. It seemed ordinary enough; it needed paint, but there were plenty of places like that. It was strange to think that there was a discussion going on inside about whether or not the inhabitants would volunteer to spend time in gaol.

I asked Rodie the difference between investigators and negotiators. "Negotiators deal with other companies and their clients, and they only pick up a case once the investigation is complete," he said. "Here, because it involves a United client, it's a job for their own investigators. Unless it's very unusual, they will be expected to sort out a deal by themselves."

Suddenly his communicator bleeped urgently. At the same time Jeannie stuck her head out of the truck window and shouted, "Boss, urgent message coming through." Rodie turned away to talk on his mobile, then swung back and motioned for us to get back in the truck. I heard him telling the United investigators on his mobile that they were leaving to deal with an emergency. They must have protested, but he dismissed their objections. "You told me you didn't need us inside, so you can do without us outside," he said. I noticed that Tina, who hadn't been taping while we were hanging around, carefully recorded this exchange.

Jeannie now showed why she was the unit driver. She handled the heavy truck as though it was a high-performance sports saloon. As we hurtled through the streets, siren and lights going hard, Rodie gave his orders. "There's a stand-off between Rexy's lot and the Green Hill bunch at the Junction. Six/nine are nearest, but the Castle has asked us to back them up, especially as I know Rexy well. Menotti," (I learned later he was the six/nine team leader) "has metalled up and taken the heavy stuff out. I don't want us to do that but put your hats on." He looked at me. "Tina, give our guest the spare kit."

She just had time to dig out a vest and helmet from a box behind her before she was tumbling out after Rodie, Archer and Shuts as we suddenly stopped by another patrol truck parked on the edge of a desolate cross-roads. As I strapped my armour on, I asked Jeannie, who was clearly going to stay with the truck, if these gangs were armed. "Probably, and even if they aren't we always assume they are." That was the most I'd heard her say in two hours.

Rodie wouldn't let me leave the vicinity of the two trucks, even though there was a lot of coming and going by the two patrol units over the next hour or so. I managed to work out that the Green Hill gang were gathered in a grim block of flats and boarded-up shops across what must have once been a square but now looked like a bombed-site, while the gang led by Rexy were closer to us in a cluster of derelict warehouses. Apparently there had been a brief exchange of gunfire between the two sides before the security patrols arrived: this had cleared the area of any passers-by, and intensified the desolate, empty character of the place: however no further gun battles took place while we were there.

Subsequently I put together a fair idea of what was going on. The patrol team were more relaxed after the tension of this shared experience, and were a bit more willing to talk. The Junction, as it was known from the time when trams and buses used the square as an important transport interchange, although none ran there now, marked the border between the turfs of the two rival gangs. Such borders were not, it appeared, normally a problem, since they were accepted by all concerned: the trouble with the Junction was that it was the only convenient area for some distance for a grubby street market, based on barter and stolen goods, the only kind of shopping available in the worst parts of SAD Six.

Who controlled the Junction market had been an issue between the two gangs for years and had regularly provoked violent incidents. Stavros, when he had taken over the SAD Six franchise, had early on decided that he wasn't going to tolerate this, and had negotiated a deal whereby Rexy's gang were given the overlordship of the market. He had compensated Green Hill with a privilege elsewhere. Unfortunately, this did not, in the view of the Green Hill gangsters, prove to be as profitable as the Junction market (though God knows the Junction profits must have miserable enough): and today they had returned to reassert themselves.

Rodie and Menotti had, for now at least, resolved the conflict, by threatening in the crudest and most brutal terms to call for reinforcements and blast the Green Hill gang from their position in the flats with their superior firepower; and the gang had very sullenly withdrawn. Rodie had told Rexy that the patrols recognised his rights but insisted he should let them deal with it, which he had, not surprisingly, been happy to accept. Green Hill was part of the 6/9 unit's quarter, but Menotti had nothing like the co-operative relationship with that gang that Rodier had with Rexy's crowd. Indeed, according to Tina, Menotti would have dearly wanted a firefight with Green Hill, had half-expected them to reject the patrol's demands, and had been disappointed when they hadn't.

Surely, I said to her when we were discussing this, killing and wounding a number of gangsters and (probably) innocent bystanders as well, would have been a dangerous and perhaps counter-productive tactic, likely to make security work more difficult in future; there was bound to be retaliation.

Tina looked puzzled. "What retaliation? None of these people have insurance, there would be no come-back from anyone. And anyway, most people in the area would be glad to see them dead."

"What about their friends and relatives? Wouldn't they want revenge on you and your colleagues?"

She shrugged. "They might, but we would have to live with that. The units that cover Green Hill, and not just Menotti's team, are in almost permanent war with that gang. Two gangsters were killed in a fight a couple of months ago. The Commandant doesn't like it and will probably discipline Menotti for the way he handled the gang, but this is the worst bunch in SAD Six so he can't do much about it."

"Are all security units as heavily armed as you are? I don't just mean in a SAD like this one, but generally, throughout the country?"

"Not at all. It is only in SADs that we can go around like this. For a start in many normal districts there are no patrols at all – no one company would have a comprehensive franchise. People don't like seeing armed security teams driving around their streets. Most security officers carry no more than clubs, and that is for self-defence in emergencies. Normally we can only use weapons once a negotiation has been completed, and even then, we usually don't need to. What you see here is very unusual in our country."

That was, I thought to myself, presumably why working here seemed to attract the psychopaths. But I was puzzled by the implied absence of firearms among the population at large. Given the libertarian nature of this country, anyone who could afford to must have been able to buy such weapons: so why weren't guns more widely used?

"Oh, lots of us have guns, that's true. But we hardly ever fire them, except in sport or hunting. Your insurance is almost always automatically invalidated if you shoot somebody, except in clear self-defence, and is definitely invalidated if you shoot a security officer. You would have no protection in such circumstances against reprisals by the victim's insurers and security teams. That is a very powerful deterrent, believe me. Though rather less so to these thugs down here, since they don't have insurance anyway. But then they can't buy guns from the armouries, and can only get them by bartering or stealing, which is not that easy."

This struck me as a bizarre outcome. Most people could, and apparently did, have guns, since in this lawless country there was nothing to stop them buying them, but they couldn't easily use them because of the constraints of their insurance policies. People without insurance found it impossible to buy guns but if they managed to steal them, or get them in a barter exchange, they were far less constrained about using them. Weird, or what?

One useful thing did come out of my morning at the Junction.

Rodie brought Rexy and a couple of his followers over to the two trucks at one point, for some kind of discussion which took place out of my earshot. However, the gang leader must have recognised me off the television, because he came over to talk. He said he'd read what I'd written about schools, and, since he was very angry about the lack of schools in his area he would like to talk to me about it. I kept my surprise to myself and willingly agreed. I told him what time I would finish at the Castle that afternoon, and he said he would send someone to pick me up at the gates.

Archer and Shuts didn't like the idea of me going off with gang scum, and said so clearly, but Rodier told them to mind their own business. "Ignore them," he said to me. "They are thick bastards whose only idea for dealing with people in this district is to give them a good beating. Rexy is nasty enough when he wants to be, but he is more intelligent than most: you will find him interesting, and you should be safe enough."

And so it turned out, after I finished my day with unit 6/7. I stood by the Castle front gate, looking hopefully around. After a couple of minutes, a slim, scruffy youth appeared as from nowhere and said, "You the European reporter? OK, this way." I followed him down two nearby streets until we came to a parked car, with a driver sitting in it. The youth signalled me to get in the back, and we drove for ten minutes in almost total silence; my brief attempts to get them to talk being met with such little success that I soon gave up.

I thought I recognised the pleasant park that I had passed with Sergeant Rodier's unit that morning; and soon afterwards we drew up outside a large house in poor condition, with several young men and boys sitting around on the steps and walls. Loud music was blasting from an upstairs window. A banner, with what looked like a red hawk on a black background, was draped across the first-floor frontage. The walls were covered with graffiti, mostly incomprehensible, but I did make out WELCOME TO THE RAPTOR HOUSE above the front door. (I learned a bit later that The Raptors was what the gang called themselves.)

I'd written about London youth gangs a couple of times, and at first little about the Raptors surprised me. I was led past sullen stares, searched roughly, and taken through a warren of rooms destitute of any furniture save screens, video and audio equipment, dirty mattresses and piles of clothing. (I counted myself lucky we didn't seem to need to go via whatever kitchen and eating area the house possessed, and that what I took to be bathrooms had their doors closed.)

However, on the second floor we suddenly arrived at what looked very like a functioning office, with computers and phones, desks, shelving and filing cabinets, and mostly young women doing the work. (Again, I learned later that the district administration had provided most of this, though some items had been stolen; and, as important, it paid the energy and telecoms bills.) My guide handed me over to a smartly dressed young woman, who already knew my name, and asked me to a sit for a moment, just as if I had been coming for an interview in any City or Canary Wharf corporate offices.

Then I was shown into Rexy's room – definitely not a conventional office. It was all sofas and armchairs, with low tables, though all in a shabby state. The video and audio equipment was rather smarter, though, like everything in Libance, not what I would have called the latest models. The one large window looked out over the park. Through one door I could see a bedroom, and off that an en-suite bathroom. Another door seemed to lead to a small kitchen area. Rexy himself emerged from this room, carrying a mug of steaming liquid, and asked what I wanted – drinks, drugs? I thought a local beer would be the safest, and he nipped back and returned with a nice cold can. We sat down on sofas across from each other and talked for more than an hour.

What interested me most about this young man was that he seemed to be engaged in the closest thing to politics that I had so far encountered in Libance. His activities weren't determined, as so many people's elsewhere seemed to be, by the complex obligations of their contracts and insurance policies, but by the deals he could strike with the organisations that shared power with him in his territory. The most of important of these were the SAD administration, Commandant Stavros and his security operation, and half a dozen charities that worked in his area. And none of these deals were of the kind that could be enforced by any court of law.

Stavros had touched on this when I had met him a couple of days before; he had talked of the 'accommodations' he reached with gang leaders like Rexy. Rexy himself was remarkably clear minded about the situation.

"Look," he said. "When I was a kid there was no hope for people like me. My father lost his job as a driver when I was very young, his insurances lapsed, the block of flats we lived in was abandoned by the property company that owned it, and finally my mother was forced to quit her job as a receptionist because the insurance companies refused to deal with us anymore. And that was typical of many people in the area. My father took to stealing, like many others, but he was pretty hopeless at it, and was badly wounded in a fight with a United security team. No hospital would take him – no money, no insurance – and I watched him die at home with no medical help at all.

"I had to quit school. We couldn't afford it, and anyway I'd stopped going most of the time because I couldn't see the point of it, and no-one was going to give me a job. So, like all my friends I joined the Raptors full time; I'd hung around with them anyway since I was eight. I was in a lot of trouble; a couple of spells in prison, but the prisons soon refused to take me because they couldn't see any way in which I was going to become a proper citizen, as they called it. I fought in the gang wars that eventually led to us becoming a SAD. More than half the boys I had grown up with were now dead. I still don't know how I survived all that.

"The Raptors was my life. They looked after me and gave me something to do. But it was a grim sort of existence. Most of the time you were hungry, dirty and recovering from some kind of physical injury. You were constantly hassled by the security patrols, and constantly fighting someone or other. But you had little choice.

"It turned out I was good at organising, and I was good at negotiating. I was OK at fighting, but plenty of others were better, though many of them didn't last that long. I did. By my early 20s I was one of the gang leaders, though anyone with half a brain who had reached that age in this district qualified as a leader. Even by then, I had begun to think that this was a bloody stupid way to live and had done a small deal with one of the more sympathetic charities in our area. We organised protection for the old people on an estate in return for regular groceries from the charity. Then there was the chaos after that mad attack, led by the Green Hill morons, needless to say, on the Castle, but some of our hard men joined in, and got themselves killed. By the time Keely Stavros arrived as the new security boss I was the effective leader of the Raptors.

"He saw the deal I had done with the charity and offered me a deal of his own. If I kept the Raptors under control, he would get his men to lay off us and our district. I said I needed more than that: I could only achieve that control if there was something in it for all the guys in the gang. Over the next few months we stitched together the current arrangements, bringing in the administrators and the other charities. Now we have this place, most of the bills are paid for us, and we get regular supplies of food and so on. In return we keep our streets reasonably quiet and peaceful. We sort out trouble. And we can collect our donations, as long as we aren't too greedy."

He saw me glance towards the ceiling, with the heavy rock number coming through.

"OK, not always quiet. Anyway, it's a better life than any other gang can offer in SAD Six. We may not have insurance, but we do have a bank account. You are warm, you are fed, you can have fun and you have a fair chance of reaching your 30th birthday. But that's all. No prospect of getting out of here, of having a decent life and a family. That's where schools come in."

Schooling was pretty well non-existent in SAD Six. I already knew that Isaiah Raeburn had refused to build any of his Knowledge Factories there, and I could see why. Rexy told me that there was one conventional school in the moderately decent bit of the district (not that far from The Raptor House as it happened) but only children from normal families with parents with jobs and insurance could afford to go there, a tiny proportion of the overall population. The religious charities ran a couple of free schools for members of their churches or mosques: there were various self-help efforts organised by desperate parents on a very modest basis ("the semi-literate teaching the illiterate," said Rexy) and even small groups for younger children run by The Raptors themselves; but in effect the majority of children got little or no formal education.

Rexy wanted to know what happened in England. I explained about state education and how much tax we paid, and he looked depressed; not much hope to be had from that model in Libance. I asked about the non-religious charities. Couldn't they run some schools? Rexy said some of them had talked about it to him, but it always turned out to be too expensive when they went into it in detail. And then I had my great idea. A conventional school would indeed be too expensive, but adapting the Knowledge Factory model wouldn't. There were plenty of empty buildings in the district. One of them, using Raptor members as labour, could be converted into a factory school. The marginal costs to Raeburn of plugging a few hundred SAD Six kids into his primary literacy and numeracy courses would be low, and almost certainly affordable by a charity. The Raptors could provide the security teams at the school and share the admin tasks with the charity. It would be basic stuff, but a start.

Rexy got the point instantly, but questioned why Raeburn would want to do it. I said because he loved new ideas and because it would be good for his reputation. He still looked doubtful, but asked if I could fix a meeting. Of course, I said. In my enthusiasm I had no doubt I could persuade Raeburn to at least try this as an experiment. In my turn I asked why none of the charities had thought of working with Raeburn in this way. Probably because they disapproved of him, said Rexy. But that wouldn't be a problem; if I could deliver Raeburn, he could deliver a charity.

And so I found myself as a kind of broker of new do-gooding ventures; not a role I had ever envisaged in England.

Before I left, I raised one other topic with my new partner. Why didn't people like him think about going off to the Island?

He sort of smiled. "How much do you know about the Island? Not a lot, I guess. Well, none of us know that much, but what we do know is that life is hard there, very hard – much harder than being a Raptor in SAD Six. And you have to do what you are told to do by the Island bosses. No good having ideas of your own or trying to argue with them. That at least is what the very few people who have come back from there say. Yeah, it's the sort of thing you talk about as a kid – I'm going to run away to the Island, get away from all this shit – but when you learn what it is like you pretty soon give up that idea. At least I did, and so did most of my mates. I only know of one guy who did leave to go there. And I have no notion of what happened to him."

What he said made sense. But it also made me even keener to find out about the Island for myself – if I could.

Chapter Fifteen

As it happened, the crisis meeting of the top Guardian people and their advisers that Rilka had asked me to go to took place in the evening of the day on which the Constitutional Court had indeed voted to allow Proposition 72 on the United/HGP merger to proceed. The actual vote had been 2-2, with Justice Ackerman, the former United man, abstaining on the grounds of potential conflict of interest; but as Rilka had predicted, it didn't matter because the acting Chair of the Court, Schneider, had cast his deciding, second vote in favour of the referendum proposal.

One of those attending the Guardian meeting, which took place in the boardroom in the Group's head office, was the lawyer Timo Jankel, who had so confidently assured the rest of us at Rilka's lunch party several days earlier that the Court would definitely reject the proposal. He was unabashed; how could anyone have known that Riccardo was going to drop dead like that? Other guests from that day were also present on this occasion: Stilo, the NDP official, Elli Dyvers, the Guardian executive, and of course Rilka herself, though her husband was bedridden with the 'flu and had sent his apologies. Kris Myer had also turned up. The meeting was led by the Guardian Group board chair, an elegant woman in her mid-60s called Dr. Irene Gopiak.

Rilka had obviously passed on my argument that they needed to decide how to play the referendum; whether to maximise the No vote even though they knew they would lose, or to ask people to abstain, to reduce the legitimacy of the outcome. Gopiak started the meeting by referring to their decision to adopt the latter course, on the grounds that the Competition Court might be encouraged to look at the merger sooner rather than later as a result. They discussed how exactly they would go about this for half an hour or so, and then Gopiak asked me for my views.

"If you want to undermine the validity of the vote, then you have to really bang the drum," I said. "You have to make people understand that this is an exceptional event, way out of the ordinary, and that they should treat it as such. In short, you have to politicise it. I suggest you call for a Voters' Strike."

This disconcerted them. After all, they had long since abandoned real politics, and there hadn't been a strike in Libance since the Revolution, because such action would be a breach of contract, and hence illegal. "Precisely," I said. "Your argument is that the Proposition is in truth illegal, a breach of the social contract as expressed in your Basic Law. It is only a piece of opportunism by the pro-United faction in the Court, in forcing a decision while missing a key member, that has let things get this far. Therefore, the proper response by all citizens who are prepared to put the public interest above their own narrow pecuniary benefit is to refuse to take part. A Voters' Strike."

They actually applauded this bullshit. Myer leapt up in his enthusiasm and said he would use exactly the same ideas in his next speech. Rilka beamed at me with what looked like parental pride. Dr. Gopiak congratulated me on my insight, and we spent the next hour discussing how to present this novel idea to the electorate. Then I produced another bombshell.

"Of course," I said, "securing a very low turn-out will give Kris Myer total justification for getting the Senate to overturn the referendum result. That stops the merger dead."

This time they looked at me in puzzled silence. Then Myer said, "But as I explained to you when we met, Bob, the Senate vote is a formality, purely ceremonial. We never reject a referendum result."

"You haven't done so for years," I replied, "but you agreed with me that you have the power to do so. It may be unprecedented, but this is, as we are saying, an unprecedented and scarcely legal situation. You will be acting unusually, but unlike your opponents, within the law."

Dr. Gopiak turned to Jankel. "Is that right, Timo?"

I had been conscious throughout the evening that Jankel disliked the way I had become the hero of the hour, and fully expected him to rubbish my idea. He looked at me thoughtfully for a moment and then said that I was indeed correct. The Constitution gave the Senate the job of approving all referenda decisions. The fact that the Senate had never rejected any of them did not alter that constitutional truth. However, it wasn't clear to him that a majority of the Senate would agree to such a proposal.

"That's up to Mr Myer," I said. "Obviously I am assuming that the polls are right in predicting a victory for the NDP."

Myer shook his head again. "It is not as simple as that, Bob. There will be pro- and anti-United people in all four parties. At this moment I couldn't begin to say if there would be a majority in the Senate for such a bold initiative."

"OK. In that case can you fix it so that at least all the NDP successful candidates are against Proposition 72?"

Myer looked at Stilo, who slowly nodded his head. "I think we could," Stilo said. "I know what most of those who have got through the votes so far think about this, because obviously everyone is talking about it. It would mean putting three or four of them who are expecting to be in the top half of our list to the bottom for the final round, which will surprise both them and a lot of other people, but I am sure I could arrange it."

"What about the other parties?" said Dr. Gopiak. "Could you talk to your opposite numbers and get them to do the same?"

"Hang on a moment," I said. "We need to keep this idea under wraps. We don't want the United camp to learn about it. This must come as a surprise. God, if it was made an issue at the Senate elections who knows what would happen? You might get people voting about something real. You could lose the Senate as well as the referendum."

Dr. Gopiak smiled but otherwise ignored my sarcasm. "Yes, of course this very interesting suggestion must remain a secret between us. No-one must speak of it outside this meeting. Kris, we don't have to decide whether we will ask you to do this until after the elections. But it would be a very good idea, Josep, if you could quietly make sure that at least we have a chance of mounting this coup by fixing the NDP lists in the way you indicated."

That signalled the end of the meeting. I was hoping for a lift home from Rilka, but she surprised me by proposing that I honour my agreement to take her to dinner. The bedridden Tomas would be tucked up asleep in his own room and wouldn't be expecting her for hours yet. She had indeed provisionally booked a table at one of her favourite (but not too expensive) restaurants, which was rather presumptuous of her but she was sure I wouldn't mind.

And so the evening developed. Over what was indeed a good dinner she commented favourably on my recent Tribune column on the Libance addiction to voting, and took it for granted that I would write in support of the Voters' Strike. I said I would certainly report it in due course but might not feel it right to declare a view one way or the other. She didn't begin to understand such scruples, and confidently declared that she would persuade me otherwise at the appropriate moment.

I decided to tell her at that point about Dirk Caldor's request for a meeting. Rilka looked momentarily disconcerted, but brightened up and said that I must find out as much as possible about his plans and pass them on to the committee.

"Look," I said, "I have rules about this. Anything Caldor says on the record I will pass on. Anything he puts on a confidential basis will remain confidential. I may be helping you out as a friend but as a journalist I have to keep some things back. I hope you understand that."

Rilka clearly thought this was ridiculous, but she saw there was no point in pursuing the subject at that stage and moved on. She said she had spoken to the Guardian Security captain who had just taken over the Island Causeway watch, and he would be happy to see me whenever I wanted. (He was the self-same Captain Reinhardt whom Friya had mentioned, a coincidence which set me wondering.) And she asked about progress on the TV documentary. I told her it was going well, we had focussed on a couple of possible themes, and I had been contracted for a further two months at a higher rate – "so I could afford this dinner" – a crack which she ignored.

Just before coffees Rilka said she needed to go to the toilet. When she returned, she handed me a small carrier bag containing a small present which I was to open when I got into the car. She would of course drive me home.

When I opened the bag in the car as we left the car park, I found a silk bra and panties, slightly warm. I looked at Rilka quizzically. "Thank you very much," I said. "Er, what am I supposed to do with them?"

Her eyes were twinkling. "Just keep them for now. They are mine. My present to you is that I am taking you home and not wearing any underwear." She took hold of my hand and put it on her thigh. "See for yourself."

She wasn't lying. I stroked her gently and trusted it wouldn't take her mind off her driving.

It wasn't long to my flat, but when we arrived, we were both in a state of some excitement. "I hope you are going to invite me in to see your new home," said Rilka.

"With pleasure." However, seeing my new home didn't turn out to be her main objective. As soon as we were in the hall, Rilka pulled me to her and kissed me hard. "Fuck me now, right here," she demanded. I did; and then we did it again half an hour later in my bedroom, only in a slower and more exploratory fashion.

It was nearly midnight when she left, but she didn't seem concerned. I assumed Tomas was used to his wife being out late. I was uncertain what to say as she went, but, consistent with the way she had managed the evening, Rilka did it for me. She kissed me and put a finger on my lips. "Don't say anything. I enjoyed myself, and I could tell you did. At some point we may want to do this again, and if we do, I am sure we will find a way of telling each other. I look forward to seeing you after your visit to the Causeway and my friend Captain Reinhardt."

And she was gone.

Chapter Sixteen

The next day, by an unfortunate coincidence, I met Friya for dinner, the first time for days. I was very nervous about somehow giving her cause to wonder what I had been up to; I am not a particularly effective deceiver of women. Luckily, enough had happened since we had last met to arouse and retain her interest without us straying into tricky territory (like had I seen Governor Delene recently?).

First thing that morning I had gone to visit Isaiah Raeburn and had got him seriously interested in opening a knowledge factory in SAD Six in co-operation with Rexy's gang and some supporting charities. He hadn't wanted to start a conventional operation when he'd looked at the district a few years previously, but the novel approach I suggested got him excited. Not only would it be a challenge in itself but if it was successful, it would improve his reputation, show he wasn't just the money-grubbing businessman he was normally painted as. He had straightway spoken with Rexy on his video phone, and I had enjoyed watching the two of them hitting it off immediately.

Friya too approved of my idea. "It is very interesting, Bob, the way you are able to think about things quite differently from us," she said, after I had given a lengthy account of my trip round SAD Six with the security unit, and of the meeting with Rexy as well as the follow-up with Raeburn. But she was even more impressed with my description of my long meeting with Dirk Caldor that had taken place that afternoon.

His office had called to ask if I could reschedule it at short notice. They gave some excuse or other but I reckoned it was more to do with United's success at the Constitutional Court on Proposition 72. It suited me perfectly since I was booked to go north for my trip to the Island Causeway station the next day, and getting the Caldor interview out of the way would leave me free to remain in the north for as long as I wanted to.

The United headquarters were in the centre of town; a big brick building in the Gothic style of a hundred years ago, which gave it rather more distinction than most more recent Libance buildings. I expected Caldor's office to be in modern chief-executive mode: large, with a polished glass or wooden table for meetings, a comfortably lush leather sitting area, a giant flat screen on the wall, and a vast flat desk with nothing on it but a comms system and a keypad. (I always wondered why corporate bosses seemed to need to suggest that paperwork was either non-existent or so swiftly dealt with no trace was left in their vicinity.)

Caldor's room was big enough, but was filled with bookshelves, almost like an old university professor's room. His desk had a laptop and a chunky comms system and was piled up with papers. There was no meeting table; just a couple of ancient sofas with a coffee table between them. (At one point in our lengthy conversation I joked that I had thought when I came in that I was coming for a tutorial. Caldor said he had deliberately kept the office in the traditional style when he took over precisely because so many people regarded him as a restless business visionary who would change everything overnight, and this was an easy way to give them pause.)

After he had grilled me on my life and work in England and why I had asked for asylum, he asked if I had worked out why he had asked to see me. I shrugged and said I assumed it was something to do with the coming referendum on the merger. He shook his head.

"No, no, though we can talk about that later if you wish. No, I have been very struck by some of the insights about Libance that you have revealed in your columns. One of the troubles with being as cut off as we are from the rest of the world is that we have lost an accurate sense of ourselves. You are the first person in a long time to point out certain features of our way of life, features that bother me but which most people don't even seem to notice, let alone worry about.

"Two things in particular that you have written have intrigued me. First, that we have in effect replaced paying taxes with paying enormous insurance premiums, and that it isn't obvious we have gained from this: and secondly, that far from being a radical exciting place, where the future is being forged, we are a very old-fashioned and rather sleepy country, way behind the rest of the world. Why do you think this is? And is there a connection between the two?"

"I don't know if there is a connection; I haven't really thought about it in those terms," I said slowly. "As to being old-fashioned despite your Revolution and your lack of any form of government, I suppose it is in part due to what you have already mentioned – that you are cut off from the rest of the world, so that the technological and economic changes that we are going through simply haven't got here: and also that your habit of holding votes on virtually everything must make it very difficult to get agreement to make big changes."

Caldor leaned forward and stabbed his finger at me in an excited manner. "Exactly. Far from being revolutionaries, we are a deeply conservative and risk-averse people. Those who dislike a new idea or a proposal for a new venture are always more numerous than the few who understand and favour such ideas, and far more likely to vote than those who are either only mildly supportive or who don't care much either way. It is almost impossible to get agreement to build a new road or railway, to expand an airport, to increase the number of flights, to build new offices or factories. There are not many parts of the country where we can build new homes, and they are usually in places where people don't want to live anyway.

"Of course, the first time a new venture is proposed to the whole country you can quite often win the vote. Most people aren't going to be directly affected in a negative way, and they like the idea of the positive aspects. But that's of little help to you when the proposal moves on to being considered by those local associations or districts which are going to be directly involved. Then it is usually very difficult to get their consent, unless they are poor and think the new development will improve their lot. And even then, it isn't usually enough. What's the point of being able to build new factories or warehouses in a place if the neighbouring districts turn down the new roads you need to service them, or who threaten to increase the charges on the existing ones so much that it makes the whole business uneconomic? And of course there is no law, no government, which can force those who object to accept the new developments, even if it is in the overwhelming interest of the country as a whole.

"So scarcely anything new on any significant scale has happened in years, unless it can be achieved using old, abandoned sites or converting existing buildings in areas which won't be affected by the change."

"I hadn't thought of it like that," I said. "That's 'Not In My Back Yard' on a grand scale. That must have serious economic consequences. But Tomas Kryk – you must know him, he's the Guardian banker – was telling me that the Libance economy has worked perfectly well for years."

"Pah, Kryk, he is just a banker. His idea of an effective economy is low inflation, modest level of debts and financial stability. The fact that there is scarcely any growth and that no-one gets much richer doesn't worry him at all."

"How does the Great Insurance Phenomenon tie into this? I mean you run the biggest insurance operation of the lot, and it's about to get even bigger. That must mean what's happening here, which you don't seem to like, must be at least partly your fault."

Caldor grinned sardonically. "A clever point, Mr Rowgarth. Indeed, it is, as you say, partly our fault in the big insurance companies. Essentially my colleagues in the industry as a whole share Kryk's perspective; they like financial stability and steady returns, and happily accept very low growth. Why shouldn't they? It keeps life far cosier – far less competitive. If your company is doing roughly as well, or as badly, as your competitors then no-one can really complain. And if you are the main motors of the economy, as we undoubtedly are, that leads, in my view at least, to stagnation."

He paused and seemed to be thinking. After a moment I chipped in.

"What about the other point you mentioned?" I said. "That in effect, insurance premiums replace taxes, but that in the end you pay out probably the same amount but without the redistributive effects of progressive taxation?"

"Well, it's probably true, though I know of no academic study which proves it. You claim you gain in fairness;, we claim we gain in individual freedom and the ability to choose, but basically services cost what they cost. I doubt there is much to debate, though I was struck by the novelty, at least in Libance, of your claim. But I want to return to your other argument, which is much more interesting, to me at least.

"Do you not think it surprising that a country with no government and no taxes should turn out as conservatively as we have done here in Libance? We have of course quite a wide range of incomes, but not nearly as great as exist in your world, as I understand it. Why should that be? Surely, we should have a handful of very, very rich people and a great mass of the poor? But we don't."

I shrugged and said I hadn't really thought about it like that.

Caldor leaned forward and looked at me with surprising intensity. "But I have, Mr Rowgarth, I have. We are excessively democratic. When everyone can vote on everything, the conservatives win almost every time. Those who want change are nearly always in a smaller minority than those who fear it, even if they are both minorities. On many things the great mass of people is indifferent. And so the status quo triumphs. Once a society reaches a certain level of prosperity, it is very hard to move on if there is a universal right to veto change in its detail."

"But how does that stop people getting very rich? Entrepreneurs must make a fortune here."

"Hah! The conventional assumption. Innovation in most things requires you to construct new buildings, to change the infrastructure in some way. Bad luck! Voted down in the districts affected!"

"But some things don't need that kind of new activity. What about financial services? Some of the biggest fortunes in my country have been made out of them in recent decades."

Caldor smiled grimly. "Indeed, the voters have no say in these matters. But that is where the insurance giants come in, and the banks. We act as blocks on many new ideas, both culturally, – we have grown used to viewing innovation with suspicion – and practically; our low rates of growth have limited the surpluses we have available to invest boldly. It has been a vicious circle. We do not like risks."

I shook my head. "I find this all very hard to believe."

"I assure you it is true. Which is where Proposition 72 comes in. By an extraordinary piece of luck, I may be about to break this vicious circle. An accident has suddenly allowed the chance to put it to the vote; and for once those who will benefit outnumber those who will lose out. Once it is passed, and once we have merged with H & P, then, my friend, we can begin to break out of this conservative fix we are in. The new giant company can change the rules unilaterally. We can find ways to bypass the voters, and where we can't, we can probably muster the majority of our clients to vote the way we need them to. At long last Libance can deliver the real fruits of its Revolution. Innovation will be welcomed and funded and will happen regularly – at last."

"But you are in breach of the Basic Law, surely? You are creating what is in effect a giant monopoly."

"I disagree with that, though it is, I admit, arguable. But even if the Court finally reaches that conclusion, it will take a good few years to do so. And in that time, we can change enough to fundamentally destroy this culture of conservatism."

I recalled what Rilka Delene had said about Caldor's probable game plan, and this seemed to fit her apprehensions pretty closely. But she hadn't of course seen it with Caldor's revolutionary ambitions.

"Do people know this is what you want to do? And how have you persuaded United and H&P to take this route? Surely there are plenty of what you call conservatives on their boards?"

"You are right, of course. No, very few people know what I intend to do, and many would have been frightened if I had spelled it out. My board colleagues, and the managements of the two companies, see the narrow benefits of being the biggest player in town, but they have as yet no sense of the truly powerful changes we can achieve. They didn't think we would get away with it – nor did I, to be honest – but went along with it because they didn't think it would do any harm. I was playing a longer game; I wanted people to start to get used to the idea and hoped to win a second referendum in a few years' time. But Riccardo's death has wonderfully changed everything."

I looked at Caldor as straight as I could. "Mr Caldor, you have been very interesting and very frank with me. Why have you told me all this? I can go out and write it in the Tribune and probably cause you real difficulties."

He smiled. "Well, yes you can write it. I will of course deny I said anything along these lines. I will say that you are a foreigner who has come here with your own strange ideas, and thanks to these you have completely misunderstood our intentions. A few people might not believe it, but most will either not read your piece or will not care about it. They will want the discounts on their premiums far more than getting worked up about the implications of wild ideas about changing our culture in some way.

"And anyway, I do not think you will write it, at least not in a damaging way. I think you agree with my view, that we are indeed messed up by our negative conservatism. Your reactions will be complicated, and it will be far too difficult to put them down honestly in a journalistic column. So you will wait and bide your time to think about it and get it right. And that will be after the vote."

And that was pretty well the end of the interview. We chatted and joked briefly about the Libance attitude to sex and drugs – I said I hoped he wasn't including these on his list of reforms – and I left.

In many ways Caldor was right about my views. I did agree with much of what he had said, and it would be very difficult to write his ideas up in a way damaging to him. But he didn't seem to have any idea about my connections with Kris Myer and the Guardian chiefs, or if he did, he didn't seem to take these particularly seriously. He certainly had no inkling of my suggestion of using the Senate to block him. I found myself in a rather odd position; intellectually I was inclined to his side, but in practice I was trying very hard to frustrate what his side was trying to do.

Of course I didn't say all this to Friya. I didn't mention the idea that Myer would block the United referendum result if they won, and I didn't go into Caldor's calculations about what I would do with his honest account of his motives, but I summarised the rest. She was more sympathetic than I expected to his criticism of the risk-averse Libance culture.

"That's true, Bob. I have often thought how difficult it must be to get people to agree to new things happening in their own area. But surely Caldor doesn't hope to change things just because he gets away with his merger? How will that work?"

I was actually too tired by then to make his arguments in detail, and we left it in a rather unsatisfactory state. In fact, I was too tired to try very hard to persuade Friya to spend the night with me. She was pretty unreadable on this subject on this occasion, giving away nothing as we said goodbye to each other at the door of the restaurant. She wished me well at the Causeway, said I should give her love to Captain Reinhardt and looked forward to hearing all about when I got back in a week's time. She gave me a surprisingly enthusiastic kiss and strode off to her car, looking back once with a gentle smile on her face. I was suddenly both exhausted and depressed – and too tired to worry about it. I got back, ignored the messages on my screens, went straight to bed and slept what my mother called the sleep of the just. Well, she got that wrong anyway.

Chapter Seventeen

My trip to the Causeway splits nicely into two parts; my time with Reinhardt and his teams, and, a complete surprise, my extraordinary visit to the Island itself. But that comes later.

Travelling north was interesting. It was good just to get out of the capital; but the flight arrangements were strikingly old-fashioned in some ways. Ticketing was online of course, and easy; the claim that it was like taking a bus or train was justified, in that even with hold baggage I didn't need to be there more than half an hour before departure. And that was largely because the security checks were casual to the point of non-existent. No-one asked for my passport or ID card, nor screened the baggage at all. I asked an airline worker why this was, and he was puzzled until I explained that I was 'the European' and that we did things differently over there. It turned out that the security systems they had set up in the last century had fallen into disuse gradually without any adverse consequences.

"Why would anyone want to hijack a plane here?" he asked. (We agreed that the circumstances of my own unintended arrival were irrelevant, since I'd been on an Air France flight.) "We don't have any political terrorists of the kind you describe, nor religious ones either. Nor criminals – what would anyone gain by taking over a flight?" I couldn't answer that question, once again. It did frequently seem that Libance had all kinds of mundane advantages over life in the rest of the world.

We touched down at a small northern airport, and I was in my hired car within 15 minutes. It was decidedly cooler up here – Friya had rightly advised me to take some heavier clothing – but the countryside was pleasantly green, with a few small farms here and there. God knows how their inhabitants survived without any government subsidies: I made a note to ask about this when I next had a conversation with someone who might have an answer. The airport served a town that lay inland, but my route took me away from it.

After half an hour of driving without meeting another car, I found myself on the main road between the Causeway and the south, with a bit more traffic on it, though nothing like what we had even in the remoter parts of Europe. After another twenty minutes I entered a village, with a number of new developments, mostly warehouses. The Causeway wasn't signposted, but it didn't matter since the main road took me to what was clearly the security headquarters: a large modern block dominating the small central square. The sea could be seen behind the buildings; and so could the Island itself, looking much nearer, and much bigger, than I had imagined.

While its nearest point was considerably less than a kilometre away, the Island's coastline ran rapidly towards the horizon in both directions. My view was limited by the village buildings, but I could make out wooded low hills rising from the coast, with no obvious sign of either dwellings or traffic. Not that the fine drizzle that met me as I got out of the car improved the perspective much.

I had stopped in what looked like the main car park just off the square, though it wasn't very full, considering it was early afternoon. I was booked into the main hotel in the area, but I wanted to touch base with Reinhardt if possible and confirm a schedule for the next couple of days before I checked in there.

Given that the only firm arrangement had been an interview with him at nine thirty the next morning, I was lucky: he turned out to be available when reception called him on my arrival. He came down himself to collect me and made a favourable instant impression. He was a man of middling height and build, in his mid to late 30s, with thinning brown hair; but he had a powerful presence, with twinkling eyes, a strong handgrip, and a firm but cheerful smile. "Welcome to this Godforsaken outpost," he said. "I've heard a lot about you – and I have even read a couple of your articles. Come upstairs and have something to drink."

"You've certainly made your mark," he said as he loped up the stairs. "I've had phone calls from Friya Alling, Governor Delene and the Tribune features desk, all pressing me to help you and telling me what a good man you are. Not sure anyone can quite live up to all that."

We sat down in his office, an undistinguished medium-sized space with basic furniture and equipment. He kept it reasonably tidy, though there were three piles of papers on his desk. He saw me looking round and summing it up in my head, and he smiled.

"Not the best office in the world," he said. "But then we share our space with three other outfits. When you're here for three months in twelve there's no point in personalising anything. It's been like this for years; I can't remember when it was last painted. Last time I was here I was a junior officer and just had a busted locker for myself. At least everything in this room locks up, and I have a spare seat for visitors."

He poured out some tea from a flask. "I'm not short-changing you," he said. "We've still got our date tomorrow morning. But let's use half an hour to work out a schedule for you now. How long have you got and what do you want to do?"

I said I guessed the main thing, apart from talking to him and some of his men, was the twice-weekly market, the next session of which I knew would take place in two days' time. Reinhardt said I was in luck: the Island market people would be led by Xerxes, one of their chiefs; he had got to know him on his previous tours of duty, and he was sure he would be happy to talk to me. I was about to press him on how the Islanders organised themselves but decided that would be better when we had a longer session the next day. Instead, we used our time to work out which of the Guardian security troopers I should meet. We shook hands and I left to collect my car.

My hotel was pretty basic. My room wasn't much bigger than the one I'd had at the Guardian Central prison when I'd first arrived, and not as neatly designed. I booked myself dinner, largely because Friya had warned me that there were no restaurants in the village, not because the advertised menu was in any way compelling, and wandered out to explore.

It was a strange place. There had clearly been nothing here until relatively recently. Apart from the security HQ there were bleak barracks and flats for the couple of hundred security troopers and their support staff; the handful of warehouses I saw on my way in; and perhaps half a dozen streets of modest homes, with three shops, a small bank and an even smaller post office in the square. The village was situated on a small hill above the sea; beneath it, and built out over the beach, was the large but cheaply constructed market hall. On one side of the hall was the road leading down from the village; on the other a sort of large barbed-wire tunnel enclosing a track which ran for two hundred metres to the start of the causeway, itself demarcated by an imposing gatehouse, with the sea on three sides of it. (I realised later – it was high tide when I saw it first – that the causeway was exposed on the side facing the Island at low water.) A second open track ran down to the gatehouse from the other end of the village, with a barrier and check point just before it merged with the wire tunnel at the main gatehouse itself.

It was easy enough to guess the functions of the two tracks. The one enclosed in a tunnel was for the Islanders bringing their produce to the market and returning with their purchases; the other for those, presumably, mostly security troopers, going to and from the gatehouse, or, in a very few special cases, being taken out to be left on the causeway.

I walked through the village (the rain getting harder as I went) to the open track and started down it towards the checkpoint. I was about a hundred metres away when a couple of troopers came out of their hut and shouted for me to halt. Their uniforms were similar to those worn by unit 6/7 in SAD Six, but they were more lightly armed, in itself an interesting reflection of the levels of relative danger in the two postings. I decided it was neither the time nor place to start a conversation, and turned back, making an apologetic wave as I did so. Clearly, casual visitors were unusual here.

I had slightly more luck with my attempt to visit the market hall. Here at least I could get to the building and walk part of the way round it. The hall itself was locked, but I could see through one of the windows into the large space, with various unadorned stalls set out in a skeletal fashion. Outside was a very large car park, divided into two by another barbed wire fence. I guessed one was for the Libancers, the other for the Islanders and their vehicles. Both were empty. The spray from the waves crashing against the walls mingled with the rain in a truly disconcerting manner.

As I returned to my hotel, I realised I could see the causeway appearing above the retreating tide. It was wider than I had expected and ran clearly across the narrow sea onto the Island, with the track on the other side briefly visible as it climbed through the woods. But there was still no sign of human life there.

My dinner was poor, but restfully quiet. There were half a dozen other guests, all male: a party of four, and two single diners. All looked at me with varying degrees of curiosity, but none approached or spoke to me. For once I was spared the routine of comparing Libance and Europe. I ate my meal as fast as I could, went up to my room and fell fast asleep.

Chapter Eighteen

My session with Reinhardt the next day was useful and informative, though not quite as much as I had hoped, or indeed, expected. We started in his office, and then went out to the gatehouse, where he eventually handed me over to a couple of his troopers. I must have had a good couple of hours with him.

I certainly got a better sense of the origins of the security operation at the Causeway, which had been going on for more than 20 years. For several years after the original two 'refusenik' families, called Duggan and Fantoni, apparently, had moved to the Island there had been nothing in the way of a control point. However, as the 'outlaw' population grew two things happened: there was internal conflict on the Island itself, and a couple of serious raids on the mainland in which local farmers were attacked, homes burned, fields damaged, livestock stolen. Security teams had on both occasions crossed over and killed those whom they decided were the offenders; not members of the original families, incidentally. However, the National Insurance team, which had handled the second incident, set up a small guard post at the mainland end of the causeway. This had frustrated a third attempt to raid the mainland some months later, but this episode led to the development of another 'security protocol', whereby the big four companies obtained dispensation from the Courts to create a permanent shared arrangement.

Modest to begin with (since it was paid for out of their profits), it grew in size, first to manage both the voluntary and involuntary traffic to the Island, and then, within the past ten years, to handle the markets that sprang up once the Islanders had achieved a reasonably settled existence. It was this latter development which had forced the building of the warehouses, the barracks and the market hall complex; fortunately for the insurance companies, they could recompense themselves in part from levies imposed on the traders.

This rotating Causeway duty was, according to Reinhardt, one of the drearier features of life as a security officer. For a start it was very predictable and very static. Often the most exciting incidents were managing the rows that broke out between the traders, not that there were many of these. With over a hundred troopers in his charge he had to find ways of dealing with the boredom. Fortunately for the sport-inclined, there were playing fields nearby, and the barracks had a gym and small pool. Reinhardt organised regular football competitions of a four-week duration, changing the team compositions for each series. In the evenings there were regular quiz team events; and two sex apartments nearby were kept busy, though the troopers' modest pay rather reduced their ability to indulge themselves as often as many would have liked. A similar issue arose with gambling and gaming – aspirations outran financial capacities. Drugs and drink were less of a problem, in the sense that the Guardian security team code was quite strict in its requirements, but of course the actual problems when a trooper breached them could be more difficult. "In fact, the most challenging part of this job is the amateur psychiatrist one," said Reinhardt. "After my three months here, I will either be a damn good counsellor, or I should be fired."

What surprised me was how little interest Reinhardt showed in what was happening on the Island; neither the daily activity nor the big picture much attracted him. "Look, they are basically wasted people; they have opted out of our society, so they can get on with whatever they want over there without me worrying about it. They can't much affect me, whatever they do. There's maybe three hundred of them over there, the majority adult males, but they don't agree with each other and couldn't organise a concerted attack on us. And even if they did, we massively outgun them."

He said this while we were standing on the edge of the causeway itself, and his statement of fact was visibly no boast. The gatehouse was the most solid construction in the village, a three-storey tower built of large concrete slabs, with heavy automatic weapons installed on both the roof and behind protective slits in the walls of the floor above the gateway itself. Any attackers coming along the causeway would have been massacred. There were two formidable solid gates, one at each entrance to the tower, which would have needed directed artillery hits to demolish them; these were both bolted and locked each night, and when necessary, "not very often," according to Reinhardt, during the day.

I asked whether the Islanders had boats, and whether there had been any raids from the sea. "No raids that I'm aware of," said Reinhardt. "I think they do have a few rafts and rowing boats, possibly even a couple of sailing dinghies, but they have never been seen by the teams here, so I guess they keep them out of harm's way. Of course they have nothing with an engine, since they have no fuel for such a craft. We have two fast motor torpedo boats moored in that boathouse," and he signalled to a building I hadn't really registered before, about half a kilometre away along the beach, "and these do weekly circumnavigations of the Island at a decent distance, just to check nothing threatening, to us, at least, is going on; but they never stop to land on the Island."

All this was pretty complacent, but it sounded justifiable enough; and I turned to the subject I'd nearly raised the day before: how the outlaws organised themselves on the Island. I'd got the size of the place; roughly 15 miles on a north-south axis, and eight miles across east-west, giving roughly three people per square mile, if Reinhardt's estimation of the population was correct. Not exactly crowded, anyway, though possibly nearing the limits of what a disorganised, almost primitive, lifestyle could sustain.

He was annoyingly uninterested in this, to my mind, fundamental aspect of Island life. "I know you want to know about this, and I'm sorry I can't help much. I guess it's because you're a journalist, though I don't recollect any Libancer journalist wanting to delve into it. You can ask Xerxes about it, he'll be here tonight, and we'll have dinner together if you like. All I know is they seem to live in small groups, some with women and children, some men only; that the accommodation is generally rough and ramshackle; that almost all of them grow vegetables, some have chickens, and a few have pigs, cattle or sheep. They bring their surplus products over here twice a week to exchange for stuff they need but can't make or grow themselves – tinned food, clothes, batteries for radios and torches, fuel for heating and cooking, tools like hammers, saws and axes, cheap medicines. Occasionally, a few books, pens and paper, even old-fashioned board games. Since they don't have any gas or electricity, they haven't got any of the consumer electronic equipment that we have grown used to over the past century, except for a few items that can run off batteries, of course. We strictly limit what they can buy and check the wagons going back extremely carefully. And I only know this because I study the trading lists very thoroughly each market day. I really have no idea how they actually get on with each other. There hasn't, as far as I know, been any murder over there in recent years, but even if there has – so what?"

I had to admire, at least in one way, the ruthless manner in which he focussed his attention on only that which he thought he had to; idle curiosity was clearly not one of Reinhardt's qualities. So I asked him about this man Xerxes; how long he'd been an outlaw, how he'd become one of the Islanders' chiefs, did he seem cheerful or was he bitter? That sort of thing.

"God, the questions you ask. You can ask him yourself tonight. I met Xerxes on my last tour here a couple of years ago, chatted to him a bit, and got to know him enough to quite like him. Basically, he comes here with a group of traders once a fortnight. They seem to have sorted out a pattern which keeps the hostilities (between them, not with us) under control, and he is clearly the leader of his little group. I think he went over about ten years ago – don't know why, never asked him – and he seems to have not just survived but got himself into what must pass for a cosy position in that place.

"Maybe he is a good farmer, or maybe a brutal gang leader with some muscle at his command. Maybe both. He is bright enough and strikes good bargains in the market. He clearly keeps in with the Duggan/Fantoni families, who as far as I can tell still have some kind of dominant position on the Island. Apart from anything else their clan occupy most of the big house in the centre of the old estate – Mortimers, it was called, and for some reason still is. But I don't ask questions, and he doesn't volunteer information readily. I think you'll get on with him, but I can't promise he'll open up to you. Libance and the Island have a basic deal – we don't interfere with them if they keep themselves over there, and they don't tell us what they get up to."

And there we left it for the time being. I spent a fairly useless hour with his two troopers, who were OK in an ordinary kind of way but who told me little I hadn't already gleaned from their boss. In the afternoon I stayed in my hotel room sorting out my notes and trying to work out how to deal with this rather fascinating character I was going to meet that evening. At least I was fascinated, even if no-one else in Libance seemed to be.

When I went down in the late afternoon to get some air it was very noticeable how much livelier the place had become. For a start the hotel was full, presumably with traders for the next day's market. The market hall was open, and a medley of sounds drifted up to the village itself. It helped that, though the weather was overcast, it wasn't raining. The Libance side of the car park was three-quarters full, with a mixture of cars and vans and trucks of various sizes; and I noticed that on the Islanders' side there was a couple of what must have been covered horse-drawn wagons, though the horses (if that was what the draught animals were) were being kept somewhere else.

I wandered down to the market hall, and on the spur of the moment went inside. By great good luck one of the security troopers at the entrance was one of the men I had met earlier, and he let me in without a problem. I wasn't at all sure his colleagues would have done the same without his say-so, and I could see why. There must have been a dozen troopers checking lists, rifling through material, asking questions and generally harassing the traders, who were taking all this rather sullenly. It did not appear that harmonious relations existed between them – certainly not that evening.

The hall appeared to be divided unequally between what was obviously the Libance sector and the Islanders' much larger area. The home team, as it were, were piling up the hardware that Reinhardt had described that morning – tins of food, batteries and so on. I found my security chum and asked when the Islanders would arrive to set out their stalls and was told the train of wagons would arrive around nine in the morning. He said they would be assembling at Mortimers that evening and would set off very early the next day – all except Xerxes, who always turned up the night before with his list of the Islanders due to attend the market.

So I went back up to the dinner with a basic idea of these novel arrangements. Reinhardt had booked a small private room in my hotel, and he and the Islander were there chatting when I arrived. Xerxes was a big man in his early 40s, with a great beard and a mass of dark untidy hair. His clothes were old, heavily patched and ill-fitting, and his boots looked very battered.

He had small squinty eyes which looked at me warily as we shook hands. I had half expected to smell the stink of the unwashed, but there was nothing like that. (I learned later that he had a private deal with the security captains to have a bath in the barracks when he came over each fortnight.) "It's good to meet another outsider," was his slightly surprising welcome. "These people think they have all the answers," he said, nodding towards the captain. "At least you will have a different way of looking at things." Reinhardt grinned at him but said nothing.

The meal was no better than the one I had endured the day before, but Xerxes wolfed his food down with enthusiasm. "Proper cooked food," he told me. "When you don't have real ovens, you learn to appreciate their value."

I asked him what kind of meals he had on the Island. "Me? Well, my group make our own cheese. We have enough potatoes for most of the year, and green vegetables for all of it, though they're pretty limited in the winter months. We have boiled eggs at least twice a week. Fruit is abundant though seasonal – we are good at bottling ours, which makes a big difference out of season. Chicken, pork, lamb and beef are occasional, and mostly stewed with vegetables. In fact, most of our daily meals are stews hung over a slow wood fire. A couple of our lads are decent fishermen, and we usually have fish cooked over the fire once a week."

"That sounds very healthy," I said. "What about bread? You haven't mentioned that."

"Nah, we don't grow wheat or any kind of corn. I think there was an attempt once, but no-one seemed to want all the fuss of harvesting, grinding, milling and baking – not with the kind of improvised equipment that's available. We take back loaves and so on from the markets, but they only last a day or so each fortnight. Real treats of course, but not basically part of our diets."

"Why once a fortnight? I thought the markets were twice a week."

Reinhardt interrupted at this point. "Essentially there are six different Island groups that come to the Causeway markets. Xerxes here, and Carl Duggan, they each bring their wagons over every fortnight. But the other days are shared between four smaller groups, who each come once every four weeks."

"And we don't really trade with each other, not for stuff we've picked up here at the Causeway," said Xerxes. "So bread is a luxury."

"Does each group bring the same products with them?"

Xerxes and Reinhardt looked at each other, and Xerxes nodded to Reinhardt.

"Not really. Big groups, like those led by Duggan and Xerxes, bring something of everything that's farmed on the Island – that's why their days are busy each week. But the others are smaller, and their produce is more limited, often no more than the surplus fruit and vegetables they have picked that week."

"In one way we've been very lucky," said Xerxes. "The Mortimers, the family that lived on the Island before the Revolution, did a bit of farming, but basically they maintained the Island as a great hunting estate, full of deer, pheasant and boar. When they quit it became almost wild. Then the Duggans and Fantonis turned up after a few years, and since they were farmers, they started to work it their way. Turns out the climate and the soil are unusually good by comparison with what you find over here on this part of the mainland. The result is that if you put the effort in you can do quite well. Of course, most of the people that came to the Island over the years weren't interested in making much of an effort, at least until they found themselves starving. Even now it's very patchy. Some places are doing OK, others find it all a bit of a struggle."

This seemed like a good moment to ask the question I was so keen to get answered – how did they govern themselves? Especially as they had refused to co-operate with Libance society, which was in many ways the least governed place on earth.

"We don't have a government. Or a leader. There are a dozen or so groups of very different sizes. The biggest lives at Mortimers – that must be over a hundred strong, and it's run by the Duggans and Fantonis. My group has 70 people in it, and we live in twenty huts a few miles from the big house, on the edge of the old estate. Then you get much smaller groups of 20 or so, and I think there are even a few odds and sods living either on their own or in twos and threes.

"Each group has its own rules and way of life, its own leaders. By and large we have learned to live and let live, but you have to be on your guard pretty well the whole time. You never know when you might run across someone who decides to have a go at you."

I wanted to know more, much more; but Xerxes' patience was running out by now, and he suddenly said, "Look here, I don't feel up to this tonight. If you are so interested, why don't you come back with me for a couple of days and see for yourself. I assume," and he looked at Reinhardt at this point, "your men would let him back onto the mainland when he returned?"

Reinhardt looked as surprised as I felt, but he glanced at me, and then shrugged. "If Bob Rowgarth wants to put himself in your hands for a few days then I see no reason why we shouldn't let him back. It's a bizarre offer in my view, but then he's a European and, as you say, sees things rather differently from us."

I was taken aback by this sudden offer, and the casual way Reinhardt had agreed to it. I hadn't dreamed of visiting the Island itself, and for a few seconds my flustered amazement must have been obvious. Then all my journalistic instincts kicked in, and I said, sure, great, what a superb idea, let's do it. Both men nodded; Xerxes said I was presumably going to visit the market the next day, but at any rate I should be ready to leave with the wagons at four in the afternoon. And that was it.

We carried on talking, though my mind kept returning to this fantastic opportunity. Luckily they asked me about my experiences thus far, so I could concentrate for a bit on SAD Six, and on the Knowledge Factory visit. Xerxes was particularly interested when I mentioned I thought I'd got Raeburn to agree to a novel schooling arrangement with Rexy's gang; he said giving an education to the forty or so youngsters on the Island was a real problem, but he didn't pursue it much further than that.

Then Reinhardt asked about the prospects for the proposed merger between the United and Health & Prosperity companies, and if I thought Proposition 72 would be carried now the Court had cleared the way. I said it looked as though it might be, though of course I didn't let on about my involvement with the rearguard action being explored by the Guardian executive team. I spoke briefly about my interview with Caldor – Reinhardt was very impressed that he'd asked to see me. I'd expected the captain to share the gloom of Rilka Delene and her friends, but he seemed remarkably relaxed about what might happen, and unworried about any consequences for him and his career. "They can't rewrite the security protocols. It took them ages and several expensive trips to the Courts to get them agreed years ago. They work fine. No-one will want to shake them up. The Guardian security company is the best and will remain so."

I could think of various ways in which this could be excessively complacent, but it was neither the time nor the place to get into that argument. Anyway, Xerxes was looking tired, so we broke up the conversation soon afterwards. I was ready for bed, but Reinhardt stopped me after Xerxes had gone to his room. "I hope you know what you are doing, going off with him tomorrow. It's lawless over there. I don't want to be leading a security troop in to avenge your death in a week's time."

"Look, I accept there is a bit of a risk. But if I stick with Xerxes, which I will, I should be OK. You said yourself there hadn't been any murders there recently, as far as you knew. Xerxes isn't going to want anything to happen which will disrupt his fortnightly visits to the market here. And anyway, I doubt I would have any claims under my insurance on you for help in the circumstances."

That got a grin out of Reinhardt. "No, I guess not. But I don't want Friya or Rilka harassing me for letting you get yourself killed with me standing by and letting it happen."

"I'll write you a note saying you warned me thoroughly and I still chose to go."

"Fair enough."

And we parted on that note. I don't think he was really worried about me for my sake, more for the potential impact on his reputation: but I was guessing that he didn't really think anything untoward would take place. I was quite proud of the way I used the insurance conditions argument to convince him. I was turning into a Libancer, sort of.

Chapter Nineteen

Next morning, I got up early so that I could breakfast and be ready to watch the arrival of the Islanders' wagon train. At around half past eight, I positioned myself on the road above the market hall, with a good clear view of the causeway (which, slightly to my surprise, looked as though the incoming tide would cover it within half an hour). Within a few minutes I suddenly saw a line of carts and wagons appear on the slope of the Island opposite. I counted seven of them, drawn by mules, donkeys, an ox and (a smaller one) two goats. There were also a couple of handcarts being pushed by young men. All the larger carts seemed to be carrying two people; I think there were sixteen outlaws, all male, in all.

They made their way steadily across the causeway, sloshing through the seawater that was continuously encroaching. Fortunately, the weather was overcast but dry, with little wind to whip up the sea. Within ten minutes the train was safely over. The leading wagon was through the gatehouse but stopped 50 metres on the road leading to the market hall and parking area. (I soon realised this was to allow the last handcart to clear the water flooding over the causeway.) Xerxes emerged from the gatehouse with a couple of security troopers with clipboards, and they worked their way down the line of wagons, presumably checking against the list of names he had supplied the previous evening.

After about quarter of an hour, Xerxes came back to the front of the line, and it moved off and into the parking area beside the market hall. Then began the task of unloading the fruit and vegetables and carrying them into the hall, presumably to be laid out on the tables organised the previous night. A number of Libancer traders stood watching – none, noticeably, offering to help. The outlaws had cleared their carts within twenty minutes, and by 9.15am the market was up and running.

As he had promised the day before, Reinhardt collected me from the hotel around 10, and took me down to the market. "For the first hour, both sets of traders wander around checking what each side has available, and making their calculations about what they want and what their priorities are," he said. "Then the Libancers make a set of detailed offers to buy from the Islanders, quoting prices in US dollars. Obviously, there is excess demand for some goods and insufficient for others. The lucky traders then have two choices; they can either increase the notional price by 10 per cent, then another 5, and so on in what is in effect an auction, until they have cleared their wares; or they can produce a list of goods that they want and see if they can get most of these at less than the advertised prices.

"Those Islanders who have at this stage got surplus produce then slowly renegotiate with the Libancers, and at a lower price. This first stage, which looks as though it is about to start, lasts until lunchtime, a moveable feast which can start as early as noon or as late as one thirty."

A trooper sitting on a platform above the loaded tables suddenly rang a bell, and the Libancers, some two dozen of them at least, who had been standing on their side of the line which divided the hall into its two sectors, rushed forward and a burst of noise erupted as the haggling around the Islanders' tables began.

"After lunch, which takes around half an hour, it is the turn of the Islanders to seek out the goods on this side of the market," continued Reinhardt. "Actually a lot of stuff is pre-ordered at a negotiated price, so it doesn't take anything like as long as the morning trading. Look at Xerxes: that's what he will be doing now."

The large outlaw chief was talking to three Libancers in front of tables loaded with cooking oil, batteries, bread, and what looked like a handful of specific items: a couple of pots and pans, some rain-capes, a batch of notebooks. They were comparing lists and prices, and it looked amicable enough.

"The real fun comes around half past two," said Reinhardt. "That's when the exchange of goods takes place. We, the security team, hand out toy currencies to both sides – quite an experience for all of us, since we don't usually handle money in any shape or form. Both sides use these according to the written agreements they have made earlier in the day. It should work perfectly, but it doesn't always – there are sometimes arguments, and what are, in effect, renegotiations. Actually, Xerxes is pretty good on this; he checks the various agreements over lunch to see if there are discrepancies which he can sort out separately before the exchanges actually start. Some of the other groups aren't nearly so efficient.

"In the final hour the Islanders sell off most of what they have left for whatever they can get; their produce won't keep, unlike the goods sold by the Libancers. Then everyone hands back the toy dollars. They clear up, sweep the hall, stack the tables; the Islanders load their carts with their purchases and are ready to be checked out by four or half past at the latest. We look through everything as it goes through the gatehouse. We don't want anyone doing side deals on guns or dynamite. But they are usually all safely back over the water by five at this time of year. In the winter the trading is finished by lunchtime, and the wagons are on their way by two pm; but then the Islanders don't have anything like as much to sell in the winter."

"What about the tides?" I said. "Don't they affect the trading times at all?"

"Not really," said Reinhardt. "There is usually only an hour at high tide when it is seriously difficult to cross the causeway, though it can be worse than this in bad weather. The Islanders vary their coming and going a bit to maximise their trading time, but it never usually stops the market completely. They really need to make it work, as their stuff rots if they miss their turn."

It seemed a rather loaded game to me: the Libancers with goods that weren't going to go bad if they took them back to the warehouse, the Islanders with highly perishable produce, all traded according to a phoney currency. But I reckoned it must be worth it to the Islanders, even if they generally got a poor deal.

I wandered around until mid-day, watching the market activity and trying to get into conversations with the traders: but mostly they brushed me aside, either because they were too busy haggling or because they were suspicious of a European who claimed to be a journalist; neither category was at all attractive to these hard-faced

Libancers. From what I could see the action seemed to bear out Reinhardt's account. I often looked out for Xerxes, but he had disappeared for a good hour, and seemed busy when he got back, so I decided to leave him alone until we set off for the Island. Eventually I did manage to speak to an ageing Libancer for a short while. His life seemed routine: buying greengrocery twice a week at the market, selling it over the next days in the town near the airport, buying the goods he needed to trade once a week and storing them in one of the warehouses, bringing them to market as needed. I learned that the Libancers were licensed by the security consortium, to keep the numbers under control, which suited him. "The Island produce is generally very good, and we effectively get a great price for our stuff, so I make a decent living doing this. The competition is predictable and not very difficult; there's only three of us greengrocers in the town, so no problem there. Much better than when I started, when we didn't have the Island as a supplier." He didn't mention it, but I recalled a comment that Reinhardt had made; the big supermarkets were not interested in this low-rent bartering process. It prompted an intriguing thought about what might be a unique circumstance for preserving traditional small shops.

I grabbed a couple of hours sleep in the early afternoon, since I wasn't at all sure I would get much over the next few days. I spoke to Friya on the phone; she was surprised, shocked, even, when I told her what I was going to do but made no attempt to dissuade me. Reinhardt had lent me a sleeping bag, and on his advice, I was taking four litres of bottled water with me, as well as toilet paper and a torch and batteries. "Just remember they don't have any public facilities or utilities over there. You are going to have a couple of days of a really primitive existence." I left most of my stuff in my big bag at the hotel and had packed what I thought I needed in a rucksack I had bought that morning. I tied the sleeping bag underneath it. I also purchased four bottles of wine as potential gifts for Xerxes. The purchasing was all done electronically, of course.

I went back down to the market hall at 3.30pm, which was just as well since it had finished early, and the Islanders were packed up and were already being checked through the gatehouse by the security troopers. Xerxes had put his wagon at the back of the line and waved me to join him. He introduced me to his companion, a young man of a rather wary disposition. As our goods were checked by the security men there was an exchange of bad jokes about the unusual guest the Islanders had, and that I shouldn't expect to come back any time soon, or indeed at all.

We crossed the causeway in a few minutes, Xerxes and I riding perched on the driving seat, the youngster walking alongside the mule. The tide was out, and the raised road stood well above the sand and pools of seawater. As we started to climb the slope on the other side I looked back and saw the village houses spreading up the hill above the gatehouse. The Libancer traders were themselves leaving the car park, and I could pick out the individual vans and trucks.

I suddenly realised we had been joined by an escort party of around a dozen men, variously armed with clubs and makeshift spears; a couple of men carried bows and quivers full of arrows. They must have been waiting for us out of sight on the hill. Xerxes saw my surprise. "Don't worry," he said. "We are very unlikely to run into trouble. But if we didn't have this protection we would risk being attacked. For some of our friends the temptation to get their hands on what we've got in our carts might be too much."

This was my first insight into the way in which the Islanders felt compelled to live, constantly on their guard. Over the next 48 hours I would regularly notice this characteristic. As it turned out, there was a kind of stable equilibrium on the Island, but it was hard won and undoubtedly brittle.

Though everyone I met was curious about me, they didn't express any views about my presence once they knew Xerxes had personally invited me. The apparent indifference was in strong contrast to the flood of questions I got from most people on the mainland.

Getting to what I guess I will call the homesteads that housed Xerxes' people took over two hours of steady walking, so that we arrived about an hour before sunset. (Not that there was one to see in the grey cloudy sky.) The track was clearly visible all the way, understandably so when I realised it was in regular use each week. However, it was very rutted, with the wagons and carts trying as best they could to stick to the most convenient wheel tracks. We passed at least two makeshift camps that I could see, both of them some way off from the track: Xerxes said they were the homes of two small groups of outlaws. I could make out a few chickens near one of them, and patches of what seemed to be cultivation, but no people. Apparently, there was no friendship between either of them and Xerxes' group, so no-one wanted to come out and wave a greeting, though Xerxes reckoned a couple of men from each camp would have been hidden near the track, watching the return of the market wagon train.

Xerxes was far more forthcoming than he had been the day before and indeed, he continued in this relaxed mood through most of my two and a half days on the Island. I learned he had been 'offered' the Island by a team of security troopers eleven years earlier, after a long sequence of trouble with the various security companies. His parents had split up soon after he was born, and he had been brought up in a provincial town by his mother and, since this was before the Revolution, with irregular maintenance payments from his father. His mother had remarried quite quickly, and she soon produced a couple of half-siblings.

His stepfather had soon resented what he had felt was his subsidising of his stepson's upbringing. (Listening to Xerxes' account, it dawned on me that this must be a regular phenomenon in Libance life, and I made a note to write a future article on the subject.) The boy had gone to a rough school, where the combination of his own negative attitudes and his parents' indifference meant he left with no qualifications. For the teenager and young adult, the turmoil of the revolutionary years had been 'good fun', in his words, but when the country began to settle down, he found he was worse off – no settled job, a wrong attitude and now no welfare state to help him. By the time Xerxes was in his mid-twenties his stepfather had grown tired of his mother helping him and had got him put in gaol.

I could have predicted the subsequent pattern. Enforced labour, badly done; refusal to undertake any formal education; spells of tough living on the streets, punctuated with increasingly acrimonious returns to various prisons; decreasing engagement with the minimum requirements of Libance society (insurance policies in particular).

Eventually his performance was assessed by the security 'forum', the partnership of the insurance firms and their security teams which met regularly to look at the hard cases their teams were dealing with, and this group had decided that dumping him on the Island was the only course available. (It was the first I had heard of this organisation, and I made another note for a future subject.)

Xerxes had known no more about the Island at that point than most Libancers; he had never contemplated being forcibly sent there. He had been shocked and frightened by the decision but in a way it had been the making of him. By great good fortune he had been picked up by some of the Fantoni men when he had walked across the causeway (after sitting in a sulky panic for a couple of days outside the original unfortified gate which marked the boundary of Libance). It was at the height of one of the wars between the farmer families and the criminal gangs that had plagued the early years of the outlaw regime, and the farmers needed every new hand they could get.

Now Xerxes' years as a streetfighter were a help rather than a hindrance. He acquitted himself well in a couple of violent incidents soon after his arrival at Mortimers, and, by the time (a few months later) that the farmer families had imposed themselves on the remnants of the gangs, he had become the number two to Carl Duggan, the farmers' hard man. "They were interesting times," Xerxes told me. "The Duggans and Fantonis had brought a number of rifles and hand guns over with them years earlier, but of course they found it very hard to replace the ammunition." (I would have thought it would have been impossible, but something about Xerxes' manner at that point in our conversation persuaded me I shouldn't pursue this topic.) "So it was a basic rule that the guns were kept at the big house, and used very sparingly on the odd occasion that a gang chose to attack the buildings. We never took them out on raids, in case we were beaten, and some gangster would have the present of a gun and a few bullets. This meant we were little better armed than our opponents, which certainly tested our abilities."

He never gave me a systematic history of the endemic violence, though his individual anecdotes were vivid enough, but I got a rough understanding of the way life on the Island worked. Essentially the two original families chose those new arrivals that they reckoned would fit in with their highly patriarchal regime at the big house, and let the others go off and create their own camps well away from the main estate. (They chose almost all of the small number of women who had either made their way to the Island or had been dumped there.) The numbers living in and around the big house grew: children were born, but a greater increase came from the newcomers the two families accepted over the years. The farming was reasonably well organised, and the trading across the causeway raised the quality of life from very primitive to a bit better than subsistence.

About four years ago there had been a new kind of crisis: the numbers were becoming too great for effective management by the family elders, and tensions increased. Xerxes struck a deal with the two original families: he would take about a third of the group living in and around the big house and move to what had been a small hunting lodge, by then rather derelict, a couple of kilometres away on the edge of the estate. Their way of life would be run more openly, but they would be committed allies of the Mortimers regime, and would fight alongside them if any violence broke out with the other outlaw camps. The Duggan-Fantonis agreed; they provided the breakaway group with tools, bedding, basic furniture and plants and seeds, and a few animals. Xerxes and his motley troop moved out over a month or so, putting up tents and shacks around the ramshackle lodge, and then worked hard to create vegetable gardens within the negotiated boundaries. "I had had my eye on this ground for a while," said Xerxes. "I thought it could do the job, and I was right."

The first couple of years of independence had been very hard. Although it had been the more adventurous spirits that had opted to join him, some people cracked under the strain and went back to the big house; another dozen had died, some of whom might have survived if they had stayed at Mortimers. But then came the turning point: they had an excellent food-growing season, Xerxes' trading skills secured them enough essential stuff in the markets, four children were born and survived, "an immense psychological boost, even to the great majority of men who hadn't had anything to do with it"; and the new settlement began to become something like a living community.

I got a quick sense of the homesteads when we arrived, but a fuller one the next day. The core was the partially ruined hunting lodge, which had some dozen rooms in use, with another three derelict rooms in which rough shelters had been rigged up. In addition, there were three old bathrooms – no running water, of course – where people took water from the nearby well to wash themselves in a disciplined rotation almost every day. (The well had been built at the same time as the lodge, over a hundred years earlier.) Around a third of Xerxes' group lived, or at least slept, in these rooms. The rest lived in tents and rough-built shacks around the lodge. These were scarcely weather-proof: Xerxes told me that on several occasions in the past four years heavy rains had driven everyone into the lodge, where everyone crammed together, wet and miserable for days on end. However, for most of the time people endured the conditions outside; most of the tents and shacks had raised wooden decks on which the sleeping bags or bedding were laid, which kept them dry enough.

They had dug out two sets of latrines, the larger of the two for men and the smaller for the few women and young children. Each day the waste was collected and carried off to pits at the far end of the settlement, and the latrines were washed through. Nonetheless the smell was pretty strong, though the inhabitants had clearly grown accustomed to it.

Cooking was done in two places: inside the lodge in bad weather, and in a much bigger area outside when it was dry. At first they had kept a fire going continuously, but had soon realised that they were using up the local timber far too quickly, and now only lit the fires on Saturdays and Sundays, a strange (and isolated) celebration of 'weekends', which seemed to recall days-off that had once meant something to them. Vegetable stews and soups were cooked in a couple of giant metal pots, and eaten over the following days, either reheated in pans over portable gas cookers (if Xerxes had traded enough canisters at the causeway market) or supped cold. Tinned food brought back from the market was a regular supplement, often consumed cold as well. Everyone ate together at big communal tables, and the entire population was fed in two shifts three times a day. I discovered Xerxes had been exaggerating considerably in his description (at the dinner with me and Reinhardt) of regular cooked meals of fish and meat; these happened very rarely (though I think a bit more often with the Duggan-Fantoni clan at Mortimers). His group had at least twenty chickens, and a half a dozen cows; they made crude cheese each day, which with a couple of eggs a week per person furnished their breakfasts. The loaves they brought back from the market were eaten within a couple of days. For the rest of the time they ate dry biscuits, purchased each fortnight.

It was a readily obvious irony that these people, who had almost all rebelled against the particular way that ordinary Libance individualism worked, now had to live in a profoundly collective manner in order just to survive. When I made the point to Xerxes he laughed and shrugged. "OK, so it is much, much harder here than on the mainland. And yes, we have very predictable routines which we all have to follow. But we are truly free here; no giving up half our income to the insurance companies just to keep going. No security troopers keeping us in line." I didn't find this convincing, but it was interesting that over the couple of days I spent in the settlement no-one seriously groused or indicated they would have liked to go back to the mainland.

(In fact, I found out later, when I was back in Libance, that a few people did manage to return to mainland life each year. Neither Reinhardt nor Xerxes had mentioned it, but once a year penitent Islanders put themselves forward for return: they were assessed by a panel of the four security companies, their relatives and friends in Libance were contacted and, depending on the results and the assessments, a few were allowed to go back home. I found no evidence that any of these 'returners' had subsequently misbehaved and been put back on the Island again.)

The men all had beards, the length varying according to age; obviously shaving was an unnecessary luxury in terms of razor blades, shaving cream and water. And it was striking how ragged both men and women were. Both sexes dressed in patched-up jackets, sweaters and trousers, adding or taking off layers according to the temperature and the weather. Essentially everyone was almost always cold at night, and truly warm only in the summer sunshine. A persistent, strong, stale smell hung around everyone I met; Xerxes may have benefited from his bath at the causeway inn, but his clothes were as scruffy and unwashed as everyone else's.

When we got to the settlement Xerxes took me to a smallish tent outside the lodge, and introduced me to its inhabitants, two middle-aged men and a younger one in (I would guess) his late 20s. Caleb, Rigby and Dieter were the only names I was given, the older two having been on the Island for ten or more years, while Dieter was a relative newcomer, having been dumped on the causeway three years earlier. They were surly and suspicious, having had no inkling of my impending arrival. However, Xerxes explained my exotic background, and in effect ordered them to treat me civilly for the two days I would be their guest.

I now wished I had thought to bring a few tins of food or beer with me. I had already given Xerxes his wine but I hadn't given much consideration to how, and with whom, I would be lodged. In fact, the three of them gradually got used to me. I was very prudent in my behaviour and forewent my usual journalistic eagerness to ask a string of questions, so that by the time I left we were, if not bosom friends, at least on reasonable terms. At any rate they made room for my sleeping bag and kit on the rough wooden deck of the tent.

I found that, in between the conversations with Xerxes (which happened whenever he felt like having them), I was expected to share the work of my three hosts. By good luck this didn't include (in the time I was there) cleaning out the latrines. On both days we got up at sunrise and joined the long queue for the two bathrooms in the lodge, having collected a bucket of water from the well first, and taking a second empty bucket to catch the dirty used water when we had finished. I carried this with Dieter, the younger man, what felt like a good half mile to a specific place in the vegetable gardens and dumped it on a patch of carrots. On our return we joined another queue to collect breakfast; boiled egg, cheese and bread brought from the causeway market the day before, and a mug of black instant coffee, and took this to join one of the long tables full of people outside.

All this took nearly two hours. At eight o clock on the first day Dieter and I went out back to the area where we had taken the dirty water, picking up hoes from a store en route. Caleb and Rigby would normally have joined us but today they were part of the team taking the wagons and animals used the previous day back to Mortimers. (Apparently this was a regular arrangement – the Duggan-Fantoni clan kept almost all the transport on the Island.) We spent a couple of hours steadily weeding the rows of vegetables; I counted at least a score of men dotted around us doing the same thing.

Mid-morning we had a break. I was stiff from all the unusual exercise. After half an hour we should have gone back to the hoeing and weeding, but it began to rain and the others grabbed their tools and ran back to the lodge, with me inevitably bringing up the rear. There everyone packed into the lodge itself and sat around chatting or playing cards, and Xerxes took me off to what turned out to be his room for a long talk. After an hour or so, the rain stopped, and Xerxes said I ought to get back to work – he smiled as he did so – and I found my three companions (the older two had got back from Mortimers by now) in a small gang cleaning and maintaining the weapons in the settlement's so-called 'armoury'.

I counted at least fifty spears of varying quality and all roughly made, most of them with what seemed like big, long nails fastened crudely into stout branches that had been cut into shafts at least seven feet long. There were hundreds of arrows, similar in design to the spears but with much shorter and smaller shafts, though the nail-like points looked the same as those used for the spears. There were perhaps twenty bows, most of them home-made; I did notice two professional-looking jobs and wondered where they had come from. Caleb said the bows were effective at distances of thirty yards or so. The arrows lost momentum rapidly thereafter, but he had seen three men killed at that distance in his time on the Island. Finally, there was an array of crude clubs, lumps of wood of various lengths, some with nails jutting out from them at their head ends. In addition, there were several axes, hand saws, hammers and other tools, and a sharpening stone. It was all carefully arranged and logged; Xerxes, or one of his lieutenants, issued weapons to those on guard duty each day, and collected them in, and locked them up, each night. Then they handed out weapons to the night watch and repeated the collection and logging process in the morning. I assumed the padlocks and keys had been purchased at the market.

Half of this armoury had been brought with them from Mortimers; the rest had been added since. Xerxes and his four lieutenants all had big proper knives – no-one quite knew where these had come from – and there was a suspicion that Xerxes had a revolver, though no-one had actually seen him with it. The outlaws who lived in the smaller camps around the Island had their own versions of these weapons, though on a much smaller scale. There hadn't been any actual fighting or raiding for well over a year: the last occasion had been when a gang of six men had stolen some vegetables at night, and Xerxes had led a punitive force against them. It might have been difficult to know which particular gang was guilty but one of the raiders had torn his jacket and left some distinctive fabric behind. (This surprised me – nearly all the ragged clothing they wore looked indistinguishable, but apparently this garment was bright yellow and well known.) Twenty-five men equipped with clubs, spears and bows had gone to a small camp five miles away and killed all six inhabitants, recovering most of the vegetables when they were there.

I was appalled when I heard this. Six men killed for stealing vegetables! My reaction must have shown: Caleb grinned (sort of) and asked what I thought Xerxes' squad might have done instead. I stuttered something about seeking payment of some kind, but this was greeted with derision by the others in the armoury. Later I raised it with Xerxes, who said simply that killing was the only deterrent; anything less and their farm grounds would have been raided regularly.

At midday we broke for the communal lunch of vegetable stew. Xerxes called me over to sit with him and his 'wife', a woman called Lee who must have been in her thirties. She had a two-year-old daughter with her, by the name of Elsa. At first, I assumed the father was Xerxes, but it eventually became clear that this might not be true. Lee told me (after Xerxes had left us to talk on our own) that any one of four men could have been the parent.

The picture I got of life for the few women in the settlement was bizarre, a kind of mix of sex-slavery and feminist independence. Most of them had a man who was regarded as their 'husband', usually someone senior in the gang, who effectively protected them. However, they were expected to share their sexual favours around, though I never quite understood the basis on which they did this. It wasn't prostitution as such – no payments were possible – and the women appeared to choose their partners most of the time, but it did appear that on occasion individual men who weren't being picked could insist on having their turn, as it were. It seemed that if you hadn't had sex in a month, you could have a woman to fuck on some kind of rotating system. One way or another she had had sex with all the men in the settlement.

Lee had clearly got used to this and didn't find it particularly remarkable. She made the men use condoms (regularly bartered at the market) until she decided she wanted a child, and she kept this up until she conceived. (She had two older children who had stayed on at Mortimers after she decided to move out to the lodge four years previously. She visited them once a week and seemed comfortable enough with the arrangements.) If she felt any particular affection for anyone then she kept it to herself. "It would be too dangerous and disruptive to have an obvious emotional relationship with someone," she told me, "and certainly not with Xerxes."

They shared some of the daily work with the men, preparing and cooking the food, rough cleaning the shacks and rooms, washing up and so on, but they didn't do any of the farming, nor did they clean the latrines. However, they did collectively look after the children during the day and had the responsibility for teaching them both the rules of the community and basic reading, writing and arithmetic. They took it in turns to sleep in the children's dormitory, with the job of dealing with any night-time disturbances.

"Actually we develop our strongest emotional relationships with other women," she said. "That doesn't get in the way of surviving, though it can lead to occasional problems when two women fall out with each other. And yes, we do have sex with each other sometimes." I didn't really get the chance to discuss the prevalence or otherwise of homosexuality in the camp; Lee indicated there were three or four men who were suspected of it, but the prevailing ethos ruled out any open displays of affection, whether straight or gay.

That struck me as one of the most important aspects of Island life: the effective prohibition of any one-to-one deep relationships, certainly for the men. They had to work to regular routines, nearly always in teams; survival did indeed depend on it. Rivalries and competitive instincts were suppressed or contained. People who had been sent to the Island because they wouldn't conform to mainland life found themselves having to subscribe to an even harsher collective system.

After lunch I went back to the hoeing and weeding for another couple of hours, as the rain had stopped, and then we had time to ourselves. Xerxes called me up for another long conversation about both his life and the way the Islanders organised themselves. He had a small room of his own, with a narrow bed and some basic furniture, including a safe, and a small table and a couple of chairs. It was, as he said, a combination of office, living room and bedroom.

What turned out to be the main event of the day came next. At around six o clock all seventy or so outlaws assembled for the daily meeting in an open space outside the lodge. People brought waterproof sheeting or just blankets to sit on the ground in a rough semi-circle facing a table and five chairs, where Xerxes sat, flanked by his lieutenants. I parked myself with Caleb and the others towards the back.

Xerxes opened the meeting by introducing me, obliging me to stand up so everyone could see me. "This is Bob Rowgarth, a European journalist who is seeking asylum in Libance." There were murmurs and grunts of astonishment at this. "Yeah, I know, asylum. You might think it refers to a madhouse. Actually, it means a safe haven – somewhere that you can live because you are too frightened to live in your own country. I don't know what Mr Rowgarth is frightened of, and why he thinks Libance might be a better place to live" – this won more grunts and a couple of hoots of derision – "but anyway he writes articles and makes TV shows and people on the mainland seem to think he is pretty good at this. I met him at the Causeway and suggested he should come here and see how we live; he might be able to write us up and get rid of a few of the mad ideas Libancers have about us."

Xerxes waved for me to sit down, and then got on with the meeting proper. Various men and women got up and gave reports in turn on the areas they had worked in that day, answering a few questions prompted by their remarks. Then one of the lieutenants read out the list of duties for the next day and answered, or tried to, various comments and even a couple of protests, though Xerxes brushed these aside. Finally, he offered the chance for anyone to say anything they wanted to, an offer which was declined. (I gathered later this was the general pattern, unless some kind of emergency had happened.) Then everyone got up, picked up their sheets and either wandered off to their tents or rooms, or hung around chatting and talking.

Soon afterwards everyone was back for the evening meal – vegetable stew again. I took the chance to talk to other outlaws, and though their individual stories had their particular details they essentially followed very similar narratives. The overwhelming impression I got was of resigned acceptance of a dull, hard and uncomfortable existence. Only a couple of younger men echoed Xerxes' claim that Island life was freer and better than their former lives on Libance.

By eight the light was fading, and most people started to drift back to their bed areas. I thought I might get another session with Xerxes by torchlight but he had disappeared and I decided it would be more sensible to go to bed myself. I chatted briefly to a couple of the nightwatchmen – they made it clear this was the most boring job of all – and then got back to Caleb and his companions in their tent. By nine they were all asleep and snoring, and, rather to my surprise, I too dropped off pretty quickly. I was clearly wiped out by the unusual physical exertions of the morning.

Chapter Twenty

Next morning, I went through the same washing and watering routines with Dieter and had the same breakfast as the day before. It was a sunnier day, however, (though still not very warm), and I had an idea that would be slightly tricky to pull off. I had, very quietly and discreetly, been filming life in the homestead with the camera phone the TV station had given me. There wasn't that much since it was very difficult to use the camera without being noticed. On the previous day I had spotted a small hill a shortish distance from the gardens where we had been working, with a clearing at its summit, and it had given me an idea.

I hadn't been able to get a signal hitherto on the Island, not surprisingly, but I thought it might be worth a try on the hill-top; and if I succeeded, I could email the films to the Metro people. So, when we took a break from our weeding the beans in the garden area at around ten o'clock, I told Caleb I was going for a piss, and would be back shortly. Of course, it would take me far longer than that to climb the hill and make the call, but I reckoned I could deal with any consequences when I got back.

I strode off into the woods, and as soon as I was out of sight I ran as fast as I could through the trees and then up the hill. It was sometimes tough going as there were no paths, and the undergrowth was occasionally difficult to get through, but after some twenty minutes I reached the clearing at the top. I worked my way round to the opposite side of the hill, as I didn't want one of the gardening outlaws to glance up and see me, and switched on my phone. To my relief and surprise, I got a signal, but for some reason couldn't get the TV folk at any of the Metro numbers I had. So I tried, and got, Friya on her mobile at work.

"Bob, what a surprise. How wonderful to speak to you. What are you doing on the Island? Are the bad guys treating you properly?"

and so on, for longer than I needed at that particular juncture. I told Friya I wanted to send her the sequences I had taped and asked her to send them on to my Metro contact. She was very excited at this and promised to do it straightaway. I was just about to switch to mailing the clips when she remembered something exciting of her own to tell me. "Something very astonishing has happened. Kris Myer has called for a mass boycott of the Proposition 72 referendum, the one on the insurance merger. He said we needed a Voters' Strike. What do you think of that? Everyone is talking about it here."

"Yeah, I knew he would. I suggested it. It was my idea."

That set her off into yet more excitement, but I managed to cut her short by saying my batteries were running low and I needed to download the sequences quickly. Fortunately, the contention ratios in the north were not a problem, and I finished faster than I expected. I told Friya I was returning the next day and we agreed to meet the following evening for dinner.

Caleb and his colleagues were very suspicious when I rather breathlessly came back out of the woods nearly an hour after I had left them. I said I had seen some wild boar, had followed them for a while until they had suddenly sped off, and then had struggled to find my way back. I doubt that any of them believed me, but Caleb just said that Xerxes wanted to see me urgently and I should go back to the lodge. They sullenly said they didn't know why, and rather obviously turned their backs on me to continue with their work.

I found Xerxes in his room. His mood was decidedly unfriendly. "Where the hell did you disappear to?" he said without ceremony. I didn't try the wild boar tack but said I had strolled up the nearby hill to get some sense of the neighbouring areas. "And what about our friendly neighbours? Meet any of them, did you?"

"I saw no-one. And I didn't expect to."

"On this Island no-one just wanders off to look at the view. It is very dangerous, in more ways than one. You could have run into people who would have no idea who you were and what you were doing: and in such circumstances they would kill you rather than ask you questions."

I tried to protest that I had seen absolutely no-one, but he simply carried on.

"Alternatively, it would be very dangerous for you because you met some of our neighbours by pre-arrangement. And any such pre-arrangement would necessarily be a hostile act as far as I and my people were concerned."

"Oh, come on. How could I have made any such arrangements? I hadn't intended coming here until you suggested it three days ago. And I haven't been out of sight since then until now."

"How do I know how long you had been at the Causeway? You could have made a deal with that rabble that went to market last week."

"That's fantastic. Reinhardt himself told you I had only been there a couple of days. Is he in this conspiracy too?"

Xerxes simply looked at me. "I have a very good reason for doubting your word. And I don't believe you climbed that hill just to see the view. You had better come up with a better explanation."

I was becoming very uncomfortable. I realised I had taken Xerxes and his regime rather too lightly. I was definitely not in a civilised Libance home or office here. The outcome of this conversation could be very serious indeed.

I took out my camera phone from my jacket pocket and put it on the table.

"OK, you are right. I went up the hill to see if I could get a signal for my phone. I did, and I had a conversation with a woman I am friendly with. Look, you can see the number I called." And I switched it on and pressed the recall button.

Xerxes picked up the phone and studied it. It only then occurred to me that he might know nothing about the latest mobile phone technology, since he had been out of circulation, as it were, for more than ten years, and they had moved on rather a lot in that period. "It's much more than just a phone," I said rather too eagerly. "You can send and receive emails, surf the web, take pictures, get the latest news."

"Show me," he said. So I did, or at least as much as I could, given there was no active signal in the lodge. I had not intended to reveal the filming I had done in his camp, but when I told him how you could take pictures, he started to play around with it, and suddenly saw the frames I had been taking in the past two days.

"So, Mr Journalist, you have been busy here I see. Very nice and interesting pictures of our home here. And no-one knew you were doing this. Even more important, I think, no-one gave you permission to do it."

I had no answer to that.

"How do you get the power for this? Batteries?"

I explained about the charger; when he pressed me, I pulled it out my bag. "I'm afraid it won't work here. You don't have any electricity."

He picked up the plug and cable. "No, but I could of course recharge the batteries every two weeks at the Causeway hotel." He looked at me. "Whatever it was you were doing on the hill, I don't think I approve of it. How can I, since you didn't tell me about this camera and the pictures you were taking? However, you cannot have been contacting anyone on this Island, since no-one has such equipment, and as you say, the call you made is shown here, and the time you made it. So we do not have to kill you. However, I must keep this smart little gadget and its charger. And as you also say, I can at least keep up with the news, even if I have no-one else to talk to.

"You will leave tomorrow first thing. The men from the north camp are coming to collect a couple of wagons from Mortimers today, and I have arranged for them to pick you up after breakfast on the way to the Causeway."

I was shaking as I made my way back to the empty tent where my sleeping bag was. The casual reference to killing me truly unnerved me. I was very lucky that Xerxes had taken such a fancy to the mobile. It wouldn't be of much use to him that I could see, but clearly he liked the idea of having one, the more so since even the Duggans and Fantonis wouldn't have anything like it. And I wondered about the deal with the men from the north camp. When had he done that?

I had calmed down a little when the tent flap was pushed back, and Lee came in.

"You have been in real bad trouble," she said. "But I am glad to learn that Xerxes is not going to punish you."

"Not half as glad as I am."

"I expect not. In fact, he feels he has been a little harsh on you, So he has sent me to you in compensation."

It took me a moment to understand what she meant. "Sent you to me? And what are you – we – supposed to do?"

She grinned, and pulled her jacket off, and then her sweater. "What do you think? Or are you not interested in me?" Now she was completely naked above the waist, with her ample breasts bobbing around cheerfully. She grabbed me and pulled me to her. She felt me through my jeans. "Oh yes, you are interested. That's good."

My head was whirling at the roller-coaster of events. I had been very close to being executed, and now I was being offered a free fuck.

Fortunately, I coped.

Chapter Twenty-one

Lee and I were having a cup of instant coffee, sitting at one of the long tables outside the lodge kitchen (this seemed to be a privilege she could exercise occasionally) and chatting away cheerfully when a sudden commotion caught her attention.

"My God, they have got Daguerre and Christiansen." Two men were being noisily dragged towards the lodge by four armed guards. I couldn't make out what they were shouting about, other than that the two men were volubly denying something or other, and they disappeared inside the building.

She had gone pale. "I didn't believe Xerxes would do this," she said. I tried to ask her what she was on about, but she rose and refused to answer. "Can't tell you now – maybe later," and she too disappeared into the building. Men were running towards us from the fields where they had been working, and women and children tumbled out of the lodge itself. Everyone was shouting and gesticulating, but I still couldn't make out the reasons. More armed guards appeared and prevented anyone from entering the main building.

Slowly I began to understand that the two men had been in effect arrested, and seemed to be accused of betraying the settlement to hostile camps. It wasn't at all clear what they had precisely done, but it did seem as though there would be an immediate trial of some kind later that day. The crowd were divided in their reactions, some refusing to believe the two men could have done anything wrong, others uncertain, and the rest – almost half, I would guess – assuming they must be guilty. I saw Caleb standing and arguing with a group of men, and went up to him. He still seemed suspicious of me and wasn't that interested in explaining anything in detail, if indeed he could have done.

"There will be a trial, after lunch, probably." I asked about procedures, who would be prosecution, who the judge, what kind of jury. He laughed. "We will be the jury, for what that is worth. Xerxes and his lieutenants will be prosecutors and judges. Daguerre and Christiansen will defend themselves. And then they will be executed." Then he returned to his argument with his mates.

After my experiences over the past couple of hours that did indeed seem a likely outcome. A man came out of the building and said people should get what lunch they could and be ready for the trial in an hour. The normal meal discipline had broken down; some people did manage to find bowls and a pot of cold vegetable stew, but I didn't bother to join them. I wandered off to the side and sat on a rough log. No-one was interested in me; they were all in a state of considerable excitement.

After a while Lee came out of the lodge and went and joined a group of women. She spoke earnestly with them, then spotted me, and after another couple of minutes broke away from her group and came over to me. "It's as bad as I feared. Xerxes saw a couple of men from the far northern camp yesterday – they were on their way to Mortimers to collect some wagons – and it seems like they tipped him off about a couple of our guys who had been in contact with them over several weeks, promising to let them have some of our produce in return for drugs. God knows how the north campers get hold of drugs, if indeed they do, but anyway Xerxes took it seriously and checked out people's movements over the past couple of months. It turns out only Daguerre and Christiansen have been away from the lodge on their own for long enough to get to the north camp and back in this time. They were supposed to have been going to Mortimers a few weeks ago, but late last night Xerxes went up to the big house and they denied having seen them."

"That is highly circumstantial," I said. "Surely they can't be convicted, let alone executed, on evidence as skimpy as that."

"Don't know what 'circumwhatsit' means but believe me those guys are as good as dead now. Of course, what makes it worse is that there is a rumour starting that they are gay, which won't make them very popular with our crowd."

"Jesus, that probably explains what they were really doing when they were out of camp here. Giving each other a good buggering, I bet."

Lee looked thoughtful. "Well, why should the north campers make up this story if you are right?"

"There are various ways of answering that. First, how do you know the northerners did tell Xerxes anything? You've only his word for it. Second, the northerners could be trying to stir up trouble, and picked on two men, who they knew would be suspect anyway, and peddled a pack of lies about them. Then again maybe they are telling the truth, but the real villains have been very smart, and Xerxes has simply got the wrong guys."

"Pity you aren't defending Daguerre and Christiansen. Which reminds me, Xerxes said to tell you that you weren't going to be allowed to attend the trial. You will be taken to one of the back rooms in the lodge and kept there under guard while it is going on. I think he thinks you might have another camera hidden somewhere and he certainly doesn't want this trial being broadcast across Libance."

How did she know about my camera phone? Had Xerxes told her?

And so it was. I spent more than three hours stuck in a small room, though it looked as though eight people usually slept in it, on that dramatic afternoon. The door didn't lock – nothing much did around here – so a couple of men with spears kept guard. They were as pissed off as I was about missing the excitement. We also missed the killing of the two men, but I was glad of that.

I got a couple of versions of what happened later, from Caleb over dinner, and from Lee after dinner, when she took me for a walk around the lodge and its immediate grounds. "Xerxes is pretty mad with me," she said, "but he's feeling vulnerable right now. I don't think he expected so many people to protest about their innocence both at and after the trial. He has got too much to worry about without picking on me for taking you for a walk."

"Why should he want to do that anyway? I thought it was his idea that you should be nice to me. Compensation, you called it this morning."

She screwed her eyes up at this but didn't answer. Instead, she launched into her account of what had happened at the trial, which was close enough to Caleb's version, though each had its own particular observations.

The form had been much as Caleb had anticipated (which suggested similar episodes had occurred rather more than once every ten years). The trial took place in the normal meeting area, and with much the same lay-out, except that Daguerre and Christiansen sat on a couple of chairs at an angle to the table where Xerxes and his colleagues were sitting, with four guards armed with spears and clubs standing behind them. Xerxes stood up and made the accusation, treason, which was simple enough, and then ploughed straight into his account of what he thought had happened. Basically, Daguerre and Christiansen had taken advantage of their supposed trip to Mortimers a few weeks earlier to visit the north camp instead and strike a deal for drugs. Xerxes had learned of this from north campers the day before, though not the names. (I wasn't surprised that the northerners hadn't been able to describe what the alleged dealers had looked like, since pretty well every adult male was near-identical in their beards and patched-up rags.) His men had checked the diary of movements they kept in his office (I hadn't realised he'd kept such a record), and Daguerre and Christiansen were the only two who had had an unsupervised break long enough to have got to the north camp and back in the relevant time.

The two accused then tried to give their version. They had gone to Mortimers, but had only been there a very short time, and had dealt with a young man whose name they didn't know. They had brought back the medicine they had gone for and given it to Xerxes. (He didn't remember this at all.) They had never met any north campers on their own, ever. They would never steal the camp's vegetables. They had never had any interest in any kind of drugs.

Various people from the community had asked them questions, most, though not all, hostile. Xerxes and his fellow judges had then conferred very briefly – three minutes was Caleb's guess – and then Xerxes pronounced them guilty. He called for two votes: the first to endorse the verdict, the second the punishment of execution. He got a majority for both, but not without considerable disagreement and protest, which had clearly unnerved him. Perhaps he felt he had to assert himself, because he ordered the guards to strip the two men – the clothes would be useful – and tie them to two trees. He then picked up a spear and thrust it several times into each of them and summoned the guards to finish them off. The corpses were cut down, loaded onto a handcart, and taken away to be tipped onto a rubbish area where birds and animals would make a meal of them. Outlaw justice indeed.

After I had been released, I had found the whole place still in a state of subdued excitement, with people arguing over the event. By now the alleged homosexuality of the two dead men was being openly discussed. Perhaps luckily for Xerxes, many of those who thought the two men had been unjustly treated seemed to reckon that if they had been gay then they probably deserved to die anyway. We had then had an unusually good dinner. The stack of tinned food kept in store had been generously opened and made available to supplement the vegetable stew, and Xerxes had deliberately withdrawn himself and had his meal with his key lieutenants in the lodge. He was still in there when Lee had suggested our evening stroll.

Unlike when we had talked the previous day, Lee had made an effort to look attractive. She was a plain woman, but now she had put on lipstick and had washed her dark hair, which hung down over her shoulders instead of in the standard tied-up-in-a-bun style of the women in the camp. Her body, as I had discovered that morning, was remarkably attractive underneath all the stale shapeless clothing: and the harsh routine on the Island at least gave a woman a chance to maintain her figure. That evening she was alight with an unusual vitality, her eyes shining and her face smiling most of the time. It was obvious she had taken a fancy to me and was indulging it with what I took to be an unusual recklessness. And she was very direct about it.

"Look, you are a decent-looking man, you are clean – it is amazing to smell someone whose clothes and body are clean for the first time in years – you have a very interesting background, and you are here on an extremely unusual basis: I mean, you are actually going home to Libance tomorrow! Of course I want to take advantage of all this, before I go back to the endless round of generally tedious sex that I have to endure the rest of the time. So, unless I actually turn you off, why don't you just go along with it?"

I didn't want to admit to feeling a certain nervousness about Xerxes' attitude to this, and I was beginning to have my doubts that he had 'sent' Lee to see me that morning. However, I calculated that, since the camp women shared their sexual favours widely, he was unlikely to feel especially jealous; so I behaved with more gallantry than I might have expected beforehand.

She had brought us to a small shack (we must have been almost half a mile from the main buildings by then) which contained various agricultural tools, but it had room enough to lie down inside; and Lee found a groundsheet and some blankets tucked away at the back – rather conveniently I thought. And there we had sustained sex, she naked and enthusiastic, me with most of my clothes on since it was damned cold; but I did manage to match her enthusiasm in all other respects.

As we walked back afterwards, I said I hoped she didn't mind me asking, but didn't they pick up nasty sexual diseases with all the sleeping around they had to do? She looked at me with a slight smile. "As I told you yesterday, we use condoms almost all the time. There are a couple of women who have something or other wrong with them – I think they must have come over with whatever it is they have got – and the men are very careful with them. We women think we know who the suspect men are, and we make sure we are protected when we have to go with them. As to when one of us wants a child, we are very careful to restrict our unprotected fucks to men we think are OK. So far as I know, that seems to work well enough. We may have been too bloody awkward for Libance, but that doesn't mean we are stupid. Mind you, I can't speak for the rougher camps."

We walked on in silence for a couple of minutes, and then she spoke again. "I guess I will have to sleep with Xerxes tonight. He hasn't been that interested in recent months, but today's events will have fired him up. He will want to remind me who's in charge, and of course he will have all kinds of resentments about you. Not," she added, "that you need to worry about me, or indeed yourself."

I said I hoped she was right. It was getting dark as we got back to the lodge area, and most people were drifting off to their beds. We got some interesting looks, but Lee wasn't bothered. I began to respect the way she almost queened it here. She stopped some metres from the lodge entrance and turned to me. "Thank you, Bob, for us today. What with one thing and another, I shall remember it for a very long time. Try to be nice about me when you write your stories about the outlaw Island. I had thought of asking you to contact my parents and my brother and sister, but I've decided it would be better if you don't. Let's shake hands – no, don't try to kiss me – and say goodbye."

She turned, walked to the lodge door, looked back and smiled at me, and went inside.

I carried on to Caleb's tent and found him sitting outside with the young man who had accompanied Xerxes and me on the wagon that brought us from the market two days before, though it did seem rather longer ago than that. "He's got some orders for you from Xerxes. I'm off to bed." No goodnight or anything friendly.

"You don't need to wash or nuffin tomorrow. An' you don't need breakfast – I'll give yer some biscuit and cheese to take wiv you. We gotta go early to meet the norv'n wagins at the main road just arter sunrise. They're 'specting us. I'll leave yer at the water and you'll carry on over to the markit."

"Sounds fair enough. Can I say goodbye and thank you to Xerxes?"

"Nah, 'e says not. E's too busy. I'll pick yer up tomorrer."

It was then I realised that my sleeping bag, rucksack and clothing were piled up outside the tent. I carried them over to a nearby tree and hoped it wouldn't rain.

Chapter Twenty-two

The journey back to Libance the next day passed without incident, though there was a slightly sinister edge to it. I had slept badly and was awake and ready to leave at first light. My young guide emerged from the tents looking pretty rough himself, and we walked to the main road with precious little in the way of conversation. Just before we got there, he roused himself and offered some advice.

"Stick wiv me, and don' git on a wagin. Walk at the back. Then when they stop at the water to orginise 'emselves you keep goin' onto the causeway wivvout me. Don' stop nor look back. Xerxes sez not to trust 'em once I'm gone, but if you get an 'ead start goin' over the water you should be OK."

I asked him why, if travelling with these wagons was risky, I didn't just go on my own at some other time. "You saw them camps on the way in? Well, the people there'd kill yer if yer did that, an unknown bloke on his own. I'll be OK on the way back – they know me, and they all know there'll be big trouble if I'm not back by lunchtime. Ain't worth it for any of 'em. But you – Xerxes ain't goin' ter start a war over you. An' he ain't goin to waste the time of 'alf a dozen guards goin' dahn wiv yer as protection."

Which put me nicely in my place. When the north camp wagons turned up there were only half as many as Xerxes' train three days before, and the ten or so men looked at me sullenly, with no desire to engage in any kind of chat. We trudged in silence for nearly two hours; when we neared the bottom of the hill by the sea, my guide nudged me, and I kicked into life and strode purposefully past the wagons and down onto the causeway. Some of the northerners looked up angrily as I passed them, but they had to stop and sort themselves out for the gateway on the other side, and I was a good three hundred metres ahead of them when they started to cross. I reached the gates even further ahead and was greeted by four grinning troopers. I positively enjoyed their jokes and ribbing; it was a deep relief to be back and safe.

I went straight to the hotel – I had kept my room on while I was on the Island – had a bath and ordered a beautiful, substantial late breakfast from room service. Reinhardt phoned and congratulated me on my adventure; naturally he wanted to know how I had got on. I told him I would email him a report from the airport and talk to him on the phone from the capital when I got back, but I would have to dash for my flight. It wasn't strictly true, but I needed to work out how much I would say about what I had seen, and I could do that far better if I wasn't face to face with him. He sounded disappointed but accepted it.

In the end I decided that both for Reinhardt and my media outlets I would put in all the main facts but gloss them favourably for Xerxes. I would play down any difficulties I had had and omit entirely my brief relationship with Lee. I was honest about the tough quality of life and the hard existence – no-one would have expected anything else – but said the settlement worked, with decent procedures for discussing issues and events. As for the extraordinary coincidence of the instant trial, I described it as rough but fair justice, and that the great majority had voted for the death penalty. I said I wouldn't want to live there, but none of the outlaws I had met seemed to want to come back to Libance. I thought that life in the outer camps was far nastier, but I had had no experience of these.

Privately I told Reinhardt that I had freely given Xerxes the camera/phone, as I didn't want him trying to get it back from Xerxes on the latter's next visit, but gave a truer version to the Metro TV people. They were delighted with the pictures I had sent back, and happily bore the cost of replacing it for me.

Now I was faced with writing a big piece for the *Tribune* and doing a half-hour special interview for Metro, with my snatched Island pictures, which I had agreed with my editors on the phone from the airport, both to go out in three days' time. On top of that the election and Proposition 72 were both boiling up very fast. The final round of the elections was in four days' time, and the referendum vote a day later. The accounts I read in the papers on the flight back certainly dramatised the situation in what I imagined was, for Libance, a highly unusual manner (though it looked normal enough to someone reared on British tabloids). Kris Myer and his call for a Voters' Strike dominated the news and op ed pages. Dr Gopiak, the Guardian Group chief executive, and her equivalent at the National Insurance Group, had both backed him. Caldor, for United, professed calm indifference; if such a boycott occurred, it would simply give the proposition an enormous majority. Interestingly, Myer's Senate opponent, Lisja Tuller, seemed more concerned, and said that such an action would be very unwise and would cause real problems going forward.

When I got home, I found several urgent messages for me, three of them from Rilka Delene. The most immediate was an invitation to a top-level strategy and tactics meeting of the informal Guardian/NDP grouping that I had attended a couple of weeks earlier, scheduled for lunchtime the next day. Since I had committed myself to writing up My Island Story (as I called it in my head) on that day, I reckoned I could spare them a couple of hours. I also had a message from Dirk Caldor, congratulating me on the Voters' Strike idea (which he correctly assumed was mine) as highly innovative, though certainly of no practical value.

There were separate calls from Rexy and Isaiah Raeburn, both sounding very excited and saying they were going to sign a contract for the SAD Six factory school, and that Commandant Stavros was backing the idea enthusiastically as well. And I had a forwarded email from Axal, coolly letting me know that the Guardian Central martial arts team had reached the national finals.

I had just about unpacked, put my laundry on, stuck a dinner in the oven, and was relaxing with a whisky and soda, when I got a phone call from Xerxes. (My home number was in the cameraphone's contact list.) "Well hallo, Mr Journalist, you got back in one piece. I am very glad to know that. This is a very interesting telephone, which I am trying for the first time. I am sorry we parted on, shall I say, not the best of terms, but I am sure you can understand my anxieties. Doubtless you are preparing your stories about me. I trust you are not going to exaggerate what happened."

I reassured him that I was doing essentially favourable pieces in the paper and on the TV. I had been impressed with the way a hard and difficult existence had been organised, and with the way the great majority of people in the settlement worked together. I saw no reason why our disagreement on the day before should affect this judgement, and certainly had no intention of mentioning it.

"I am very glad to hear it. You have confirmed my instincts about you when we met at Captain Reinhardt's. Of course, life on the Island is very different from that on Libance. Everyone will understand that. I do not expect a sudden wave of tourists trying to come and see us as a result of your stories, but equally I do not want the security companies to feel they will have to mount a major clean-up operation here."

"Well, if Captain Reinhardt's reaction is anything to go by, they will be relieved to hear there is some semblance of order on the Island. They certainly won't care that you executed a couple of criminals. After all that is what they do too." Mentally, I apologised to Lee for this travesty of what had happened at and after the 'trial'.

"Ah, very true. An excellent point, which I trust you will make. On another matter, I gather you got on well with Lee. She is a delightful woman, and an honest one. She told me of her relationship with you. She has asked me to let you know that I have no difficulty with that. I am very happy to tell you this. We have no place for sexual jealousy here."

Finally, he asked me to call Reinhardt and get him to keep a copy of the Tribune feature when it appeared, so that he could collect it on his next market visit. He promised to telephone me with his reactions when he had read it.

I was disconcerted by Xerxes' ability to unnerve me even at this safe distance. What I had said about the article and TV interview was certainly what I intended to do, but I vaguely felt that Lee would only be safe so long as Xerxes didn't dislike what I wrote for the Tribune. This was a pressure I could have done without.

I had poured myself another whisky when the doorbell went. It was Rilka, on a surprise visit, on her way home, she said. She looked at my drink and asked for the same. "I have sent my driver off to get his dinner. He will be back in an hour." An hour, I thought – half an hour to exchange news, and half an hour for a fuck? Except it then happened the other way round.

Rilka was almost as keen to swap news as she had been to swap sexual roles a few minutes before. "Tomorrow we will learn how successful Josep Stilo has been in organising the final election lists in our favour. This is the most thrilling Senate election in years. It really matters that Kris wins and wins well. All that publicity about not voting in the referendum – it has made him the most famous person in Libance by a mile."

"Don't you mean by 1.5 kilometres?"

She grabbed my genitals and gave them a slow squeeze. "Careful, funny man, or I will make you perform again." She carried on but stroked me with increasing vigour while she did so. "It will be very difficult to know about the Progressives' list, and the two smaller parties, though I think we have got some help there. And how do you think we will do on Proposition 72?" And at this she ducked down and sucked me with enthusiasm.

"Careful," I said, gasping slightly. "I'm not sure I'm up for this. Anyway," I said, pulling her head up gently, "I was reading that since at least 20 per cent don't vote in normal Senate elections, then Caldor will need to get 60 per cent of people voting yes to be able to claim a minimal moral majority. And the prospect of the Yes vote being so high will almost certainly reduce the willingness of some of his supporters to make the effort, out of laziness if nothing else. I know everyone votes electronically at home, but you still have to find the site, register, confirm your registration, encrypt your vote, and then do it. It will too much bother for quite a few, I suspect."

"My, you have studied our system. I hadn't thought of it like that. I don't know what you mean, not being up for it. You look promisingly firm to me."

"Pure show. There's an empty penis and uninterested testicles right now."

"Well, in that case," she said, rolling on top of me and sitting astride my face, "you will have to use your tongue as cleverly as you did before." I don't think I had to be that clever; just hanging on in there was sufficient. Thankfully she came soon enough.

"Now I must rush. Tomas and I are out at the theatre. And I must wash before I go."

She was in and out of my bathroom remarkably fast for a woman, but still managed to look the smart matronly Governor she had been when she arrived. "Bye dear, see you at the Guardian tomorrow lunchtime."

I slumped back on my bed. And even though it was scarcely seven in the evening, I fell asleep almost immediately. And slept for nearly eleven hours. In the morning, I found that the oven had, thank God, switched itself off, leaving a frazzled baked meat cold and very unappetising on the middle tray. I threw it in the bin and went out for a real, big breakfast.

Chapter Twenty-three

"I'm not sure," said Friya, "that I truly understand the position of the women on the Island. You say that they are better people than the men. They have real emotional relationships with each other. They don't have to work in the fields, but they have to look after the children, and as far as possible teach them as well. But at the same time they are effectively unpaid prostitutes, both the 'partner' of specific men but also regularly available to any man who wants them. Have I got that right?"

We were dining out in one of the capital's better restaurants. (I was spending a little of the bonuses I had been promised by both Metro TV and the *Tribune*.) Basically the meal was going well; we were visibly enjoying each other's company. However, I was getting a bit of a grilling on both my couple of days with the outlaws and the imminent political crisis.

"Yes, pretty much. I'm not quite sure I'd call them unpaid prostitutes, but that is certainly arguable. And I don't know about the women at Mortimers, the big house where the original families live. But the women I met certainly didn't seem ground down, or second-class citizens."

"From your description everyone, except the chief – Xerxes, I think that is what you called him – and a few of his sidekicks, seems to have a been second-class citizen. I think you are allowing the fact that you quite enjoyed yourself to colour your account. Though quite why you enjoyed sleeping on a plank of wood in a tent with three men who didn't like you, weeding for hours on end, eating only boring vegetable broths and coming dangerously close to being killed, I'm not at all sure."

"Look, I don't think it is Paradise. But they were making a bit more of their lives than anyone here had led me to expect. It isn't some gangster-dominated anarchy. The violent thugs are kept under control and have to scrape a living like everyone else."

"Tell me something. Obviously no-one gets paid. They don't have bank accounts. So how do they decide who does what, who does the hard work and who gets away with not doing very much?"

"Well, in that way perhaps you are right about Xerxes and his lieutenants. They are very much in charge and are the only ones who carry their own weapons. They have the keys to the armoury, too. And they don't seem to do much of the hard graft in the fields, though I believe they do some of it sometimes. But they don't live any better than anyone else. They eat the same food, wear the same rags, sleep just as roughly as everyone else. And they have one vote each in their assemblies, just like everyone else too." I chose to ignore my gift of wine as a one-off, as well as Xerxes' theft of my phone.

"But why do they put up with it? I mean most people would give up after a couple of months and come back home to Libance."

"Most of them, remember, wouldn't be allowed back. The security troopers dumped them there, and for good reasons – they didn't fit in with life here, even the prisons. Or perhaps I should say, especially the prisons. A few of them are ideological about staying and living there;: the Duggan and Fantoni families, I guess, and certainly Xerxes, who thinks life is much freer on the Island."

"It certainly sounds as though it might be as far as he is concerned. But doesn't anyone else change their mind and try to come back?"

"Apparently a few people do. Once a year there is a very discreet assessment made of those who have changed their minds and applied to come back. I'm told that a very few are accepted, and that apparently it works out OK back here. But most of the people I met, and I guess this would apply generally on the Island, know they wouldn't get through an assessment, for whatever reason, and have decided to make the best of it."

Friya suddenly smiled. "I know what happened. You had sex with a woman, and you enjoyed it. You men are all the same at bottom. A good fuck, and the world is a nice place, at least for a couple of days."

I looked at her for a moment, and then gave in. "Well, OK, I did. And I did enjoy it I suppose. Not sure why. I mean she wasn't at all attractive to look at, or indeed to smell, to be honest, but she did have a pretty good figure and was remarkably full of life. And she came on to me. I wasn't looking for sex at all."

She was still smiling, thank God. "I can well believe she took the initiative. You must have seemed a godsend. A good-looking, intelligent but exotic man, and clean above all, particularly in comparison with her usual companions – well, I'm surprised the women weren't all queuing up for you."

And she laughed and shook her head at me. Fondly, I hoped. "Anyway," she said, "I've got some news for you. I got a message today that your asylum application will be considered in ten days' time. So then we will know." And she looked at me strangely.

This took me aback. I knew of course that someone in authority would make a decision at some point, and I had been assuming that when it happened, I would be relaxed about whichever way it went, largely because I thought that I would leave the country anyway, whether by their choice or mine. But suddenly I felt a real concern.

"God, that's soon. Will I be called in for an interview?"

"It doesn't look like it. The security forum have appointed a special committee to look at your case. The woman who told me the date also said that the paperwork I had sent them was all they needed, and that they didn't want anything more. I imagine they will have got their own copies of the *Tribune* articles you have written in the past few weeks."

"Why don't they want to see me? And who is on this special committee?"

"They will be fairly senior people from each of the four security companies. I told you when we first met at the airport that an asylum application was an extremely rare event. This process seems fair enough, even if it has been specially invented for you. And why would they want to meet you? The circumstances are clear enough. You make it sound as though you would want to persuade them directly yourself. That is hardly an objective procedure."

"Oh, I don't know. I just want to make my case, I suppose."

She smiled gently and reached over to hold my hand. "Don't worry, Bob. There is no reason why they should reject you. I am sure you will be granted asylum."

This was reassuring, but more for what it said about Friya's feelings for me than about my official chances. It was true that I couldn't think of a reason why I might fail. But even more disconcerting was the growing realisation that I now cared a great deal about not failing. I gripped her hand tightly. I had a wonderful feeling that I was falling in love with her.

This didn't mean we would agree about politics any more than about life on the Island. Friya was not as taken with Myer's call for a Voters' Strike as I had expected. In fact, she sounded like Lisja Tuller, the opposition candidate for Senate Leader. "I think it is a dangerous idea. Voting is the lifeblood of Libance. You can do it several times a week if you want, and though most of us aren't quite that keen, we do recognise our responsibility as citizens. Proposition 72 is desperately important. I know the Constitutional Court took a surprising decision to let it go ahead, and that in a way that was an accident because of the death of Riccardo, but nonetheless the proper procedures are taking place. It almost looks as though my side know they will lose and are trying in some way to invalidate the result in advance."

"There may be some truth in that. Certainly, I know your side thinks that far too many of their own clients will be persuaded by the bribe Caldor is offering – the substantially reduced insurance premiums if they vote Yes – and probably enough for him to win in a straight vote. But that would be very short-sighted of them. This is a revolutionary move by Caldor. He has a big vision if he wins. He wants to shake up what he feels is a conservative, risk-averse culture which basically stops anything new happening, and to liberate entrepreneurs and their like, knock down the barriers to change. Actually, in some ways I think he is right. But it is a cheat's revolution – he isn't saying any of that in public, he wants to do it by stealth. A couple of million people get cheaper insurance, and probably only for a couple of years, and bingo! Quite soon you will all wake up and find you can't just vote to stop things you don't like that mess up your back yard, that there are all kinds of adverse consequences that none of you are currently debating or even thinking about. If there was a real, open argument going on, then maybe I'd agree with you. But there isn't – and your proper procedures will be by-passed damn quick if everyone simply followed your line."

"If this is true, and Caldor told you all this, you should write it, Bob. It is terribly important, and I don't instinctively know what I think about that kind of consequence. But leaving that aside, how exactly will a Voters' Strike help? OK, it might just give some grounds eventually for the Competition Court to find against Caldor, but that will take a good two years if precedent is anything to go by. Surely there must be more to it than that?"

I was now in a real difficulty. This was of course precisely what the inner group at the Guardian had been talking about at lunchtime. And I, along with everyone else at the meeting, was under strict instructions to keep quiet about it.

"Look, Friya, I am going to have to trust you on this. You must not repeat what I am about to tell you to anyone, not even your best friend. There is indeed more to it. If Caldor fails to win a majority of those entitled to vote, entitled, not those who actually voted, then Kris Myer will get the Senate to reject the referendum result. Of course, he will have to win the final Senate Leader election, but we already believe from the candidates selected so far that he will have enough support in the Senate for a No vote. I know the Senate endorsement is normally a formality. But the law says they are entitled to vote on every referendum, so …"

Friya had smiled gently when I mentioned her 'best friend', but her expression changed dramatically as I continued. She looked incredulous at first, and then admiration swept across her beautiful face.

"You mean the Senate will have to take this seriously, and not just as a way of providing entertainment for the television viewers? What a hoot! And here I am going on about following the proper procedures. Well, that will be doing it with a vengeance. How wonderfully exciting!"

I was very grateful for her positive reaction. "Well, it's a logical move, as well as being a total surprise to everyone, I hope. Of course, we can't be sure that we will have a majority for this action after all the rounds of the Senate elections are over. Josep Stilo – you know him, Myer's numbers man – told a meeting I was at this lunchtime that he was 99% certain the NDP senators finally selected would support Myer, and that he had had discreet conversations with the minority parties and reckoned that a majority of their likely winners would probably back Myer as well, though since he couldn't actually say what he had in mind this was a bit speculative. We are assuming all the Progressives will oppose any such move, though some of them are certainly against Proposition 72. Whether that would be enough to make them go this much further, who knows?"

"You and your colleagues have been working hard. I assume Governor Delene is part of this team, and I suppose you have had a few meetings with her. Ah well, this is so serious I suppose I will have to live with that. It will totally change the way I watch the final rounds of the elections. Will you come and watch them with me?"

"I would love to, but unfortunately, I agreed to join Dr Gopiak and the others at a party at the Guardian headquarters. Why don't you come with me to that?"

"They wouldn't invite a mere agency official like me."

"Oh bollocks, if you came as my guest no-one would argue about it."

"I think at least one person would. However, it is a nice idea. Perhaps I will buy a new outfit to wear at it."

"That's settled then. You'll come. I'll get you invited."

Friya was gazing thoughtfully at the ceiling. I imagined she was thinking about her new dress. But she wasn't.

"It's not just the election results we should be worried about, is it? Caldor could still block us even if Kris Myer knows he can get a rejection through the Senate."

"Eh, what do you mean? How block us?"

"The security franchise for the Senate building is currently operated by United's troopers. They will be there for at least another month. Certainly, during the time Proposition 72 will have to be voted on."

"So?"

"So," she said slowly, "if I were Caldor I would make sure Kris Myer couldn't enter the building on the day of the vote. I would instruct my troopers to keep him out. And I would do it on the grounds that Myer was trying illegally to frustrate a referendum vote."

"But he couldn't do that. That would be outrageous, preventing the duly elected Senate Leader from going about his proper business."

"Would it be any more outrageous than the Senate suddenly changing the constitutional practice of the past 20 or more years and reversing a referendum decision? It seems to me both actions are legal, as you call it, and both are equally reprehensible. But Caldor would still end up the winner."

I looked at her in total shock. I had thought I had wrapped this problem up neatly with my idea, but I was beginning to see the force of her argument. And I could see even more clearly that Caldor would think of it himself within minutes of Myer announcing what he intended to do.

"Ok, so he stops Myer attending the Senate on the day of the vote. So what? His deputy can simply move the vote in his place."

She smiled. "Oh dear, this is where our light-hearted treatment of the Senate suddenly makes life difficult. The Senate Leader always proposes the vote on referenda, those that the Senate is actually interested in. If he or she isn't available, there is no vote, and the referendum is automatically passed without any discussion. Most referendum decisions go through the Senate in this way, and no-one cares because the vote doesn't mean anything – except to provide some good fun with rival performances to entertain the viewers. If Myer isn't there, Proposition 72 will go through on the nod."

"You're joking," I said, but I could see she wasn't. I was beginning to feel desperate. "OK, so we get the Guardian security teams to accompany him to the Senate. If necessary, we would fight our way in."

"We couldn't do that. The security protocols forbid it. No security company can interfere with another one when it is holding one of the public franchises. Just as no-one could have stopped Captain Reinhardt letting you go over to the Island with Xerxes, so no-one could stop the United troopers doing what Caldor tells them to do. Of course, normally this is not a problem. No-one tries to do anything as outrageous as our scenario."

"You mean there will be no way of getting Kris Myer into the Senate building if the United security troopers decide to stop him, and if he isn't there then there will be no vote on the referendum result?"

"That is what I said. Of course, you can check it out with Dr Gopiak and Governor Delene and the others, but I am sure I am right."

"I will have to. We must be able to think of something if that is what Caldor will do. Though I am buggered if I can think what that is."

"Why are you sometimes so coarse? It doesn't suit you, you know."

"Me, coarse? Who was it who said 'fuck' so cheerfully ten minutes ago?"

"I admit it was strong language, but at least it was a direct and literal use of the word. I am not sure anyone will want to bugger you, as you put it, in the middle of a serious tactical discussion." She paused. "Though I suppose one person might want to do it soon after."

"What are you on about? You keep hinting at some sexual activity or other involving me. You are the only person in Libance who I want to fuck – pardon my coarseness – but you won't say yes."

"Yes, you do, don't you? And I want to too."

"You do? That's fantastic. What about all that stuff you were on about last time, trying to work out whether you trusted me or not?"

"Not whether I trusted you, but whether it mattered if I trusted you. And I have decided it doesn't matter."

"Oh, I see. OK, so whether you trust me doesn't matter. But, purely out of curiosity you understand, can I ask if you do trust me?"

"Mm, on the surface, yes. But deep down, no."

I thought for a moment. "Well, since sex happens mostly on the surface, I guess that's OK then."

"That is exactly the kind of sensible response I would expect of you, Bob. So – shall we go? After you have paid the bill, of course."

I should have been totally delighted by this turn of events. And in one sense I was. But I was hit by other, conflicting feelings too. I felt bad about the sex I had had with Rilka Delene – not that I hadn't enjoyed it, but that I had not done anything at all to discourage her, just lapped it up when she offered it. Even more, I was now worried about Friya's saying that it didn't matter if she trusted me, and then that she trusted me 'on the surface', whatever that meant. Damn it, I wanted her to truly trust me, as deep down as it could go. It did matter to me, suddenly very much. She didn't seem to care about me screwing Lee on the Island, and it sounded as though she thought Rilka and I were having regular sex and she didn't seem to care about that either. But actually, I wanted her to care, and care very much.

We took a taxi back to her place, she chattering confidently, me torn by a combination of nervousness and exhilaration, which persisted right through all the rituals of having a drink, kissing and fondling, undressing each other and getting into bed. I was even more knocked out by her beautiful body than I had been on my first visit nearly a month earlier, when we had sat opposite each other naked. She wasn't as aggressive as either Rilka or Lee, and I was almost apprehensively gentle. My nervousness didn't actually disable me, and ultimately it lent a heightened intensity to the whole thing, but it certainly made me very sensitive to every moment and nuance. Needless to say, I finished before she did, but she allowed me to bring her to orgasm afterwards.

"Thank you, Bob," she said, smiled sweetly, whispered, "Good night," rolled over and fell asleep almost immediately. I lay there, looking at her and wondering what on earth was happening to me. Eventually I too fell asleep. When I went to the toilet in the middle of the night, I was still in an excited but twitchy state. I don't generally remember dreams at all, and in truth I didn't this time either, but I felt as though I had been going through a whole history of strange, vivid stories, and woke up hardly refreshed at all.

Friya had been up and about for nearly an hour. I had neither shaving kit nor a toothbrush with me and felt uncomfortably dirty. She said I shouldn't worry about it and should go home straightaway and clean up if I wanted to. I asked when I could see her again, and she said I could pick her up to take her to the election night party in three days' time. That seemed an awfully long time away, but she said we would both be busy, and it would pass in no time. I was too unsettled to find any counter arguments.

It took me over half an hour to walk back to my flat. It seemed extraordinary to me that the workaday world was carrying on as normal. Perhaps fortunately, I had messages from both the paper and the TV people reminding me of deadlines and meeting times which brought me back to the daily life of the rest of the world. And I did remember to call Dr Gopiak to ask for an urgent meeting.

Chapter Twenty-four

It was only later that morning, when I was on my way to Metro TV to record the interview about my time on the Island, that I suddenly realised that neither Friya nor Rilka had talked about the need to notify that busybody outfit that allegedly kept all the data on sexual encounters in Libance. Each of them – though I remembered my first long talk with prison governor Rilka in particular – had made it sound as though we should get these episodes into the records at the Institute as soon as possible, but neither of them had mentioned it to me following the sex we had had in the past couple of days.

There seemed to be various ways of interpreting this. They could each have felt that as long as they reported it by themselves, then this would be enough; effectively they would both be covered, they needn't bother me about it. But this seemed unduly secretive, particularly for Friya, though I could believe Rilka might do something like that. Alternatively, they could have decided to leave it for a while. Rilka had given me the impression in that first talk that this was quite common, although people usually got round to putting these encounters on the record in the end. It could even demonstrate that in reality there was widespread evasion of this obligation and that neither of them intended to do their duty because they didn't feel the need to.

Interestingly, while I didn't much care which of these explanations fitted Rilka, I was concerned about the motivation for Friya's action, or rather lack of it. I positively wanted her to give the information to the Institute – and for me to do it too. I decided to raise it with her when we were going to the election party.

The TV interview went well enough. I was relaxed and spoke sufficiently succinctly and simply to make most of it useable, though since they got well over an hour's worth of my thoughts for a half-hour show, there was no way most of it would get into the final programme. The producer showed me the pictures I had managed to shoot on the Island, which were better than I had feared, though of course I had never got anyone speaking clearly enough to be heard. He told me they had sent a crew up to the Causeway to shoot wall-paper material, and that they had also got a decent interview with Reinhardt. He showed me the clips they intended to use, which were generally fair, though the captain was rather more sceptical about me personally than I would have liked. All the material would be edited that day and broadcast in peak time that evening.

Dr Gopiak had rearranged her schedule, and that of a few others too, I guessed, to summon an emergency meeting at lunchtime in response to my phone call about Caldor's potential 'killer' block on our Senate coup. Though Kris Myer was too busy preparing for the election shows the following day to get there, he sent Josep Stilo; and Rilka Delene, the Guardian woman executive called Elli Dyvers whom I had met at Rilka's Sunday lunch, and the self-satisfied young lawyer, Timo Jankel, had also cancelled whatever they had intended to do to get to this meeting.

"My, this is fun, Bob, seeing you three times in three days," was Rilka's greeting. "We really should have these crises more often." Fortunately, no-one else was around when she said it, though it meant we did have to kiss far more sensually than I wanted to.

As we started on the sandwiches and nibbles the company had provided, Irene Gopiak got straight to the point. "Bob phoned me with an alarming thought he has had about Caldor's likely reaction once Kris announces his intention to get the Senate to veto the referendum result. Since we currently plan for him to do this in two days' time, immediately after the referendum result is declared, we need to think about what we intend to do now. Bob, please repeat your ideas for everyone's benefit."

I hadn't mentioned to Dr Gopiak that it had been Friya, not me, who had thought of this, and her preamble, plus the presence of Rilka, now inhibited me from giving due credit to Friya. It was just too complicated to explain why I had breached the agreement we had solemnly reached the day before with someone I would have to refer to as my girl-friend. So I mumbled a vague disclaimer, and then ploughed on.

"I understand that Caldor's security company currently has the six-month franchise for guarding the Senate building. There doesn't appear to be anything to stop him ordering the guards to prevent Kris Myer entering the Senate on the day of their vote on the referendum, which I gather will be sometime next week. If Myer doesn't show up, there will be no vote; Proposition 72 will simply be added to the list of half a dozen other referenda results up for automatic approval, which will go through without debate and without a vote. Of course, there will be uproar if Myer is physically barred from getting in, but there will be no recourse, and Caldor will have won. He can anyway justify his action simply on the grounds that, though it is theoretically possible for the Senate to veto a referendum result, they haven't done so in more than twenty years. So one unprecedented action simply provokes a second one. End of story. We will have lost."

Stilo, Rilka and Elli Dyvers looked at me, stunned. I think Jankel smiled very slightly. Gopiak spoke.

"That is it in a nutshell. Does anyone disagree that Bob's scenario is highly plausible? I thought not. So, can I have proposals for what we do, if indeed we can do anything?"

After a moment, Jankel decided to offer his views.

"Well, well, what a stroke of bad luck. If any other company had been on Senate duty …" He paused briefly. "I suppose we can think about meeting violence with violence. The protocols prevent our security people getting into a gunfight with the United people, and I very much doubt if they would even consider it. I assume, Irene, that is why you haven't invited any of them to be here right now?"

Gopiak nodded. "Quite right," Jankel continued. "We would be completely circumscribed if we tried to take advice from them. So do we have any other likely lads who can muscle Myer past the guards?"

Dyvers broke in. "Look, before we start trying to hire our own hoodlums, can we just go back a bit? Why do we think Caldor will behave like this? Aren't we being a bit premature?"

Gopiak responded, "Elli, he might not think of this, or choose to do it even if he did think of it. I have to say, from everything I know about Dirk Caldor, he is very likely to both think of it and do it. But we are here, not to debate whether he will or won't, but to come up with an answer if he does do this."

Stilo followed her. "I agree with Irene. I think we would do something similar if the roles were reversed. Indeed, our proposal to veto Proposition 72 is something similar anyway. As someone who is, essentially, in the entertainment business with a bit of politics on the side, I find the idea of a mass brawl on the steps of the Senate building very appealing as a TV event, but not very helpful in guaranteeing the result we want. Where would we find our crowd of fighters? How could we be sure they would win? We could massively damage our reputations, provoke all kinds of unpleasant consequences – as individuals, we would almost certainly lose our own security insurance provisions – and still end up without achieving the Senate veto."

Then it was Rilka's turn. "Josep paints a gloomy but, I think, accurate picture of what would happen if we tried to recruit enough people willing to take on the United troopers. Frankly we are unlikely to find many recruits, and even if we did, they would almost certainly be defeated in their attempt to storm the building. But let me try a variant of that idea on you. Suppose we got a large crowd together, not to fight the troopers, but to protest their actions outside the Senate. This would distract the security team, perhaps so distract them that we could smuggle Myer in some other way. If we could get him in in time, he could still propose the vote, and we would have won after all."

We all looked admiringly at her. This sounded more promising.

"Very interesting, Rilka," said Irene Gopiak. "Let us assume we can get enough protesters together as you suggest. How exactly do we smuggle Myer in?"

Jankel now came back in. "It is a very neat idea, Rilka. Many congratulations. I believe there are at least six entrances to the Senate building. Obviously, the security at each of them will be particularly tight that day. We could either get a much smaller team of thugs to deal with the guards at one of the minor entrances: or we could cheat our way in via, say, the service entrance. We could send Myer in with the post, for example."

Gopiak smiled. "I think Kris is too well known to get away with a disguise as a postman, Timo. But let's look at both these possibilities. First, the small team prepared to take on a small unit of troopers. How many do we need? Where do we get them from? How do they escape the consequences of killing United troopers?"

They all shook their heads. None of them seemed to know the right kind of people for this job.

"Well," I said, "here are a couple of thoughts. There is the Guardian Central martial arts team. There are probably enough of them. Whether they would want to – don't know. Perhaps rather more promising would be the Raptors. They are a rather smart gang in SAD Six. Your man Stavros is in charge of that SAD. So I guess he would turn a blind eye to enough of them leaving the SAD to take on the troopers."

"Of course, we all read your column about Rexy and the Raptors," said Gopiak with a smile. "And these Raptors do sound a real possibility. I think we should look at that option before we consider anything else. So here is what I suggest. Bob, you get down to SAD Six and talk to Rexy and his gang. Don't be too precise – we don't want Caldor learning what we are thinking about. Rilka, can you talk to Commandant Stavros. I am sure you know him. Josep, we need a detailed plan of the Senate building. Kris can get you that. Timo and Elli, please think about the security team implications of this – what the consequences might be. You must do all this today. We can meet here again for breakfast at eight."

After this clear set of instructions, we obviously had to break up and get on with our new tasks. It was no problem for me, as I had the time to get down to the SAD. The others would have to jettison any commitments they had in their diaries. As we were leaving, Rilka managed to get me on my own briefly. She took my hand warmly and kissed me again. I got myself free politely.

"Well done, Rilka. That was a brilliant idea of yours."

"It is all down to you, Bob. The others were good, too, all except that wimp Elli. I have never seen our team think so originally, so creatively, before. You have clearly had a big influence on us. Let us go down to SAD Six together in my car. We can combine business with pleasure."

Inwardly I groaned at this. I could guess exactly how Rilka envisaged combining these two imperatives. But I could scarcely object. In the event I responded to her fondlings on the journey adequately enough from her perspective, and with admittedly guilty pleasure for myself. I was amazed at how freely she was willing to behave in the presence of her driver, even with the curtains pulled across the screen between us – he must have had a good idea what was going on.

In between the sex I managed to phone Rexy – luckily he was available that afternoon – and Rilka managed to get an urgent appointment with Commandant Stavros. She dropped herself off at the Castle and told the driver to bring me back in an hour and a half's time. "Long enough for you? Great, see you then."

The driver took me across to the Raptors' gaudy-looking building, muttering about being forced to drive over such shit roads in such a shit area and then being fucking expected to hang around for an hour. Passing a couple of SAD Six armoured trucks en route made it worse. "Christ, even the fucking troopers are scared here," he said. He was working himself up so much at the prospect of being hijacked and slaughtered that I told him to go away to somewhere safer and come back on the hour, and he drove off in a happier frame of mind, to the accompaniment of the jeers and cheers of the young men and women hanging around outside the building.

Rexy welcomed me with what looked like sincere enthusiasm. He raved about his new business partner and friend, Isaiah, who had, on his side, clearly taken to Rexy too. Apparently, they had checked out a couple of empty buildings that might make an educational factory, and Raeburn had already sent some of his team to do a proper survey and costing of refurbishment. A four-party meeting with Commandant Stavros and the main SAD charity had been set up for next week, and Rexy had got his own team of young men and women trying to fit Raeburn's demands for staffing to their ability to meet them. It all sounded wonderful.

However, when it came to my turn to sketch out what I was after, this new educational venture effectively killed any idea of co-operation by the Raptors. "Look, Bob, a month ago we might have done it," said Rexy. "I could have found ten guys who would have been excited by the idea and willing to take it on. Sounds like you could have organised the guns and the several cars we'd have needed to fool the street cameras; you say you could square off Stavros; and we could no doubt have come to a deal over our rewards. We would have run the risk of getting caught. But now – no way. Anything like that gets pinned on us, and the new school is dead. That's just too important to me. It is the best chance ever for us to break free of the shit that drowns us. I am very grateful to you for making the introductions, but this favour is way too much to ask in return."

I gave up trying to change his mind. Indeed, I was privately relieved at his new interest in respectability and would have made the same decision in his place. We parted on good terms – he promised to watch my TV report on the Island – and shook hands. I had to wait ten minutes in the road outside, as Rilka's driver had clearly decided it was better for me to wait in such dangerous surroundings than him, and I prepared myself to give Rilka the disappointing news.

"I'm not surprised," she said as we drove back to the Guardian Central prison. (Fortunately her lusts seemed to have abated.) "Keely Stavros would reluctantly have tried to ignore the Raptors leaving the SAD discreetly for half a day, and blessedly he didn't ask me why we might need them, but he said he thought Rexy was now so keen on this school idea that he wouldn't want to take the risks that my request implied. Like a good SAD commander, he clearly understands the people he is dealing with. I'm afraid we will have to think of something else."

As we approached the prison where I had spent my first days in Libance, I casually mentioned that I had got an invitation for Friya Alling to come with me to the election night party that Dr Gopiak was hosting. Rilka went very still for a moment; then she turned to me and smiled. "Ah, of course. Friya Alling and you seem to be close. Well, it will be very nice to meet her. I know she has a good reputation in the agency. I cannot expect to be the sole object of your affections, no need to say."

She looked out of the car window and picked up her bag. "Well, here we are. I have told the driver to take you to your home. I will of course be watching the programme tonight. Best of luck for it and see you at breakfast tomorrow." She smiled brightly and got out of the car without any kind of farewell kiss. I watched her walk into the prison without turning round; then the car moved off.

I watched the programme alone after dinner. It seemed pretty good, I had to admit, though I was put out to see they used a particularly critical passage from Reinhardt that they hadn't shown me earlier. In it he said that 'as a European' I was bound to take a different view of many things about Libance, including the peculiar role played by the Island and its outlaw inhabitants. It didn't totally undermine the impact of the rest of the piece, but it allowed any viewer who felt so inclined to feel that I was exaggerating.

I took some congratulatory calls afterwards from the few people I knew in Libance, and then opened up rather more emails from people I didn't know. Most of these offered congratulations as well. There was nothing from Rilka. Friya rang later; she had been working when it had been transmitted but had caught up with the recorded show when she got home. "My, Bob, how handsome you looked. And so brave and believable. Those people seemed better off than I had imagined, though I don't think I like their justice much." I asked her what she thought about Reinhardt's contribution. "Oh, he was handsome too, wasn't he? I think he was a typical security trooper. And then trying to say you were bound to get things slightly wrong. That was entirely irrelevant."

That made me feel better. I told her I had got the invitation for her to the party, and we parted on warm, affectionate terms. When I woke up next morning, I immediately grabbed the *Tribune* from the front door, and saw that it had given me equal space on the front page with the latest election news. Of course, the other papers had used my TV interview, but for the *Tribune* I had written an enhanced version of my bi-weekly column and offered the fullest explanation and description of my experiences, more even than on the TV, since I was totally in control of what I wanted to say.

I had to rush off to the Guardian building, where Gopiak's gang, as I was beginning to think of us, were assembling again for another session. Everybody (including Rilka) was complimentary about both the programme and the newspaper article. "It made me think," said Dr Gopiak, "and in particular it made me wonder why none of our journalists has tried to do what you did in all the years that the Island has been a haven for outlaws. The best explanation I can come up with is that the Island is so convenient for us all that we prefer to ignore it. All our journalists assume that there is no news to be found there. Now you come along, and suddenly we find we are very interested indeed."

She turned to the main point of the meeting, and Rilka and I swiftly reported our unwelcome news. It was echoed by Jankel and Dyvers, who both indicated that they thought that SAD dwellers were likely to be tracked down through the surveillance records that logged all movements in and out of the district. I wasn't so sure of that, but there was no point in debating it. Only Stilo had been successful; he produced an excellent map of the Senate building, which clearly showed the half dozen entrances.

"So, back to first square," said Gopiak. "Let us consider our alternative idea of smuggling Kris into the building. Here is the service entrance that Timo mentioned yesterday. Kris Myer tells me that endorsement of the various referenda votes normally takes place on the first full day of business, which he says is next Tuesday. I asked Josep to discreetly find out what regular deliveries the Senate has on that day. What did you get, Josep?"

Stilo produced sheets of paper, which he passed round. "Here is the list. There are some twenty or so regulars: more than half the deliveries occur before noon, when any referendum vote will take place. They are very varied but see what you think."

We all looked rather blankly at names of food shops, stationers, mail delivery companies, cleaners and so on. "Irene," said Jankel, "how on earth do we choose one of these?"

"First, I think we must see how many of these companies have close links with our group. I can see four of them already. Then we must consider how easy it will be to conceal Kris in their trucks or vans, and whether he can get out of them without being spotted by security guards. And we will have to think about whether we can afford to let various people in these companies know in advance what we are trying to do. Quite a tall order, I fear."

We debated the various choices we had. Fairly rapidly we came down to the mail company, which was a well-known part of the Guardian group. They used large vans, and someone could at least in theory be concealed amongst the bags.

"I said he could go in as part of the post," said Jankel.

"Yes, Timo," said Rilka, "but we have two problems. First, an organisation which calls itself Guardian Express is bound to be thoroughly searched by United security men on that day of all days. Second, the men who make the delivery will have to be in on the deceit, and they will be very vulnerable afterwards when Caldor gets their names and seeks revenge. In fact, I doubt they will take part."

"This is very true, Rilka," said Gopiak. "But I think Guardian Express is still our best hope of getting Kris into the building that day. Bob, I have been thinking about your programme. Those outlaws you met; they have one great advantage over the rest of us: they will not be traceable by United at any point. Is there any way you could persuade two of them to come here and take the places of the postal workers on delivery that day? I recognise we will have to reward them well, which might be difficult since they don't have bank accounts. But what do you think?"

I didn't immediately respond, which gave Jankel the chance to jump in. "You are right, Irene, that they are not traceable, but how on earth can Bob get in touch with them without going back to the Island? That will take days to arrange, and we have to have this sorted out by next Monday."

"Actually, I might be able to talk to Xerxes sooner than that," I said. "He has got my old mobile phone. I can text him or voicemail him to call me. The signal is unpredictable but knowing him I bet he goes up the hill at least once a day to play with it. But what exactly will I say to him?"

"First, find out if he is willing to send a couple of men, preferably ones you met out there, who are able to take the places of the mail drivers," said Gopiak. "If he is, tell him we will send a motorboat to pick them up from the Island. I know people I can trust to do this. They will be met in Libance and driven here. We will put them up in one of our own homes. I haven't yet worked out the best way for them to take over the driving of the van, but we can worry about that later. We will of course have to smarten them up – shave their beards, in particular. They will be briefed on what they need to say at the security gate, and they will drop off both the mail bags and Kris Myer. Then they will drive back to the mail depot, where we will pick them up and drive them north to the port where they landed, and they will be returned to the Island. It will all be done in two days.

"You must ask the chief – Xerxes, isn't it? – what he wants in return, but I don't envisage a problem with this. That is what you should say."

I wasn't totally convinced. What would happen if the United troopers searched the van and found Myer? But I nodded in agreement. The others also seemed enthusiastic about Gopiak's proposal, though whether this response was genuine or simply sycophantic, I couldn't tell. What I could see was that the Guardian top team were becoming increasingly desperate in their planning.

We broke up at that point. Irene Gopiak reminded us to get to her election party that evening in good time (I caught Rilka's eye briefly as she said it but couldn't interpret her expression). Elli Dyvers took me to her office so I could call Xerxes' mobile. I left a message asking him to ring me as soon as he could. As I finished, I heard Elli on her phone talking to someone about having the boat ready next Monday morning.

"That's OK," she said, when she'd finished. "They are set up for a mystery trip. You will of course have to get the landing place on the Island from Xerxes, if he wants to go ahead with the deal. I assume you will need to be with them to bring them down here, so I suggest you go up with the car and driver I am provisionally fixing for Sunday and stay in the same hotel. Is that all right with you?"

I hadn't thought about this, but I saw she was probably right. I would need to be part of the team collecting the outlaws, if indeed we went ahead with Irene's plan. I was still worried about the point

Rilka had made, that the United security team were almost bound to search the van and discover Myer, but Gopiak had confidently postponed worrying about this aspect until we knew if Xerxes was willing and able to deliver the crucial outlaw element.

I left the Guardian building and walked first to the *Tribune* offices and then to the Metro television studios, to get the reactions of my editorial teams and their bosses to my efforts, and to sort out some of the stuff that always happens after big stories. Both the paper and the TV news people were in a state of excitement. My Island exclusive, today's Senate elections with Kris Myer's contentious recommendation to the voters, and then tomorrow's big referendum – they hadn't had three successive days of serious news like this in a long time.

I ran across Josep Stilo as I picked up a canteen lunch at Metro. He told me that he had briefed Myer on our latest proposals, and he had come up with a simple but brilliant idea to divert the attention of the United security teams on the Senate vote day. He, Myer, could pre-record a 'live' interview in the morning, which the studio would play out as live exactly at the time he was being smuggled into the Senate. This sort of delayed broadcast happened in television for one reason or another quite often anyway, so the TV people wouldn't be particularly surprised, but anyone watching would assume Myer was actually in the studio at that time if that is how the TV company billed it. Crucially this would include the United bosses and their security people.

I realised instantly that if the security guards at the service entrance were watching this event when the Guardian Express van had to be checked they would be very unlikely to search the bags. The man they would be looking for would, as far as they were concerned, be elsewhere – in the TV studio. It would transform the situation, always provided we could persuade Xerxes to co-operate.

By mid-afternoon I was home and had just dozed off for a nap when my phone rang. It was Xerxes, slightly uncomfortable with this technology that had changed dramatically in the past ten years. "Hallo, Mr Journalist. How interesting to get your message. Most unexpected. Why exactly do you want to talk to me?"

"Xerxes, thank you very much for calling me back so quickly. I want to put a proposition to you. Some very senior people here would like to hire the services of a couple of your men, and for a couple of days next week. If you agree, they will be picked up by motorboat from the Island, brought to Libance, driven down here to the capital, put up for the night, and then, the next morning, asked to put on mail delivery uniforms and to drive a mail van into the Senate building. There it will be unloaded, and they will bring the van back to the depot. After that we do it in reverse, driving them back and getting the boat back to the Island. Oh, and they will have to shave their beards – mailmen don't normally look like Russian hermits.

"In return, the senior people will reward you and your community in any way that is convenient for you. That's it. Not difficult, I think, and no risk to your men. What do you think?"

There was a pause. Xerxes had clearly not anticipated such a request.

"I am suspicious. This sounds very simple. Why should it need two of my men?"

"We need two people who cannot subsequently be traced by the security companies. Though this is not a dangerous venture, something very, very important depends on it – and there are powerful people who will lose out very badly as a result. They will spare no effort to find out all the details, and where possible take revenge on those involved. The security system at the Senate takes photographs of everyone who comes and goes. Any Libancer driving the van would be recorded, and thus be identifiable. No records will exist of your men – and therefore no comeback will be possible."

"I am still suspicious, but also now very intrigued. Please tell me more about these angry powerful people, and what you will have done to make them so angry."

"I am sorry, I cannot at this stage do that. We will tell your men when they are here, and they of course can tell you when they return."

"I do not like that, but let it pass for a moment. These rewards: how generous will you be?"

"Because it is very important, I think my friends will be very generous. How much do you want, and how do you want it delivered to you?"

"Ha, here we have big difficulties obviously. We cannot use electronic money. We have no bank accounts. I could perhaps give you a big list of things we would like, but how will you deliver them here? And would we get these goods before or after this little adventure?"

"We could bring some stuff in the boat, and land it when we pick the men up. We could let you have the rest when they return. We might be able to open an account for you which you could draw on when you are at the market – some real money, over and above what you can achieve through barter."

"Hm, I will have to think about this. I am still very suspicious, and you refuse to tell me things that are clearly of great importance to you and to this adventure. Also, I must think about our rewards. It will help a bit, your idea of us getting stuff before even the men have got on the boat, but basically, I must trust you for the rest, and in particular for the money in the account."

"Xerxes, if you agree, I can set up the account beforehand as well, and you can check that we have put an agreed amount into it before we collect the men."

"How can I check? I am not going to the market for another ten days."

"You can do it by phone," I said wearily. Clearly, he had missed a lot of changes in his years on the Island. "Though I suggest you don't use the phone much before all this; we don't want you running out of batteries."

"Use the phone? This is the first conversation I have had. You have several numbers listed which I could ring I suppose, but what would be the point? Hello, strange person, I am an outlaw and I live on the Island? I don't think so."

"Well, I am glad of that. Listen, when will you call me back? We will need to pick your people up on Monday morning – that's only five days' time. There is a lot to do beforehand if you are going to help us. Oh, and I assume there is a place where we can land easily?"

"Yes, Mortimers has a landing stage. It is old, but it will work, I think. I will have to include the Duggans and Fantonis in this, I suspect. OK, I will call you back during our morning break tomorrow. But I do not like it, that you will not tell me what this is about."

And thus we left it. On balance, I thought he was more interested by the end than he let on. I fell asleep easily enough.

Chapter Twenty-five

Well, the election night was exciting enough. Not just the result: Myer's victory margin was tighter than any of us had expected. However, for me, the really tense part was the meeting between Friya and Rilka at Irene Gopiak's party.

Friya had said she would drive us to the Guardian headquarters, rather than having to rely on getting a taxi back when we needed it. I tried to persuade her that any inconvenience in hanging around for a cab would be more than outweighed by the freedom to drink, but she insisted she was happy to remain sober. She called round for me at 7pm and looked beautiful. I had never seen her in her party gear before, and the effort she had made had been well worth it. Her brown hair had a subtle reddish sheen which caught the light in attractive flashes; she had applied her make up with great care, so that her eyes looked bigger and wider behind her glasses, and her mouth was even more succulent than usual. She was wearing a deep, dark-brown dress that was an elegant variation on the standard little black number, and which showed off her cleavage to great advantage. Gold earrings and a simple but striking gold band necklace, together with a dark brown bag with gold fastenings completed the effect. I stood and gaped when I opened the door.

"Thank you, Bob," she said to my rush of compliments on how she looked. "Well, it is an important night. A girl must do her best on such an occasion." She was so glamorous that it did seem a touch inappropriate to raise the question I had prepared as we drove to the party, but I was sufficiently nervous about her possible response not to want to postpone it. She smiled when I put it to her directly.

"I thought you had forgotten about our Libance peculiarities," she said. "Well, we were careful enough. I doubt any accident will happen. To be honest, I didn't want to raise it with you straightaway.

I thought we could leave notifying the Institute for a while. But of course, if you want to, then we should."

"Hey, look, I'm not trying to step out of line here. If it's what you would do with a Libance man, then let's do it ourselves. When in Rome, and so on." Actually, I was very keen to do it, but I felt slightly worried about looking too enthusiastic.

"Then let's leave it for a while. Libance will survive, and so will we."

There must have been a hundred people at the party when we arrived. Irene Gopiak welcomed us warmly and was graciously charming to Friya. (I had briefly updated her on my conversation with Xerxes that afternoon, which she discreetly acknowledged with a "and thank you for your telephone call earlier, which sounded quite promising.") I spotted Josep Stilo and took Friya over and introduced them.

"Miss Alling, is it? Delighted to meet you. You look more than good enough to be on television. Please allow me to introduce you to Kris Myer later this evening."

Friya blushed and said she would love that. "Now, now Josep," I said. "None of this casting couch stuff here. Tonight is the peak moment in Libance democracy. You above all should be behaving yourself with dignity."

"On the contrary, my dear Bob, tonight's entertainment is the equivalent of the Hollywood Oscars, not the presidential elections." Looking around at the mass of well dressed, sparkling guests all animatedly talking and laughing, with big screens on the walls showing some kind of sophisticated variety programme, I thought he was right, though I didn't say so.

"So how come you're not with the great man right now? I thought you would be sweating in a hot studio gallery."

"Ah, my work is done. We got all our people through earlier, in the first part of the show. Not that it was a surprise. No, the results were much as I predicted. We have 44 senators, the Progressives 28, and the minority parties 12. That will be good enough for our purposes." And he gave me a conspiratorial wink. I didn't believe people really did that, but Josep certainly kept the cliché alive. "Irene insisted I came here. All that remains is the vote for Leader of the Senate, and

I can do nothing to help that. Kris and the Tuller woman will be performing in half an hour, and then we have an hour of voting – and the result!"

Stilo was grabbed by a rather aggressive man in a smart suit that was decidedly too tight for him, and Friya and I were left briefly alone. "An hour doesn't seem very long. Can everyone get through in that time?"

She nodded. "We all have specific call centre numbers to phone or email. There are over fifty of them, and they can handle thousands of calls and messages each in that time. We have lots of practice at this. No-one wants to wait too long for the result. I promise you it will work."

"How do you stop people repeat voting, or swamping the system in some way?"

"You have to give your personal number for yourself first. Once logged, it cannot be used again in that voting round. I suppose people could try and invent numbers and vote more than once, but you'd have to be lucky twice – first that you had got the right call centre, and second that the right person hadn't voted yet. Why would anyone bother? There's never been any evidence of such bad behaviour in the past."

This gave me one reason why Gopiak and Myer had decided to wait until after the referendum to announce his plan for the Senate to reject Proposition 72. The system for voting for the senators seemed very vulnerable to a determined attempt to undermine it, and such an announcement could well have provoked that response.

I went to get some drinks from the bar. As I turned to go back, I saw that Rilka Delene had joined Friya, and they were deep in conversation. I wanted to hurry over and join in – a protective instinct towards Friya, I guess – but something in their manner gave me pause. They looked very engaged in whatever topic they were discussing. At that moment Timo Jankel wandered up and joined me at the bar.

"Ah, now," he said, looking at my drinks, "let me guess who is driving tonight. Not you, I think. Where is your beautiful companion? I have heard about her already and would love to meet her."

"Over there, talking to Rilka."

"Well, she is indeed very striking. I would suggest you took me over with you, but they look quite seriously involved in something. Perhaps they are talking about you."

"And why should they be doing that?" That was of course my deepest fear, but I wasn't going to admit it to Jankel.

"But Bob, you are the centre of so many conversations at the moment. Still, I think we should give them a little more time on their own. I gather you had a useful telephone conversation with your new friend on the Island this afternoon."

"Yeah, sort of. He's thinking about it overnight. I shall get his response tomorrow. I hope he doesn't want anything too much or too difficult in return."

"Money shouldn't be a problem. If Caldor does what we fear he will, then we will find whatever it takes to get our outlaws over here to do the job. If he doesn't then we will cancel the operation. By the way, I have been thinking. It will be impossible to open a bank account in the names of any outlaws, so I suggest we do it in the name of Captain Reinhardt. Your man Xerxes clearly trusts him, and he can arrange to spend whatever he wants through the good captain. I am sure the latter won't attempt to siphon off anything for himself, but if he does, he will face very severe penalties. Xerxes will need a second contact, but any of us in Irene's gang will do for that.

"And I gather you are deputed to travel up north again. You must take documentary evidence with you of the account and how much is in there. Timing is tight, but Irene can make things happen five times as fast as any normal person."

"You guys are going to have to work all this kind of thing out and make all the arrangements. I'm just the go-between."

Jankel looked at me, and then across at Rilka and Friya. "And you do your going between so very well, Bob. I think the ladies have had long enough to discuss whatever it is that has got them going so intensely. Please introduce me to the lovely Miss Alling."

We went over, and I gave Friya her fruit juice, with apologies for the delay, and introduced her to Jankel, who was polite and complimentary in response. Rilka had her usual strong presence; but, while she looked smart and attractive, she knew she could not directly compete with the more alluring appeal of her younger companion. She smiled at Jankel and me. "Friya and I have been having a most interesting discussion – about politics, and sex, largely. We find we agree about the first but have some differences on the second. However, I doubt it would be sensible to repeat these to you. Don't you agree, Friya?"

"I am sure you are right, Governor. I don't know Mr Jankel, but I would be surprised if he wasn't, like Bob, rather vain about his masculinity, and there is no need to massage their egos in that way at all."

"I am not sure that everything we said could be regarded by them as complimentary, but I agree they have a remarkable ability to hear only what flatters them."

"Vain? Susceptible to flattery? What, *moi*?" said Jankel. "After all the time we have known each other, Rilka, I am mortified to think you could attribute such characteristics to me. And I have come to regard Bob, in the short time we have known him, as the model of modesty."

"Dear Timo, such elegant affectation of injured pride. But you do not mind, I know. You would far rather be labelled vain than boring. As for Bob, he may be modest on the surface, but deep down he is convinced he is right about most things. Is that not so, Bob?"

"Rilka," I said, "how can you say that? In my short month in Libance I have been overwhelmed by how often I have had to review, indeed revise, my judgements about how best both to run a country and manage one's life. My convictions are in turmoil."

"You are merely following the precept of your famous English economist, Keynes – when the facts change, I change my mind. That is not modesty, it is the supreme self-confidence of the observer who thinks he is being truly objective. And indeed, you have some justification: your insights have been, and doubtless will be again, invaluable to us all."

"Thank God for that. Well, clearly, I will have to wait to get more details about your differences on sex." Friya blushed slightly; Rilka's eyes narrowed perceptibly. "But it's very good you agreed about politics. What precisely was the issue under discussion?"

"Well, the most important thing was Friya's inadvertent revelation that it was she rather than you that anticipated what Caldor might do when Myer unleashes his thunderbolt in two days' time. I have to admit I was ashamed of you, taking the credit for this important foresight."

Jankel raised his eyebrows. "Yes, I admit I glossed over that," I said. "Though that wasn't out of any desire to win brownie points. I didn't want to open up a discussion about precisely why I had breached the agreement between us to keep these matters to ourselves."

"I'm sorry, Bob," said Friya. "In the excitement of tonight I had forgotten your instruction to keep quiet about it. It just came out naturally in my conversation with Governor Delene."

Rilka patted her on the arm. "No, no, Friya. You are not at fault. We should be grateful to Bob for bringing you into our charmed circle in this way."

It was, I had to admit, an impressive performance. Rilka had effectively wrong-footed all three of us and put us on the defensive. Any jealousy she felt about Friya and me, if indeed she felt any, had been magnificently subdued. At that moment her husband came over and joined us. "Tomas, here you are at last. This is Friya Alling. She works for Western Guardian Security, at the airport amongst other places, and she was the first Libancer to meet Bob when he arrived. Bob has taken supreme advantage of this piece of good fortune and has brought her to this party tonight. Friya, this is Tomas Kryk, my husband. He runs a bank."

"Miss Alling, delighted to meet you. Bob was clearly very lucky to get you as the person who welcomed him to Libance. Rilka, Timo – the final show is about to start. Irene has got seats for us to watch it. Bring your drinks with you and let us go and cheer on Kris Myer."

We moved off to a small screening theatre down the corridor. About half the party stayed behind to watch on the screens in the main room, but we were clearly expected to take more interest in the contest itself, and duly watched with (largely) quiet attention.

It was an extraordinary election ritual. Myer and Tuller each had solo ten-minute performances, and then they sat together to be interviewed for the final ten minutes. Myer went first and did what was presumably a variant of his standard gig – effectively a stand-up comedy routine, with lots of good jokes, none of which were remotely political as far as I could tell. He rounded it off with a highly competent song, which he accompanied on a guitar, and won great applause from the studio audience. (Kryk whispered to me that these were selected by the TV company, supposedly on a non-partisan basis, but that Josep Stilo had as usual managed to infiltrate a good number of Myer supporters.)

Tuller chose a very different approach. She did a rather good presentation of her life and opinions, linking short clips of video. She came over as decent and thoughtful, and as someone with a nicely quiet but sharp sense of humour. It seemed to me much more appropriate to the matter in hand, though I didn't feel able to say so to my friends. She was clapped, not as rowdily as Myer had been, but to my mind with rather greater sincerity.

What did surprise everyone was the final interview sequence. There was not a lot either of the candidates could say in the time available, but whereas Myer looked surprisingly nervous, Tuller handled herself confidently. The main point of interest was the exchange on Myer's call for the Voters' Strike on the next day. Myer blustered rather pompously about the need to show that on such an important matter the Proposition, which should not have been accepted by the Constitutional Court, was discredited. Tuller argued that irrespective of the virtues or otherwise of the proposition it was everyone's duty to vote on it, and that if it was as discreditable as Myer suggested then people could simply turn it down. Myer got agitated about voters being bribed to vote against their real interests, which Tuller refuted straightforwardly – voters would work out for themselves where their interests lay, and it was patronising to assume they wouldn't or couldn't.

I thought she won hands down, and our group looked rather uncomfortable as the show concluded with a call from the presenter to vote now – the lines are open! I was surprised that all – except Friya – commented purely on the stylistic differences, and how Myer had not been up to his usual standard. For her part, Friya simply said that she thought Tuller had made good points, and she hoped it wouldn't mean Myer lost the vote, or indeed that the strike he had called for would be rather less solid than we expected. Then, like everyone else except me, they all got out their phones or handsets and emailed or voicemailed their preferences.

The discussions continued over the hour of voting, during which time we ate the excellent food Irene's people had got ready for us. I found Stilo and asked him what he thought the outcome would be. He didn't seem particularly worried. he agreed Tuller had done well and that Myer had not been his usual excellent self, but said that in his experience people made up their minds weeks or even months ahead of the vote itself, and that there wouldn't be many last-minute people switching their votes on the basis of the final show. "Many people log their votes in advance – you can do this at any time during the day if you want – and I reckon we will have a clear lead amongst those people."

In the event he was right, but only just. We finished eating as the grand finale started on the TV screen. The presenter went through the familiar tease of delaying the announcement of the result, but at last declared it: Lisje Muller: five million, nine hundred and sixty four thousand, three hundred and seventy two votes: Kris Myer: six million, one hundred and fifteen thousand, two hundred and eleven votes. There was tremendous applause in the TV studio, and of course we all cheered and waved enthusiastically too. But, straight after, people turned to each other and all seemed to be saying the same thing – wow, that was close! Much closer than we expected! A majority of less than 200,000 – I thought Myer would win by more than a million!

Our little gang was divided about why it had happened and what it meant for the referendum the next day. Stilo looked shaken, and said he was very concerned that the strike would be a failure, a view supported by Rilka and her husband. Jankel however said that the important thing was that Myer had won, and that tonight's event was very unlikely to have an impact on whether people voted or not on the Proposition. I said that I thought it showed that Libancers were more interested in the politics and less in the entertainment than people had led me to believe, but they all pooh-poohed me on this:

Lisje had come across much more sympathetically than anyone had expected, and it had very little to do with anything political. In which case, I said, then Jankel was probably right, and we shouldn't conclude that tonight's result would have any effect on tomorrow's referendum. But they wouldn't accept this either.

Suddenly I felt very tired, and quietly asked Friya if she would mind leaving the party, even though Kris Myer was expected at any minute. She looked disappointed but agreed to go. We made our farewells, amid the customary clamour of "Oh, are you going so soon? It was lovely to meet you, Friya," and so on, which dragged out our departure for what seemed an age. We sought out Irene Gopiak and thanked her; she was her usual pleasant self and asked me to call her the next day as soon as I had spoken to Xerxes. As we got into Friya's car, we saw a small convoy arriving, and glimpsed Myer, the damaged victor, and his entourage going into the building.

I apologised to Friya for taking her away early as she drove us to my home. "I'm sorry, love, but I am both drunk and shattered. The past few days have suddenly caught up with me. It was a great party and will clearly go on for another couple of hours, and I am very sorry that we missed your hero Myer, but I am desperately tired."

"That's all right, Bob, I can see you are exhausted. Let us get you into bed as fast as we can."

My eyes were closing as I grunted assent. I struggled to rouse myself, and said, "What exactly were you and Rilka saying to each other on sex? I'd love to know."

"I am sure you would, Bob, but not now. We can discuss this when you are sober."

I feebly protested but must have fallen asleep as I did so. I can't really remember how Friya got me out of the car and into bed. When I awoke the next morning, she was gone. I didn't know whether she had slept at my place or not. I found a note which asked me to call her during the day. She had signed it with three kisses, for which I was extremely gratified.

Chapter Twenty-six

I spent a good couple of hours over breakfast going through the newspapers, taking in the TV and radio news bulletins and checking at least some of the blogs on both the Senate elections results and their calculations about that day's referendum. I was struck by how little comment there was on the narrowness of Myer's win, though there was a good deal on how impressive Tuller had been. Nor did many people read across from that narrow victory to any forecasts about the referendum. In that sense Jankel's relaxed views seemed justified.

Just as I was getting ready for my phone call from Xerxes, Friya rang. I hoped it was to explain what had happened to her that morning, but she glossed over that. "No, really, Bob, I have been thinking about what you will say to Xerxes. Surely you must go ahead with your plans even if Caldor doesn't respond to Myer's announcement tomorrow about the Senate vote next week. Why should he say anything about what he intends to do? If he does want to physically prevent Myer getting into the building, he need do nothing until Tuesday morning. Therefore, you must get your Islanders over here and ready to act anyway. And the Guardian must pay for them, even if they do not turn out to be needed."

"Hm, that isn't what Jankel anticipated. But I take your point. If we don't act as if we think Caldor will take preventative action, we will be in no position to deal with it when he does. Thank God someone is thinking straight about this. That's the second time you have spotted what we should do. You should be doing our job for us."

"No, no, Bob, Dr Gopiak has got enough good people around her, she doesn't need me as well. But I wanted to tell you in case all of you decided to relax too early. I will see you for dinner tonight. And fingers crossed for the Voters' Strike."

Friya's call had been timely, because when I spoke to Xerxes, half an hour later, I realised I should commit to a definite plan.

"Well, Mr Journalist and Conspirator, we are willing to provide you with two men for three days. I assume they will not be asked to do anything violent, since you haven't mentioned that, and I think you would have done." No, no, I said, nothing violent at all. "Very well then. You will send your boat to the old jetty at Mortimers – it is marked on your maps – to arrive at ten o'clock Monday morning to pick them up. You will return them by six o'clock in the evening on Wednesday, though of course you can bring them back earlier if you wish. They will follow your instructions. In return we wish to receive thirty thousand dollars, and I would like to know how you propose to make this available to us."

I made a rapid calculation and decided that at $5000 a day per man this was not grossly expensive, particularly as Xerxes had presumably to involve the Duggan-Fantonis in some way as well, but thought I ought to be rather guarded about it. "That's a lot for what we have in mind," I said. "I will have to check with my bosses, though I will recommend we accept your proposal. As to how we will give it to you – what do you think of the idea of opening an account at the Guardian National Bank in the name of Captain Reinhardt, which he will not use himself but will let you use to purchase goods that you want? Of course, you would have to keep in contact with him once he has finished his round of duties at the Causeway, but you have my mobile phone for that. And if there is anything you want us to bring with us on Monday, we can do that too."

There was a long pause before Xerxes replied. "I see the advantages of that suggestion. I would trust Reinhardt to do this, and it would enable us to use the money for purchases when we need it. I had been thinking of some complicated arrangement at the market, but that would involve many traders and they would begin to ask questions that you might wish to avoid. Yes, that suggestion seems a good one. I would like you to give me a telephone number for the captain so I can confirm that he is happy to do this, and also that the account has been opened before Monday morning. Incidentally you will know the two men who will be working for you: Caleb and Dieter, your friendly sleeping companions when you were here. You will have to get them shaved once they land in Libance. So – please confirm with your bosses our arrangement and get me the good captain's number. I will call you back at five o clock this afternoon. And I will also have a list of items for you to bring with you."

I got on to Irene Gopiak immediately, and she was happy with the outcome, even when I made Friya's point about having to commit to paying the Islanders even if Caldor didn't attempt to block Myer at the Senate next Tuesday. "I have been thinking about how we should proceed on Tuesday if the worst happens," she said. "I have spoken to the head of the Guardian Express group and the office manager here in the capital. I did not explain exactly what we are doing, but they understand we wish to take over the delivery of the post to the Senate on Tuesday. We will pick up a couple of mailman uniforms from the manager on Monday. The manager will change the rotas around, so that in the end no-one will actually be scheduled for that run the next day, but no-one should notice. We will take our two special mailmen to his office on Tuesday morning, and they will be given the necessary documentation. The manager will take them to the van, which they will drive out of the yard. Incidentally, I think you will have to give the two outlaws some driving practice on Monday – we don't want them crashing the van. That would be most unfortunate. They will be accompanied by you, and you will bring them to our main offices here. Myer will then be concealed beneath the bags, and taken to the Senate – without you, of course. Josep Stilo will be waiting at the service door in the Senate. If our drivers reverse the van up to the door Myer should be able to get out and into the Senate without being seen. Stilo says the Senate mail room handlers will not cause any trouble – Myer is very popular with the staff."

She made it sound all very straightforward. She confirmed that Myer's idea of the pre-recorded 'live' broadcast would be agreed with the head of the Metro studio late on Monday; not that he couldn't be trusted but it was just safer to keep this particular idea on ice as long as possible.

"I will speak to Captain Reinhardt immediately, the new account will be opened, and the deposit made today. Your friend Xerxes will get all the reassurance he wants. I think we are as well prepared as we can be. And really, Bob, we all owe you an enormous debt of gratitude for your help in this."

She said Elli Dyvers was making the final arrangements about the car and the hotel for Sunday night, and I should talk to her about these. Elli would also arrange the tidying up of our Islanders, get them photographed for the ID cards and look after them in the capital on the Monday night. I could see there was a real benefit in running one of the major security companies. I spoke to Elli a couple of hours later, and she told me to be at the Guardian headquarters building at 9 in the morning on Sunday. I would be accompanied by a Guardian security officer on my journey north, and they would put together whatever list of items Xerxes gave me that afternoon.

This all seemed very efficient and left me with nothing more to do for the next couple of days, other than writing up a column on what I thought Caldor would do once he had won the referendum. I got on with that immediately, since it was a foregone conclusion Proposition 72 would pass when the result was announced at 6pm that evening. I checked the voting channel, but all it said was voting was ongoing. Interestingly, given Myer's call for a boycott, they left out the usual mantra about making sure you voted in time. They must have thought it was too partisan in the circumstances. The column was due with the Tribune the next day, for publication on Sunday morning. I decided I would incorporate a section on Myer's intention to get the Senate to vote the Proposition down after he announced it on Saturday morning. It was all a bit tight, but fortunately I knew what I wanted to say.

I began to think about what Friya and I might do on the Saturday. I assumed she had the day off, and for the first time I could hope to spend a day with her doing normal Saturday things like shopping, going out for a walk somewhere pleasant, taking in a film or the theatre. I decided to call her and ask if she was prepared to spend all day with me in this way.

When I spelled out my ideas she laughed. "Well, well, Bob, that does sound wonderfully normal. I had begun to wonder if you ever did anything like that. I will have to re-fix some things I was planning to do, but that isn't a problem. Of course we can have the day together. Let us plan it when we meet tonight for dinner. And let me cook for you at my place, rather than going out to a restaurant. I will enjoy that."

The sudden prospect of an ordinary weekend, well, Saturday, at least, was so enticing I found myself reacting almost as an adolescent, so intense was the pleasure and excitement I felt. I wrote out a shopping list – trickier, given what was likely to happen in the first half of the week, than I had expected – researched the movies and plays, and looked at a map of the city to check out parks and similar walking possibilities. I looked at the weather forecasts available in the papers, on the TV and on the web; all looked reasonable for a day of wandering around. I was so wrapped up in all this that the phone call from Xerxes at five o'clock sharp almost surprised me.

"Good God," I said, "I didn't think you kept clock time so precisely up there on your Island."

"Normally, we do let it slip, I agree. We fit in with the seasons. However we are making very important business, I think. I know how business people regard punctuality. So I am checking my mobile phone clock very carefully. You are properly prepared, I hope."

In fact, we sorted the remaining matters out very swiftly. He had already spoken with Reinhardt, who had been rather taken aback by the earlier call from Irene Gopiak – "I do not think the captain usually gets telephone calls from the top person in Libance" was Xerxes' comment – but who could confirm the arrangements and the arrival of the $30,000 in his new account. He didn't ask what was going on; his professional discipline helped him out on this. Xerxes gave me a list of stuff he wanted brought over on the boat, and that was that. I told him I would be coming with the boat, and he said he would look forward to seeing me again. It was becoming all strangely mundane.

I had just enough time to pass on the list of provisions to Elli Dyvers before settling down to watch the announcement of the referendum result on the six o'clock news. It was obviously being treated far more elaborately than was usual for such events. Very unusually, the chairwoman of the Referendum Authority, which organised and supervised the entire range of Libance voting, made her announcement live on the steps of her office. The Proposition passed with 4,520,702 votes in favour and 535,612 against. Immediately afterwards political experts gave their views, which were that the vote in favour was lower, and the vote against higher, than expected, though of course this did not affect the result. Apparently, there were nearly 14 million people over 18 in Libance and therefore entitled to vote. Caldor had got roughly 32% of the electorate to vote in favour, though 90% of the votes actually cast.

He came on to look and sound very cheerful about the ninety per cent, and dismissive of the large number of absent voters. "I have all along said that the so-called Voters' Strike was irrelevant. The Proposition has been passed overwhelmingly. We will start getting on with the merger on Monday. I am very grateful to all those who voted in favour." Irene Gopiak and others said that it was a sad day for Libance, but that they hoped the Competition Court would take into account the large number of abstentions when they came to consider the effects in due course. A couple of pundits said they thought Lisje Tuller's performance in the Senate election finals might have persuaded a couple of hundred thousand people to vote yes who might otherwise have abstained. They also speculated that many people who would benefit from the merger hadn't bothered to vote because they could see it would get through easily, though this provoked a rather tedious legal argument about how any court could work this out if it ever needed to. No-one talked about the Senate vote on Tuesday, though the news presenter did say that Kris Myer had been unavailable for comment.

Rilka called me as I was getting ready to go out to Friya's place. It showed, I reflected, her unerring capacity to time things awkwardly for me, but she was calm and businesslike. We swapped views on the result, both saying it was useful that fewer than a third of the electorate had been in favour, and then she said she was going to be at the National Democrat Party headquarters next day when Kris Myer would declare his intention to veto the result. "I assume you won't be there, Bob. I know you journalists like to pretend to be impartial and objective at such times, even for something as historic as this will be. But of course, you will be doing something much more important on Sunday."

I was mildly surprised she knew about my being on the boat trip, but it scarcely mattered. We finished with me saying vaguely I hoped to see her soon, and she agreeing equally vaguely. After I had put the phone down I told myself that I had got away pretty lightly.

Chapter Twenty-seven

As it turned out, I hadn't. When I got to the Guardian head offices just before 9 on Sunday morning, I was welcomed by Elli Dyvers – and Governor Rilka Delene. "Well, Bob," said the Governor with a confident smile, "here's a pleasant surprise for you. I have decided I need to go with you to help you in this important task. We will drive north in my car, and two security troopers will accompany us in the SUV carrying the stuff Xerxes wants, and which will bring back the young men he has selected for us. I am sure you will agree this is a good arrangement."

"Governor, it is always good to have you as a guide and adviser on any job I do. It is a surprise but a very pleasant one. I am properly grateful." And I nodded a greeting to Elli, who was looking quietly amused at this development. I wondered quite what Rilka had told her when she fixed this deal for herself.

I was in a tremendously good mood, and I wasn't going to allow the unexpected presence of Rilka to dent it. My Friday night and the whole of Saturday with Friya had been even better than I had anticipated. We had had a luxurious Friday evening, eating and fucking and watching the TV screen and drinking and fucking and smoking dope and fucking and sleeping – eventually. We didn't discuss the current Libance political crisis, but instead had talked about our lives; mostly, our past lives. We were, I think, a bit apprehensive about the future, and didn't want to let our conversation get out of control.

We had woken up late on the Saturday morning, had made a sexual shambles around our breakfast, which effectively became lunch as well, and then decided that we had missed the chance of doing our household shopping and instead went out for a long walk along the riverside and back through an enchanting park. (I recognise that the park was probably ordinary enough, but I was enchanted, so it deserves the adjective.) We talked about the films and books and plays we had seen and read. Libance seemed to get most of the stuff that came out in Europe and the USA, I am not sure how, though it always appeared rather later than it did in those two markets.

By great good luck we found an off-beat American film on in a central cinema which was both romantic and funny and appealed to both of us, and which I had missed in London; we went to the late afternoon showing, came out in the twilight and Friya recommended a nearby restaurant. The food was delicious – OK, it might actually have been pleasantly ordinary, but in my mood, it was transformed into a gourmet delight – and we got back to Friya's home around ten in the evening. We were exhausted but not, it turned out, quite satiated.

My 9am start at the Guardian offices meant I had to leave Friya very early to get back to my flat and collect what I needed for the journey north. I took my taxi ride afloat on a glorious sense of well-being, which kept going through my packing and the second ride, to the Guardian. As I got into Rilka's car (having met the two troopers and checked out the list of goods provided by Xerxes) I was still in a great mood.

Rilka must have detected it but made no comment directly. The streets of the city were quiet and remained so as we got onto the motorway north. We chatted in a desultory manner, and then Rilka asked what I had made of Kris Myer's dramatic public appearance the day before. I had completely forgotten that he had planned to do this – indeed the entire event had passed Friya and me by in our long morning of pre-occupation with ourselves. We hadn't watched the TV news all day, nor had we caught a radio bulletin either.

"Er, do you know, I didn't see it," I mumbled rather shamefacedly. "Did it go as planned?"

"You didn't see it?" Rilka looked at me with disbelief, which slowly hardened into what almost felt like mocking contempt. "My, my, the great outcome of your ingenious plan, the revolutionary moment when we do as you suggested and turn the political and constitutional world upside down, and you missed it?" For a moment it looked as if she was going to ask what on earth I had been doing, but for whatever reason she didn't. I just shook my head and looked out of the window. "Was it OK? Did Myer do it well?"

Rilka didn't answer for a moment, just drove on steadily. "Yes, yes, he was good. Very good in fact. The party organisation had prepared well. The news reporters found a significant majority of the elected senators ready in principle to support him in vetoing the referendum result. Lisje Tuller said this would be a very serious step, but she stopped short of saying it was unconstitutional or anything like that. She was clearly taken aback but behaved with real dignity. Most interestingly, Dirk Caldor didn't appear on TV or say anything in the papers. The reports just said he was unavailable for comment. A junior spokesman from the United group waffled on about a completely unprecedented action and people wouldn't accept such an outrageous action by the Senate, blah blah blah – he looked completely out of his depth, poor lamb. And there is more of the same in this morning's bulletins and the papers. A mixture of surprise, shock, some predictable outrage and a lot of admiring support. Have you looked at the blogs? No, I thought not. Well, they are a similar mix. A divided response, but much as we expected. And nothing from Caldor."

"So we don't know what he will do, or even if he will do anything," I said.

"Are you surprised?"

"No, not particularly. Fri— I spoke to Dr Gopiak about having to carry on whatever Caldor said or didn't say in response to Kris, and she agreed. Which is after all why we are still driving north. We have to act as though the United troopers will block Myer right up until the moment he mounts the Senate steps on Tuesday – and only then will we know."

"Yes, Irene told me of your latest conversation. You made a good point. Timo Jankel was all for calling the whole thing off and saving the money, but we made him see sense after a while. You have a column in the *Tribune* tomorrow, don't you? What will it say?"

I thought of my article sitting unfinished on my laptop and wondered quite how I had managed to forget to see what Myer had actually said the day before. "I will write it when we get to our hotel.

You don't happen to have a transcript of what Kris said, do you? It doesn't matter, I can check the internet when we get there."

"Ah, you will be busy when we arrive. I had hoped to show you the little harbour and our boat. Perhaps we can still find time for that."

We drove north steadily, mixing idle chatter with quite lengthy periods of silence. Rilka seemed to be thinking hard, inasmuch as it was possible to make such a judgement about someone who wasn't saying anything much, but the mix of the silent and the mundane suited me. At one point, Rilka confirmed my guess that this motorway must have been built before the Revolution; I said I couldn't see how any contractor could have got all the many necessary community agreements after it and we had a brief discussion about the merits of road-pricing schemes. Needless to say, the tolls we paid on this motorway seemed excessive to me.

We passed two largeish cities and a number of small towns, though these began to give out the further north we got. I took over the driving for the last part of the journey. Shortly after swapping places, Rilka suddenly asked if I believed in God.

"No, not really."

"Not really? How can you 'not really' believe in God? Either you do or you don't. I certainly don't."

"OK, OK, I don't." I paused for a moment. "I have to say I haven't detected much religious thinking or activity amongst the Libancers I have met so far."

"Well, you have tended to mix with our elites, and any religious beliefs are in a small minority amongst them. But there is a larger proportion in the population more generally. There is a similar groundswell in favour of charismatic and evangelical groups as I have read about in the US and Latin America and parts of Africa. Fortunately for us, we don't have any Muslim immigrants. Indeed, we have escaped the various migrations of the past half century almost entirely. I suppose it is a beneficial if unintended consequence of our largely self-imposed isolation from the rest of the world. Before the Revolution we were too far away, and not particularly prosperous enough, to be of interest, and afterwards it became just too difficult to get here."

"Lucky you, to have missed the war on terror, 2 major global recessions and, what was by all accounts, an appalling pandemic."

"Indeed. However, back – if we may – to not believing in God. I am interested in how you develop your ethical code if it is not based on any religion. I am sure you must have such a code."

"Well, I think it probably is based on religion indirectly. Culturally the British have retained at least some of the basic behavioural attitudes that developed when they were a Protestant country, even if most of them don't actively subscribe to any kind of Christian belief anymore. Obviously, the commandments against stealing and murder live on in the law. Respecting your parents – well, that isn't obligatory, but I think it sort of survives as a natural human thing to do. Coveting your neighbour's ass, if we take that symbolically rather than literally, is again something that if you do it you tend to do it quietly. Aspirations to own an abundance of glossy material goods are not as widespread as you might think, in my view. We are inundated with advertising, and the pressure on parents that comes from children wanting what their friends have can be pretty insistent, but I think most people strike a sensible balance between trying to get a decent share of the good things in life and busting your bank credit with crazy consumer spending.

"Sex, of course, is more tricky. The old monogamous pressures, reinforced as they were by specific Christian injunctions, have largely collapsed throughout Europe. People struggle to find their own individual accommodations. But I suspect most of us want to behave decently towards our lovers and partners. Does that owe something to past religious beliefs? You tell me."

"I recognise what you are describing," said Rilka. "Indeed it fits closely enough with what I and my friends believe. Theoretically of course, as citizens of Libance with no government, hardly any laws and no taxes, we are even freer from religious or ethical constraints than you are. Nor do we have any formal obligations to worry about the welfare of our fellow citizens. But I think we too struggle, as you put it, to find ways to behave decently."

I wasn't quite sure whether the cheerful lust she had shown for me quite fitted my sense of her behaving decently, but I recognised my own complicity in the encounters and kept the thought to myself. Rilka however hadn't finished.

"Would you say we had any obligations towards each other?"

"Obligations? I don't know – it rather depends on what you mean by obligations. I treat you decently, I hope. And I have no complaints about your behaviour to me."

"Let us assume we agree about that. But what about our obligations to other people: are we breaching those in any way by what we do together?"

"I'm not sure we are equally bound in that respect. You, after all, are married, with children. I am a single man freshly arrived here with no such baggage. I mean, I left my ex-wife and children in London, so they don't count in the same way."

"Oh, I realise you think that about your family. I am not sure I agree but let us leave that. Why do you assume I have breached my contract with Tomas and my children?"

I shrugged. "Well, I guess he wouldn't be delirious about knowing about the sex with me. I wasn't really including your children in this. I don't think you have any intention of leaving them."

She smiled to herself. "Ah, my intentions. What do you know of those? Come to that, what do I know? You of course do not feel the need to concern yourself about what I might intend to do. And why should you? As you say, a freshly arrived single man with no baggage. The epitome of freedom. But why do you seem to assume that Tomas knows about the sex between us?"

"I don't. But you risk him finding out. And I doubt he would like it if he did."

"Well, let us just say that risk is mine to worry about. But what of you – and Friya Alling? Do you run the risk of her finding out about us?"

I squirmed inwardly at this. I certainly did not want to talk about it. "If you don't mind, I would prefer to keep what I say and do with Friya to myself."

"So – now we have come up against an ethical boundary. We cannot blame God for this one. But is it a manifestation of so-called decent behaviour, or just a way of avoiding embarrassment?"

"I'm not embarrassed. I just don't feel obliged, as you put it, to share my thoughts with you."

"Clearly you don't. But she is quite happy to talk to me about you."

"What? Oh, you mean that conversation you had at the party the other evening. Well, I don't think it is an analogous circumstance. She came with me, people knew that; she would naturally respond to any questions you might put to her, as she had no reason to suppose they would be anything other than innocent. Whereas you and I have a history here; not a long one, I grant you, but enough to cloud the issue."

"My, you are sounding unusually arrogant, pompous and complacent. Do you know what we said to each other?"

"No, I don't." But I was beginning to wish I did.

"Then I don't think you can make judgements about the innocence or otherwise of our conversation."

I fought back the strong temptation to ask her for the details of her conversation with Friya. I had decided not to ask Friya herself; there had never seemed to be the right moment, and I was vaguely aware that she might refuse, or the details would not turn out in a way I liked, and this had meant I had left it unexplored. But I hadn't expected Rilka to deploy it against me in this way. I was stuck.

Then Rilka smiled. "OK, Bob, I will let you off the hook. You are a decent man, and you don't really deserve this grilling. We are going to turn off this road in a few minutes, so be prepared."

Twenty minutes later we arrived at a small seaside village, which looked as though its inhabitants made modest livings out of fishing and a small tourist trade. We pulled up at a shabby hotel opposite the harbour, and checked in. Rilka and the two security troopers were going on to a Guardian-owned jetty and boat sheds half a mile out of the village, to sort out the boat and pack the goods ahead of tomorrow's early departure. I stayed behind to finish the *Tribune* column and email it to the features desk by my 4pm deadline. I managed it – just – and then lay on the bed, fell asleep and was out for over an hour.

I was woken by a phone call from Rilka, saying she and the troopers were proposing to eat an early supper, and inviting me to join them. I agreed. I was slightly surprised; I had fully expected her to set up an intimate twosome for us.

Over supper, which was an awkward affair as far as I was concerned (though Rilka found it easy enough to banter with the troopers about their working lives and Guardian insider stuff more generally), I did manage to ask her about the likelihood of our movements being traced by the United people fairly quickly. She was quite calm about it. "Our phone calls are all made on Guardian networks. It will take them a couple of weeks to go through the procedures needed to get the details from our people. Similarly with the road toll information. Of course, the movements of both vehicles are traceable, but they would need to know not only our route, which they might get by elimination, but also the details of the vehicle registrations. That in itself wouldn't take too long, but I would guess it will be at least three days at the earliest before they can get enough information to make a shrewd guess about the purpose of our trip. And that's if they start with accurate presumptions. By which time our Islander guests will be safely back in their outlaw refuges."

I had previously discussed the prospect of United action against me, and the Guardian people involved in this exercise, with Irene Gopiak, and she had convinced me that even if Caldor and his investigators did manage to work out what we had done there was no case they could bring. "What is the nature of the complaint? That the mail company used a couple of outlaws deceitfully? Who was injured by this? No-one. What contractual arrangements were breached? None. The mail was delivered – end of story."

Afterwards I lay in bed contemplating the ironies of life in Libance. A series of what in any normal country would constitute dubious – where they weren't downright illegal – actions of one kind or another could happen here without redress. Caldor exploits the accidental death of a Supreme Court justice to get a referendum which under normal circumstances would be ruled out. Myer and the Guardian group call for a voters' boycott of the referendum, and then Myer proposes to breach all the de facto rules of the Senate to block the result. Caldor (if he does) physically prevents Myer getting into the Senate to move the vote. The Guardian team hire a couple of outlaws to masquerade as mailmen and smuggle Myer into the Senate anyway (if we succeed). In between Metro TV puts out as live a pre-recorded interview with Myer to confuse the viewers, and Caldor's people in particular. In this country it would all, apparently, be permissible because no law or regulation prevented it. Ridiculous, all of it.

They weren't the only thoughts that kept me awake. I was acutely conscious of Rilka in the next room. I strained my ears to hear her undressing and getting ready for bed. I waited for the phone call which would summon me to her room. When it didn't come, I wrestled, with mounting desperation, with my desire to call her and ask to join her. It would be a first: she had so far taken all the initiatives. It would, as she would doubtless tell me, be in breach of my 'obligations' to Friya. Worst of all, she might turn me down.

In the end it was that prospect which decided me. Whether or not she gloated or was regretfully sympathetic, I couldn't face the idea of either. I masturbated in a small fury of frustration. Sleep – when it eventually came – was a relief.

Chapter Twenty-eight

This is the article which that appeared in the *Tribune of Libance* under the heading **The Return of Real Politics**.

"One of the most fascinating aspects of life in Libance is the way you have eliminated conventional politics – or you had until Saturday. On that day the Leader of the new Senate, Kris Myer, made an announcement that astonished the country. He said he would move the rejection of the recent referendum decision to permit the merger of the United and Health & Prosperity insurance groups in the Senate. He seemed confident this resolution would be passed tomorrow.

The shock of course comes from what in any other country would be a normal political move. Here in Libance, however, you have gone so far down the road of making politics a subsidiary of the entertainment industry that this – apparently entirely legal – manoeuvre causes admiration and outrage in equal degrees. The idea that the Senate might actually activate its hitherto dormant right to reject a popular referendum result is entirely novel.

It is however not exactly a one-off. Last week we had the final rounds in the general election of Libance Senators, which coincided with the United merger referendum. Kris Myer and most of his National Democratic Party colleagues had called for a boycott of the referendum – another highly unusual tactic. This was because they believed that normally the referendum proposition would have been disallowed by the Constitutional Court, and it only scraped through thanks to the sudden death of Mr Justice Riccardo. Mr Myer made much of his boycott in his senatorial election campaign. Since he won this, one must suppose he feels the boycott and his intention of using of his Senate majority to frustrate the referendum are both democratically justified.

To me, an outsider, this is just what one would expect of a politician fighting for what he believes in. But here it is so unusual it almost justifies the label of a 'coup' that United supporters have given it. By reawakening the Senators to their historical but long forgotten task of using their powers seriously instead of as a way of making us laugh, Mr Myer, an outstanding entertainer himself, is entering an entirely new world, and one without precedents or obvious parameters. Let us hope he and his colleagues can cope with the consequences.

However, there is an extra dimension to this story which has attracted little if any attention. Everyone seems to assume that Dirk Caldor, the United chief executive, sought the referendum result simply for the commercial advantages the hitherto unacceptable merger would give his company. While this must be partly true, it is not, in my view, the main purpose. For what Mr Caldor wants to do is to wake this country up from the deep conservative sleep into which it has, in his view, fallen. Economic activity is sluggish at best. It is hard, if not impossible, to get the necessary approvals to start major new businesses, build new roads or railways or airports, indeed build anything new much at all unless it simply replaces an old house, factory or office.

This is, he argues, the unintended consequence of the glorious Revolution of thirty years ago, the Revolution which abolished taxes, government and all but basic laws. Everything is put to the vote of all the adults in the country. At any one time there are a dozen votes under way. Of course, people are so used to voting that many of them don't take it that seriously. Many of them in fact rarely vote at all, unless they themselves feel threatened by the proposals; then they push their buttons with great determination. The result: most new projects are turned down. In Britain we have a phrase for this: Nimbyism – Not In My Back Yard. Nimbyism, it seems to me, turns out to be the (unacknowledged) ruling principle of Libance life.

In my conversation with Mr Caldor a couple of weeks ago, when he outlined his idea of trying to change this deep-seated mindset, he didn't say quite how he intended to go about it, other than that the United/H&P merger was the necessary starting point.

Now it looks as though this will fall at the last hurdle. So while I am intrigued by Kris Myer's bold move to veto the referendum in the Senate, I will also be sorry to see Dirk Caldor's visionary strategy for shaking things up come to a sudden end. But at least a genuinely political arena has opened up, which he and others like him can seek to exploit.

Libance is about to discover the fun of real politics.

Chapter Twenty-nine

"Well," said Lee to me as we stood on the crumbling jetty soon after 10 the next morning, watching the outlaws taking the goods for Xerxes off the motor launch, "here's a turn-up. Bet you weren't expecting to see me again this morning."

Indeed I wasn't. Our party had set off after an early breakfast in the Guardian's boat, an old naval vessel which nonetheless moved at good speed through the choppy seas south of the Island. I had phoned Friya almost as soon as I had woken up, feeling guilty about failing to do so the previous evening. She had been calm enough, commenting favourably on my latest *Tribune* article which she had just read over her breakfast, and wishing me well on my day of adventure. I didn't mention the presence of Rilka; there was no easy way to do it over the phone. Not that it really mattered, of course.

Neither of us, nor the Guardian troopers, nor indeed the half dozen crew, spoke much on the journey. The early morning mists cleared steadily, and the captain was confident of pushing on at speed. "There's no-one out here in this mist," was his view, which seemed a touch complacent to me, but which proved true enough in the event. The tension palpably rose when we saw the coast of the Island, and as we proceeded round the western shoreline towards where the map showed Mortimers Landing to be, up a long inlet. The captain ordered two of his men to man the heavy machine gun sited below the bridge: only Rilka and I stood on the deck looking out towards the oncoming coast; everyone else took cover below decks.

Fortunately, the tide was full, and we were able to come up alongside the long pier which ran out from the shore. I recognised the bulk of Xerxes among the dozen people gathered on the pier, though the rest looked indistinguishable in their ragged bundles. It wasn't until we were hove to, and men were tying up the ropes we threw them, that I suddenly saw that Lee was one of the waiting party.

"Hullo again, Mr Journalist," said Xerxes as we jumped off the boat. "What a good job you gave me your mobile phone, I think. And this is Commandant Delene, I believe. It is very nice to see you again, Commandant, though I do not think you remember me."

Rilka clearly didn't, though given the years since they could have last met it was not a surprise. It turned out she had been on the final panel hearing his case before he was sent to the Causeway. Xerxes couldn't have known she was coming with me, and he understandably didn't know of her greater rank, but it was still remarkable that he instantly recognised her.

Rilka was impressively confident and relaxed meeting this bunch of miscreants, shaking hands and being cheerful throughout. When Xerxes explained that he had switched Lee for Dieter at her request the previous day, "It did not seem to me it would matter to you, Mr Journalist, since though you have not told me what you want us to do it cannot be beyond this woman, whose competences you are already aware of," and this with a beaming smile of complicity, Rilka had brushed away my feeble attempt to protest.

"You are quite right, Chief," she said to him. "I am sure Lee – that is your name, isn't it, dear? – is more than capable of what we need from her."

Lee and I had only the briefest of conversations. I was acutely aware of Rilka's amused interest in my evident discomfiture, and in less than a quarter of an hour we had unloaded the goods and were ready to depart with our two guests. Xerxes bid farewell to his companions with heavy-lidded benevolence; "I am sure you will be fascinated by your trip but equally sure you will be glad to be back here in three days' time," and was graciously complimentary to both Rilka and me. "Well, Mr Journalist, you have set up an excellent relationship between my people and the Guardian insurance company. I am truly grateful to you." It was as though my rough expulsion from the Island only a week before hadn't happened.

My last sight of Xerxes was as we turned out of the inlet and Mortimers Landing. I couldn't of course really discern this, but he still seemed to be faintly and mysteriously smiling as we disappeared from his view. Dieter and Lee stood close to me on the rear deck. They gazed back at their colleagues stolidly, and without any visible emotion. Not surprising, I suppose, given they would back with them within three days.

As we sailed back to the mainland, I listened to Rilka briefing the two outlaws on what we wanted them to do. She made it sound mundane and very easy, though I suspect they saw the potential dangers that she was ignoring. After we got back to the capital, they would be driven to Elli Dyvers' home, where they would spend the night. Elli would have a couple of Guardian Express uniforms and two fake identity cards ready for them; Rilka took their photographs on her handset and said she would email these and their size details through to Elli once we had reached the mainland.

On Tuesday morning they would drive to the Express sorting depot, where they would be met by the manager and taken straight to the mail van scheduled for the Senate trip. Their job was to drive it to a particular office building, escorted by an unmarked Guardian security vehicle, where they would pick up a special passenger. He would hide behind the sacks of mail in the van, and they would drive to the back entrance of the Senate building.

Rilka assured them that the security guards would let them in without a fuss. It was a daily visit, and sometimes they looked in the back of the van and sometimes they didn't, but it wouldn't be a problem either way. They would then drive the van to the back door and reverse it up to the threshold. They would be met by Josep Stilo and a couple of hand-picked post room staff; the van would be emptied, and their passenger would slip into the building.

They would then drive out of the yard, pick up their escort and be taken back to Elli's house. They would change back into their normal clothes – she couldn't avoid grimacing slightly when she mentioned these – and be driven back to the northern fishing village, where this boat would be waiting to take them back to Mortimers Landing that evening. It was all very straightforward.

Dieter made one comment and asked one question. He would need some driving practice to make sure he could do it, particularly the reversing manoeuvre, since he hadn't driven for several years. And if it was so easy, why were we going to the hassle of hiring outlaws in this manner? Why not use the normal PO staff? Rilka said he could drive her car for part of the way back, and that they couldn't get Express staff to do the job because once it was discovered that we had used the mail van in this way, which would take a couple of days at least, in her view, these staff would be vulnerable to revenge attacks from United security people, whereas Dieter and Lee would not be traceable.

I noticed that neither of them asked who their special passenger would be, and why he had to gain entrance in this way. I doubt Rilka would have told them, but it certainly made things easier that they didn't even try to find out. And she never mentioned the possibility that, if Caldor didn't try to stop Myer the following morning, none of this elaborate scheme would be needed anyway.

When we landed Rilka took me aside. "I think you should go back in the guards' car, not with me. I will take these two with one of the guards. We will go directly to Elli's place, while you can go to Irene's offices, report back and get your instructions for tomorrow."

"My instructions?"

"Yes, she wants you to be in the escort car. I don't know why – is there a problem?"

I shrugged. "Not that I can see. I suppose it might be fun to be in at the finish."

"Good. Well, I'll say goodbye for now. The best of luck. When we next meet Myer will have won the day, one way or the other." And she kissed me on the cheek.

As I took turns with the security trooper to drive us back to Libance City I realised I was grateful not to be stuck with Rilka and Lee on the long trip. I wondered whether their women's intuition had suggested that I had had sex with both, and that Rilka at least had found it more comfortable to be without me in such circumstances. But maybe that was too egocentric a thought.

It was the evening before I got to the Guardian headquarters and saw Irene Gopiak. She accepted my report calmly and didn't question why Xerxes had sent Lee instead of a man. She told me that while

Caldor had not said anything publicly about Myer's intention to get the Senate to veto the referendum result, she thought he would prevent him getting into the building the next day. The papers, the TV news and the blogs had been buzzing with excitement all day at the prospect of Myer's coup, with opinion overall slightly in favour of what he was planning. Lisje Tuller had said that she was opposed to using the Senate in this way, but she had not been as vociferous about it as some of our people had feared.

"Bob, I hope you don't mind, but I would really appreciate it if you could pick Myer up from the Metro TV studios tomorrow, if it does turn out to be necessary. Currently we expect him to get there by ten, do his interview and be finished by eleven. You will have a car and driver and should be at the back entrance of the studios by ten thirty, ready to bring him here. The Express mail van will come by at around eleven fifteen and Myer will hide himself in it here. You will join the escort car, which will lead the van to the back of the Senate building – which should take quarter of an hour at most. You will park nearby and wait for it to come out; then your driver will lead our two outlaws back to Elli's house. Finally, you can come back here and celebrate our victory."

She looked tired but smiled at the prospect of success. I said I was happy to do as she suggested, but wondered – why me?

"Well, to be frank, I trust you more than most of my people to do this sensibly; you won't get too excited. Then you are known to the outlaws, which must help them a bit. Finally – and I hope you won't be offended by this – you are a bit like them; not a Libance citizen, at least not yet. If anything goes wrong, it will help us contain the damage."

I hadn't thought of it like that, and I have to say it wasn't the most encouraging thing I had ever heard, but on balance I couldn't really see it going wrong and then me having to take the consequences, whatever they might be. So, I said OK.

I was starving by the time I got back to Friya's place. She had cooked a meal for me, which I wolfed down. I described the day, but didn't mention Rilka, though I did say Xerxes had sent his woman on the trip rather than the man originally mentioned. Like Dr Gopiak, she was full of the way the story was playing out in the media and was very excited by the role I had been asked to take on the next day. We went to bed soon enough, and I am glad to say that exhausted though I was, it didn't stop us enjoying ourselves thoroughly.

Chapter Thirty

We woke early next morning. I was far more apprehensive than I had expected to be, and Friya was bouncing with excitement. "Ooh, I do wish I could get down to the Senate instead of dragging myself off to the airport for boring duty," she announced over breakfast. "Today is a historic moment. I would love to be there when it all happens!"

"Well at least you can watch it on television. I will be stuck in a car doing nothing much except looking out for my two tame outlaws. I can follow most of it on the car radio, I suppose. Not the most historic way to take part in this glorious event." However, I decided I would go to the TV studios via the Senate building, and Friya offered to drop me off on her way to work. I didn't really expect Caldor's troopers to let Myer in, but I might just be able to see the outcome for myself.

As it turned out, Friya had to let me out a couple of blocks from the Senate, as troopers had already set up traffic diversions. None of this had stopped a large crowd gathering in the plaza in front of the Senate steps. I struggled to find a place from where I could see most of what was happening, eventually standing on the steps of a large office building facing directly onto the Senate. By nine o'clock there must have been some ten thousand people crammed into the plaza, which seemed extraordinary to me. Most of them appeared to be Myer supporters. When I spotted Axal and a gang of young people in the crowd, I began to realise this was an organised event. I was even more surprised when I saw Rexy and many Raptor men and women near the front. Clearly the Guardian machine had worked hard to bring out as many of its supporters as it could this morning. Presumably they were there either to cheer Myer into the building, or to protest if he was refused admission.

However, Caldor and the United machine had been just as hard-working. There were at least a hundred of heavily armed troopers in their dark green uniforms carefully distributed on the steps of the Senate. (Caldor must have cancelled all leave for his men in the capital.) Tough steel and concrete barriers prevented the large crowd of demonstrators getting onto the steps themselves. I noticed that a route, protected by the same barriers, had been created through the plaza, presumably to allow senators and their staffs to drive up. At the edge of the plaza, where the cars would enter this improvised roadway, they had erected formidable-looking gates. All this must have been done overnight, and it strongly suggested Myer would be stopped.

I couldn't believe that, in such a situation, Myer would be expecting his supporters to try to rush the security troopers. They would have great difficulty climbing over the barriers and would be easily picked off if they tried it. While I didn't want to think about the slaughter that would ensue if any such attempt was made, I realised there was no law or restraint which would prevent the United men opening fire without warning.

Fortunately, the crowd seemed in a good humour, chanting and singing snatches of Myer's best songs. I guess they thought he would be admitted.

We soon found out that he wouldn't. Around nine, a stream of cars and taxis began to arrive. They were slowly processed at the gates, dropped their passengers at the steps, and then moved away. The Senators and their staff either looked amazed at the crowd (if they were Caldor people) or at the barriers (if Myer's supporters). Just before nine thirty, a large dark green car was stopped at the gates and refused permission to proceed.

The crowd spotted this and became agitated. Then Myer got out, to a great cheer, and was clearly arguing with the troopers. The crowd began to chant, "Myer In, Myer In." The mass of troopers on the steps suddenly took up defensive positions, weapons ready to fire. Myer climbed onto the roof of his car and raised his arms for a hush. (He ignored the cars piling up behind his vehicle.)

"Comrades!" he yelled. "You can see what is happening. These United troopers are refusing to let me in." A great roar of anger and disapproval from the crowd. "This is highly illegal. I am the elected Leader of the new Senate. These men have no right to stop me entering. We all know why they do, of course. They fear that if I am admitted the Senate will pass the resolution that is down in my name today: the resolution overturning the fraudulent referendum result which would allow the merger of United with Health and Prosperity insurance. This takeover should have been stopped by the Court, but thanks to the corrupt judges, and their reduced numbers, it wasn't. So only the Senate can do the job our constitution requires.

"You can see how desperate Dirk Caldor and his minions are. They have taken advantage of the fact that United holds the current Senate security contract. All these troopers have been brought here to make sure I do not get into the Senate today." He paused, and there was another angry roar.

"Do not, I ask you, resort to violence. These men have guns, and you don't. But I do ask you to stay here and continue your protests peacefully. Libance needs to see the full illegality of what is being done today by Caldor. I am now going to the Metro television studios, where I will demand the right to speak to the people directly. And then I will be back. Let us see if Caldor has the nerve to continue this unlawful activity when he sees the people's anger!"

Yet more shouting, and clapping. A great chant of "Myer In," went up. Myer waved, got down off the car roof, and disappeared inside. His car slowly and awkwardly manoeuvred itself about, and drove off past the queue of vehicles waiting to get in. His supporters in the queue joined in the waving and shouting, leaning out of their windows as he passed. I realised the whole thing had been taped by TV and radio news crews that I hadn't earlier noticed, and that there was live coverage from small OB units located at the side of the plaza.

It was interesting how easily Myer slipped into a conventional political rhetoric about lawful and unlawful activity, both because such language couldn't have been used for many years and because I couldn't see what laws were being broken – the country didn't have any to break.

I would love to have stayed on to see what the crowd did, but I needed to get away myself, particularly if I was going to have to walk to the TV studios, since I didn't think I would get a cab. In the event it was easy enough to find a taxi, once I'd got clear of the streets around the Senate plaza and I arrived well before my scheduled time of ten thirty.

Irene Gopiak had told me to ask for Christine Abbass, the TV company's senior executive whom I had met at Rilka Delene's Sunday lunch a month earlier. She came down to reception and took me off to a side room where coffee and croissants were available, and which I enthusiastically attacked.

"Kris is here," she said. "Everyone believes he is getting ready to do a live interview at half past eleven, and doubtless this information has already got to Caldor's people. In fact, he is being interviewed now by our star news presenter with a two-camera crew in my office, and they will be finished by eleven o'clock. We are broadcasting live coverage of the situation inside and outside the Senate at the moment, with plenty of comment from all sides. It is actually great TV – we haven't had anything like it for years. At around 11.30 we will interrupt this and go 'live' to the tape of the interview we have already done. It should keep Caldor and the United team happy; they will think Kris is missing the crucial call for the veto resolution in the Senate, which Josep Stilo has confirmed is set for mid-day. So it is down to you and your outlaw mailmen to get him in by the back door."

At this she smiled, whether in pleasure at the beauty of the scheme or more cynically at the prospect that if it failed it wouldn't be down to her or her company, I couldn't tell. She added that the people doing the interview at the moment would be kept in her office, looking at the material and so on, until it was transmitted as live. This should keep the reality safely concealed for long enough.

"So far, so good," I said, and I asked about my car and driver. Christine said she would take me down to the back entrance where they were parked. I asked how Kris would get down there without being spotted. "He will use the executive lift, which we have kept locked off for him. I will bring him down, and out to the car park. He will be wearing a hooded coat and has a pair of glasses to put on, but I doubt anyone will see us anyway. You will make the switch to the

Express mail van in the executive area of the Guardian insurance offices. Irene has made special arrangements which should mean there won't be any trouble there."

It all seemed clear enough. When we got to the car, I noticed we had Rilka's personal driver, who nodded to me. I guess they knew he could be trusted. There was a tense twenty-minute wait, and then Christine and a hooded figure appeared, walking rapidly to our car. Kris Myer got in, in a clearly excited state. "Greetings, Bob," he said. "The adventure continues. Let's go!" And we moved away swiftly. I asked how the interview had gone. "Oh, fine," he said. "I can't now remember much of what I was saying, but it doesn't matter anyway. As long as they all think it's live!"

It took us ten minutes to get to the Guardian headquarters. The security people clearly expected the car and waved us through. We drove down to an enclave in the underground car park and pulled up. Irene Gopiak and Elli Dyvers were waiting for us, and Kris and I got out. We exchanged greetings in a quietly tense way; the climax of the operation was approaching rapidly. Elli said that the TV and radio people had only just realised that Myer had to present the resolution himself or it would not be taken. There was a great deal of highly excited commentary, and the crowd in the plaza were getting rather alarmed – and alarming. "We have got Zaslofsky and Marchmont down there to speak to the crowd and try to calm them down," said Irene. (These were key people in Myer's entertainment business, well used to show business appearances and widely popular.) "I don't know if they can work their magic, but I hope so." For the first time she seemed upset, facing a potential outcome they hadn't planned for.

Myer himself seemed unconcerned with what the thousands in the plaza might do. "I told them no violence," he said. "And within little more than half an hour we will have won." We all tried to look reassured, but we could see that if the crowd erupted, and the troopers opened fire we would have a disaster on our hands.

Thankfully we heard, then saw, the Express van driving into the car park. Dieter turned the wrong way and Elli had to run across, shout at him and get him back on course. They pulled up alongside us, and Lee, looking quite handsome in her postman's outfit, cheerfully stuck her head out of the window and said, "Well, here we are. Where's our passenger? Don't keep us hanging about."

Elli and Irene were already opening the van's back door. Kris divested himself of his hood., coat and glasses and climbed in. Between them they sorted out the sacks and got him awkwardly hidden behind them. Irene looked at it, sucked her lips, and said it would have to do. She slammed the door shut and told me to get back in the car I had come in, which, it turned out, was also going to be the escort car to the Senate. "The best of luck," she said, and shook my hand. Elli was issuing last-minute instructions to Dieter and Lee, who just nodded. She jumped in beside me and we set off, back out of the car park.

I had had no time to talk to the two fake mailmen, but I knew what we had to do – get them to within a hundred metres of the back entrance to the Senate, park, and let them proceed in as normal a manner as they could manage. If all went well, they would come out in under ten minutes, drive a little way down the road and wait for us to overtake them and lead them back to Elli's house.

We had the radio on, which kept veering in an excited manner between the situation in the Senate chamber, where business had started, and the rowdy scenes in the plaza outside. The showbiz stars were having some effect on the crowd, it seemed. Then the radio suddenly switched to broadcasting the 'live' TV interview with Myer. Elli and I burst into laughter together as we heard it and hugged each other spontaneously.

Rilka's driver suddenly said, "This'll do," and he pulled over to park. We were at the back of the Senate building, and we realised we could hear all the shouting and roaring that was happening round the front. It was eerily quiet back here; there were just a few people walking along, and no crowd outside the back entrance to the Senate. There was however a significant group of troopers, looking rather itchy-fingered. The Express van passed us, and pulled into the Senate entrance, where it was halted by a single barrier. The troopers looked at it but didn't move towards it. We could see a couple of security guards come up to the driver and passenger windows. There was a brief conversation, and then they went round to the back of the van. Lee got out, came round and seemed to be joking with the men. She took her time to open the door, joshing one of the guards in particular, and touching his arm. They looked in briefly, and then she shut the door, and they all went back. The barrier was lifted. Lee didn't seem to get back in the van, which drove on into the courtyard.

Elli and I looked at each other. "Oh my God," she said. "It looks like they have got in."

"It certainly does. So now we just wait."

The radio coverage was getting ever more hysterical, interrupting the Myer interview to give up to the minute comments on the countdown in the Senate chamber. We were listening intently when Rilka's driver suddenly said, "Hallo, looks like we've got problems." Four troopers were coming towards us, clearly set on talking to us. "What shall I do? Shall I take off?"

"No," said Elli. "Stay calm. We are doing nothing wrong."

"Look," I said, "let's say we've been sent by the Guardian group to keep an eye on what is going on here. We have other colleagues round the front. They can't do much about that."

The troopers came up and the driver and Elli wound their windows down. A standard interrogation followed. 'Who are you? What are you doing here? Can't you see there's a near riot round the corner? I would clear out if I were you.'

Elli handled the situation well. They saw our identity cards – a couple of the troopers got mildly excited when they realised that I was the European journalist who had been to the Island – and she agreed to move out. There had been no real trouble, except that as they left and were walking back to the entrance, our driver said, "I couldn't really interrupt you, but a couple of minutes ago the mail van came out of the Senate yard and drove off without stopping. They went round that corner up there."

"Shit," said Elli. "They must have seen us with the troopers and decided they couldn't stop to wait for us. Let's go and see if they have pulled up nearby." As we passed the Senate entrance we simultaneously heard Kris Myer on the radio proposing the Senate resolution overturning the referendum result and saw instant confusion among the troopers, who must have been listening too. An officer was speaking in agitated tones on his radio.

There was no sign of the Express van as we turned the corner. We drove to the next junction, looked in every direction, but still nothing. "Perhaps they are going straight to your home," I said. "Maybe they have a map with them, and don't want to wait in case we have been picked up by the troopers."

"Maybe," said Elli. "But I don't think they have a map or know how to get to my place. Anyway, we don't have much choice." She told the driver to go as fast as he could to her home and got out her phone to call Irene. Then she stopped and looked at me with a broad grin. "But they did it. We all did it. Kris has got in and got to the chamber in time. Caldor is well and truly stuffed." And she hugged me even more enthusiastically.

Chapter Thirty-one

I picked up as accurate a version as I could, of what had happened over that Monday and Tuesday, from conversations with Irene Gopiak and Kris Myer, and from interpreting both the public statements and visible actions of Dirk Caldor and, to a lesser extent, Lisje Tuller. However, one important aspect of the story remained a complete mystery.

The Guardian team had indeed put a great deal of energy into assembling a large demonstration outside the Senate on the Tuesday morning. Ever since Kris Myer had announced what he intended to do at the Senate on the Saturday, they had rallied as many people as possible through their security organisation, their insurance clients in the capital and their own employees. (These were told on the Monday there would be no loss of pay if they attended the demo the following morning.) It was billed simply as an enthusiastic way of supporting Myer as he went to the Senate: there was no suggestion that people might be encouraged to attack the United security troopers if they tried to stop him getting in. (For Axal and his fellow prisoners, it was a great morning off, and, similarly, for Rexy and the Raptors it was a wonderful opportunity to get outside SAD Six without any hassle.)

However, when this organising became public on Sunday, it enabled Caldor and the United people to set up their extra security operation openly, justifying it by the need to keep the Senate properly protected. They put the barriers in on the Monday, and the traffic diversions late Monday evening. It wasn't at all clear that their security people had any right to extend the Senate contract in this way, but they got away with it since no-one wanted to make an issue out of it. But Caldor never said a word about intending to stop Myer, and in my view he was right to leave this to the last minute. Lisje

Tuller was interviewed widely, and said she would oppose Myer's resolution, but gave no indication that she didn't expect him to be in the chamber to present it. Indeed, I think Caldor didn't tell any of his Senate supporters of what he planned to do. Why should he? They had no role to play if he succeeded.

The media, and pretty well everyone else, was astounded when Myer was turned back at the Senate gates on Tuesday morning. At first no-one could understand why, but within an hour the commentators and news presenters had learned that if Myer wasn't present to formally put his resolution when the referendum came up for approval, then it wouldn't be put at all, and the United merger would automatically go ahead, unchallenged at this last hurdle. For half of them this was a great coup which they applauded and for the other half an outrage which they couldn't believe. Some of the latter were suggesting that Myer would simply bring the resolution forward at a later date, and other similar fantasies. Irene Gopiak made sure there was no formal comment from anyone senior in the Guardian group, though she allowed her lower-level press and PR people to scramble around for whatever instant views they could come up with, largely (she told me) to ensure that Caldor's team thought that their manoeuvre had not been anticipated.

In a similar way Myer's TV interview kept the United team thinking they had already won their victory. On screen, Myer appeared very excited about the unprecedented behaviour of the United troopers in stopping him, and late in the interview, when asked about the failure of his attempt to veto the merger if he was kept out of the chamber, simply blustered and fumed away without answering the point.

In Myer's view, that delayed 'live' interview was critical in getting him into the Senate via the back door. He had travelled from his rendezvous at the Guardian HQ, hunched up and uncomfortable, in the back of the Guardian Express mail van, hidden behind the dozen or so sacks of mail. (Actually, half of these were full of newspapers and paper rubbish; the real number of mail sacks was felt to be too few to give him decent cover, and the extra sacks had been put together at the Guardian office on the Monday and added, along with

Myer, at the Guardian offices on Tuesday morning, which I hadn't noticed at the time.)

This could have been a dangerous move, provoking the security guards to inspect the sacks more closely since there were twice the usual number. Myer was acutely conscious of this as he sat huddled, listening to the conversations going on between Lee and the guards when the van halted at the security barrier. In the background he could faintly hear himself on the TV screen the guards had in their gate hut; they had been watching the TV coverage of the events as they happened. As he told me, at that point he had been convinced the guards would find him: they were dealing with a couple of Express people they had never seen before, there were twice the number of mail sacks as normal, and it was a Guardian vehicle – more than enough to merit a complete search, in his view.

But it didn't happen, largely because he could tell the guards assumed that since he was there live on the TV he couldn't be in the van. And Lee had clinched the scam by her flagrant flirtation with the guards. This had started with comments on the photos on the fake cards, proceeded via a couple of raunchy remarks as they walked round to open the van door, and climaxed with what Myer took to be a clear offer to give both guards a hand job in their hut while the van was being unloaded. This had so appealed to the two guards that they gave only the most cursory glance inside and shut the door instantly, to be able to get on with this quite unexpected opportunity for sexual gratification.

Dieter had then driven the van across the courtyard and reversed it up to the mail room entrance. Josep Stilo then opened the back of the van, and Myer scrambled out, effectively concealed by the van door. No-one had been looking; the two guards and Lee were inside the hut, and the force of additional security troopers (not that Myer had been aware of them) were probably working up their interest in the escort car in which Elli Dyvers and I were sitting.

Myer and Stilo had then walked rapidly through the corridors and up the stairs in the Senate building, meeting no-one on the way; they all seemed to be either in the chamber or glued to their TV screens and sets. Myer had decided not to enter the chamber by the main door, but through a side one at the back: in his showbiz way he wanted to keep his presence unobserved, if he could, for the few minutes before the Senate chairman would call the votes on the referendum results.

It worked brilliantly. Even watching the video playback later, I could feel the palpable tension in the chamber as the chairman closed the preliminary business and announced, "Item Three: Proposition 72; that the merger of United Insurance with Health and Prosperity Assurance be approved. The people have already assented in the referendum held on May 25, by 8.564 million Yes votes to 1.202 million Noes. We have a motion that the Senate should reject this result. I call on Senator Myer, in whose name this motion stands, to speak."

He paused. For a second there was a silence so intense you could have held it in your hand. Some people were looking round or staring at Myer's empty seat in the front row. Most were simply fixated on the chairman, as were the TV cameras. Then a loud, familiar voice came from the back of the chamber. "Thank you, Mr Chairman," said Myer very clearly, as he strode down from where he had been standing by the side door. "I recognise this is a highly unusual procedure in this Senate. I believe I have ten minutes in which to make my case. Oh, and I apologise for arriving late and missing the earlier business." And he arrived at the podium to gasps of astonishment that rapidly changed into wild cheering from the NDP group and their allies.

The bedlam continued for minutes, with Myer standing there smiling broadly as many of the Senators cheered, applauded and stamped their feet. There was bafflement and some consternation on the faces of Lisje Tuller and her supporters, and there were a few very angry Senators. Though the TV reports didn't catch this, Stilo told me that a couple of them slipped out, he assumed to talk to Caldor on their mobiles outside the chamber.

Myer really enjoyed this highly theatrical moment, and, for a man who was essentially a TV entertainer and businessman, he handled the strange new language of political principle very well. He justified reviving this long dormant habit of subjecting the referendum result to serious scrutiny and, he hoped, a rejection, by the constitutional gravity of the situation and the improper (not, I noticed, illegal) way the Proposition had passed. Unlike in his TV debate with Tuller a few days earlier, he spoke with confidence and authority. When he had finished, he was cheered and applauded all over again.

Tuller made a decent job of replying, but she knew the votes were against her. She emphasised that the referendum result, though distorted by the NDP boycott call, had been legitimate, and rehearsed the benefits of the merger. But she did not attack the idea of the Senate breaching all custom and practice by behaving in this unusual way, and, most surprising of all, she congratulated Myer on evading the United security blockade, which she deplored as excessive and unwarranted. It was a dignified and impressive performance, and way beyond what the Libance Senate was used to.

Far too many senators wanted to join in this novel experience of actual, meaningful political debate, but the chairman called a halt soon enough; he too knew what the result was going to be and didn't see the need to prolong the situation. Stilo had done his side of the business well: Proposition 72 was rejected by 108 votes to 63.

Over the next few days there were lengthy discussions in the media, at respective commercial and party gatherings, and at myriad private dinners, about what had happened and the implications of this extraordinary sequence of events; and I will deal with some of this later. But while most Guardian people were celebrating Myer's amazing appearance in the nick of time, a few of us were trying to find out what had happened to the two outlaws and the Guardian Express mail van that had enabled him to achieve it.

When Elli and I had realised we had lost the mail van, she tried to call Irene Gopiak, but her line was inevitably busy, as Myer's dramatic appearance in the Senate chamber was causing mass excitement at the Guardian. Eventually, having failed to raise two or three other people, she left a message on her own office machine, hoping her PA would pick it up soon. "Let's go to my home," she said to me. "That must be where they have gone."

But it wasn't. We were both getting very worried. Then Gopiak called, and after mutual congratulations on the triumph, she said she would speak to the Express depot manager and, if necessary, get instructions out to the security troopers in the city to look out for the mail van. She told Elli to stay at home in case the outlaws turned up, but suggested I would probably like to join the party at the Guardian offices. "Oh, and bring that nice Friya Alling as well," she added.

The disappearance of Lee and Dieter nagged away at me through all the celebrations and congratulations that long Tuesday. Myer was all over the TV news, but he was careful not to give any hint of how he had managed to get into the Senate and past all the United security troopers. I discovered later that Caldor's people had worked out within a few hours that the Express mail van was the likeliest vehicle Myer had used, though by that time a Guardian security team had found it parked in a side street – inside the SAD Six boundaries, and, inevitably, empty. It was immediately brought back to its depot and given a thorough, but fruitless, going over.

Had the two outlaws planned their disappearance all along? Once the van had been found, we cast around for how they might have contacted someone in Libance City. They hadn't got any mobile phones of their own, but when the calls made from Elli's landline were checked she found a number that she didn't recognise but which had been called just before midnight on Monday evening – after she had gone to bed and had assumed her outlaw guests had done so too. It turned out to belong to an elderly couple living in the next district to SAD Six, and these, as we discovered once the Guardian security team had visited them on Tuesday evening, turned out to be Lee's parents.

And this was as far as the Guardian search for Lee and Dieter got, which cast an interesting light on the strengths and weaknesses of the Libance view of law and law enforcement. The old couple admitted readily enough that they had been completely surprised to hear from Lee, whom they never expected to see again, and overjoyed at her plan to visit them on the Tuesday morning. They were surprised too when she and her companion turned up in Express mail uniforms, which they changed out of into some ill-fitting clothes belonging to the parents. Lee had said that the Guardian security people would be after them, that they hadn't done anything wrong but that they would need to disappear for a while. She promised to get back in touch in due course. And then they had gone.

It was impossible to tell whether or not they were lying about their ignorance of where their daughter was and what she was doing, but I suspected they weren't. In any event there was nothing the Guardian investigators could do. The old couple were not in breach of any contracts, and their protection contract with their own security team (United, of course) effectively dissuaded the investigators from getting rough with them.

I learned from Commandant Keely Stavros a couple of days later that, though he had been charged with trying to find the two outlaws, he doubted they would surface. "Chances are they are being protected by one of the gangs. Even Rexy and the Raptors might be looking after them, and frankly it isn't worth my while to offer much for information. Irene Gopiak might be curious about why they ran off, but she won't want to pay anything to find out. And you will have seen for yourself how half the population in SAD Six manage to live without identity cards, credit cards and insurance."

A bit later Captain Reinhardt reported back on a conversation he had had with Xerxes, when he next came to the Causeway Market. Xerxes had been highly amused at the escapade, though he claimed to have been completely unaware of any plan by Lee and Dieter to disappear after dropping off Myer. "They honoured the contract we had with you," he said to Reinhardt, "so I don't see that you have any grounds for complaint." I wasn't at all sure about his plea of ignorance; I suspected Lee had been switched with Caleb at the last minute precisely because she had told Xerxes she wanted to seize the chance to get back into mainland life, on her terms rather than at the benevolence of a security panel hearing. Timo Jankel tried to persuade Dr Gopiak to reduce the amount given to Xerxes in the special bank account, but she demurred. "Timo, you are being very mean-spirited. The job we paid for was done, even if those tasked with it chose to finish it in an unexpected manner. The Express group got their van back undamaged. Dirk Caldor may have a fair idea of what happened, but he can take action against no-one. That money was very well spent. I wish more of our funds were as profitable."

Irene Gopiak's assessment was spot on, except in one respect. Dirk Caldor did find a way to exact at least a partial revenge.

Chapter Thirty-two

The remainder of that week was one of the best of my life. I was a hero to the Guardian people, who treated me to a series of celebratory parties and dinners (not just for me, of course, but I was regarded as a central character in their festivities): there was increased interest in my press and TV work: and best of all, Friya and I had a truly wonderful time. Though we were both going to work (she more regularly than me), we were together all the remainder of each day and night, usually at her place.

I realised I had begun to appreciate life in Libance far more than I had expected to. It was by no means perfect, not by a long shot, but it seemed to suit me. There was a strangely attractive combination of anarchy and conservatism, a blend that had become institutionalised after three decades of post-revolutionary experience. Friya noticed the change. "My, Bob," she said, "you have altered your views, haven't you? Where has all that sarcasm about our way of life gone? No more jokes about the insurance companies that run our society, or telling us that Dirk Caldor is right, and we need to be shaken up?"

"Hang on," I said. "Just because I am enjoying myself hugely with you doesn't mean I have lobotomised my principles or my beliefs. I still think this place is crazy." But I wasn't sure I did think that anymore. And one good thing about that was that I was sure I would now put on a much more convincing case at my asylum hearing, which was scheduled for the week after Myer had won his victory in the Senate.

As Friya had told me all those weeks ago, asylum applications were very rare indeed in Libance, and the security and insurance companies had taken a while to agree on the format, but at long last they had decided. The hearing would take place in front of a panel made up of senior officers from the United and National security companies, an executive from the Health and Prosperity insurance company, and a Senator. It would be clerked by an official from the Constitutional Court. No-one from the Guardian group would be on the panel, since they were my insurers, but I could, and would, offer testimonies from the Guardian Central prison, the TV studio and the *Tribune* newspaper. Normally I would have been accompanied by Friya, as my representative designated in the airport contract, but she said that since she had decided to log our relationship with the Human Behaviour Institute it would be better if someone else came with me. Thinking in European terms, I thought I had better have a lawyer, and asked for and got Timo Jankel. Irene Gopiak volunteered to pay for his services, which I thought was rather decent of her.

Though Friya at first said she shouldn't really do it, in the end she agreed to rehearse me the day before the hearing. She went through the paperwork I had been sent. "Essentially, Bob, they will have the part of the Basic Law document that the clerk considers relevant; that is this paper here. It's not exactly clear why he thinks this covers your case, but anyway it says when a foreigner seeks admission to the country, they must demonstrate that they have sufficient funds to support themselves; that they have a fit and proper sponsor; they must have a clear departure date; and that they have, or will have, obtained full insurance cover. Finally, they must not breach any contract they enter into; if they do their admission will be immediately revoked.

"I think this is meant for the few foreign businesspeople who come here each year, not someone like you seeking to live here permanently. But I guess it is the best guidance we have."

"Hell, I don't have a departure date – obviously I don't. Isn't that going to invalidate my application straight away?"

"No, I don't think so. In a note appended to the Basic Law extract, the clerk says this criterion cannot be considered in this case."

"Phew, that's a relief. I guess I score fine on the rest of it: funds, sponsor, insurance cover, no breach of contract. So what else do they have to consider?"

"Well, obviously they will have to develop a view of you as a suitable person to become a Libance citizen. Provided you don't slag us off in your normal manner you should be able to charm your way past that hurdle."

"No problem. As you yourself have pointed out, my opinions have changed significantly. I will keep my residual sense of your craziness to myself."

"Hm, you have written several columns about us. I don't recollect anything too damaging in them. Can you think of anything?"

That gave me pause. I rapidly went over in head what I had written. Luckily nothing felt as though it had savaged Libance or its customs; at worst I had given the impression that Libancers were quaint or eccentric. It hadn't seemed sensible to slag the country off, as Friya so nicely put it, at the time, and I was now very grateful for my own forbearance.

"No, I think they are OK. So – anything else to consider?"

"Very unlikely. They are allowed to consider material provided to them secretly, but this is a provision that should not affect you. It is a procedure normally used in breach of contract cases, where one party fears the consequences of publicly revealing their views in a specific instance. It can occur in a case between an employer and employee, or one involving sexual partners. You are fine on both fronts. Metro TV and the *Tribune* have given glowing testimonies to your abilities, and as your sole sexual partner I promise you I have nothing secret to say to the panel." And she grinned at me.

I grinned back. "I should hope not. That is, there are things that should be kept secret, like that weird but nice bout of separate masturbation that we went in for on our first date, but I know what you mean."

We then spent a happy hour role-playing my appearance, Friya asking tricky questions and me answering them as straight as I could, though all too frequently we collapsed into laughter at what seemed absurd questions and even more absurd answers. And then we went to bed.

The hearing the next morning was in the offices of the Health and Prosperity insurance company executive, who was to chair the panel. We were in a meeting room which had been set up in interview mode; the four panellists (two of them were women, including the

Senator) on one side of a long table, Jankel and me opposite them, with the clerk sitting to one side. The chairman took us through the procedure he intended to follow, the criteria they would apply, the opportunities I would be given to raise points of my own. He listed the documentation they had been presented with. After the hearing the panel would adjourn and reach their decision by the end of the day. A courier would bring the written decision to my home. There was no appeal against it.

It all went off smoothly enough. There was a slightly rough exchange between Jankel and the United security officer over the departure date requirement, but the clerk intervened to rule in my favour, and the chairman accepted this without demur. There was some confusion over who exactly my sponsor was, but Jankel ended the discussion by saying firmly that Dr Gopiak was my sponsor and that he was authorised to make this clear. Again, they seemed to accept this. My funds were deemed adequate. My insurance documents were nodded through. And I formally promised not to breach any contract I entered into.

The next phase was more unpredictable. They fired questions apparently at random, but since this was the personality section, that seemed fair enough, and I was confident I had presented myself in a favourable light (which Jankel subsequently confirmed). The United officer brought up Proposition 72 and the Senate's rejection of the positive referendum result. I said there had been merit in the positions of both sides, and I had written as much the previous week. I did not feel it was my job as a foreigner to take one side or the other.

The last phase was given over to me. I spoke warmly of my esteem for the country and referred to my articles in which I had made this clear. It was an unfortunate episode that had brought me to Libance, I said, but out of that adversity I had found new hope and new challenges, and I was deeply excited at the prospect of settling down here. I didn't want to lay it on too thick, nor to take too much time in flannelling them, but to make clear my sincere admiration for the place succinctly and briefly.

The chairman thanked me and asked if there was anything that I felt relevant that we hadn't discussed. I said no, there wasn't. The woman Senator repeated the question, varying it slightly. "Please think about this carefully, Mr Rowgarth. You understand the wide range of our questions, from the professional to the narrowly personal. If there is anything you feel we should know, please tell us."

I paused. Was she getting at anything in particular? I thought hard but couldn't see what she might be driving at. We had talked about most of the things I had done, much of which I had written about: the schools, the SADs, my trip to the Island, my views on their showbiz politics and the nimbyist consequences of so many referenda, the way everything was recorded electronically somewhere – I couldn't see that we had left anything of substance out. So I politely said, no, thanks, I think we've covered everything.

Then Jankel and I left. I thanked him, and he congratulated me on my performance. "You didn't mention your involvement with us at the Guardian, helping to get Myer into the Senate, and so on. I think that was very wise. It would have raised all kinds of questions. And I don't see how they would know about it anyway."

We parted on good terms, and I went back to Friya's place, and prepared a celebratory supper. She came in around six, and asked how I had got on and had the courier arrived yet? I said no he hadn't, but it seemed to have gone well, and Jankel had thought so too.

We were just sitting down to a drink of wine and a smoked salmon starter when the courier arrived with the letter. Friya signed for it and gave it to me. I opened it and read it. The shock was tremendous, far, far worse than I should have expected, given that I had originally set out on this course as a convenience, and fully intending to leave after a few months.

"They've turned me down," I said. "It's a clear no."

Friya looked distressed. "Oh, my love, how terrible. How truly terrible. Here, let me hug you. What reasons do they give?"

"I don't know," I said. "I can scarcely look at them."

"Let me see." She took the letter and read it rapidly. "They give two reasons. First, that you secretly helped the Guardian group develop their policies around the referendum and the Senate vote and did not admit these to the panel. Second, that you are having an affair with Governor Delene, and did not acknowledge this either. On both counts this lack of openness on very important matters clearly indicates that you are very unlikely to honour contracts that you enter into. This disqualifies you from becoming a citizen of Libance."

"Helping the Guardian? Having an affair with Rilka Delene? How did they know about these? And why should such activities disqualify me?"

Friya looked tight-lipped. "Well, clearly you do not see how keeping such things quiet would indeed disqualify you, though I can see it. As to how they found out, they summarise the evidence on which these interpretations are based. Here, look for yourself." And she thrust the letter back at me.

I read it with a growing mix of outrage, misery and bafflement. The Guardian involvement was detailed in a confidential paper from Dirk Caldor, in which he listed his evidence, starting with the discovery by the troopers guarding the Senate of me and Elli Dyvers sitting in her car outside the back gate of the Senate during the riots, and going through a list of telephone calls I had made or received either on my mobile or landline to and from various senior Guardian people, most frequently Irene Gopiak. His note admitted that the content was not known. However, none of these calls could be related to articles I had written, and the incidence was at its greatest in the ten days before the Senate vote.

"How did they get this list? And anyway, it's all pretty circumstantial. They can't convict me on just these phone calls. I could have been discussing anything."

"They are not 'convicting' you, as you call it. They accept that there could be other interpretations for the phone calls, other than the one Caldor puts on them but recognise that it is a credible one; however, and what is much worse, you did not raise this yourself."

"But they never asked me."

"Are you sure? Was there nothing on Proposition 72, and the Senate vote?"

"Well, yes, but I answered that positively and neutrally."

Friya shrugged. "And what about your affair with the Governor?"

I looked back at the letter. "That seems to be based on two things. Apparently Delene herself refers to it in a confidential appendix to the Guardian Central testimony – but Caldor wouldn't know that. It seems the panel checked with that Human Relations Institute; she must have recorded our few fucks there. Not that she bloody told me. Caldor says that I must have journeyed up with her to that northern village Sunday week back, because they have the record of my phone call to you on the Monday morning. They picked up on this journey because her car and a Guardian security escort were logged going through all the district traffic monitors, which led them to check the records of phone calls from the village. I guess that was part of their investigations into how Myer got into the Senate. Brilliant – they caught me instead."

"And did you?"

"Did I what? Have an affair? Yes, but it was nothing. It pretty well all happened before you and I got ourselves together. God, you aren't upset about this, are you?"

"Before we became an item, as you put it so sweetly a couple of days ago? But your journey to the north was after our wonderful Saturday together. You never mentioned going up with Governor Delene in her car and staying the night with her in that small hotel."

"But I didn't know she was going until I got to the Guardian on the Sunday. I didn't mention it because there was no significance in it whatsoever. We both behaved as though we knew our brief – very brief – fling was over. We never even touched each other. You can't believe anything else, surely, even if those bloody panellists did."

Friya suddenly relaxed and smiled gently at me. "Bob, it doesn't matter what I believe or don't believe. I told you that days ago. Trusting you is not important. I have enjoyed our short time together wonderfully. It truly has been brilliant, as you keep calling it. The real significance is that the panel discovered your other affair, gave you the chance to admit it yourself, but you didn't – and now you must pay the penalty. It is all very sad. But what I believe is completely irrelevant."

I looked at her aghast. "You're using the past tense. You make it sound as though our relationship is over."

"Well, isn't it? The last part of the letter gives you a fortnight to make your arrangements to leave, but I notice they also refer to a cargo flight to Newark in four days' time. Since these flights are rare enough, I think they want you to catch it."

"Jesus, I can't cope with this. You are giving up just like that and trying to put me on a plane in a couple of days! I didn't expect any of this, and I don't want it. There must be something we can do. Get Dr Gopiak to intervene. That's our best bet."

"I think in the circumstances, where you are in effect revealed as a secret Guardian agent, she will find such an intervention impossible."

"This is insane. I kept quiet about my informal work with Gopiak and company because the Guardian people wanted me to, and now you tell me they won't want to know me. And the panel get all pompous about what was little more than a one-night stand with Delene. That is absolutely Victorian. I know you don't have laws, but it looks like you don't have any justice either."

Friya came over and put her arms round me. "I am desperately sorry for you, Bob, and for us. I thought you were the best man I had ever met. I know I said trust was irrelevant, but I was beginning to love you, nonetheless. It is very, very sad."

I burst into tears. "Shit, Friya, I can't bear it. I can't bear the thought of leaving here, leaving you behind. I never expected this." And I continued sobbing on her shoulder.

We went on like this for a while, me sobbing and ranting, she soothing me and kissing me gently. Eventually I pulled myself together. "I'm sorry I have let go like this. I can't help it. It isn't dignified, I know. I bet seeing me like this will at least help you to get over me."

"Don't be silly, my love. Let us go to bed. We won't have many more times after all."

It seemed the best available advice. In bed, I was passionate and needy. Friya was accommodating, and compliant – and distant. I pretended I didn't notice the distance, but the fact of it said it all.

Chapter Thirty-three

When I got back to my flat the next morning, I found emails from the Guardian people (Irene Gopiak and others), the TV station and my *Tribune* editors, all regretting the asylum panel decision and asking if they could be of any help in my last few days. Apparently, the decision had been on the news the previous night and again that morning. I hadn't checked any news programmes in my shock and grief. Looking at the online news made it all feel done and dusted: I was a non-person, on my way out. From hero to victim (or quasi-criminal, depending on your point of view) in less than 24 hours. Shattering.

Amongst the messages was a short note from Rilka Delene. She expressed surprise and regret at the decision. She didn't ask or offer to see me before I left, but I decided I needed to have it out with her. I called her office, and within the hour they came back and said Rilka would see me at Guardian Central the next day.

I hadn't expected any message from Dirk Caldor, but half-way through the morning I got a phone call from his PA, saying he would very much like to see me. I thought about it, and then agreed: that too would take place the next day.

I spent the rest of the day sorting out my finances, claiming my final expenses and trying to make sure that the fund of dollars and euros that I had built up in Libance could be turned into real money for me to take with me when I left. This was harder than you might have thought, and I wasn't absolutely sure that I would get this sum at the airport, but I had to hope that it would be okay.

I agreed to pay rent on my flat for another couple of weeks so that Friya could arrange to sell a few bits and pieces I had purchased. I also cancelled my insurance deals and got refunds. I decided to risk falling ill or getting run over in the next couple of days.

That evening Friya and I had another rather miserable night. We tried to cheer ourselves up but didn't make a very good job of it. Neither of us slept very well. She had to leave early for work. I had a rather desultory breakfast and then set off in good time to walk to Caldor's offices. It was a cloudy dreary day and fitted my mood rather too well.

I went to his office without any idea of what he would say, aside from any formalities. He hadn't seemed from my limited experience to be the kind of man who would arrange this last-minute meeting just to gloat that at least he had made someone in the Guardian group suffer. Instead, he said he wanted to explain in more detail why I had failed in my asylum application. He did remind me of a university professor handling a student after he had failed his finals.

Indeed, he was professorial throughout – no gloating at all. Basically, he said I was dishonest on key questions, so that adding them all together, no-one on the panel felt that I was the kind of person they wanted in Libance. The deceits were over failing to acknowledge the part I played in the Guardian's successful overturning of the merger referendum, [there were several of these actions, over at least three weeks]; and a blunt refusal to admit to the affair with the prison governor, and subsequently failing to file the business with the Institution with its very important record of such transactions. I was taken aback by the knowledge he had of what had been intended as secret. When pushed at the end if I wished to say anything, I had declined the offer, thus missing my chance to give my own versions of these events.

Though it was tempting to give an answer now, I didn't do it. I would gain nothing from it, and I had no idea how he might use such material. It dawned on me that Rilka was the source of these wretched own goals, a conviction that grew into a certainty as I made my way home. I instantly decided not to keep my appointment to see her; my anger would not be contained if we met, and I would probably have beaten her up, thus losing any chance to get out on a rare future cargo flight; and then to find out just how harsh a real prison might be. I was frustrated, raging with an angry sense of being trapped.

When I got home, I tried to calm down, but it was difficult to achieve this. There were the big boxes packed with the stuff I'd collected in my tours, my suitcases full of my clothes, and everywhere the desolate detritus of an impending dreary exit. Not the environment for mature reflection.

Then, to cap it all, I had a call from Friya saying apologetically that she was working late that evening and that she felt therefore that it would be best for me to finish my packing alone; she didn't know when she would finish and so therefore, she would go home to her flat and get a good night's rest. She would get up early tomorrow and bring me fresh rolls from the artisanal bakery near her and make me breakfast in bed.

I was devastated. I would be leaving in two days' time and yet she was coming up with a feeble excuse, restricting us to just one more night together. I remonstrated with her, telling her she was cutting our remaining time together in half; every minute was precious, in my mind at least. She paused, then said that she absolutely agreed, and, in exchange as it were, she told me that she had got the afternoon off tomorrow and could therefore come to me then.

I said nothing for a moment; I had assumed she would get the whole day off for us, and now found that I had suddenly lost half that time as well. However, I felt it was better to express enthusiasm for that supposed bonus, and we ended the call on a positive note.

Sleep that night was poor and patchy, my lover absent and me with, at best, 36 hours left in Libance. I finally fell properly asleep around 5am and had to be shaken awake by Friya, standing next to my bed with the smell of coffee and warm bread filling the room. I was torn between having immediate sex and eating breakfast; the latter won after Friya insisted that our sex would be hot at any time, but her carefully arranged breakfast was getting colder by the minute.

In one way the sex was good, fierce and frantic one moment, caressing and gentle the next: but behind it I was paranoid, the mood of yesterday unresolved. And so it remained throughout that day, me on the edge of sullen aggression, she with a continuous false jollity; and I had no wish to initiate what was bound to be a fruitless discussion.

That evening was different again; I was determined to avoid both tears and sobs, a determination broken when Friya herself started to cry, her whole body convulsed with unchecked emotion. Once we had both calmed down, she suddenly raised the prospect of me coming back to see her on a visitor visa. I questioned if such a thing existed in Libance, to which she said that such visas were granted very occasionally to the few US businessmen who had to come here to negotiate or finalise an import deal, and she couldn't see why I couldn't get something like that; to which I suggested she should instead come to the US, sponsored by me if necessary; and so on, down the road to the ultimate mirage of marriage, a prospect which gave us pause; and then we went back to tears and hugs and clinging to each other, as if to defy the troopers who would come for me within a few hours to separate us.

Exhaustion brought sleep eventually, and when we awoke, we were both back in the formal mode of the day before; my paranoia resurfaced, Friya chose to be distant, and so we presented no problem to the United security troopers who had been assigned to take me to the airfield. We didn't kiss; we shook hands; hugged briefly; I got in the car; sat in the seat that was given to me; we waved to each other: the car started and moved off.

And that was that.